9.95

THE LIFE, HISTORY AND MAGIC OF

THE CAT

THE LIFE, HISTORY AND MAGIC OF
THE CAT

by FERNAND MERY

Translated by Emma Street

Madison Square Press
Grosset & Dunlap Publishers . New York

Second Printing, 1969
by Grosset & Dunlap, Inc.

Copyright © 1966 Editions Robert Laffont
Translation © 1967 Paul Hamlyn Ltd.

Published in 1968 in the United States
by Grosset & Dunlap, Inc.
51 Madison Avenue, New York 10010

Library of Congress Catalog Card No.: 68-10647
All rights reserved

Published in 1967 in England
by Paul Hamlyn Ltd.
Drury House, Russell Street, London, W.C.2.

First published in France
by Editions Robert Laffont
under the title *Le Chat*

Printed and bound in Italy by Ilte, Turin

CONTENTS

1 THE ORIGIN OF THE CAT

You can visit the caves of Eyzies, Lascaux and Altamira. You can look at every detail of the frescoes of Tassili des Adjjer or the excavations of Chou-Kou-Tien. From Chaeroneia to Kenya or Java you can examine all those archaeological sanctuaries where there are relics authenticating the passage of man and his animals from pre-history to today. Nowhere will you find a trace of the cat.

There are no small felines in the rock paintings or rock carvings of paleolithic times. There is not a tooth nor a vertebra of a cat in the Kjokkenmöddinger or 'kitchen-middens', those rubbish-dumps of the small Neolithic cultures of Northern Europe where fragments of shellfish shells and broken tools are found mixed in with the bones of deer, wild boars, dogs and birds. In the pile-built, lake-villages of Mooseedorf in Switzerland and in the caves of Thayngen the only feline skeletons to be found are those of the occasional lynx. The only pre-historic representation of a small feline so far discovered is on the wall of a grotto in Asia Minor, and even this is questionable.

The dog, the reindeer, the bear and the horse had for millenia been the companions and servants of man before the domestic cat appeared on the scene.

Where did it come from? Who were the ancestors of Shakespeare's 'harmless necessary cat'?

The most natural explanation might seem to be that the domestic cat descended from the European Wild Cat (*Felis silvestris*).

In fact, this mistake was made for generations. The first to refute it, in 1736, was the Swedish botanist Linnaeus (Carl Von Linné). This was all the more remarkable in that he could never have seen a wild cat. *Felis silvestris* is not a particularly rare animal. It is found in a great many regions of Britain, France, Spain, Italy, Germany and Central Europe. But it is completely unknown in Scandinavia and Ireland.

Linnaeus gave a quite definite opinion. But it was not until Temminck, in the middle of the nineteenth century, that the issue was finally settled: the domestic cat is not a tame version of the European wild cat.

WILD CATS THROUGHOUT THE WORLD

EUROPE

The wild cat of the European forest and woods differs in many ways from the domestic cat. The main morphological difference is the wild cat's wide skull with clearly convex profile and a very marked orbital cavity. It has a heavy-jowled appearance, black lips and green eyes. Its tail is club-like, short and thick, ringed six times and black at the tip. Its body is massively built, muscular and covered in thick fur. It often weighs 12 to 16 pounds and apparently, in Eastern Europe, even 26 to 28 pounds. Its characteristic coat colour is a yellowish-grey on the back and sides which turns paler under the belly, with stripes that are always in a vertical direction. Lastly, the underneath of the paws is protected as far as the digits by a wide, thick, callus pad, which joins up at the back with a smaller but still thick metacarpal pad. There is, of course, such an enormous range of difference in the weight, colouring, and even the degree of wildness of the domestic cats that roam the towns of Europe, that these physical distinctions alone do not distinguish the wild cat from the domestic cat. But there are other differences.

The habits of the European wild cat are different from those of the town cat. The wild cat feeds very irregularly. As autopsies have proved, it can swallow, very quickly, an enormous quantity of meat, and then remain for several days afterwards without taking in anything at all. Similarly, it drinks

Types of cats: plates from Buffon's Histoire naturelle *published in the late eighteenth century*

a great deal, but infrequently. In the winter it is less active, but does not hibernate. And a recent study has shown that the wild cat scarcely ever moves out of an irregularly shaped territory whose extreme points are only separated by about half a mile as the crow flies. But the most interesting point of all arises when one interbreeds wild with tame cats. It is certainly possible to cross domestic cats with all kinds of wild cats. But the progeny are fragile and delicate throughout their lives, often die young, and rarely succeed in producing a second cross-breed generation. This point, more than any other, seems to set the domestic cat apart from the various wild species.

In mentality the wild cat is one of the great predators. It is a terrifyingly wild animal, ferocious, savage and utterly intractable. In Scotland, where wild cats have always been wide-spread, the peasants up till the end of the Middle Ages were authorized to destroy them at will and use their fur for clothing. Hundreds of stories are told of how these cat-hunts turned into battles between equals; of how the cat turned on the man, chased him back into his home, and fought with him there to the death.

The European wild cat and the domestic cat are completely different species. Further, the wild cat should not be confused with 'feral cats', which are usually domestic cats run wild, sometimes a mixture of wild and domestic.

Wild cats are rare in the Mediterranean islands. But the occasional specimens found in Corsica, Sardinia and the Balearic Islands have been classified as *Felis libyca*, a species that also inhabits Africa and Asia.

So *Felis silvestris* is certainly not the only wild cat in the woods and forests of Europe. And, of those small felines that we can consider really wild, there are numerous varieties throughout the world.

ASIA

The small *Neofelis nebulosa* (Clouded Leo-

The bobcat of North America. During the Pleistocene age the lynx inhabited Britain. Its disappearance from central Europe is fairly recent

pard) lives throughout southeast Asia, from the Himalayas to Formosa. The natives of Borneo and Sumatra call it Rimoau-Dahan. The name itself miaows. Its tail is thick and woolly, and has earned the cat the name of 'tiger with a fox's tail'. Its body can be over a yard in length. Its coat is yellow in ground-colour, and is marked with wide dark discs clearly delineated by a rather indefinable colour that varies from a dark blue-grey to an almost black, olive green. Two other cats that have less conspicuous markings are *Felis manul* (Pallas's Cat) of Russia, China and the great Tibetan steppes, and *Felis viverrina* of Ceylon, Malaya, Java and Sumatra. The latter is smaller and is called the Fishing Cat because it feeds off fish and water snakes. Temminck's Golden Cat of southeast Asia and Sumatra is quite unusual looking because of the combination of its elaborately patterned face and its plain-coloured body. This ground colour is a rich golden-brown, giving the species its name.

Asia has two kinds of lynx: the Northern Lynx and the Caracal Lynx. The Northern Lynx is also found in North America, but the Asian and American animals, although of the same species, are two different races. The caracal is only 18 inches tall, but is a very powerful animal.

Finally, any list of Asian wild cats must also include the Chinese Desert Cat and the Rusty-spotted Cat, as well as the Sand Cat, Jungle Cat, Marbled Cat, Bay Cat, and the Flat-headed Cat.

NORTH AMERICA

The wild cats of North America are the Northern Lynx (*Felis lynx*), which is found in the coniferous forests of Canada, and the Bobcat (*Felis rufa*), of southern Canada, the United States and parts of Mexico. The bobcat is smaller than the lynx, but they are alike in that they both have short tails and tufted ears. Cats signal each other by moving their tails or their ears, and although their short tails put the lynx and the bobcat at a

A young genet. It is quite like a feline in that it has retractable claws and a taste for rats

This margay, which lives as a pet with its mistress Mrs Merill, is exceptionally tame

The serval, an African wild cat, is particularly irascible

Mrs Merill's margay, 'a hurricane from the equator'

disadvantage in one form of communication, their long black ear-tufts compensate them for this deficiency.

They are both night-hunters, utilizing their extraordinary powers of vision to prey on rodents, birds and deer. The lynx will attack much larger animals, especially in deep snow, where it can move more easily than its heavily-built victims—such as the moose or reindeer.

The bobcat, which often makes its den in the roots of a fallen tree, stays close to home when food is abundant, but in hard times it may patrol areas 50 miles apart.

The Puma (*Felis concolor*) is of the wild cat family, but in North America it is almost as big as a leopard. These big pumas, known as cougars or mountain lions, are formidable hunters. The pumas of South America are much smaller in size.

CENTRAL AMERICA

The best known of the Central American wild cats is *Felis pardalis*, the Ocelot. Its fur is a very pale yellow, regularly marked with black spots running down the line of its back like the links of a chain. It is found from Texas in the North to as far south as Brazil. All attempts to domesticate it have been in vain, and any docility achieved is only temporary and apparent. Its reflexes are too unpredictable for it ever to be suitable for human company.

There does exist in Central America, however, a small cat, living in the hottest areas, which seems to have some potential as a domestic pet. This cat, *Felis tigrina*, or the Little Spotted Cat, is known by various names, perhaps because there seem to be several varieties within the species. Mme Falken-Rohrle, the great Dutch specialist, owns a variety of this species which the French call *oncilla*. In her 'Cattery van Mariendaal', Mme Falken-Rohrle is breeding little Mexican *oncillas* with Margay Cats (*Felis wiedi*, also from Central America). She has succeeded in turning them into

almost acceptable house pets by letting them live with domestic Abyssinians. But, she warns: 'It is in complete disregard of any value you may attach to your furniture, curtains or knick-knacks!' Her experience and that of Mrs Merrill, who lives with another hurricane from the equator—a margay that tyrannizes her New York apartment—show that perhaps, some day, with a great deal of time and patience, these small Central American wild cats may be tamed.

Mme Falken-Rohrle seems to be on the way to achieving this aim another way. It was in her cattery, for the first time and completely by chance, that a small cross-breed kitten was born as a result of the mating of a tame Abyssinian with a wild *oncilla*. Not knowing whether this kitten was the result of a straight mutation or a genuine crossing of two breeds, Mme Falken-Rohrle repeated the experiment, this time on purpose. And now the small cross-breed 'Gloria' is no longer a unique specimen in the world. For the same Abyssinian fathered on the same *oncilla* mother three more cross-breed kittens, and all are doing well.

SOUTH AMERICA

The ocelot, margay and little spotted cat are all found in South America as well as in Central America. There is also the *Felis yagouaroundi* (the Jaguarondi), which is found from Mexico to Paraguay. It is not yet possible to be absolutely precise about either its habitat or its coat, but one detail is particularly interesting. The individual hairs of its coat are tri-coloured. They are dark grey at the root, deepening to almost black, but becoming a lighter grey again at the tip. As a result, the coat has a totally different appearance, depending on whether the fur, which is short and closely packed, is bristling or lying flat. Because of this difference in its appearance the jaguarondi was classified as two distinct species and was sometimes called the Eyra Cat (*Felis eyra*), but this is no longer an acceptable differentiation. The

other species to be found in South America are the Kodkod, the Mountain Cat, Geoffrey's Cat and the Pampas Cat. Within the species mentioned, there may be as many as thirty or forty varieties of climbing, tree-living cats in South America. But they are even more difficult to classify and describe than to catch alive. And to breed them is more impossible still.

Attention was drawn for the first time to the cat in American prehistory by Gallenkamp in 1960. In his study of the Mayas he speaks of a discovery (in 1937) in the Sandia Mountains which dominate New Mexico, and mentions a grotto containing bones that may date from around 10,000 BC. These are a mixture of the bones of bears, dwarf dogs, camels and other animals, together with those of sabre-toothed cats.

AFRICA

The *Felis serval* is a beautiful animal which is found from Algeria to the Cape of Good Hope. It is taller and stronger than the European wild cat. About a yard in length, it has an elegant body, a short tail and a coat of thick fur which is beige, tawny or reddish in ground-colour, more or less regularly spotted with black and lighter in colour towards the end of the limbs. Its ears are large, long and tapered like those of the lynx except that the ends are not really pointed, and are without the lynx's characteristic small plume-like tufts of hair.

The *Felis chaus* (Jungle Cat) is magnificent but extremely shy. It lives as easily at a height of 8,000 feet in the East Indies as in thickets and thorny hollows by the sea in Africa. It has small black plumes of hair at the tips of its ears.

The fur of the *Felis libyca* (African Wild Cat) is tawny in colour or slightly greyish, and is similar to the hare's fur with its flecks of black at the tips. The back is striped with four fairly dark lines, and the paws, ringed with black two thirds of the way up, appear gloved with a lighter colour at the end.

Le Serval

MADAGASCAR

Does there really exist a separate species of wild cat in Madagascar? The question is not settled yet, but it is probable that there is.

The Malagasy Academy has in its collection a magnificent tabby cat that is clearly bigger in size than the biggest domestic cat, although where and in what circumstances it was captured have been forgotten. As additional evidence, it is worth noting that the Malagasay language distinguishes between the *piso* which is the domestic cat, and the *kary* which is thought of as wild.

These are the most important of the African wild cats. Which of them is the most direct fore-runner of the domestic cat? It is very difficult to be certain. It could be descended from the famous 'gloved' *Felis libyca* of the Libyan desert, or possibly even from a mutant of this. Again, it could be descended from a species that no longer exists. We have a few skeletons of such species, but they do not throw much light on the problem. As a result of their haphazard matings, and their adaptation to changes in all the conditions affecting their survival, all the various species of cats, and particularly the domestic cat, could have undergone considerable modification over such enormous periods of time.

The most probable answer is that the domestic cat is the result of some mutation in one of the wild felines of Libya or Nubia, and of a long and progressive domestication of this new animal by the Egyptians, who must surely have been struck by its exceptional gentleness.

DOMESTIC CATS THROUGHOUT THE WORLD

EGYPT

People have tried to trace the origin of the domestic cat back to the Ethiopian cats that Sesostris is said to have brought with him

Detail from an Egyptian fresco in a tomb at Thebes dating from 1500 B.C. This cat is already tamed and trained to hunt ducks

18

into Egypt after his conquest of Nubia. Ancient Egypt is certainly the cradle of the first tamed cats. But from which period and under what conditions? Champfleury (author of *Les Chats*, 1870) and others trace the presence of the first domestic cats back to the eighteenth dynasty (about 1590 BC). But there were cats in the service of man as early as during the fifth dynasty (about 2600 BC). This is proved by a picture of a cat, its neck imprisoned in a wide collar, in the tomb of Ti.

Suppose that one day a wild cat of a type not previously known is captured. For any number of possible reasons (aesthetic appeal, character, etc.) it is kept. It is used for breeding and brought up. The Egyptians, with their acute powers of observation, stubborn patience and natural zoophilia mixed with respect and fear, succeed in soothing, taming and finally in training their new animal. The result would be the domestic cat. Man has always achieved the domestication of animals by turning a lucky discovery to account; by slowly harnassing and developing the natural aptitudes and instincts of a new species for his own use.

From that time on, fed and protected artificially, the cat must have come to appreciate the advantages of living under the same roof as his masters. And in accepting this new life in their company he would come to indentify himself so closely with them that he would make their enemies – the rats – his enemies. Rats, the classic plague of Egypt, along with snakes and other wild life of the Nile, would be his prey. Instinct and training together would lead him to search them out and surprise them with a kill. By the end of the Middle Empire (2100 BC) the cat as fisher, hunter and ratter was already appreciated and widely used.

That the cat was used so early should not be surprising. The Phoenicians and Cretans of the same period had already learned to make practical use of another wild animal,

*A stylized Egyptian bronze.
Egyptian sculptures are usually
more realistic*

the dolphin. And the taming of the dolphin, abandoned at the end of the Cretan civilization, has been taken up again recently by the most modern countries.

From the X Dynasty on, the domestic cat occurs more frequently in Egyptian art. A cat can be seen in a frail skiff, sitting by a hunter on the point of hurling a boomerang, and watching for ducks and other water birds to take flight as a trained goose decoys them. Again, in a fresco of 1500 BC, one cat holds three birds prisoner while another scoops up a fish with a practised claw. Finally a XIXᵉ dynasty papyrus shows a dead woman making a last libation at an offering table over which three animal deities preside: the dog, the snake and the cat.

At all levels of life the cat is important. During the XXᵉ dynasty Egypt is in political anarchy. The cat by now is a familiar totem of the people. They call him 'Myeo', a name that could not be phonetically bettered. He has become part of their lives. They make him a witness to their sufferings. In satirical papyri he is their associate in criticizing the regime. But at the most practical level, his life as a domestic animal is still the same. And in the harshest hours of his life the poorest fellah never fails to set aside a portion of his meagre meal for the household cat he loves – and will come eventually to worship as a god.

With the founding at Bubastis, of the XXIIᵉ dynasty, peace, prosperity and order are temporarily restored to Egypt. As social organization evolves, the status of the cat continues to rise. The services he has provided in the past have secured him the affection of princes and humble people alike. Now they promote him. The cat is given a task which previously was reserved for lionesses – that of watching over the temples. Because of his resemblance to these large savage cats he is on his way to becoming a major god.

Finally, in the figure of Bastet the cat-headed goddess of maternity and all that is feminine, the cat achieves incarnation as an imperial god. At Bubastis, the priests of Pacht (another name of this cat-headed Goddess of Love) watch night and day the behaviour and attitudes of their sacred cats. And from the slightest purr, the faintest miaowing, the most discreet stretch or the least alteration of posture, they draw their predictions.

THE NEAR EAST OF ANTIQUITY

Were any other countries at that time familiar with the domestic cat?

The Assyrians have left no record of them. The Chaldeans were overtly hostile to their few wild and domestic cats. The Hebrews, the nearest oriental neighbours to the privileged and envied Egypt, seem to have been determined to ignore 'the sacred beast'. The Hebrews, of course, were far too concerned with making a stand against the worship of false gods to have any interest in the cat. Do the Bible texts prove whether the cat was known in Palestine or not?

In a passage from the First Book of Samuel (XXXII, 5) some have tried to see, in relation to the two words *satus Haret*, the origin of the cat's name *haret* given by the Hebrews to the cats (?) of the tribe of Judah. The first point to make is that this Bible verse contains neither *satus* which means 'race', nor *cattus* which means 'cat', but *saltus* which means 'forest'. Next, reproducing the Latin text and the translation: *Dixitque Gad Propheta a David: Noli manere in proesidio, profiscere et vade in terram Juda. Et protectus est David et venit in saltum Haret'*. The English Revised Standard Version reads 'Then the prophet Gad said to David, "Do not remain in the stronghold; depart, and go into the land of Judah". So David departed, and went into the forest of Hareth'. This *saltus Haret* has not been identified. It is

An Egyptian bronze of a mother cat and her kitten

Detail from a fifth century Greek bas-relief of the battle of Marathon

thought to be a forest in which David could easily hide, and it is hard to see what a cat could be doing in this verse.

The other text which is often quoted for this purpose is an extract from the letter of Jeremiah to the exiles that occurs as an appendix to the book of Baruch (VI, 22). Describing the lifeless statues of the heathen idols, the prophet says: '*Supra corpus eorum et supra caput eorum volant noctuae et hirundines et aves similiter et cattae.*' The English Revised Standard Version reads: 'Bats, swallows, and birds light on their heads, and so do cats'. Now this word *cattae* has two meanings. According the Ernout and Meillet Dictionary of Latin Etymology, it means both 'wagtail' and 'cat'. If it was in this phrase being used with the meaning 'cats', it would have the form 'catti', not 'cattae'. But if *cattae* is taken as meaning 'wagtail', the phrase can be translated as follows: 'About their bodies and about their heads fly bats, swallows and birds like wagtails'.

To sum up, this famous text has nothing in it about cats at all. The Hebrews have never spoken of the cat. The only possible reference that scholars of Old Hebrew are prepared to admit is that it could have been the cat that was meant by Isaiah's phrase 'the demon of the Desert'. This is rather a brief reference.

ARABIA

The Arabs have kept cats from the sixth century AD. According to legend, Muezza, the favourite cat of Mohammed, was asleep on his sleeve. Finding himself obliged to go away, the Prophet preferred to cut off this part of his clothing rather than disturb the animal's sleep. When he returned, Muezza, to thank him, bowed. Mohammed then passed his hand three times down the length of the animal's back, giving it from that time on (and to all cats forever) the capacity always to fall on its feet. And ever since then, Muslims, for whom the dog is unclean, have had nothing but indulgence for cats.

ANCIENT GREECE

Europe was slow to discover the domestic cat. According to Herodotus' *History*, the Greeks were the first to import Egyptian cats. The Greeks had the same difficulties as the Egyptians in preserving their harvests from rodents. For better or worse, they had recourse to various small, carnivorous animals such as the weasel, the ermine and the stone-marten. This last blood-thirsty dandy they called in those days *galê*, the word which later came to mean 'cat'. These are all relatively easy animals to tame, and they are small enough to be able to follow rodents right down to the ends of their holes. Unfortunately these ferocious killers destroy quite indiscriminately chickens, pigeons and even goats as well. The Greeks, therefore, went off to Egypt and stole the cats that the Egyptians refused to let them have. As a result, there grew up a squalid system for petty theft, series of clandestine voyages of recovery, and a succession of diplomatic incidents.

Unfortunately, the Greeks never took the trouble to select the best cats for breeding. It is not surprising that documents on the introduction of cats into Greece are so rare, and the dates of the animals' adoption so uncertain. In Crete, however, in the palace at Cnossos, faience wall-tiles dating from the First Minoan period (1600 BC) depict hunting cats beside some wild sheep. Cats also appear on the facade of the palace at Hagia Triada.

The word *galê* still presents a linguistic problem. It certainly means 'cat' both in Modern Greek and in poetic and in post-Classical Greek. But in Archaic Greek it means first and foremost the 'weasel' or 'polecat'.

A Roman mosaic of Hadrian's time

An Asian caricature

Images from the temple of Go-To-Ku-Ji in Tokyo, where most of the cats are represented with a paw raised, an attitude symbolizing their ability to attract luck

There is some evidence from art and literature that the domestic cat was present in classical, if not in archaic times. From the fifth century BC a bas-relief of the battle of Marathon already shows a cat held on a lead by its master and about to confront a dog. The word cat (*kattos*) occurs in the fifth century in Herodotus and in Aristophanes (*Acharnians*, 425 BC). It occurs in the fourth century BC in Callimachus' *History of Animals* where there is a passage that, translated, reads 'It also ate the "cat" of which the small mice were afraid'.

So, wherever they came from and however few there were, there had certainly been domestic cats in ancient Greece for a long time before Alexander the Great conquered Egypt in 332 BC.

ANCIENT ROME

No matter what Cicero or Pliny said, Rome had not developed any interest in zoology, and was too proud of her supremacy to deign, even via the Athenian lesson, to take any interest in the attributes of the cat. Not a single cat's bone has been found at Pompeii, in spite of the fact that it was regularly visited by Greeks from Egypt. Those mosaics and paintings from Pompeii that show cats are Alexandrian both in style and in origin. Some wall paintings in Etruscan cemeteries clearly show cats on tables playing with partridges. But in the patrician Italian homes, where so many kinds of animals were at liberty, there is not a trace of a cat. The first very rare domestic cats would have arrived in Etruria at the end of the Republic.

When Spain asked Rome for help in getting rid of a plague of rabbits, all the latter could think of was to send ferrets. These are the ancestors of these ferrets from North Africa, that are still at large in Cantabria, the Canary Islands and the Balearic Isles. Their characteristic is to turn yellow in winter.

Rome understood so little about the uses of the cat that her rough soldiers and their vain leaders never understood the feelings of the Egyptians for their cats. Once when the Nile area was occupied by Caesar and his army, a Roman soldier was mobbed and murdered savagely in a street in Alexandria. The crowd, accusing him of having accidentally killed a cat, threw themselves on him, lynched him and dragged his corpse the length and breadth of the town. Deaf to the Roman threats of severe reprisals, the Egyptians rose, and resistance began. It did not stop until the deaths of Anthony and Cleopatra, when Egypt, at last effectively defeated, became a Roman province; and the cat, formerly worshipped, was now ostracized.

GAUL

For a long time only *Felis silvestris* was known in Gaul. The domestic cat certainly existed there in the fourth century AD, but the Gauls seemed to take no interest in it. In the fifth century, however, in Paladius, the word *catus* appeared in Low Latin. An equivalent of this word also existed in Celtic and Old English. It is probably in this period also that the domestic cat first set foot in the Low Countries near the old mouth of the Rhine, where the Romans founded a tribe called 'The Friends of Cats'.

SCOTLAND

The introduction of the domestic cat into the northwest of Europe had a more romantic history. Again it begins on the banks of the Nile. When the Greek general Galsthelos, who commanded Pharaoh's army, was defeated by the miracle of the parting of the waters of the Red Sea, he fled to the far end of the Mediterranean, eventually reaching what is today Portugal. There he founded the kingdom of Brigantium. With him was his wife Scota, Pharaoh's daughter, who had

Detail from a sculpture at Mahabalipuram in India

In Peru between A.D. 500 and 1000, the cat-god Chavin was used as a decorative motif in the pottery of Nasca

brought her cats with her. Centuries later Fergus I, a descendant of his, became undisputed ruler of a great kingdom even further north, and in memory of his ancestress the beautiful Scota he called his country Scotland. And so, the story goes, there arrived in Britain the very distant descendants of those mascot cats that the beautiful Scota led out of Egypt.

INDIA AND THE FAR EAST

Several centuries after Christ, some of the countries of Asia began to import domestic cats. India was the first to introduce the cat into religion; but it is difficult to be precise about the exact period. There are, however, several unquestionable pieces of evidence, as for example, the head of a cat belonging to the Museum of Peshawar. Orthodox Hindu rites have for a long time obliged each of the faithful to feed at least one cat under his roof. The law of Manu specifies that 'He who has killed a cat must withdraw to the middle of a forest and there dedicate himself to the life of the animals around him until he is purified.'

Much later cats were introduced into Japan, probably in the sixth century AD at the same time as Buddhism. It was the custom to keep at least two cats in each Buddhist temple to protect the manuscripts of moral treatises against the mice. Legend has it, however, that cats were officially introduced into the country as late as the reign of the Emperor Idi-Jo (AD 986–1011). In the year 999, it is claimed, on the tenth day of the fifth moon, in the Imperial Palace of Kyoto a white cat imported from China gave birth to five pure white kittens. The court was so moved by this unusual event that the Emperor decreed that these charming animals must be brought up with as much jealous care and attention as if they were infant princes.

Centuries passed and, cats being very prolific, hundreds of thousands of cats were born and bred in their turn. There grew a tradition of cherishing and spoiling them, walking them in the gardens on leads, leaving them to choose at will their own place on the softest satins and choicest silks.

Japan, however, is the country of the silkworm, and mice are very fond of silkworms. It was inevitable that cats would come to be used in the war against these natural enemies of Japan's traditional industry. Action became necessary. But the Japanese, such friends of their cats, thought it would be sufficient for the mice just to know that there were cats about, and therefore, the action took the form of some naïve strategems. Cats were drawn on the doors of houses. People bought cats of bronze, wood and porcelain. The mice ignored them. Each year this plague against the harvest and the silkworms became more menacing. By the thirteenth century, because of this defaulting in its important duties, the cat, in the eyes of public opinion, changed from an almost sacred being into a wicked, useless, cruel and egoistic demon. In the fourteenth century it at last became necessary to place these beautiful blue-eyed pets squarely in front of their responsibilities. The court resigned themselves, without much hope but with regret. In 1602, worn down at last, the government passed stringent decrees: all adult cats were to be set at liberty and it was forbidden to buy and sell or even make gifts of them under penalty of heavy fine.

So the cats of Japan fell from their aristocratic pinnacle and became members of the working class. They remained over the centuries the friends of artists and the common people, but discovered at last their natural destiny in the destruction and warding off of those enemies of their country, the rodents.

Pottery from a coastal civilization in Peru, between 1200 and 400 B.C., depicts the cat-god Chavin

A Peruvian Paraca cloak of the first century A.D. is decorated with a painting of a cat-man

AMERICA

Where and when did the domestic cat discover the New World? Rafael Larco Hoyle, director of Peru's Archaeological Museum, is convinced that the cat was the supreme deity of the Mochicas, those Indians of the Andes whose civilization preceded that of the Incas. This archaeologist, to support his thesis, refers to some very old pottery in the shape of a cat's head with the attributes of either a soldier, a musician or a sorceror. But this might easily be a representation of a wild cat.

Our first record of the attempted introduction of the domestic cat into America is the remarkable but true tale of a French missionary who turned up amongst the Huron Indians. As a pledge of friendship he offered the chief a handsome pair of large French ratting cats. The Indians accepted the present without stopping to wonder if these cats were any different from the ones they already knew as wild and harmful. And so, thinking that these new animals would

A vase shaped like a cat's head from the Mochican period of Inca art

From Mexico: Judas represented in the form of a wild cat's head

soon destroy their game, they left them to die. Hunting cats? There were already plenty of them wandering around the countryside, feeding themselves on the odd rat, squirrel or field-mouse out of the hordes of rodents that regularly devoured the crops. And so the fat cats of Father Sagard succumbed without issue. Not until whole colonies such as Pennsylvania were overrun by a plague of black rats was it decided, in 1749, to import domestic cats into the Americas—no matter what the price.

Today, there are 35–36 million of these cats in the United States (and over 20 million dogs). But who knows? Suppose that that sceptical Huron chief had had more confidence in his French missionary visitor, and that the Indians, trappers, hunters and warriors, had, with the aid of those cats and their descendants, become an agricultural people who knew how to preserve their harvests intact? The destiny of the American Indian might, in some measure at least, have been changed.

2 THE CULT OF THE CAT

Ancient Egypt was the first to discover, among the many small wild cats of Africa, the one which was to become the domestic cat the world over. She not only selected it, bred it, loved it and used it, but eventually came to venerate and worship it, placing it at the head of her hierarchy of animal-gods. With the exception of the vulture, no other of her sacred animals is so richly and completely documented.

THE CAT AS DIVINITY

In Egypt from the XII° dynasty on (from almost 2000 BC) the cat was the object of an established cult to which princes, priests and common people alike contributed. This cult was centred in Bubastis, a town of Lower Egypt on the eastern branch of the Nile which has since silted up. Bubastis is today a heap of ruins known as Tell Basta. Here the cat, already having been dedicated to a variety of different divinities, received its final consecration in the effigy of Bastet, the goddess with a cat's head. The goddess was a disturbing creature whom every Egyptian woman wished to resemble in the strangeness of her gaze, her slanting eyes, her supple loins, her noble posture and her animal abandon. The most beautiful artistic reproductions of cats that we know today are those on the tomb of the sculptors Apuki and Nebanin, who were famous during the reign of Amen Hotep III and to whom we owe the famous Colossi of Memnon.

Suppose a cat died a violent death at that time? If it happened in the street, the passer-by who discovered the corpse would hurry away crying out aloud his grief. He had to prove by his tears that the accident had nothing to do with him. For anyone guilty of having, even accidentally, killed a cat was liable to the death penalty.

Suppose a cat died a natural death under a family roof. The inhabitants of the house shaved their eyebrows and lamented loudly for hours. The eyes of the beloved deceased were piously closed. Its whiskers were firmly pressed down against its lips. And then it was wound round with a mummy's wrappings. According to the district of the coun-try, precise rules governed the funeral laying out. In some places, fragments of painted cloth replaced the eyes, now forever closed. In others, two small artificial ears stood up from the head, giving an appearance of attentiveness to this now immobile face. Elsewhere, turquoise collars were wound round the neck of the sacred beast. Then came the embalming of the mummy. Depending on how rich its masters were, it was either buried or placed in a true sarcophagus. There is still one of these to be seen in the Cairo Museum. It is the empty stone that once contained the mummy of a cat which had belonged to a grand master of the order of architects. His name and his titles appear in the epitaph he had engraved on the stone in memory of his favourite cat.

In the middle of the nineteenth century a complete cemetery was excavated at Beni-Hassan, and found to contain three hundred thousand embalmed and mummified cats. What was the fate of this unique discovery? Not a single archaeologist took the trouble to ensure that they were preserved. Twenty tons of mummified cats were piled up, transported to Alexandria and loaded on to a cargo boat going to Liverpool. A copy of the *English Illustrated Magazine* at that time gives the incredible details. The remains of these pricelessly old cats were turned over to the farmers of England, at a price of four pounds the ton, to be used as fertilizer.

Three hundred thousand cats from one district were lost to science. And biologists have scarcely been able to find a few hundred mummified cats from over the whole world to aid them in their studies of the first domestic cats.

The Egyptians pushed their cult of the cat to the point of aberration. The Persians, in the year 500 BC, laid seige to Pelusium, which used to stand where Tisseh, near Port Said, stands today. All the tactics and efforts of Cambyses, their leader, were being blocked by the fierce resistance of the Egyptians, and the Persians were beginning to lose heart. Then Cambyses had an idea. He ordered his soldiers to search over the whole region for eight days and seize the

The Egyptian goddess Bastet, who symbolizes femininity and maternity

*Egyptian mummified cat
of the Roman period*

*Two mummified heads of cats
of the Roman period*

greatest possible number of cats, and to hold them prisoner without doing them any harm. Three days later, when the moment of the attack arrived, the Egyptians, thunderstruck, saw panic-stricken cats surging in from all sides. The cats raced ahead of the Persian Army, in which each soldier calmly advanced, holding in his arms like a shield or buckler a living cat. Counter-attack? Let fly a single weapon at these adored cats? They would risk injuring ten cats in trying to kill one Persian. What subject of Pharaoh's would have taken the responsibility on his life in this world or the next of so dramatic a sacrilege? Pelusium capitulated without a single blow having been exchanged.

THE CAT AS SYMBOL

In Japan, cats are most particularly venerated after their deaths. In Tokyo, they have their own temple, the temple of Go-To-Ku-Ji. It is small in size, but perfectly proportioned, and concealed by foliage. It is typically Japanese, both in style and in the material used, which is crossed battens of wood. It opens with a great doorway, a kind of lattice barrier, flanked on both sides by two less conspicuous, bell-shaped entrances. This temple is served by priests who wear sacred vestments and intone gentle religious chants for the repose of these small feline souls. Before entering Go-To-Ku-Ji it is traditionally necessary to pass before the famous 'guardians of duty' who remind visitors that to live is to pray, work and forget oneself in thinking of others, and that the death of a simple cat is, as much as the death of a human being, an event requiring gravity and respect.

At the heart of the temple, on the altar, appears the most astonishing assembly of cats, sculptured, painted and carved in relief. Cats on cloth and paper, in porcelain and bronze. There they are crowded one against the other, frozen motionless and mounting guard. And each one has its small right paw curiously raised to the height of its eyes as if to greet the visitor or attract his attention. This is the classic way of representing 'Maneki-Neko', the small female cat who lures and enchants people, brings happiness and ensures good luck.

Almost all the cats in this necropolis welcome you this way – in a seated position with one paw in the air. However, at a turn of a passage, one comes up suddenly against a completely different type of statue. It represents the 'Spirit-Cat', symbolizing in one image all the cats buried in this district. For the Japanese Buddhist, to bury his small companion in this temple or nearby, and to offer at this altar on the same day a painted or sculptured likeness of this cat, is both to offer homage to fidelity and to gain a very reassuring pledge of tranquillity and good luck for himself in his own lifetime.

The cemetery stretches out around the altar. The graves are covered with tablets inscribed with prayers for the souls of the cats, and with invocations to Buddha, God of Wisdom and Peace, whose image appears in the corner of each tablet. The purpose of all that appears on these tablets is to wish the dead cats the swiftest possible attainment of Nirvana, as this will mean that the human soul of which each animal was merely the earthly shell will have achieved at last its final perfection.

But, as there is not a religion in the world that manages on thoughts and words alone, so, under the great doorway at the entrance to the temple, there are set out for sale all kinds of sculptured cats, in hardwood, stone and black marble. Any of the faithful can purchase here the statue they find that most resembles their dear departed. The more wealthy cat-owners, however, disdain these prefabrications. A rich man usually commissions a statue to be specially made during the lifetime of his favourite cat.

The 'Spirit-Cat' in the temple of Go-To-Ku-Ji in Tokyo represents all the cats buried in the temple cemetery

It is only in Japan that the cat has this religious significance after its death. And although one might suppose that this cult of the soul of dead cats originated in ancient times, it is interesting to note that the temple of Go-To-Ku-Ji was built barely two hundred years ago. The choice of the cat to figure in this cult seems to have been simply the choice of an animal that was symbolically pure enough to act as the messenger between Buddha, the unique and the perfect, and the five hundred million Asians who adore him.

It is worth noting, however, the curious fact that Buddhism, which was taught in India more than four hundred years before Christ, advocated the protection of all animal creatures *except* the cat. This precept of early Buddhism was not governed by motives of hygiene, aesthetics or ignorance but, according to Louis Léon de Rosny, a scholar of eclectic Buddhism, it was due to the belief that 'this small domestic feline, when called like all the other animals to attend the entrance of Buddha into Nirvana, fell asleep on the way and arrived too late for the ceremony'. In any case, the sentence appears to have been not without appeal, because in the Buddhism of today the cat, like all other beings, can attain Nirvana.

Before Islam the Arabs adored a golden cat. The Koran, however, is more practical, advising that the cat be respected and not chased from either mosque or tent. But at least one ancient custom remains. Elian J. Finbert claims that the faithful of the mystic brotherhood of Siddi Heddi entice into their sanctuaries ownerless cats, fatten them up and once a year eat them during the course of a ritual feast, even though Islam forbids the eating of all carniverous animals.

They are not the only ones to feast on cats. The Dutch daily newspaper *De Telegraaf* reported, on March 1966, a story which the Brussels correspondent of *Le Monde* passed on to France on 6 March under the title:

*From the studio of Hans Baldung
Grien : a cat takes part in a witches'
Sabbath*

'The artificial Paradises of Anvers: from sadism to gastronomy'.

'The town of Anvers was the scene of action of a group of "ecstatics" of between eighteen and forty years old, who, advocating new methods of releasing the mind, proceeded to the collective massacring of cats. The classic drugs no longer allowing them to achieve ecstasy, these debauchees took to cats, preferably black ones. The animal would first be hung by a rope for twenty minutes. If it succeeded in escaping this martyrdom, it was sent through a door which, on being closed violently, crushed its head. It was then dismembered and cut into small pieces under the haggard eyes of the members of the sect relishing the spectacle.' Finally, and always, according to *De Telegraaf*, 'the cat was cooked and eaten'.

Such a story, told in the middle of the twentieth century and in a highly civilized Occidental city, may make the history which follows less incomprehensible

THE CAT IN DIABOLISM

From the first days of her triumph, the Christian Church wished to ignore the cat, in reaction to the pagan religions that had adored it. Egypt had made a god of it. The Greeks had consecrated it to Artemis (Diana) whom the church thought of as the Devil's consort.

In Europe, the Church denounced the cult of Freyia and Holda, which flourished during the fifteenth century. These cults practised rites in which, it was believed, the goddesses appeared every night; one in a chariot drawn by twenty cats and the other followed by a cortege of virgins, either riding astride tomcats, or else disguised in their skins. Working themselves into a frenzy by screaming out the battle cries and howlings of cats, the adepts at these reunions gave themselves over to wild and extravagant orgies. It seems that these Sabbaths, that reunited the initiates one day in every week, always proceeded in the same fashion. The witch arrived disguised as a black cat and riding a broom or a sow. The Devil presided over the festival and, accompanied by sounds from the violin of death, women with cats tied to their petticoats danced with sorcerors amid cries of 'Har, Har, Sabbat! Sabbat!'

In Indre, a district of France, this sabbath of cats took place at the foot of a cross, but cats with the slightest trace of rustiness or brown in their black coats could not participate. In Maine, an ancient French province, only cats at least eight years old were admitted to the annual sabbath.

In Finistère, especially at the time of Advent, the cats left the houses as night fell and gathered at some square or cross-roads, from which there soon arose into the night screams and ominous howlings as the animals fell upon each other. The peasants who had stayed out late brought back tales that these insults, vociferations and blasphemies were clearly uttered in the Christian tongue.

'Only imbeciles,' claims *L'Evangile du Diable* (The Devil's Bible), 'do not know that all cats have a pact with the Devil.' Nobody knows what they gained by this, but this book of black magic claimed that one thing was certain: the Devil invited all cats to feast with him at Mardi Gras, and that was why it was so rare to encounter a single cat on that day. 'You can understand why cats sleep or pretend to sleep all day long, beside the fire in winter or in the sun in the summer. It is their task to patrol the barns and stables all night, to see everything, to hear everything. And you can deduce from that why the Evil Spirits, warned just in time, always manage to vanish away, to disappear before we can see them.'

The same 'Bible' gives two precise recipes: one to enable you to watch, if not participate in a Witches' Sabbath and the other to make you invisible. The first instructs you to mix together a hundred grams of lard, five grains of hashish, a pinch of hellebore root and one crushed sunflower seed. You are to smear this ointment on your neck and ears in the

The black cat has always caught the imagination of the Western World

evening before going to bed, and at the same time think very hard of what you wish to see or experience at the Sabbath.

Narcotics were frequent ingredients of these recipes; henbane, datura and the poppy were widely used. It is easy to see how these drugs, combined with the general fanaticism and obscurantism of the period, could have disturbed and excited the mind, transforming simple trees tossed by the wind into a gigantic witches' roundelay.

The second formula makes a person invisible. For this you take a black cat, a new cooking pot and an agate stone and put them all on the fire in water that you have drawn from a fountain at midnight. 'Put the cat in the pot, hold the lid down with the left hand, let it boil for twenty-four hours and then, having placed the meat in a new dish, throw it over your shoulder and watch yourself till you no longer see yourself in a mirror . . . .'

Poor black cat! In their fear of evil spirits, men have always made it an object of fear or hatred. Even the Chaldeans, believed to have been the world's greatest inventors of philtres, talismans and evil spells, believed that a cat the colour of the night was the most disquieting omen of all. When they saw one they used to cry aloud 'Hilka! Bescha!' (Be off, accursed one!)

For the Christian the black cat was always Lucifer's messenger. And sometimes they revenged themselves on the black cat for the fear they had of the Devil. A great deal of folklore concerning the Devil and black cats centres around bridges and crossroads. The Devil was often invoked when a bridge was about to be built, because people thought that only he could be audacious enough to throw an arch out into open space to bind together two steep river banks. This is why there are so many bridges named 'The Devil's Bridge' throughout Western Europe. But when the Devil's payment was due, the Christians almost always managed to trick him. One story tells how a Breton bishop, Saint Cedo, met Lucifer at a certain bridge

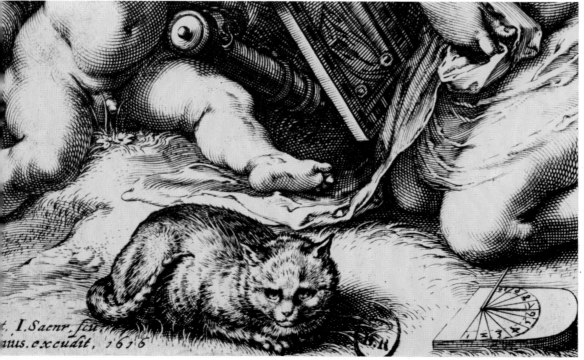

and learned that the inhabitants of the country around had, without much serious reflection on the matter, contracted with the Devil to hand over to him the first passer-by who crossed their bridge. The bishop handed over a black cat as payment and the furious Devil was obliged to accept, for the cat had certainly been the first to cross the bridge.

In Brittany there are said to be tempting treasures at the cross-roads which the black cats guard at night. In order to gain these treasures one must sell one's soul to the Devil, and the contract must be signed with the little finger of the left hand dipped in blood.

In the Midi, in the thirteenth century, a bull of Pope Gregory IX accused the Cathars of the crime of breeding black cats, cats the colour of Evil and Shame.

Black cats and witches were inseparable, as we can see from the reports of numerous trials for witchcraft. Jean Bossu has drawn attention to some of these, including the trial, in 1586, of the witch Anna Winkelzipfel. She was burnt at Bergheim, having been found guilty of disguising herself in the skins of black cats and entering the room of Jacques Potter with the intention of doing him harm.

In 1681 the French dramatist Regnard, returning from a voyage in Lapland, told how the sorcerors of the snows boasted of their power to turn evil-doers into black cats.

In Obernai, the old women of the country are still believed to have the power of turning themselves into black cats in order to slip into the stables more easily at night to harm the cattle.

Charlatans and rogues made the most of these beliefs. The charlatans took heavy fees from the simple people who came for their ridiculous and often dangerous advice. Smugglers, thieves and counterfeiters spread rumours of phantoms and apparitions, of secret meetings between cats and the Devil, with the sole purpose of keeping the people

of the neighbouring countryside from the various lairs where these rogues hid their booty and the tools of their trade.

Britain and America had their witches and their witches' cats, but these are not as startling as their continental counterparts. Cats were only one type of 'domestic familiar' that a witch might have. Others included dogs, goats, rats, pigs and just about any other kind of small animal that happened to be about. Similarly, although we find evidence of animal sacrifice in Britain, the cat was not singled out for the honour. A dog or a hen were just as likely victims. In fact, the English authority on witchcraft, Pennethorne Hughes has ventured to suggest that the cat's predominance in folk memory has less to do with ancient pagan belief than it had with the simple fact that old women – who were the most likely to be suspected of witchcraft – kept cats.

One bit of witchcraft which seems to have been a Scottish speciality was the ability to cause a shipwreck by tossing a cat into the sea. A famous incident, at the end of the fifteenth century, was the apparent attempt to kill the King and Queen by means of 'cat conjuring'. The witches, accused of treason, confessed that they had caused the storm in which the King and Queen were very nearly shipwrecked. First they christened a cat and then they bound to it several joints from a dead man. The next day they threw the animal into the sea. The result was a terrible tempest the like of which had rarely been seen before.

THE SACRIFICE OF CATS

The black cat had associations with evil other than that of being Satan's only representative to the human race. Long before the time of the Church's curse, and certainly at the time of the Gauls, the sacrifice of a cat – replacing, no doubt, an even more ancient human sacrifice – was thought to be the simplest, most certain and most apt method of keeping away evil fortune. This belief

According to an Indian rite a reincarnated soul could be liberated by throwing a black cat into a furnace

The disturbing black cat

The devil seemed to love the company of the cat (nineteenth century)

probably has many origins.

At Metz, a town in the Moselle district of France, a Bohemian woman who had been accused of witchcraft and condemned to be burnt at the stake, was secretly saved from death by order of the bishop. Under cover of the dense smoke, a cat was substituted for the woman. This cat, howling and half-burnt, succeeded in escaping and disappearing into the crowd, who were then convinced that they had seen the soul of the dead witch pass by. From that day the people of Metz believed that all cats were bewitched animals. Soon the custom of sacrificing cats *en masse* took hold in various parts of Lorraine, spreading to many other places and rapidly becoming an annual ceremony.

It was also in Metz in 1344, that thirteen cats were burned alive in an iron cage as a remedy for an epidemic of St Vitus' dance. One day the good people of Metz woke up with an irresistible need to dance. The men leapt and bounded about; the women spun like tops. This madness spread into the streets, and rapidly took over whole quarters of the town. No remedy could quell the symptoms of the disease. The epidemic was at its peak when there arrived in the town a pious knight-at-arms. Finding the performance rather unusual and wanting a better chance to observe it, he took lodgings at an inn. Hardly had he stretched himself out on his bed when he saw sitting in the fireplace a very large and intensely black cat. The animal was staring fixedly at him out of gold-coloured eyes that flamed and flickered with light. Always ready to do battle, our knight jumped to the foot of his bed, made the sign of the cross, seized his sword and flung himself at the wild beast. There was no need to strike. At the sight of the sign of the cross the cat leapt out of the hearth spitting blasphemies and disappeared into thin air. Carefully sheathing his sword, the pious knight fell to his knees and prayed to

Heaven: he had seen the Devil!

The next morning the epidemic had miraculously ceased. It was then that the magistrates decided that the best way to hunt Satan out of his feline shape was to burn the cat alive. They proceeded to organize a ritual burning. For a long time afterwards, on every Eve of Saint John, the people of Metz commemorated this victory by lighting a great bonfire and throwing on to it the fateful number of thirteen living cats. The ceremony always followed the same course. The governor and the municipal magistrate marched with great pomp, preceded by halberdiers and torchbearers, to a fixed place on the Esplanade. At the appointed hour these two vested representatives of military and civil power paraded three times round the mound of faggots, to the top of which had been hoisted the heavy iron cage loaded with victims. With the same gestures, each of the two leaders threw a lighted wax torch on to the pile. Immediately, the people broke loose and flung themselves into a dance round this roaring, crackling mass of flames. It was not until 1773 that Mme d'Armentières, wife of the Governor of Trois-Evêchés, succeeded in obtaining a reprieve for the unhappy animals and putting a stop to this cruel game.

It has been recorded that a similar custom was celebrated in the Seine-et-Marne district of France. On the twelfth of July 1739, the Mayor of Melun and his municipal magistrates also paraded three times round a pile of faggots which the mayor then lit. As the flames rose up living cats were thrown on, and afterwards the numerous spectators collected scraps of charred wood to take back home as a charm against lightning.

In Paris, from 1471, Louis XI used to attend the fires of Saint John with great flourish and ceremony for the simple pleasure of watching two dozen cats burned alive. Almost all the kings after him followed

Lithograph by Goya

this example. Henry IV and Louis XIII took great pleasure in the festival, whose origin was doubtless more ancient than that of the French Monarchy itself. Louis XIV, however, went only once, in 1648. And he was the last sovereign to observe this manifestation of popular feeling, this festival against which Saint Eloi had stood up in vain in the seventh century, and which, according to the seventeenth-century theologian Jacques Bénigne Bossuet, the Church reluctantly supported only because it knew that the practice of cat-burning had stubbornly persisted for centuries: if it was going to exist anyway it was better a Christian rite than a pagan one.

THE CAT AND MAGIC

Not all the beliefs and superstitions involving cats are as dramatic and horrible as those associated with the practices of Western European diabolism and black magic.

Titus Flavius, who lived for a long time in Alexandria, described what happened when children of Egyptian families fell seriously ill. The relatives would shave their heads and sell their hair for the equivalent weight in gold or silver. This money they would take to one of the guardians of animals and commission him to make offerings to one of the sacred beasts. If the offering was destined for the cats, the guardian would convert the money into milk straight from the cow and into fish which he would cut into slices. To call the cats each guardian had his own particular way of clacking his tongue. The cats were kept in the interiors of the temples, separated from the public by hangings of woven gold. When they heard the call they would swarm up, often eagerly and in great numbers. At the sight of them the guardian would begin to intone a kind of soft chant and, respectfully raising the golden veil, he would leave the relatives the task of reading in the sacred stare whether their child would

From the legend of a prince who threw a white cat's head and tail into the fire to conjure away evil luck

An adulterous Turkish woman condemned to be drowned with a living cat

recover quickly or whether there was no hope.

In magic practices, the function of the cat is often that of a fetish, lucky charm, mascot, talisman or amulet. A very ancient custom demands that, to ensure the solidity of a building, a living cat should be walled up and built into the foundations. Some of these cats have been discovered in the ruins of medieval castles, or during demolition work there. They have been found effectively mummified, dessicated and emaciated but perfectly preserved either because they were sealed off from humidity or because death from hunger and thirst always entails a degree of dryness that stops putrefaction taking place. There is in the veterinary college of Alfort the dessicated corpse of a cat which was found before the First World War between the ceiling and floor of an old seventeenth century house in the Rue Mouffetard.

In Russia, Poland and Bohemia, it was

thought that to bury a cat alive in a field of corn would ensure the best harvest. In the French province of Béarn a kitten buried in the earth was believed to purge the ground of weeds. In Anjou, newly-born kittens are never destroyed. They are brought up until they are three months old, and then let loose into the streets of the small market towns. How many other beliefs are similarly the product of an irrational quackery? J. G. Frazer, in his work on myth and folklore, *The Golden Bough*, relates that in France and Germany at the beginning of each summer, the following rite occurred. Plump cats, representing the spirit of the crops, were covered in flowers and crowned with garlands and eaten on the first day of the harvest!

In the Vosges it is held to be enough to slip the left paw of a black cat into a hunter's game-pouch to stop him aiming properly.

For a long time the people of Lyon talked of the evil power of a restaurateur whose black cat stew was famous. It was believed

that if this innkeeper secretly wished to bring bad luck on one of his clients all he would have to do would be to take, on any slight pretext or other, two steps backwards!

According to the old folklore of Finland, cats had the responsibility of carrying the soul of those who died to the kingdom of the dead. But in the American South, it is widely believed that if a cat should so much as sniff at a dead body, a disaster would fall upon the whole family. This superstition stems from yet another, which holds that a cat will mutilate a corpse. The only fact to support this belief is that cats do sometimes show excitement in the presence of the dead. In Holland, it is thought that people who dislike cats are pretty well certain to be carried to the cemetery through rain. They also believe that those who look after cats badly and neglect them will have umbrellas at their weddings.

Almost everywhere the black cat is believed to have the evil eye. In Sicily, they

have a saying that there is trouble if a black cat comes into your house; chase it off immediately, because it is no messenger of good fortune. In the Ozark country of the American Midwest, many people believe that it is good luck if a strange black cat visits a house, but very bad luck if it decides to stay. And, just as a black cat crossing one's path always means bad luck in this part of the country, it is sometimes also said that seeing a white cat on the road brings good luck. Finally, if an Ozark family keeps black cats about the house, all the daughters will be old maids.

The national epic of Finland, the *Kalevala*, relates that one day a witch entered a house full of people and began incantations. Within minutes everyone there was thrown into a sledge drawn by a huge cat who carried them off to the borders of Pohjola, that world of evil spirits and perpetual night where the noise of horses' hooves can no longer be heard and foals can live without

'The rat regrets it too late
when the cat has him by the neck'
(Anonymous engraving of the
eighteenth century)

'Here is the cat, look for the rats'

the need of grazing.

Popular knowledge has forgotten the origin of these confused beliefs, but all countries have kept a great number of proverbs and sayings evoking the power of the cat, a power that can be made use of by anyone who follows the famous recipe of Hermes: 'If you wish to see what others cannot see, rub your eyes with cat's dung and the fat from a white hen mixed together in wine.'

THE CAT IN PROVERBS

There are many French proverbs about cats. 'It is bad luck to cross a stream carrying a cat in your arms.' Perhaps it is more one's balance than one's luck that is threatened here. No less astonishing are these sayings: 'If a girl treads on a cat's tail, she will not find a husband before a year is out.' 'Whoever cares well for cats will marry as happily as he/she could wish.'

The provincial dialects are no less rich in proverbs. In Provence, they say that 'the greedy cat makes the servant girl watchful'. In Brittany 'the tongue of the cat is poisonous, the tongue of the dog cures'. In Franche-Comté, 'handsome cats and fat dungheaps are the sign of a good farmer'. And 'a scalded cat dreads even cold water'. The Arabs express the same thought in more picturesque terms: 'A cat bitten once by a snake dreads even rope'. In la Creuse, 'the dog wakes three times to watch over his master; the cat wakes three times to strangle him'. In Lorient, 'all cats are bad in May'. In Belgium an old Flemish phrase, 'the cat is in the clock', means there is quarrelling in the household.

Aesop's fox, who was unable to reach the grapes and therefore declared them to be sour, is often replaced in proverbs by the cat. A Kurdish proverb goes: 'the cat who could not reach the roast cried, "In honour of my father's memory, I will not eat it"'. There is a Turkish saying: 'the cat failed to make off with the liver and said, "I am fasting today"'. A Russian proverb repeats the theme: 'the cat who failed to reach the sausage hanging from the ceiling said, "It is not worth the trouble, today is Friday"'.

There are many English proverbs about cats such as 'curiosity killed the cat; satisfaction brought it back', and 'a cat may look at a king'.

In Italy, on the subject of the fear cats have of the water, they say that 'the cat likes eating fish well enough, but not fishing'.

In Russia the cat is accused of egotism—'the cat who scratches, scratches for himself', and of double dealing—'there is no kitten too little to scratch'. This last appears again in Spain as 'the cat always leaves a mark on his friend'.

All countries and languages have their version of the saying 'all cats are grey in the dark'. Likewise 'when the cat is away, the mice will play' is a common thought, though variously expressed in Italian, Portuguese, Spanish and Dutch. The Portuguese also say: 'wherever the mice laugh at the cat, there you will find a hole'. And the Madagascans say: 'the rat stops still when the eyes of the cat shine'.

In *Kristin Lavransdatter*, a novel set in medieval Scandinavia, Sigrid Undset recalls the Swedish saying, 'there is commotion among the rats at night on the farm where the cat is young'. The Italians put it the other way, 'old cats mean young mice'. According to Cervantes, 'the cat who miaows, hunts the less', a comment that might be applied to men as well. The Spanish have the simplest saying of all: 'un gato es un gato'—a cat is a cat.

LUCKY CATS

Belief in the supernatural power of the cat has left its picturesque mark of hundreds of legends in folklore throughout the world.

In Burma, the cat has never quite been worshipped as divine, but has at all times been the object of a cult. Because of their indolence, gentleness and perfection of colour, white cats in particular have been thought of as the image and symbol of beatitude.

During the Second World War, the Burmese were subjected to heavy propaganda on the part of the Japanese, who were trying

Il gagne le pais pas,
Ainsy s'en va le chat
doucement au fromage,
Mais a bon chat bon rat
elle ne laisse pas,
D'empescher quil n'ayt
sur elle cette auantage.

Il luy tire
les vers
du nez

a bon   bon
chat   Rat.

De bon fromage, mange peu,
si tu es sage.

Mariez vous c'est chose honneste
Ie n'en feré pas mary, mais
ne soyez pas si beste que
despouser vostre mary.

'She leaves the cheese to the cat'
(Engraving of the seventeenth century)

Caricature of the taking of Arras,
accompanied by the saying which the
Spaniards took as their motto:
'When the French take Arras
Mice will eat cats,
The French took Arras
Not a mouse ate a cat'

'Joining forces against the rat'
(a popular German image)

to paralyse the supply lines of the Allies by inciting the Burmese to oppose the construction of strategic roads. It became practically impossible for the Allies to recruit local labour. In spite of extremely high wages, after two or three days on the job the Burmese would down their tools and flee into the jungle.

This went on until an English colonel with considerable knowledge of local beliefs had an original idea. First of all the order went out to all ranks to collect the greatest possible number of white cats. In the meantime, the silhouettes of white cats were stencilled on all the army vehicles, jeeps, trucks, tanks, etc. as if this were the emblem of the British Army. It certainly proved a lucky one. The rumour swiftly spread that the English aerodromes were unassailable, for they were the refuge of the immaculate cat. The same applied to the rolling stock. No more was needed. The native population ignored the Japanese propaganda and gave the full weight of their support to the Allies.

Throughout the Midi of France there is a belief in *matagots* or magician-cats. These correspond to the *chat d'argent* of Brittany who can serve nine masters and make all of them rich. Both are black cats who have the power to attract wealth into any house where they are loved and fed well according to the following formula. First, you must catch a *matagot* by luring him to you with a plump chicken. (The *matagot* is, incidentally, a glutton.) Then you grab him by the tail (gently of course), put him in a sack and carry him home with great secrecy and without once lokking backwards. Then shut him up in a large chest, and every time you eat give him the first mouthful of your own food. Only if you follow these directions will you find, each morning, at the bottom of the chest beside him, a golden coin.

The inhabitants of La Ciotat near Marseille have for a long time believed in the *matagot* and his magic riches. Less than a century ago, the name of Coste, which is a nickname given to the *matagot*, was given to a fisherman there because he was the only one never to get his lines tangled and always to bring back a good catch whatever the weather. Today there are still people called 'Coste-Matagot' in Provence.

In England, the best-known *matagot* is Dick Whittington's famous cat. According to popular legend, Dick Whittington was a penniless orphan employed as a scullion by a rich merchant. He allowed his only possession, a cat, to go along on a journey of one of his master's ships. Then, having suffered much ill-treatment from his employer, Dick decided to run away. But when he got to the top of Highgate Hill he heard the Bow bells calling him back. He returned to find that his cat had come back with a fortune for him, and from that day he never looked back. He married the boss's daughter, his business prospered, and he finally became the mayor of London.

So the legend goes. The historical Dick Whittington was indeed the mayor of London – three times in fact (1397, 1406 and 1409) – but no one knows how true the cat story is. This very same legend – in which the cat brings his master a fortune – was known in the folklore of Denmark, Persia, and Italy at least a century before the time of Dick Whittington.

It certainly seems likely that Whittington's cat was really a cat-boat, that is, a coal and timber vessel. This sort of cat would be much more likely to bring its owner a fortune – especially in the shipping trade.

Nevertheless, most people like to believe in the four-legged cat, and so, we still hear the following story, told as if it were historical fact:

Richard Whittington, at the age of ten, woke up one morning to find himself orphaned and penniless and with only the street for his home. Without a tear, or any recrimination he started walking. He took with him his only remaining possession, a small cat that was now even dearer to him than it had been before. Moved by the boy's silent grief and his love of this animal, one of his father's creditors offered to give Richard a post. Quickly the young man showed himself to be a hard worker. He was so intelligent and cooperative that three years later his master, leaving for the coast of Africa, took the boy – and his cat – with him.

They had great success. When they arrived in that distant land they had the luck to disembark in a region infested with rats. When the first native sovereign welcomed the two merchants with their shipload of goods for sale, the rats scattered in all directions, even taking shelter under the king's couch. Dick's cat immediately gave chase, and in less than an hour there were so many corpses around that the King offered to buy the cat at any price. Dick hesitated for several days. Then, finally succumbing to this impressive offer, he decided sadly to give up his dear companion. Thus he returned to England a rich and enterprising man, the hero of a 'rags-to-riches' success story.

Whatever the true story, the legend of Dick Whittington and his cat has become part of the canon of English folklore. His cat is the hero of traditional Christmas pantomimes and plays and is a character well known to every young child.

In the Ozarks, when a girl receives a proposal of marriage and she cannot decide whether to say yes or no, she is often advised to 'leave it to the cat'. She takes three hairs from a cat's tail, wraps them in white paper and puts the package under her doorstep. The following morning she unfolds the paper carefully, without disturbing the hairs. If they have arranged themselves into what looks like the letter Y she should say yes, but if they fall into the shape of N, she would be better off single.

*The idea of a cat who turns into a
a woman is found in the legends of all
countries and peoples*

Finally, in the lowlands of Brittany, it is
firmly believed that in the fur of each black
cat there exists one hair of the most perfect
white. If you discover it, and tear it out
without being scratched, you will hold in
your hand a unique talisman, the most
powerful of good-luck charms. And it will
make you either extremely rich or lucky in
love, whichever you choose.

I particularly like this last legend. It
implies that you have sufficiently gained the
sympathy of your cat for it to allow you
patiently to search through the whole of its
coat for this one famous hair. The happiness
that can come from this unique white hair is
symbolic. It is recognition and reward for
whoever can prove so much understanding
and goodwill towards an animal that has
been for so long despised and ill-treated.

THE METAMORPHOSES OF
CATS AND WOMEN

There are many stories in the myths, legends
and folklore of the world in which there
occur transformations or metamorphoses of
cats into humans and humans into cats.

Six centuries before Christ, Aesop told
how Venus, solicited by a cat who had fallen
for a handsome young man, agreed to turn
the cat into a woman. But the creature remained, in spite of her appearance, still so
much a cat that the appearance of a simple
mouse scampering through the bedroom
was enough to make her leap out of bed.

Five hundred years later Ovid, in his
Metamorphoses, described the terror of the
Gods before Typhus, a mere son of the
Earth, who sent them flying into Egypt.
They hid there in borrowed shapes, Apollo
disguising himself as a crow and his sister,
Diana, becoming a cat.

The surnames of some of the inhabitants
of certain villages in France recall their
traditional habit of 'turning themselves into
cats' in order to exert evil power. Such are
the *chettas* (female cats) of Jainvillote and
the Vosges. Almost all the stories and legends

behind these names tell of a transformation. One such tale is that of *la chatte de la Croix des Haies*, which when told by an eloquent story-teller, can be spun out to last a whole evening.

'One evening the good Pichard was returning from Haute-Chapelle, near the pond of Bain, where he had been courting the woman he was to make his wife, when he saw at the foot of the cross in the square called *la Croix des Haies* a beautiful big white cat. She miaouwed tenderly, and crossed over to rub herself against his legs. From that day, every evening and at that same spot he would meet this lovesick cat. So it went on until he was married to Nanon, his fiancée. Months passed and Pichard forgot his encounters. Then, one night, having

woken with a start, he discovered he was alone. The beautiful Nanon was gone. Pichard found it all very strange, particularly as, in the early hours of dawn, just as he was opening his eyes, his wife quietly slipped into the bed.

'Pichard questioned her, got annoyed, threatened, sulked and, when the evening came, lay down beside her. Suddenly, at midnight, no more wife . . . but only the great white cat purring beside him in the room. Yet the following morning his wife was there again. Night after night the same thing happened. How could she get out? The door was firmly bolted. Pichard, fascinated, set himself to watch. He failed to hear his wife leave, but did suprise a small white paw slipping through the doorway to

Effigies of cats in the cemetery of the temple of Go-To-Ku-Ji in Tokyo

reach the bolt. Softly Pichard rose, and struck the brazen paw with a thunderous blow of his hatchet. A horrible scream echoed the blow.

'For eight days Nanon did not appear. Eventually she returned, her head low, her face flushed with confusion. She passed her husband, went straight to her bed without a word and wept for shame: her hand had been chopped off at the wrist!'

The variation of this story that is told in the Ozarks retains the horror, but leaves out the romance. A drunken braggart accepted a dare to sleep in a house that had once been used by witches. When he had finished his jug of whisky and was just beginning to fall asleep—at midnight—an enormous cat suddenly appeared. It howled and spat at him, so he shot at it with his horse-pistol. At that moment a woman's scream was heard in the distance, and just as the candle went out, the hillman saw a woman's bare and bloody foot wriggling around on the table. The following day he learned that a woman who lived nearby had accidentally shot her foot off and had died from loss of blood. Those who elaborate the story say that she died howling and spitting like a cat.

No doubt such stories are the basis for the gossip that is sometimes heard in these back-wood villages when a woman is suspected of being unfaithful to her husband: she visits her lover in the form of a cat. Once inside his house, the woman resumes her natural form and spends the night with him. Just before dawn she again becomes a cat and returns to her home, where she is transformed back into a woman—before her husband awakes.

In the Far East the cat plays much the same role in tales of magic. Hundreds of legends have been handed down in which cats take the shapes of old women, priests, courtesans and young girls in order to deceive their victims. It is even thought that, on reaching a certain age, cats acquire the faculty of speech. If one accepts this

On the facade of the temple of Go-To-Ku-Ji cats with raised paws represent Maneki-Neko

belief, one will not find it surprising that a cat can take possession of woman and speak through her mouth.

THE CAT IN FOLKLORE AND FAIRY TALE

There are certainly a few fairly monstrous cats in Asian legend and literature. There is, for example, the cat with two tails (Neko-Mata) who is killed by Inu Mura Dai-Kaku in a tale by the nineteenth-century Japanese author Ba-Kin. But evil cats are rare. Much more familiar are stories of 'Benefactor cats', talisman cats, the cats who look after men. They are common throughout China, Korea, Japan and the other countries of Asia.

A widespread belief among Japanese sailors is that cats of three colours (white, red and black) are able to foresee the approach of tempests. By climbing up the masts of the ships, they lead clear of the storms the wandering souls of those who have been shipwrecked and who are never at peace but drift continually on the crests of the waves. Cats are more often kept on Japanese ships than on any other ships in the world.

Another curious legend explains why the cat is absent from the zodiac. At the death of Buddha all the animals gathered round the body of the holy man and wept. Only the cat and the snake were not weeping. But the cat disgraced himself even further. At the moment when the whole assembly was plunged in the deepest sorrow, a young rat approached one of the lamps that were burning round the catafalque of the illustrious deceased and started quietly to lick up the oil. Seeing it, the cat could not contain himself. He leapt up and killed it. The action was natural enough. But to kill another being was to transgress against the orders of Buddha. It was for this crime that the cat was not included amongst the animals of the zodiac in either China or Japan.

Japan's ancient bogey-man, Neko-Baké

was an old sorceror and cannibal, who was said to take the shape of a cat in order to enter the houses of Tô-Kaï-dô to steal and eat disobedient children. Maneki-Neko was a small attractive female cat who lured and beckoned passers-by. She is the cat we have seen in the temple of Go-To-Ku-Ji, nearly always represented sitting with her paw raised as if in greeting. A great many Japanese paintings have for their subject a pair of fleeing cats. This is an allusion to a story in their folklore of two lovers who ran away to live together and were turned into cats.

The Japanese have always excelled at portraying the cat in art. Sometimes they achieve such effective realism that the works themselves are said to have a magic effect. A story of this kind is told of the famous sleeping cat, Nemuri-Neko, which was

created by the left-handed sculptor Hidari Jin Go Rô who lived from 1594 to 1634. It was so beautifully made that when it was placed in the temple of Iye-Yasu at Nik-kô, from that day not a mouse was seen there again. A painting of a cat by a certain Nitta, called the 'Nitta no Neko' also made its mark in legend. It is said to have the magic power of keeping off rats from any house in which it is present.

There are so many legendary tales from Asia that it is hard to choose which to tell. At the beginning of the nineteenth century an old fish-merchant fell into poverty as a result of a long illness. A cat took the shape of a man in order to give him two gold coins. This was his way of thanking the merchant, who had never failed to bring him some extra scraps whenever he called on the cat's master with deliveries of fish. When the

Head of the goddess Bastet, beautiful, ▶
hieratic, noble

*An illustration to the Japanese
folk-tale of the Vampire Cat of
Nabeshima*

A stylized cat of Japan

merchant had set himself up again, he called on his client and was stupefied to learn that the cat was no longer there. The master had had it killed because, he said, it had stolen two gold coins. Then the merchant understood that the stranger who had brought him the gold when he was penniless and on his sick-bed was none other than the cat transformed into human shape. He told the whole story, and was even able to produce the paper in which the money had been wrapped. The master was shocked. He saw his mistake. In order to atone and compensate for his injustice he had the cat disinterred and reburied beside a temple, giving it all the honours that were its due.

From southeast Asia we have the poetic tale of the transformation that created the famous sacred cat of Burma.

'In those days, in a temple built on the side of the mountain of Lugh, there lived in prayer the very venerable Kittah Mun Ha, the great Lama precious amongst the precious, whose golden beard had been plaited by the god Song Hio himself.

'There was not one minute, not one look, not one thought of his existence that was not consecrated to the adoration, the comtemplation, the pious service of Tsun Kyankze, the goddess with the eyes of sapphire. She presided over the transmigration of souls, which allows a kittah to relive the span of his animal existence in the body of a sacred animal before he takes up a body haloed in the total perfection and holiness of the great priests. Sitting in meditation beside Mun Ha was Sinh, his beloved oracle, a cat quite white with eyes of yellow, a yellow that reflected the golden beard of his master and the golden body of the goddess whose eyes were the colour of the sky . . . Sinh, the counsellor, whose ears, tail, nose and paws were the colour of soil, a sign of the taint and impurity in everything that touches or can touch the earth.

'Now, one evening, while a malevolent moon was permitting the enemy from Siam

to approach the sacred place, the great priest Mun Ha entered softly into the state of death, with his divine cat at his side and under the despairing eyes of his overwhelmed kittahs. It was then that the miracle took place . . . the unique miracle of the immediate transmigration. With one bound, Sinh was on the golden throne, perched on the head of his departed master. He arched himself up on this head which, for the first time, no longer contemplated the goddess. And Sihn also became spellbound before the eternal statue, and the bristling hairs on his white spine suddenly become the yellow of gold. And his golden eyes became blue, huge and profound like the eyes of the goddess. And as he turned his head gently towards the South door, his four paws, touching the venerable skull, became a blinding white. And as his eyes stared at the Southern door, the kittahs obeyed the expression in the eyes that were charged with hardness and with light. They threw themselves against the heavy bronze doors and against the first of the invaders.

'The temple was saved from profanation and pillage. Sinh, however, had not left the throne. He did not move for seven days, but on the seventh day, steadily facing the goddess and with his eyes on her eyes, he died, hieratic and mysterious, carrying towards Tsun Kiankze the soul of Mun Ha, from then on too perfect for this earth. And when, seven days later, the priests gathered before the statue to consult among themselves on the succession to Mun Ha, all the cats of the temple came running—and all were clothed in gold and gloved in white, and the yellow of all those eyes had been changed to a deep sapphire blue. In silence they all surrounded the youngest of the kittahs, who was designated in this way by the will of the goddess.

'From that day, if a sacred cat should die in the temple of Lao-Tsun, it is the soul of a kittah that takes its place for ever in the paradise of Song Hio, and the golden god.

And so it is unhappiness for him who, even without wishing it, hastens the end of one of these marvellous beasts. He is condemned to suffer for the entirety of his life. He will suffer in spirit and in the flesh. He will suffer until that time when the disturbed soul at last achieves peace.'

In India, too, the cat achieved recognition as a magical bringer of luck. The legend of the famous Patripatan is still current there. This cat was so cunning and so softly insidious that when he once climbed into the land of Devendiren in the sky (where, as we all know, there reigned twenty-four million gods and forty-eight million goddesses) in order to plead his master's cause, he became the friend of the all-powerful king of the gods and the beloved confidant of the most beautiful of the goddesses. He did so much and so well that for three hundred years he forgot to come down again to the earth. And while the prince and the inhabitants of the kingdom of Salangham awaited his return, not a person aged by a single hour during all the hours and days and years that passed. At last Patripatan returned. In his white paws he brought a complete and heavy branch of that rarest talisman-flower of Parasidam, in full flower. And from that day there was nothing but gentleness and beauty in that kingdom.

The cats of Russian folklore and legend also have a happy part to play. They are big and full of good will. They are generous, resourceful and cunning, like England's Puss-in-Boots and the French *Chat botte*. There is the cat Ivanovitch who, by his cunning in marrying a fox, came to reign over all the animals of the forest. Then, there is the tabby tom that belonged to the terrible Baba-Yaga (the witch with the legs of bare bone). This cat, touched by the gentleness of a tender-hearted girl, substituted himself for her and saved her from the wickedness of his own mistress. All are golden tales.

The rest of Europe, too, has its happy tales of cats—stories that have rid the cat of the odour of sulphur that clings to his reputation as the messenger of Beelzebub.

From Poland comes the gentlest story of all, the legend of the Pussy-Willow. A lot of little kittens were thrown into a river to drown. On the banks the mother cat wept so loud and long that the willows in sympathy consulted together as to what to do. They held out their long branches like mooring lines, and the little kittens, in desperation, clung to them. Ever since then, every spring, the willow-without-a-flower decks itself out in those gentle velvet buds that feel to the fingers like the silky coat of a small cat. In every land these soft willow trees are named after cats.

3 THE CAT AND THE RAT

Cats, rats, mice and men . . . throughout the world these are the main characters in the story of the cat.

The cat has always and everywhere been the rat's enemy, and according to Madagascan legend it was the rat who started it. The story goes like this: Once upon a time the cat and the rat lived in peace. One day, however, a great famine overtook them. There was nothing to eat, so they set off for a more fertile country. On the journey they came to the banks of a river too wide for them to swim across. Finding no driftwood to use as a raft, they dug up an enormous yam. The rat set to and hollowed it out with his teeth, making a canoe. When the boat was ready they embarked, the cat paddling and the rat navigating from the stern. But the rat, having been born with an eternal hunger, soon began to eat the edges of the yam. The cat knew nothing of this until the canoe shipped water and began to sink. Then, too late, he realized that the rat had foolishly put both their lives in danger. He meditated on revenge. In the water the rat, weak with hunger and fatigue and about to drown, begged the cat for help. 'I will only help you,' said the cat, 'if you agree to let me eat you when we reach land.' Always having a trick in reserve, the cunning rat consented. When they reached the bank the rat said to the cat, 'Wait till I am dry. While I am saturated you will not find me good to eat.' The cat believed him, and the rat used the delay to dig out a hole among some tree roots and hide. 'Now I am dry,' he cried. In vain the cat struggled, digging furiously, but the rat was safely out of reach deep in the earth. And so it was that the rat escaped and that the entire race of cats, duped, declared eternal war on the entire race of rats.

In Egypt, the cat rapidly showed itself to be a very effective weapon against the scourge of mice and rats. This precious quality must certainly have played as great a part in influencing the cat's destiny as any of its more spiritual qualities. Unfortunately, however, we have no documentation of the cat's ratting services to man at the beginning of its domestication.

Today we know more surely of the rat's great power for destruction and harm; we know what sort of diseases they spread throughout the world. In October, 1964, a desperate appeal went out from the town of Semargang in the heart of the island of Java. The teletypes of the press agencies of the world sent out the astonishing S.O.S.: 'Urgently required in Java all available ratting cats'.

It is surprising that rats are not among the ten classic plagues which the Bible says were inflicted on Egypt before Moses convinced the Pharoah that he should set the Hebrews free. Of course, to speak of rats in the Old Testament would have made it necessary to speak of cats as well, to describe their role and generally draw attention to them. But the new faith wanted to forget everything Egyptian, including the animal that they had made first a servant, then a guest and friend in their own homes, and finally a god. If Moses had called for a plague of rats the old pagan feline gods could have solved the problem only too well.

Rats! The word alone brings fear today. It is as if the memory of all the plagues, misery and destruction had been transmitted across the generations over millions and millions of years. The rat is man's contemporary in evolutionary time, and throughout the ages rats have followed men wherever they went. They followed in the wake of the great migrations of prehistoric times. They followed the historic invasions, the sea discovery routes and finally the maritime trade routes of commercial times. Ever since they first appeared on earth rats have clustered round the encampments, the rural communities, the urban societies of man. There they have flourished and increased in number, and always at man's expense—at the expense of his health, his property and all his efforts towards civilization.

Detail from an Egyptian fresco from the tomb of Menna at Thebes (XVIII^c dynasty)

All the corn of Europe's six Common Market countries combined equals the amount of the world's corn destroyed each year by rats alone! According to the figures published by France's *Union nationale des Coopératives agricoles de Céréales*, the figure is 150 million hundredweight of corn per year.

In the cities of France rats are so numerous that it is not an exaggeration to say that 'each inhabitant feeds his rat'. Feeding them costs the English economy £115,000,000 a year. In France the price is estimated at over 2,000,000,000 francs. In the United States the figure is believed to reach $500,000,000 – representing 200 million hundredweight of corn. Specialists estimate that a harvest infested with rodents can be destroyed by from 35% to 50%.

It is not hard to imagine how great a calamity an invasion of rats must have been in earlier times. What the rat does not destroy he contaminates. He adapts to all microbes as easily as to all climates. And wherever he goes he carries with him, and seems to thrive on, destruction and death.

We know next to nothing about the great epidemics that raged through Asia in the earliest historic periods. But we have some facts relating to the Mediterranean area. We know that in 1070 BC an epidemic broke out that the Bible calls 'the plague of the Philistines'. It killed more than fifty thousand people. Seven hundred years before Christ the Assyrians, having invaded Egypt, paid the price of twenty-five thousand dead from typhus. In 429 BC the plague of Athens ravaged not only the whole of Greece, but Persia, Palestine, Egypt and Syria, as well as Italy, Germany and Gaul.

Between 1346 and 1353 the Black Death killed twenty-five million people in Europe and twenty-three million in Asia. In 1665 the Pulmonary Plague ravaged London, killing half the population. It raged in Marseille in 1720, struck down the Egyptian Army in 1799, infected South America in

1900, and in 1920 produced in India a death-roll of eleven million, only to appear again in Taranto in 1945. And the source of this plague was rats! Always rats, against whom, until our own era, the only known weapon was the misunderstood and ill-loved cat! The cat is inseparable from civilization. On the continent of Europe the history of the cat is directly related to the history of the rat. According to whether the dangers of an invasion of rats and illness were menacing or receding, so were cats either cherished or persecuted.

THE RATTING CAT OF THE MIDDLE AGES

The great barbarian invasions brought rats in their wake, and Europe's first ratting cats, descended from imported Egyptian cats, began to know their golden age. From the North Sea to the Adriatic countries made laws in favour of the cats. Laws that fixed the price of cats implied official protection of them.

In France in the eleventh century, cats were so highly valued that they were listed in wills and legacies. In 1268, the *Livre des Mestiers* specified that the tax on the skins of wild cats was not the same as that on '*piaus de chaz privez que l'on dit chaz de feu ou de fouier*' (skins of private cats that we call the cats of the fire or hearth).

In the middle of the tenth century a disposition was introduced into the legal code of Wales by Howell Dda (Howell the Good), Prince of Aberfraw (South Central Wales). This law fixed the value of a ratting cat and also the penalties and fines which would fall on 'those who endangered its life, wounded it, or did not care for it properly'. The price of an animal varied according to whether its abilities had or had not been proved. A champion ratter was of the same value as a fourteen-day-old foal, a calf of six months, or a completely weaned pig. After killing a mouse, a cat was worth twice its value of the evening before. The purchaser

The migrations of the black rats and the brown rats,
as they followed the migrations of man.
Crusades facilitated the movements of the black rat between
the eleventh and thirteenth centuries, when the plague
killed millions. The brown rat appeared in the sixteenth
century, and within a hundred years had gained mastery
in Western Europe

North America: 1775

1800

Brown rats

Black rats

had the right to demand that ears, claws and eyes were impeccable, and, in the case of a female, that she was capable of reproduction and had the instincts of a good mother and was a provider of milk. Fraud or deceit in the sale of this living merchandise were severely repressed. If a cat did not give satisfaction, the seller had to either take it back or refund a third of the price he had charged. Whoever stole or killed a cat on someone else's land had to pay, either with a sheep and her lamb, or with that quantity of corn that would completely cover the corpse of the cat held by the tip of the tail so that its nose just brushed the ground. This strange law is of great interest, for it is the first historical reference to the domestic cat in Britain. It is not surprising that the British respect for cats was shown so early and so officially.

THE BLACK RAT

In France during the late Middle Ages the ratting cat was not treated with such solicitude. During this period it was completely accepted that rats should be the torture and the terror of prisoners. The Church cared even less for the prestige of the cat than it did for the welfare of the prisoners. However, in spite of the Church's hostility, the cat that was generally considered to be an instrument of the Devil continued to live in relative peace.

But then, with the return of the first Crusaders from the Holy Land, there came in the holds of their ships a previously unknown African pest: the black rat. Half a century was enough time for this clandestine immigrant to proliferate and swarm across the whole of France and into the rest of Europe. Rodents are famous for the speed with which they breed.

At the age of three months a pair of black rats is ready to breed, and they can then have from three to seven litters a year. Each litter numbers from five to fifteen. From such a couple the number of young annually produced, therefore, is between twenty and

one hundred. And when these reach three months, the reproduce in their turn. It has been calculated that within only three years a single couple could, between them and their offspring, produce millions of rats—those millions to produce more millions. It is easy to see how, with such a reproductive rhythm, the black rat managed to spread rapidly over both France and England and on into the rest of Europe, where it rapidly triumphed over the less harmful species which had until then flourished primarily around rural communities.

Fortunately, in the course of the many Crusades the same boats which had carried over the black rat also brought from Palestine more and more cats. The feline population increased. Paradoxically enough, the first to benefit were the cloisters, convents and abbeys which were infested with rodents. Cats were welcomed there with delight as much for the aesthetic and sympathetic pleasures they provided as for their utility. In Greece, on Mount Athos, the monks, in spite of being completely hostile to the female sex, made an exception in the case of female cats in order to propagate their mice-combatting feline stock.

These cats coming from the Middle East brought new blood to the stock of domestic cats in Europe. It must have been about this time that more distinct breeds began to appear.

Before such a natural enemy the black rats beat a retreat and appeared to diminish in number. The cats were acclaimed, but their success was short-lived. The common people made a mistake in beginning to love their cats, which were welcomed into both the cottages and the hearts of the people. The Church, having ignored the cat till then, became disturbed once again by the animal's charm and presence.

In Germany the rats were so numerous that only the presence of cats allowed people to sleep with any degree of tranquility. It

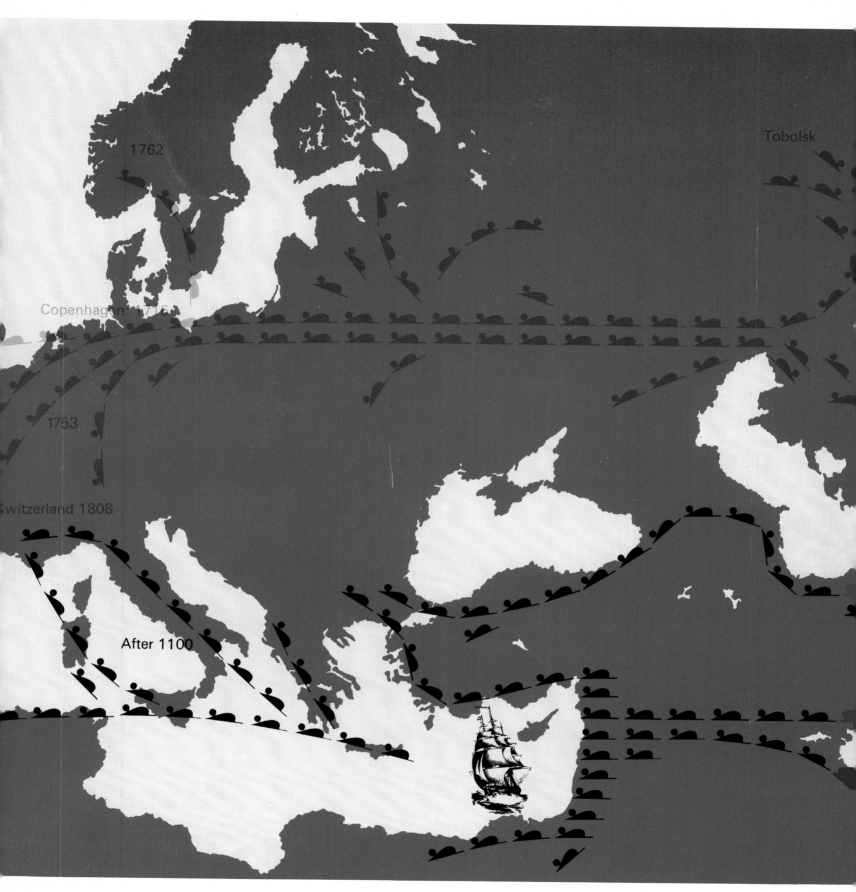

Tobolsk

1762

Copenhagen 1716

1753

Switzerland 1808

After 1100

55

was here that a pagan rite took fresh root. The cult of Freyia set out to honour the much envied fecundity of the cat, but in proceeding to unleash the instincts and excite the imagination it provoked orgies and bacchanals among its participants.

In order to attack the evil at its roots, action was taken against the cat. It became a criminal, and all crimes were heaped upon it. It was accused of being the eye and instrument of evil in this world. But the strangest thing was that the cat was rarely directly and fairly attacked, as were other 'dangerous' animals. The cat was cruelly destroyed. There were the sinister sacrificial burnings, the famous fires of Saint Jean, where cruelty was heaped upon cruelty. In some countries during these ceremonies a mast was set up in the circle of fire which was the only possible refuge for the unhappy animals. To reach this they fought amongst themselves, tearing at each other till the last of the survivors in his turn fell back into the flames. In other districts heavy cages of iron or wickerwork hampers were set high up on the brasier, and imprisoned in them five or six cats twisted in pain till their death freed them. In still other parts they were crucified

or flayed alive.

Nor did the Church's curse strike only the cats. It extended equally to those who, out of gratitude or pity, showed any friendship to cats. In 1484, under Pope Innocent VIII, the idea of the 'feline terror' knew no limits. Along with the Inquisition that reigned over Europe there spread a cat phobia that was just as cruel.

In German, Italy, France, indeed over the whole of Roman Catholic Europe except England, men and women were put to the torture, burnt or hanged because they had cared for a sick or wounded cat, or given one shelter. This hatred was not confined to Europe. In South Carolina and New England two thousand accusations of witchcraft involving cats were legally upheld.

It was during this period in Belgium that the ceremony of the Kattestoët flourished. Once a year, according to this cruel tradition, living cats were thrown from the tops of towers. The superstition served by this ceremony was the conjuring away of evil luck.

In Germany, in 1747, Archbishop Clement of Cologne published a decree which demanded that every owner of a cat have his

animal's ears cropped under penalty of a fine of half a florin.

For the whole of the eighteenth century these barbarous attitudes had free reign against the cats, who were thought to be thieves and good-for-nothing profiteers. And in the shadows of vaults and cellars and caves, sheltered by ruined buildings and tumbledown cottages, the rats continued to multiply their numbers and slowly take over the villages and towns.

THE BROWN RAT

Suddenly, in 1750, the brown rat appeared. Stronger and more prolific than the black rat, the brown rat soon became established in England, then spread over the northern half of continental Europe, up into Norway and down into Spain, finally reaching the Americas in 1775. It began its conquest by attacking the black rat. According to Buffon it did this *'en mangeant d'abord sa cervelle'* (by first eating its brain). Within a few years the black rat had withdrawn, without disappearing altogether.

The French Revolution ignored the brown rat. But in 1797 the Directory began to worry about this new and very dangerous

'The fortress of the cats beseiged by land and sea by rats and mice. More than eighteen hundred thousand rats and mice were killed'. A medieval engraving called 'The Fortress of Cats' from Northern France

A new friend?

enemy. In 1799 the first cases of plague appeared in the expeditionary army in Egypt. But Napoleon had only scorn for cats. (Later, in Saint Helena he described in his *Mémorial* the rats, 'énormes, méchants et hardis' [huge, evil and bold] that disturbed his sleep.) In Egypt he referred to all the authorities to find some modern weapon against the rats. Poisons too often killed humans as well. The most complicated traps proved useless. There was no recourse but to the cat. Once again the advice was to breed them. Their merits were praised in high places. Statistics were published showing the rodent-destroying power of a single cat: 7,000 mice or 3,600 rats in one year. But the brown rats knew no obstacle. Taking advantage of the revolutionary troubles, which more or less left them a clear field, they installed themselves in every corner. They occupied the sewers. They dug galleries through walls and battlements and tunnelled underground for miles. They came in myriads and millions. An army like this, could not be deflected by a few thousand cats. Today the brown rat (or grey rat) is everywhere. It is not only the greatest enemy of the agricultural economy, but through its fleas and lice, it is the main carrier of typhus, sodoku (rat-bite fever), the plague, Weil's disease and trichinosis, to name only the better know diseases.

Before such forces the powers of the cat failed. There were simply too few cats. They did not live up to expectations and fell into disgrace.

THE MICROBES OF PASTEUR
In the next century the genius of Pasteur was to open battle against those pathogenic agents that had previously been unknown because invisible: the infinitely small microbes that are the true pedlars of disease and death. From then on the history of cats, rodents and men was rather unexpectedly

to take on a completely new aspect. A misunderstanding grew up which was to work in the cat's favour, and it had nothing to do with the cat's rat-killing value. The reasoning behind the mistake was quite simple. Disease-carrying bacteria were, in most cases, associated with dirt, squalor and lack of hygiene. Thus, the principle seemed to arise that one must touch animals as little as possible, because they, with the exception of aquatic birds and the populations of the rivers and seas, never washed or cleaned themselves in any way! An immediate zoophobia was born. No one dared to stroke a dog or a horse without wearing gloves for protection. People would not go near the most immaculate turtle-dove or the whitest sheep. But the cat? It was known to be the only domestic animal that spent entire days licking and cleaning itself with praiseworthy scrupulousness. If there was one animal that one could accept into one's home and caress without fear it was this innocent 'fireside tiger'.

So it was that men, women and children, deprived of all intimacy with beasts, opened their doors to the cat and gave him the place

at their hearth that he had so nearly lost. As if to make up for lost time and at last do justice to the unhappy animal, people set themselves to care for him, admire him and understand him, perhaps to make him forget the miseries of his past.

CATS AND RATS TODAY
A little later there were serious attempts to wake again in this rehabilitated cat those ancient qualities that from time to time in the past had won him the interest, if hardly the enduring gratitude, of the human race. An interest was once again taken in the ratting cat. In his capacity as doctor to the port of Le Havre, Dr Loir, the son-in-law of Pasteur, was for half a century in a position to appreciate the services provided on board ships by cats. He undertook experiments to destroy a ridiculous prejudice and prove that it was not a starving cat that made the best killer of rats. On the contrary, the hostility of cats to rats was instinctive, spontaneous, a matter of sport and a leisure habit. The ratting cat hunts and kills purely for pleasure; and many are the cats who are proud and happy to take to their masters,

An old enemy

as tokens of devotion or gratitude, the corpses of their victims.

In France the ideas of Colbert were taken up again. Many administrative authorities began to set aside a special budget for the breeding and maintenance of ratting cats in museums, libraries, prisons, barracks, warehouses and stores. In Denmark and in America the ratting cat is a civil servant by virtue of his work in post offices and public transport stations. The New Zealand Post Office only crossed cats off its list of personnel in 1965. They had been introduced into the post offices in 1942 in order to hunt the rats that eat the mail, and had been allocated a weekly food allowance. Although the administration ceased to recognize them in 1965, the cats are still there. Many of the insurance companies who deal with maritime affairs refuse to pay for damage or destruction to cargoes by rats if there have not been cats on board.

The first version of the Marshall Plan envisaged the importation of ratting cats into France, which would indeed have been a historic return for the descendants of America's first cats. But in the face of the plethora of European cellar and gutter cats, the project was abandoned. In Paris there are estimated to be at least 900,000 to 1,000,000 stray cats. If adequate food were provided for just those with good hunting instincts, they would be capable of ridding whole districts of rats. The cat has everywhere been proved a better weapon than poisons or traps, better even than ratting dogs, as it is more discreet, patient and effective. This was recently proved in a biscuit factory where every weapon had been tried in vain, from fox terriers to poison gas. The fox terriers had eaten even more biscuits than the rats! Yet ten or twelve cats were enough to completely stamp out the whole army of rats in less than six weeks. In 1961 in Borneo cats were again proved to be

Peanuts, the official in charge of rat-catching at the depot in Bedford Park, Essex, has already lost an eye while discharging his duties

the surest weapons against rodents. The rice fields were infested to such an extent that all the stray cats of Singapore were rounded up and parachuted by the hundred into the fields. The crops were saved.

Since the Second World War, it is the biochemical industry that has led the vanguard in this war against rodents. But the cats still act as an ever-vigilant army against their ancient enemy.

THE
OF
DON
HALF·A
HERO
ANTHONY
HOPE
THE FRUITS
OF FOLLY
BY THE AUTHOR OF
'THE POMP
OF POWER'
HUTCHINSON

4 THE CAT IN LITERATURE

EARLY APPEARANCES

The first form of literature to feature the cat was the animal fable. Every culture has its amusing stories about animals, but the most widely-known of these are surely those which are attributed to Aesop. These fables, in which animals take on the characteristics of human beings in order to point out a moral to the human world, were part of a rhetorical tradition in Greece that, from the fifth century onwards, attached itself to the name of Aesop. New fables were added to the canon as fast as the old ones were assimilated into the folklore and popular literature of the world. Today they are amusing tales to be told to children, but originally they were intended as colourful *exempla* to be used in oratory and rhetorical composition. Writers and speakers used their fable repertories much the way modern speakers use their stocks of jokes. The difference, of course, is in the purpose of the fable. That it was amusing was secondary; its primary purpose was to demonstrate a moral principle.

The fables of Aesop that feature cat characters are not as well known as those that tell the story of the fox and the crow, or the tortoise and the hare. And where cats do appear, they are drawn in one dimension only – that of the natural enemy of mice and chickens, who are the sympathetic characters. No matter what the moral, it is always the cat that is the villain.

India's 'Panchatantra', an immense body of animal fables written about AD 300, shares many of Aesop's characteristics. The animals speak and act as men do, they exhibit human virtues and vices. Most important, the moral principles which their stories illustrate are always intended as lessons for the human world. One series of these fables tells the story of a lion king whose cynical attendants include a sly and hypocritical panther. In fact, the lion king himself, as well as the queen mother and all the little tiger attendants, are depicted as a stupid and vicious lot. The feline characters always appear in a very bad light, so it is not surprising that the most sympathetic character in the entire collection of tales is a tiny mouse. One of the few domestic cats to appear in the fables is one known as 'the devout cat'. According to the story, a duck and a hare have a terrific argument over the ownership of a home. In order to settle the quarrel, they go to see the cat, who is also a judge. This cat is respected by the duck and the hare because they have heard that she fasts all day, prays all night and will never harm any creature. When the cat sees them coming, she puts on her most humble expression and pretends to be praying. Both visitors creep up to the devout hermit with great respect. When they have told the cat their story, they ask her for a judgement. But the cat tells them that she is hard of hearing and that they will have to come closer and tell the story in her ear. Naturally, as soon as the duck and hare are close enough, the cat jumps on them and eats them both.

Animal stories are used by every age for its own purposes. The Middle Ages demanded more than the fables' simple moral instruction; they had to have didactic allegory as well. And so the bestiary was invented. These natural histories were popular because they were about animals, but they were conceived with the highest of intentions, being based on the idea that the physical world is simply a symbol of the religious world. The first bestiary was written in Greek in the fourth century, but there are several later examples. The Old English bestiary devotes itself to a study of the panther, the whale and the partridge, representing creatures of land, sea and air. The panther comes out rather well, for it is the beast that is likened to Christ himself. A later bestiary, written in Middle English, describes the lion, eagle, serpent, hart, fox, spider, whale, mermaid, elephant, turtledove, panther and the culver or dove. But

the domestic cat is noticeably absent. Why couldn't the writers of these fictitious natural histories have found a Christian application for, and moral edification in, a description of the cat?

But for such observation one must look beyond the official literature of the bestiaries to an anonymous verse written on a copy of St Paul's Epistles by a student of the monastery of Corinthia in the eighth century:

I and Pangur Bán, my cat,
'Tis a like task we are at;
Hunting mice is his delight,
Hunting words I sit all night.

Oftentimes a mouse will stray
In the hero Pangur's way;
Oftentimes my keen thought set
Takes a meaning in its net.

'Gainst the wall he sets his eye
Full and fierce and sharp and sly;
'Gainst the wall of knowledge I
All my little wisdom try.

When a mouse darts from its den,
O how glad is Pangur then.
O what gladness do I prove
When I solve the doubts I love.

For a long time the cat never made a solo appearance in literature; it was always accompanied by mice. The cat-and-mouse situation could be applied to any number of human situations for any number of reasons. Sometimes, as in Chaucer's 'Maunciples Tale', it was used to draw an observation on human nature by referring to what everyone knew was a truth of animal nature:

Lat take a cat, and fostre him wel
with milk,
And tendre flesh, and make his couche
of silk,
And lat him seen a mous go by the wal;
Anon he weyveth milk, and flesh, and al,
And every deyntee that is in that hous,
Swich appetyt hath he to ete a mous.

Others used the cat-and-mouse to make a more political point. In the fourteenth-century the story of belling the cat was told in Langland's 'Piers Plowman' for just such a reason. According to the fable, the rats and mice get together and form a council for the purpose of discussing the problem of protection from their common enemy, the cat. They decide that the only way to deal with

'The cat and the fox, like good little saints — off on a pilgrimage' — Grandville's illustration of La Fontaine's fable 'The Cat and the Fox'

Abyssinian painting of the woman who was transformed into a cat

the cat is to put a bell around its neck so that they can hear it coming. The plan is discussed, applauded and accepted, but when it actually comes to tying the bell around the cat's neck, not one of the rats or mice is willing to do the job. In Langland's narrative, this fable was used as a satire on the House of Commons and the general political strife of the age.

This moral purpose was the cat's earliest and longest role in literature. In the seventeenth century La Fontaine collected masses of fables and folk tales and rewrote them in a charming new style. Many of these fables were based on Aesop, and the Greek's attitude to cats has obviously influenced the French poet's verses. In fact, La Fontaine went a step further: not only was the cat villainous, he was hypocritical and evil. 'The cat and the fox . . . are two true hypocrites, two arch-dissemblers.' But at least he gave the cat credit for being more intelligent than the fox. In one of the fables, the fox and the cat have an argument over who is the cleverer of the two. The fox brags that he knows a hundred different tricks, but the cat replies that he himself always has only

one plan which is far better than all the fox's hundred tricks together. The debate is interrupted by a pack of dogs who suddenly appear and charge at both cat and fox. The cat, without wasting a second, scrambles up the trunk of the nearest tree and is hidden from sight by the leafy branches. But the fox, panic-stricken, runs to one hole in the ground, then to another and another. He changes hiding places a hundred different times, and when he finally thinks he is safe he smells smoke. To escape suffocation, he leaves the hole and, as soon as he emerges, is killed by the dogs. The cat, watching from the tree-top, speaks the lesson: One single, well thought-out plan is better than a hundred different untried tricks.

La Fontaine's contemporary, Charles Perrault, also enjoyed fame in the literary circles of Louis XIV's France, but it is for his fairy-tales that he is now remembered. In 'Puss-in-Boots' he has given us a cat so clever that it kills an ogre and wins its master a fortune and a princess.

In the eighteenth century the English poet and dramatist John Gay won great success with his *Fables*, in which the cat

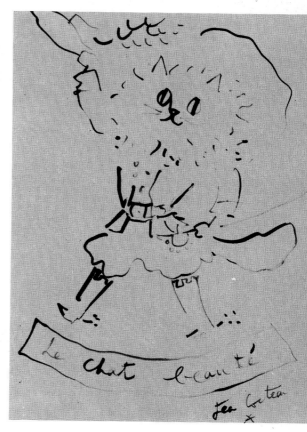

65

was frequently featured in its old role of mouse-chaser. The fables themselves are original and amusing. Instead of drawing universal morals which can be applied to all humanity, Gay satirized the court and courtiers of the age.

THE ANIMAL SPIRIT AND THE MYSTICAL CAT

The cat has served English poets as a mystical manifestation of pure animal spirit, as a nonsense character and as a symbol of the simple life of domestic bliss. But one of its strangest roles is played in a poem which Christopher Smart (1722–1771) wrote while confined in Bedlam with only his cat Jeoffry as company.

For I will consider my cat Jeoffry.
For he is the servant of the living God, duly and daily serving him.
For at the first glance of the glory of God in the East he worships in his way.
For this is done by wreathing his body seven times round with elegant quickness.
For when he leaps up to catch the musk, which is the blessing of God upon his prayer.
For he rolls upon prank to work it in.
For having done duty and received blessing he begins to consider himself.
For this he performs in ten degrees.
For first he looks upon his fore-paws to see if they are clean.
For secondly he kicks up behind to clear away there.
For thirdly he works it upon stretch with the fore-paws extended.
For fourthly he sharpens his paws by wood.
For fifthly he washes himself.
For sixthly he rolls upon wash.
For seventhly he fleas himself, that he may not be interrupted upon the beat.
For eighthly he rubs himself against a post.
For ninthly he looks up for his instructions.
For tenthly he goes in quest of food.
For having consider'd God and himself he will consider his neighbour.
For if he meets another cat he will kiss her in kindness.
For when he takes his prey he plays with it to give it (a) chance.
For one mouse in seven escapes by his dallying.
For when his day's work is done his business more properly begins.
For he keeps the Lord's watch in the night against the adversary.
For he counteracts the powers of darkness by his electrical skin and glaring eyes.
For he counteracts the Devil, who is death, by brisking about the life.
For in his morning orisons he loves the sun and the sun loves him.
For he is of the tribe of Tiger.
For the Cherub Cat is a term of the Angel Tiger.
For he has the subtlety and hissing of a serpent, which in goodness he suppresses.
For he will not do destruction, if he is well-fed, neither will he spit without provocation.
For he purrs in thankfulness, when God tells him he's a good Cat.
For he is an instrument for the children

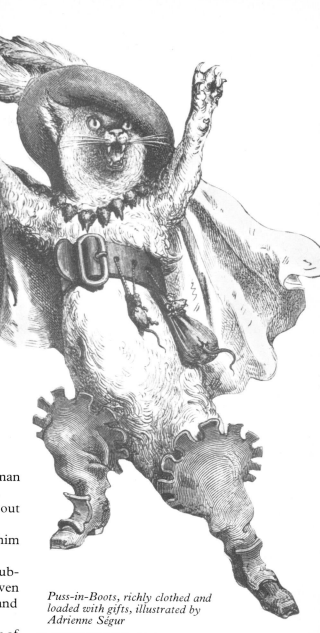

to learn benevolence upon.

For every house is incompleat without him & a blessing is lacking in the spirit . . . .

For the English cats are the best in Europe.

For he is the cleanest in the use of his fore-paws of any quadrupeds.

For the dexterity of his defence is an instance of the love of God to him exceedingly.

For he is the quickest to his mark of any creature.

For he is tenacious of his point.

For he is a mixture of gravity and waggery.

For he knows that God is his Saviour.

For there is nothing sweeter than his peace when at rest.

For there is nothing brisker than his life when in motion. . . .

For he is docile and can learn certain things. . . .

For he can jump from an eminence into his master's bosom.

For he can catch the cork and toss it again. . . .

For he is good to think on, if a man would express himself neatly. . . .

For by stroaking of him I have found out electricity.

For I perceived God's light about him both wax and fire.

For the Electrical fire is the spiritual substance, which God sends from heaven to sustain the bodies both of man and beast.

For God has blessed him in the variety of his movements.

For, tho he cannot fly, he is an excellent clamberer.

For his motions upon the face of the earth are more than other quadrupeds.

For he can tread to all the measures upon the musick.

For he can swim for life.

For he can creep.

Christopher Smart was a poetic genius, but when he wrote the above poem he was insane. He shares the quality of imaginative madness—and a feeling for feline mystery—with William Blake. Compare Smart's cat:

Aesop's fable of the cat and the cock (top) and La Fontaine's fable of the cat and the fox

For he counteracts the powers of darkness by his electrical skin and glaring eyes. . . .
For he is of the tribe of Tiger.

with Blake's tiger:

> Tyger! Tyger! burning bright
> In the forests of the night,
> What immortal hand or eye
> Could frame thy fearful symmetry?

The appreciation of the feline spirit is not confined to madmen and mystics. It can, in fact, be quite comic. In the following satirical verse, it is fairly obvious that the anonymous poet's sympathies are definitely with the sinful animal, and not with the Puritan philosophy.

> There was a Presbyterian cat
> Went forth to catch her prey;
> She brought a mouse intill the house,
> Upon the Sabbath day.
> The minister, offended
> With such an act profane,
> Laid down his book, the cat he took,
> And bound her with a chain.
>
> Thou vile malicious creature,
> Thou murderer, said he,
> Oh do you think to bring to Hell
> My holy wife and me?
> But be thou well assured,
> That blood for blood shall pay,
> For taking of the mouse's life
> Upon the Sabbath Day.
>
> Then he took doun his Bible,
> And fervently he prayed,
> That the great sin the cat had done
> Might not on him be laid.
> Then forth to exe-cu-ti-on,
> Poor Baudrons she was drawn,
> And on a tree they hanged her hie,
> And then they sung a psalm.

Many poets have been attracted to the cat's graceful affinity with nature, but W. B. Yeats went a step further and wrote a special poem about the cat's mystic kinship with the moon:

> The cat went here and there
> And the moon spun round like a top,
> And the nearest kin of the moon,
> The creeping cat, looked up.
> Black Minnaloushe stared at the moon,
> For, wander and wail as he would,
> The pure cold light in the sky
> Troubled his animal blood.
> Minnaloushe runs in the grass
> Lifting his delicate feet.
> Do you dance, Minnaloushe, do you dance?
> When two close kindred meet,
> What better than call a dance?
> Maybe the moon may learn,
> Tired of that courtly fashion,
> A new dance turn.
> Minnaloushe creeps through the grass
> From moonlit place to place,
> The sacred moon overhead
> Has taken a new phase.
> Does Minnaloushe know that his pupils
> Will pass from change to change,
> And that from round to crescent
> From crescent to round they range?
> Minnaloushe creeps through the grass
> Alone, important and wise,
> And lifts to the changing moon
> His changing eyes.

The relationship between the cat and the moon is an ancient idea. The earliest Egyptians believed that the pupils of cats' eyes waxed and waned with the waxing and waning of the moon. Later, it seems that the Egyptians worshipped a statue of a cat-god at Heliopolis' Temple of the Sun because they had discovered that the pupil of a cat's eye enlarges or diminishes according to the height of the sun in the sky. This belief never formulated itself into the scientific explanation that the pupils wax and wane according to dimness or brightness. Rather,

it was a belief that the cat was in tune with the universe. As late as 1607, Edward Topsell recorded the 'facts' in his *Historie of Foure-footed Beasts*:

'The Egyptians have observed in the eyes of a Cat, the encrease of the Moonlight for with the Moone, they shine more fully at the full, and more dimly in the change and wain, and the male Cat doth also vary his eyes with the sunne; for when the sunne ariseth, the apple of his eye is long; towards noone it is round, and at the evening it cannot be seene at all, but the whole eye sheweth alike.'

THE NONSENSICAL CAT

The nineteenth century boasted two great geniuses of nonsense—Edward Lear and Lewis Carroll—and both of them created famous cats. Lear was perhaps the truer friend of the feline world: his only companion in life was his cat Foss, who lived with him for 17 years. He wrote several nonsense songs about cats, the most famous of which is 'The Owl and the Pussy-cat'.

The Owl and the Pussy-cat went to sea
   In a beautiful pea-green boat,
They took some honey, and plenty of money,
   Wrapped up in a five-pound note.
The Owl looked up to the stars above,
   And sang to a small guitar,
'O lovely Pussy! O Pussy, my love,
   What a beautiful Pussy you are,
      You are
      You are!
   What a beautiful Pussy you are!'

Pussy said to the Owl, 'You elegant fowl!
   How charmingly sweet you sing!
O let us be married! too long we have tarried:
   But what shall we do for a ring?'
They sailed away, for a year and a day,
   To the land where the Bong-tree grows
And there in a wood a Piggy-wig stood
   With a ring at the end of his nose,
      His nose,

His nose,
   With a ring at the end of his nose.

'Dear Pig, are you willing to sell for one
      shilling
   Your ring?' Said the Piggy, 'I will.'
So they took it away, and were married next
      day
   By the Turkey who lives on the hill.
They dined on mince, and slices of quince,
   Which they ate with a runcible spoon;
And hand in hand, on the edge of the sand,
   They danced by the light of the moon,
      The moon,
      The moon,
   They danced by the light of the moon.

Lear's other nonsense cats include the 'Runcible Cat with crimson whiskers' from

Illustration by Rudyard Kipling to 'The Cat that Walked by Himself'

Edward Lear's illustration to his poem 'The Owl and the Pussy-cat'

'The Pobble who has no Toes' and a sea-faring cat who, in the company of a Quangle-Wangle, rows a family around the world.

Undoubtedly the most famous of all non-sense cats is Lewis Carroll's Cheshire Cat, who, in *Alice in Wonderland*, 'vanished quite slowly, beginning with the end of the tail, and ending with the grin, which remained some time after the rest of it had gone'. But what could one expect from a mad cat? As he explained to Alice:

'To begin with,' said the Cat, 'a dog's not mad. You grant that?'
'I suppose so,' said Alice.
'Well, then,' the Cat went on, 'you see a dog growls when it's angry, and wags its tail when it's pleased. Now *I* growl when I'm pleased, and wag my tail when I'm angry. Therefore I'm mad.'

In the twentieth century, T. S. Eliot's *Old Possum's Book of Practical Cats* stands as a monument of poetical cat-nonsense. If any of these verses make sense at all it is 'The Naming of Cats', which can be read as a joke on philosophy's traditional method of classification:

The Naming of Cats is a difficult matter,
  It isn't just one of your holiday games;
You may think at first I'm as mad as a hatter
When I tell you, a cat must have THREE
        DIFFERENT NAMES.

First of all, there's the name that the family
        uses daily,
  Such as Peter, Augustus, Alonzo or James,
Such as Victor or Jonathan, George or
        Bill Baily –
  All of them sensible everyday names.
There are fancier names if you think they
        sound sweeter,
  Some for the gentlemen, some for the
        dames:
Such as Plato, Admetus, Electra, Demeter –
  But all of them sensible everyday names.
But I tell you, a cat needs a name that's
        particular,
  A name that's peculiar, and more dignified,
Else how can he keep up his tail perpen-
        dicular,
  Or spread out his whiskers, or cherish his
        pride?
Of names of this kind, I can give you a
        quorum,
  Such as Munkustrap, Quaxo, or Coricopat,
Such as Bombalurina, or else Jellyorum –
  Names that never belong to more than
        one cat.
But above and beyond there's still one name
        left over,
  And that is the name that you never will
        guess;
The name that no human research can
        discover –
  But THE CAT HIMSELF KNOWS,
        and will never confess.
When you notice a cat in profound
        meditation,
  The reason, I tell you, is always the same:
His mind is engaged in a rapt contemplation
  Of the thought, of the thought, of the
        thought of his name:
    His ineffable effable
    Effanineffable
Deep and inscrutable singular Name.

There is also the Rum Tum Tugger:

  The Rum Tum Tugger is artful and
        knowing,
  The Rum Tum Tugger doesn't care
  for a cuddle;
But he'll leap on your lap in the
  middle of your sewing,
For there's nothing he enjoys like a
  horrible muddle.

As well as the Jellicles Cats, Old Gumbie Cat, and Old Deuteronomy:

  Old Deuteronomy's lived a long time;
  He's a Cat who has lived many lives
    in succession.
  He was famous in proverb and famous
    in rhyme
  A long while before Queen Victoria's
    accession.

But most famous of all is Macavity, the master criminal:

  He always has an alibi, and one or
    two to spare:
  At whatever time the Deed took place –
    MACAVITY WASN'T THERE!

REAL CATS
Perhaps the most famous *real* cat to be immortalized in English literature was Horace Walpole's 'Selima'. When Walpole

wrote to his friend Thomas Gray, that
Selima had died, the poet replied by sending
him the following ode:

*Ode
On the death of a favourite cat
Drowned in a tub of gold fishes*

'Twas on a lofty vase's side
   Where China's gayest art had dyed
   The azure flowers, that blow;
Demurest of the tabby kind,
The pensive Selima, reclined,
   Gazed on the lake below.

Her conscious tail her joy declared;
The fair round face, the snowy beard,
   The velvet of her paws,
Her coat, that with the tortoise vies,
Her ears of jet, and emerald eyes,
   She saw; and purr'd applause.

Still had she gazed; but 'midst the tide
Two angel forms were seen to glide,
   The genii of the stream:
Their scaly armour's Tyrian hue
Through richest purple to the view
   Betray'd a golden gleam.

The hapless nymph with wonder saw:
A whisker first, and then a claw,
   With many an ardent wish,
   She stretch'd, in vain, to reach the prize
What female heart can gold despise?
   What cat's averse to fish?

Presumptuous maid! with looks intent
Again she stretch'd, again she bent,
   Nor knew the gulf between.
(Malignant Fate sat by, and smiled)
The slipp'ry verge her feet beguiled,
   She tumbled headlong in.

Eight times emerging from the flood
She mew'd to ev'ry wat'ry God,
   Some speedy aid to send.
No Dolphin came, no Nereid stirr'd:
Nor cruel Tom, nor Susan heard.
   A fav'rite has no friend!

From hence, ye beauties, undeceived,
Know, one false step is ne'er retrieved,
   And be with caution bold.
Not all that tempts your wand'ring eyes
And heedless hearts is lawful prize.
   Nor all that glitters, gold.

The poems which Wordsworth and Keats
wrote about cats are slightly disappointing,
perhaps because they are not as romantic as
one might expect from the masters of
Romanticism. But there is no doubt that
the cats they wrote about were real ones
that they had actually observed in action
and not abstract manifestations of animal
spirit or bits of nonsense. In Wordsworth's
'The Kitten and the Falling-Leaves' the
poet watches a common sight:

But the Kitten, how she starts,
Crouches, stretches, paws and darts!
First at one, and then its fellow;
Just as light and just as yellow;
There are many now—now one—
Now they stop and there are none:

What intenseness of desire
In her upward eye of fire!
With a tiger-leap half-way
Now she meets the coming prey,
Lets it go as fast, and then
Has it in her power again...

Keats' one sonnet on a cat observes an even more ordinary feline:

On Mrs Reynolds' Cat

Cat! who hast pass'd thy grand climacteric,
   How many mice and rats hast in thy days
Destroy'd?—How many tit-bits stolen?
      Gaze

With those bright languid segments green,
      and prick
Those velvet ears—but pr'ythee do not stick
   Thy latent talons in me—and upraise
   Thy gentle mew—and tell me all thy frays
Of fish and mice, and rats and tender chick.
Nay, look not down, nor lick they dainty
      wrists—
   For all the wheezy asthma—and for all
Thy tail's tip is nick'd off—and though the
      fists
   Of many a maid have given thee many a
      maul,
Still is that fur as soft as when the lists
   In youth thou enter'dst on glass bottled
      wall.

Thomas Hardy's poem to his cat is more personal and more touching. In his 'Last Words to a Dumb Friend' he mourned the cat that had been devoted to him for years. The poem begins with his memories of the cat's 'plumy tale and wistful gaze', and then goes on to contemplate its spiritual significance:

Strange it is this speechless thing,
Subject to our mastering,
Subject for his life and food
To our gift, and time, and mood;
Timid pensioner of us Powers,
His existence ruled by ours,
Should—by crossing at a breath

Invitation card for an exhibition of the work of T. A. Steinlen, who painted cats (opposite page)

Colette at Bataclan (above)

Illustration by Dufy to a poem by Apollinaire: 'I would have in my house—a reasonable woman—a cat moving among the books' (left)

The hand and cat of Colette (right)

THE HERALDIC BLAZON OF FOSS THE CAT.

Into safe and shielded death,
By the merely taking hence
Of his insignificance –
Loom as largened to the sense,
Shape as part, above man's will,
Of the Imperturbable.

THE INDEPENDENT CAT

Perhaps more than any other quality, independence is the characteristic of the cat that is most admired by the modern world. This admiration is not simply a case of anthropomorphism. If anything it is a case of wishful zoomorphism. The cat *is* independent, in a way that humans desire to be but are not. It is a style that is both natural and sophisticated, both animal and god – a style imitated by the 'cool cats' of this world. In Rudyard Kipling's *Just-So Stories* we find a modern fable that explains how the cat won this quality. 'The Cat that Walked by Itself' compares the dog's, the horse's and the cat's relationship with men. It seems that in the beginning the dog and the horse both gave up their independence in return for food and safety but the cat made a bargain: he would catch rats and mice for man and be kind to his children, and in return he would receive milk and a place by the fireside. Otherwise he was to remain completely and eternally independent of the human race.

One of the best descriptions of this remarkable quality is found in H. H. Munro's (Saki) 'The Achievement of the Cat' from *The Square Egg*:

'Confront a child, a puppy, and a kitten with sudden danger; the child will turn instinctively for assistance, the puppy will grovel in abject submission to the impending visitation, the kitten will brace its tiny body for a frantic resistance. And disassociate the luxury-loving cat from the atmosphere of social comfort in which it usually contrives to move, and observe it critically under the adverse conditions of civilization – that civilization which can impel a man to the degradation of clothing himself in tawdry ribald garments and capering mountebank dances in the street for the earning of the few coins that keep him on the respectable, or non-criminal, side of society. The cat of the slums and alleys, starved, outcast, harried, still keeps amid the prowlings of its adversity the bold, free, panther-tread with which it paced of yore the temple courts of Thebes, still displays the self-reliant watchfulness which man has never taught it to lay aside. And when its shifts and clever managings have not sufficed to stave off inexorable fate, when its enemies have proved too strong or too many for its defensive powers, it dies fighting to the last, quivering with the choking rage of mastered resistance, and voicing in its deathyell that agony of bitter remonstrance which human animals, too, have flung at the powers that may be; the last protest against a destiny that might have made them happy – and has not.'

FRENCH LITERATURE

Montaigne was the first French author to have anything to say about cats. Curious about everything, repudiating all the conventions and the traditions of previous philosophers, the author of the *Essais* wrote: 'We condemn everything that seems strange to us and everything that we do not understand: as the judgements that we make about animals. In several ways their condition is related to ours, but of those ways that are peculiar to them, what do we know?' Contemplating the behaviour of his cat, when he played with her, Montaigne asked: 'Who knows whether she is not amusing herself with me more than I with her?' The French kings Charles IX and Henri III detested cats, and the humanism of the Renaissance was too interested in the reason of man to turn to the more inaccessible and mysterious in animals. Ronsard, the delicate poet of roses, was voicing an opinion very much current at that time when he wrote: 'There does not live a man in the world who so greatly hates cats, as I with a deep hatred ... I hate their eyes, their brow, their gaze.'

In 1616 that *'grand ami des chats'*, Richelieu, came to power, and courtiers and rhymers of little talent set themselves to praise the cat. Richelieu disdained their writings, but he was greatly amused to see his dear kittens playing with the wigs of the most notable academicians.

Guyot Desherbiers was later to write of the Cardinal's cherished cats: 'The mitred tyrant of France, Richĕlieu, whose iron arm holds the balance in Europe, finds a human heart, when he is near the mewling breed. In the rare short moments when his political torments pause, a basket of charming kittens diverts His Eminence, and many times perhaps, with a swift movement, have they avenged their barbarous master for Montmorency's death.'

The cat was celebrated in the seventeenth century by writers of secondary importance. They offered neither the cadence of Racine nor the style of Molière, but it was by this modest door that the cat entered to take its place in French literature. Among several astonishing works of fantasy is the sonnet of Voiture, composed in honour of Iris weeping for her lost cat. In this sonnet all the rhymes, for no apparent reason, are the names of provincial towns.

In the eighteenth century, under the queen Marie Leczinska, cats come more than ever to hold the freedom of the city. 'They are distant, discreet, impeccably clean and able to stay silent. What more could be needed to be good company?' But the sonnets and rondeaux so stylishly constructed, credited them only with '*fort belles manières*' (beautiful manners).

Chateaubriand, with his immense pride and his sensitivity, was a writer sufficiently cat-like in his own character to understand the animal. Indeed his wife even gave him the name of 'the cat'. Throughout his life, whether a poor exile or a rich ambassador, Chateaubriand remained faithful to the cat.

In his correspondence with the Comte de Marcellus, he confided to this friend: 'I love the independent, almost ungrateful character of the cat, which allows it to be-

*Karoun, king of cats, to whom
Jean Cocteau dedicated 'Drôle de Ménage'*

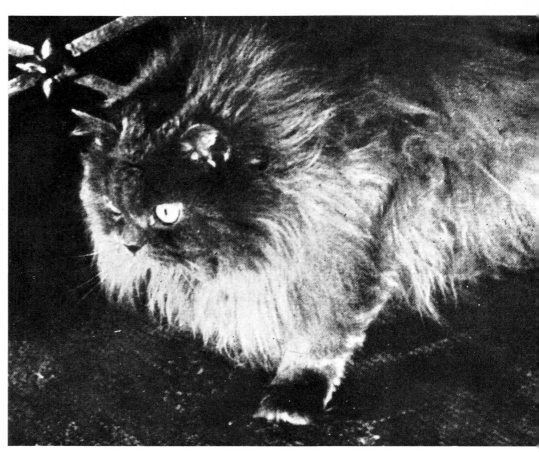

come attached to nobody, the indifference with which it moves between salons and the gutters of its origin...' 'The cat lives alone. He has no need of society. He obeys only when he wishes, he pretends to sleep the better to see, and scratches everything he can scratch.' He adds: 'Buffon mistreated the cat, I am working for its rehabilitation. I hope to make of it an acceptable and honest animal, quite the fashion of the times.' During Chateaubriand's stay in Rome as ambassador, Pope Leo XII, feeling his death approaching, made him a present of his cat 'Micetto'. Of this episode, Chateaubriand, in his *Mémoires d'Outres-Tombe*, writes in a letter to Mme Récamier: 'I have just been brought the poor Pope's little cat. It is quite grey and very gentle like its late master.' In a later chapter he writes: 'I have as companion a big greyish-red cat with black stripes across it. It was born in the Vatican, in the Raphael loggia. Leo XII brought it up in a fold of his robes where I had often looked at it enviously when the Pontiff gave me an audience.... It was called 'the Pope's cat'. In this capacity, it

used to enjoy the special consideration of pious ladies. I am trying to make it forget exile, the Sistine Chapel, the sun on Michelangelo's cupola, where it used to walk, far above the earth.'

The Comtesse de Chateaubriand, on the other hand, in a letter to M. le Moine, is more prosaically precise: 'You know that we have the little cat that the Pope loved so much, but which he made fast, because all they knew in the Vatican, in the way of sought-after dishes was cod and beans....'

Honoré de Balzac, in his ambitious and enormous portrayal of French society, *La Comédie Humaine,* found time to interest himself in the 'Peines du Coeur d'une chatte anglaise' (The heartaches of an English cat). In explaining the ways of Beauty the cat, her mistress approaches an insight into what might have been called comparative psychology if the story had been written in the twentieth century. For there is a great similarity between cat and mistress: 'Beauty, although she was so beautiful, appeared not to know it. She never looked at herself (and that is the proof of

an aristocratic education). Above all, she had that perfect insensibility that we require of our young girls and that we can only achieve with difficulty.... She waited until she was wanted before she came.... Like a true and good English-woman, she loved tea, was very grave when the Bible was explained, and thought ill of no one, which allowed her to listen to it said!.... She loved her 'home' and remained so perfectly tranquil that you might have thought her a mechanical cat, made in Birmingham or Manchester, which is the *ne plus ultra* of a good education.'

Acquérir l'amitié d'un chat est chose difficile' (It is difficult to obtain the friendship of a cat), agrees Théophile Gautier in 'La Ménagerie intime' (1850). 'It is a philosophic animal, strange, holding to its habits, friend of order and cleanliness and one that does not place its affections thoughtlessly. It wishes only to be your friend (if you are worthy of it) and not your slave. It retains its free will and will do nothing for you that it considers unreasonable.' Further on:

Decoration by Jean Cocteau in the Chapelle des Simples at Milly (near Fontainebleau)

Jean Marais and Josette Day in 'Beauty and the Beast'. Again it was Karoun, king of cats, who inspired Jean Cocteau's mask for the Beast

'Seraphita remained for long hours immobile on a cushion, not sleeping, following with her eyes with an extreme intensity of attention, scenes invisible to simple mortals .... Her elegance, her distinction, aroused the idea of aristocracy; within her race, she was at least a duchess! She doted on perfumes; with little spasms of pleasure she bit handkerchieves impregnated with scent, she wandered among flasks on the dressing-table... and, if she had been allowed to, would willingly have worn powder!'

From Baudelaire comes the famous sonnet dedicated to the 'chats puissants et doux, orgueil de la maison' (the powerful, gentle cats, pride of the household). Poets are often the precursors of later thought, and here is the strange observation of the author of *Les Fleurs du Mal* on certain physiological points, which are, a hundred years later, holding the attention of scientists:

Leurs reins féconds sont pleins d'étincelles magiques,
Et des parcelles d'or, ainsi qu'un sable fin,
Etoilent vaguement leurs prunelles mystiques.

(Their fecund loins are full of magic sparks, and specks of gold, like fine sand, add vague stars to their mystical eyes.)

From then on, men of letters gave the cat a bigger part in their works. Alexandre Dumas *fils* made himself the advocate of the cat: 'The cat, an aristocrat in type and origin, whom we have slandered, merits at least our esteem.' And he compares it with the dog who, according to him, 'is only a scurvy type, who has got his position by means of low flatteries'.

Emile Zola, in his *Nouveaux Contes à Ninon* gives us this wilfully materialistic confession of a bourgeois cat that, too happy, imprudently goes off in search of freer cats: 'You know', concluded my cat stretching itself out before the embers, 'the true happiness, paradise itself, my dear master, is to be shut up in a room with meat in it! ... (I am speaking for cats ...).'

Nothing is more false than this kind of substitution, during which the author puts himself in the animal's place and inside its skin in order to lend the animal his own thoughts. How much more true, and how much more effective, is the simple analysis of what we see, hear and experience of animals.

J. K. Huysmans, in this respect, described to perfection in *Là-bas* (1891), the behaviour of his cat, normal or pathological. Every reaction of the cat is noted, photographed and described without any personal interpretation. 'This animal was affectionate and winning, but maniac and wily. She would not permit any vagaries, any deviation, she intended that one should get up and that one should go to bed at the same time. When she was discontent, she expressed in the darkness of her look nuances of irritation which her master never mistook. If he returned before eleven o'clock at night, she was waiting for him at the door, in the en-

trance-hall, scratching the wood, miaouwing before he had entered the room! Then she would roll her langourous pupils of greeny gold, rub herself against his breeches, jump on the furniture, stand herself upright to look like a small horse rearing, and when he came near her, give him – in friendship – great blows with her head. If it were after eleven o'clock she did not go up to him, but restricted herself to getting up only when he came near her, still arching her back but not caressing him. If it were later still, she would not move and she would complain grumbingly if he allowed himself to smooth the top of her head or scratch the underneath of her neck....'

Of all the authors who have been interested in animals, none has used the power of words as effectively as Colette did to evoke in the reader that direct vision of life which was hers. And of all the animals that might have excited her curiosity, it was the cat that held her interest.

She first came to know a sympathy with cats when, in the arms of her own mother, she was called '*Minet-chéri*', or 'Darling Puss'. The fraternal association with the cat become for her 'poignant and necessary'.

'I am indebted to the species of the cat,' she said, 'for a particular kind of honorable deceit, for a great control over myself, for a characteristic aversion to brutal sounds and for the need to keep silent for long periods of time....'

Elsewhere, in *Les Vrilles de la Vigne* (The Tendrils of the Vine), which she wrote when thirty, she offers this advice: 'By associating with the cat, one only risks becoming richer....'

Among the works of Colette which feature cats are *Dialogues de Bêtes* (between Toby-chien the dog and Kiki-la-doucette, the cat) and *La Chatte* in which the characters are husband, wife and cat.

'I love cats,' wrote Jean Cocteau, 'because I love my home, and little by little they be-

T. S. Eliot's Jellicle Cats, drawn by Nicholas Bentley

come its visible soul. A kind of active silence emanates from these furry beasts who appear deaf to orders, to appeals, to reproaches and who move with a completely royal authority through the network of our acts, retaining only those which intrigue them or comfort them.'

But while offering homage to those who have written about the charm of cats Cocteau defended himself against the charge of being amongst them. 'I am not one of their maniacs. I have had one, as a matter of chance, then two, four, five, and it is quite possible that, from incest to incest and birth to birth, this little troup will become a cortège comparable with that in the story by Keats. . . .' However he did not fail to observe his cats, and he noted that none of them followed the same routine. He noticed that the white cat refused to eat if she was watched; that the doyenne only ate in the presence of the Blue Persian, but that she always refused to eat from any dish other than her own; that the son of the Siamese demanded to be fed by hand, and that the Siamese mother preferred to live in Paris rather than Milly-la-Forêt, which bored her. But Jean Cocteau is more obsessed by the mystery of the cat than he has liked to admit. Nobody has ever specified what species the beast was in the famous tale of 'Beauty and the Beast'. Yet on the screen Cocteau gives this Beast all the terrible aspect of a wild cat or a lynx, with savage fangs and claws, yet with the luminous and innocent eyes of a tender tom.

Even though he denied it, Cocteau was fascinated by the mystery of the cat, as we see in his story 'Conte vraie sur la chatte de Monsieur X' (The true story of the cat of Mr X). Here we find again the horrible accents of Edgar Allan Poe. It is the dramatic history of a solitary gentleman who is called away from home by an unexpected funeral. He gives to a neighbour the charge of feeding in his absence his beloved cat from

Spanish fables about cats are obsessed with feline greed and villainy

The French novelist Pierre Loti and his cat. Portrait by Rousseau, 1906

Anonymous lithograph of the Cat and the Cock

whom he has never before been separated. On his return, he learns that the cat has not touched a thing, but has stayed in the bedroom. Nevertheless Mr X thanks the neighbour, enters his home...

'Several days later Mr X was discovered in his bed, the cat hanging from his neck, and his open throat, furrowed by those claws, still streaming blood. The man's hands had not even tried to defend himself. They hung on the sheets. The dying cat no longer moved...' But the author adds: 'that which made the sight insupportable' (and this ending is an avowal of his fascination for cats) 'was the certainty that his jealous lady, the cat, had played out a scene of charm and had waited until the unfaithful one had gone to his bed....'

AMERICAN LITERATURE

Edgar Allan Poe, the master of the horror story, used the cat and all its mysterious associations to great effect in 'The Black Cat' (1843). In this tale a black cat named Phito discloses a murderer who has walled up the animal with the corpse of his wife. Another American author who has used the cat as a disquieting symbol is Tennessee Williams. In his short story 'The Malediction', human anguish is associated with the tragic destiny of the cat, a creature equally broken and rendered desperate by solitude

*Two eyes and fur, drawn by
Colombotto Rosso*

A young labourer named Lucio is lonely and scared on first contact with a strange town. Panic seizes him and tension coils him tighter and tighter until suddenly he is saved by a cat named Nitchevo:

'She was the first living creature in all of the strange northern city that seemed to answer the asking look in his eyes. She looked back at him with cordial recognition. Almost he could hear the cat pronouncing his name. "Oh, so it's *you*, *Lucio*," she seemed to be saying, "I've sat here waiting for you a long, long time!"'

Lucio immediately senses that a secret pact has been concluded, and that he has finally found someone to love, someone to love him.

But the strange malediction is still powerful. After finding and losing a job at the local factory, Lucio becomes ill and is confined to the hospital for a week. When he gets out he finds that his room has been taken and his landlady has put the cat out on the streets. Instinctively, he leaves the house and walks, as if led by a supernatural force, to the alley where he discovers Nitchevo. The cat is badly hurt and oddly misshapen. Lucio picks her up.

'He knew she could not go on living. She knew it, too. Her eyes were tired and dark, eclipsed in them now was that small, sturdy flame which means a desire to go on and which is the secret of life's heroic survival.... They were full to the amber brims with all of the secrets and sorrows the world can answer our ceaseless questioning with. Loneliness – yes. Hunger. Bewilderment. Pain. All of these things were in them. They wanted no more. They wanted now to be closed on what they had gathered and not have to hold any more.'

Lucio walks to the river, the cat in his arms. By the side of the river he speaks to Nitchevo: '"Soon," he whispered. "Soon, soon, very soon." Only a single instant she struggled against him: clawed his shoulder and arm in a moment of doubt. *My God, My God, why has Thou forsaken me?* Then the ecstasy passed and her faith returned, they went away with the river. Away from the town, away and away from the town, as the smoke, the wind took from the chimneys – completely away.'

A happier cat is the famous mehitabel of Don Marquis's *archie and mehitabel* (archie the narrator, being a cockroach, cannot manage the capital letters on a typewriter). For those who can bring themselves to believe in the transmigration of souls, archie offers the evidence that he was one 'a vers libre bard' and that mehitabel was once Cleopatra. But today, as archie so astutely observes, mehitabel would 'sell her soul for

Leroux's illustration of Edgar Allan Poe's 'The Black Cat'

a plate of fish'. She is now the essence of eternal alleycat, singing 'wotthehell wotthehell' and 'toujours gai toujours gai'.

GERMAN LITERATURE

In 1822 Ernst Theodor Hoffman's *Lebesichten des Katers Murr* (Tomcat Murr's views of Life) was published in Germany. This book is a most original and unusual work. It is really two works in one, because, along with the leaves of the 'Journal of the Cat Murr, philosopher and poet', there alternate fragmentary pages of the 'Life of Chapel-Master Johannes Kreisler', supposedly pages used by the cat as blotting paper and inserted in the final work by an alleged mistake of the printer. The adventurous life of Kreisler (poetic alter ego of Hoffmann, who often used this pseudonym) interrupts the history of the cat, while the thoughts of the cat, written in a tone so pedantic as to verge on buffoonery, halt any outburst of Kreisler's that is too sentimental or too personal and put a stop to the action when a plot gets too absurd. It is precisely this continual change of tone, from farcical to satirical, from ironic to despairing, this sense of the unexpected, that makes the work so fascinating. The cat Murr relates in detail the story of his youth: first friendships and first loves, enthusiasms and deceptions, evenings of carousing with his companions. And all these experiences are easily transposed from the world of cats to the world of men, especially to the world of the poet's contemporaries. Satire arises from the contrast between the gravity of Murr's tone and the banality of the experiences.

There are many other books on cats in the German language. Paul Eipper, in his *Freundschaft mit Katzen*, describes the marvellous maternal instincts of a Siamese. In Switzerland, it is the books written in German that have best dealt with the mysteries of feline psychology: Kaspar

Freuler, Edgar Schumacher with *D.. Katzenbuch*, then *Katzenjugend, Glück m.. Katzen*, etc., F. Tschudi and many others

SPANISH LITERATURE

Spanish literature, more solemn than most has not been greatly concerned with des cribing or lyricising over the cat. In Spai.. animals are either noble or despicable. Th.. bull and the horse are adulated; but wh.. would not lose face talking of the cat?

It was under the pseudonym Tomé d.. Burguillos that Lope de Vega, who wrot.. two thousand plays, amused himself in th.. seventeenth century by composing a bur.. lesque-epic poem called 'La Gatomaquia' In this astonishing parody of the Iliad an.. Tasso's 'Jerusalem Delivered', the cats, mak.. ing up the eternal trio of husband, wife an.. lover, are led into all the complications o.. the usual *ménage-à-trois*. Marrasmaquis, th.. husband, loves Zapaquilda, his wife, but sh.. is curious to know Mizifuf, the suitor, an.. of course it is this lover, whose very nam.. suggests a cat fight, who carries her off.

A relatively recent work by José Vida.. Munné, called *Psycologis de los animales .. traves los fabulistos* (The psychology o.. animals in fables), allows us to be mor.. precise about the attitude of Spanis.. writers towards the domestic cat.

On the whole, they have thought of th.. cat as a lazy animal, adverse to all effor.. that does not have its rewards, an un.. scrupulous thief, and, if not intelligent, a.. least shrewd and crafty in the extreme. Th.. fabulist Principe caught the essence of thi.. perjorative point of view in 'El raton, e.. niño y el gato' (The rat, the child and th.. cat). A small defenceless child is eating .. piece of cheese. A passing rat jumps on th.. child who, with loud cries, calls to the cat t.. help him. The cat arrives, gobbles up th.. cheese. . . and the rat with it.

Ibanez, in 'El gato y el gallo' (The cat an..

the cock) goes even further in this opinion of the egoism of felines. In this fable, inspired by Aesop and perhaps also by La Fontaine's 'The wolf and the lamb', the cat begins by trying to explain to the unhappy cock the reasons for his hostility towards him. He accuses him of a thousand imaginary crimes and, since each time the cock is able to reply, the fable ends with the cat saying, 'Then in spite of your justifying yourself more and more, there is still one great crime, and that is that I haven't had my breakfast.'

In 'Los gatos escrupilosos', Samaniego presents two big cats who discover a magnificent capon cooking on the spit. Having licked it, they discuss whether they ought to eat the spit. They argue for so long, that when the fable ends they are still hungry. The fable is amusing in its brevity, but it does not show great knowledge of cats to think them so stupid.

The Spanish fabulists de Andilla, Fernandez Baez, Joss Estremera and others seem to have given the cat an indecisive and twisted mentality. The stupidity of Samaniego's cats reappears in the Baron de Andilla's 'La gata y la gallina' (The cat and the hen). The greedy cat finds a pullet, beautifully roasted and appetising.

'There', says Andilla, 'is something to think about: the stomach evidently speaks, but reason too must have a hearing....' As a conclusion, the cat decides that, though excess may be illicit, all moderate acts, basically, can be excused. Satisfied with this point of view, she begins discreetly to eat a little white flesh, then moves from white to fat and from fat to bones, and finally has indigestion!

Other authors seem to have rhymed at will on the cat's greed and dishonesty, as well as the cruelty of the tiger that the cat hides beneath its purring. But what do we find in Joss Estremera's final fable, 'La Gata presumida' (The vain cat)? Two cats

Tenniel's illustration of Alice's cat in Alice through the Looking Glass

Illustration to Hoffmann's Leben-sichten des Katers Murr, *showing the death of Murr*

are living together in peace and, apparently, knowing all the happiness of mutual love under a cloudless sky. The male is all tenderness, consideration and attention, but the female seems to be bored. In despair, the tom wonders what he could have done to deserve this injustice. At last the female, under pressure of his questioning, explains herself: 'It is true that you love me, true that you give me presents, but you are a fool if you imagine that either cats or women will be satisfied with love or presents... that do not cause her neighbours to envy her!'

ITALIAN LITERATURE

Unlike Spanish cats the cats of Italy are made to feel at home in the narrow alleys of the small seaside villages as well as in the sunsoaked palaces of the cities. In spite of the hunger that drives them inevitably to petty theft, they are sure of an indulgent complicity and popular sympathy that the

cats of Madrid have never known.

The great poet Tasso (1544–1595), hunted from the court of Ferrara and pursued by the hostility of the princes of the house of Este, wrote a sonnet to his cat, from whom he wished never to be separated even at the worst of his destitution and misery. In this sonnet, no longer having a candle, he begs her to lend him her eyes to light up his page.

Fabio Tombari, particularly in his 'Book of Animals', talks at length about the many white cats he has brought up. One of his cats, 'Marette', was brought from China on board a battleship, and disembarked one summer evening at Pesaro in the arms of an Italian sailor. Fabio Tombari and his wife Zanze enthusiastically adopted this little grey velvet ball scarcely two months old. She rapidly became the uncontested queen of his closely-knit family of humans and cats. Till then, the only humans Marette

had known had been tough sailors, the only life, the rough and tumble existence on a large vessel of war, the only sounds the thunder of the great naval howitzers. Yet, in a few months, she revealed herself to be a great lady. 'In truth, an aristocrat', writes Tombari. 'She never miaouwed. If the wind ruffled her, she licked herself slowly over from head to foot. She spent her time running round Zanze's room, sniffing the perfume flasks, poking her nose into the silver powder bowl to flour herself over, and immediately sneezing. She had a horror of mice and avoided them; she would only settle herself on cushions of silk, she must have counted amongst her ancestors some mandarin's cat, because she adored music: Boccherini, Chopin, Debussy, amongst others. One morning Zanze played us *Jardins sous la pluie*. Marette was in the middle of amusing herself with the pompoms on the curtains and had caught her

claws in them. She tore away the lot, ran into the sitting room and curled up in Zanze's lap, the better to hear Debussy. It was in just this way that she had one evening listened to Beethoven's 'Pastoral', breathing lightly, purring mutely in order not to disturb. She lent her ear to the nightingale of the adagio, the stream of the allegro....'

Time passed, Marette grew up, and then came the revelation of love which she did not resist. She repudiated the great classics to live her life. One February day, so cold that the winter had burst the heart of a great oak, she left the ease of the hearth, fled out into the glacial buffetting wind, and did not return until two days later, dishevelled and frighteningly thin, her ribbon awry....

With the beautiful spring days, the familiar swallows returned. Several confidently entered the room, as they did each year. 'In less than an hour Marette was found stretched on the bed like a Messalina,

The cat seemed to be saying, 'I've sat here waiting for you a long, long time' (Tennessee Williams)

Mehitabel's memories, from Don Marquis's archie and mehitabel

I WAS CLEOPATRA ONCE SHE SAID.

HERRIMAN

in a great scattering of feathers, two corpses at her sides. It was in vain that she was scolded, beaten, chased away. She had tasted blood, she had killed, she continued to do so. She slaughtered chicks, two guinea-fowl, an old cock. . . . She who never went out without her rag of a ribbon, who sniffed at all the dishes like a Borgia cat, revealed herself to be what she had always been: a wild beast. . . .'

In the first days of May, Marette presented to the world a batch of five kittens, each of a different colour. Decidedly she was getting impossible. One day, it was necessary to part with her, to exile her to the mountains of Carpegna. All that was kept of her was a black kitten, far too fat, that was called Napoleon at first, then, as he almost never moved out of his armchair, rebaptised 'Mr Placid'. But, in spite of the tranquillity and peace restored to the house, it was still Marette who was thought of, Marette who must be cold, who must be hungry, and the secret wish was for the delinquent. 'Oh, if she came back, I know very well,' said Tombari, 'that Zanze would forgive her, even if she killed the chickens of half the district.'

*Cats of the streets . . . victims of
'a malediction'?*

Again from Italy, but this time under the signature of an Englishman, James Morris, comes this history of a Venetian cat whose fame was much greater than Mussolini's cat was later to know.

'He (Nini) lived in 1890 in a cafe facing the principal door of the church of the Frari, and, if you go today to have a cup of coffee in the big hall ornamented with frescos, you will see that the cat is still not forgotten. "Nini" was a white tom-cat that his master, as much in the interests of business as out of charity, exploited with such skill that he became the fashionable thing that all visitors wanted to see. If you ask the barman politely, he will get out a big album from under his percolator, dust it respectfully and allow you to look at the book of the friends of Nini. Among these visitors you will find Pope Leon XIII, the Tsar Alexander III, the king and the queen of Italy, the prince Metternich, the negus Menelik Salamen and Verdi. When Nini died in 1894, poets, musicians and artists were prodigal with their condolences; they signed their names in the book, and a sculptor immortalized the animal, whose statue stood for a long time against the wall of the shop.'

5 THE CAT IN ART

Whether or not the earliest art had significance as an act of magic is a subject for controversy. However, no one can deny that early art certainly allows us to see, over the course of time, something of the circumstances and occupations, the hopes and fears of man. If the cat does not appear in the earliest cave and rock art, this is because, being negligible as game and equally insignificant as a source of danger, it was not of the slightest interest to prehistoric man.

But with the coming of the first civilizations the cat is discovered. The Egyptians, the Hindus, the Chinese, the Japanese and the Incas seem to have wanted to express simply what surprised them, what charmed or disturbed them in this small feline that seemed so fragile yet could in turn be either impassive or violent, whose apparent gentleness could unleash lightning and savage attacks, and whose luminous stare seemed to read all secrets.

FROM ANTIQUITY TO THE MIDDLE AGES

Always in search of the highest objects of pure reason, the Greeks and Romans did not feel obliged to try to understand the mysteries of this banal destroyer of rats. Their pride could not adjust to an animal so small and yet so antipathetic to domestication. That scale of values which places man first in the ranks of all nature is continually threatened by the cat, who with one furious leap or slash of his claws can upset the scale at any minute. If he condescends from time to time, from place to place, to live without hostility beside those who call themselves his masters, it is because he happens to want to. This explains, in part, why cats are rare in Greek and Roman art. However, from the reign of Amenhotep III until the last dynasties of the pharaohs, representations of the cat in Egyptian art abounded: beginning with intimate scenes from daily life, such as cats fishing or hunting, feeding their little ones or playing with children, they ended with those formalized

Detail from La Naissance de Saint Remi, *a tapestry of the sixteenth century at Rheims. Cats have always loved hiding behind the folds of clothes*

and hieratic cats that were immobile, rigid in their divinity. The Greeks and the Romans, perhaps together with the Etruscans and Assyrians, preferred grander and more spectacular models, such as tigers, lions, panthers and cheetahs.

The French philosopher Alain said, 'Two things are aesthetically perfect in this world, the clock and the cat.' And yet the cat has always been thought of as extremely intractable artistic material. Its musculature hardly shows through its fur. Its gestures are all finesse. Yet its more abrupt and extreme movements are lacking in majesty and do not fit well with the solemnity of marble or stone. Its silhouette cannot easily be summarized in a few characteristic traits. Perhaps this is the reason that the cat never appears engraved or modelled on ancient coins or seals.

For a long time the cat only appeared in the decorations of churches amongst monstrous gargoyles and demons, symbolizing all the crimes and vices of mankind. A column in the cloister of the cathedral of Tarragona provides an exception. This thirteenth century work represents what is called *la procesion de las ratas*. The rats seem to be in procession to bury cats that are only pretending to be dead. A curious meaning is attributed to this: the unspoken wish of humble people one day to see their masters die, and the obliging co-operation of the latter, who welcome an experience of this kind in order to be certain of the true feelings of their servants!

From the tenth to the fourteenth century cats rarely appear in the paintings of western Europe. Very occasionally found in sculpture, they are practically absent from drawings. One cat does appear in the album of Villard de Honnecourt, but the mediocrity of the sketch contrasts strongly with the excellence of other sketches by this master.

There is an awkwardness about the cat which the usually subtle miniaturist Pol de Limbourg places in the '*Février*' of the *Très riches heures du duc de Berry* (about 1412).

Detail from a drawing of cats and dragons by Leonardo da Vinci

From the Annunciation *by Tintoretto : a wicked-looking cat under a wicked-looking cloud*

Drawing by Villard de Honnecourt, thirteenth century. Between the tenth and fourteenth centuries cats were very rarely represented and were very awkwardly done when they were

Detail from the Annunciation of the Virgin *by Jan de Beer from the fifteenth century. This painting scarcely resembles a cat at all*

But he has here inaugurated a long series of cats that we later find associated with the comforts of the fireside, the hearths of cottages or castle chimney-pieces and peaceful ideas of tolerance and quietness.

THE SIXTEENTH AND SEVENTEENTH CENTURIES

It is not until the sixteenth century that a few cats begin to be represented for the sake of their beauty. In Italy the drawings of Leonardo da Vinci are still the most beautiful that we have of cats. Barocci was bold enough to introduce a cat into *The Holy Family*. In Germany, Albrecht Dürer engraved a very beautiful cat in his celebrated *Adam and Eve*. In its calm and gentleness this cat symbolizes conjugal unity, and is set in contrast with the baseness and depravity of the serpent.

Among all the monstrous beasts in his *Garden of Delights*, Hieronymous Bosch

Detail from Virgin with a Cat *from the fifteenth-century cathedral of Saint-Omer. Sculptured cats were very rare at this time*

Always ready to play, even in an Italian painting of the fifteenth century. Detail from The Virgin of the Bird

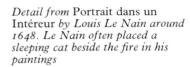

Detail from Portrait dans un Intéreur *by Louis Le Nain around 1648. Le Nain often placed a sleeping cat beside the fire in his paintings*

placed an unexpected and charming cat, sleek and well-fed, walking with its head held high and its tail as straight as a wax taper. In the *Adoration of the Magi* (Van Beuningen collection, Rotterdam) Bosch painted another cat, this time bristling and terrorized by people trying to catch it. Bosch, a visionary and a moralist, seems to set the wisdom of the good and tranquil dog against the spirit of evil represented (once again!) by the bird-killing cat. Brueghel the Elder, who loved animals, did not forget cats. He placed one in *The Death of the Virgin*, another wearing a collar of small bells in *Netherlandisch Proverbs*, and a black and white one, leaping and bounding as it hunted, in his *Procession to Calvary*.

Jacopo Robusti, better known as Tintoretto, painted a cat, wicked and on its guard, under a cloud in *The Annunciation*. He painted another, heavy with evil

thoughts, in his *Last Supper*. In the famous *St Jerome in His Study* by Antonello da Messina, there is a very beautiful cat sitting beneath a towel that hangs on the wall. In the *Prayer* by Nicolaes Maes (1632–1693) in the Rijksmuseum, in Amsterdam, a cat is trying desperately to reach the table and take hold of the cloth with its paw. In one of the most beautiful of the works of Ghirlandajo, *The Last Supper* (Florence), Judas Iscariot sits in the foreground with his back to us, while Christ and the other apostles face us. At Judas' side is a sad-faced cat that represents the Devil. A bas-relief by Gellini uses the same symbol. There is a cat in a painting by Paolo Veronese in the Louvre, and another in *The Annunciation* by Lorenzo Lotto at Recanati.

There appear to be no cats in the works of Rubens. There are perhaps only two in Rembrandt, and both of these appear in a

representation of the Holy Family (1640, Paris, Louvre, and 1646, Kassel, Gemälde-galerie). Both seem very much at home in these visions of purest domestic happiness. The cats of the Dutch minor masters are purely decorative, episodic rather than symbolic. Jan Steen, however, in *After the Drinking Bout*, does paint a beautiful cat. Are we to think that the reason cats are so rare in the sumptuous interiors of this period is that the rich bourgeoisie were afraid of a cat's claws getting at their costly satins and velvets?

In the work of Louis le Nain (1593–1648), however, there are several cats–including one under the chair in *The Dairywoman's Family* (Leningrad, The Hermitage) and a black and white one happily placed in the middle of his famous *The Peasant Family* (Louvre). David Teniers (1610–1690) introduces a few cats into his popular scenes.

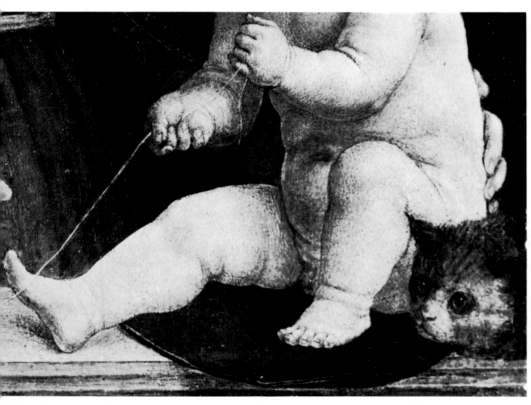

Detail from Chat et Gibier (Cat and Game) *by François Desportes*

Two pictures from Etude de Chats *by Watteau, who knew how to capture the grace of a cat's postures*

Detail from La Jeune Fille au Chat *by J. B. Perronneau shows a contented and loved companion*

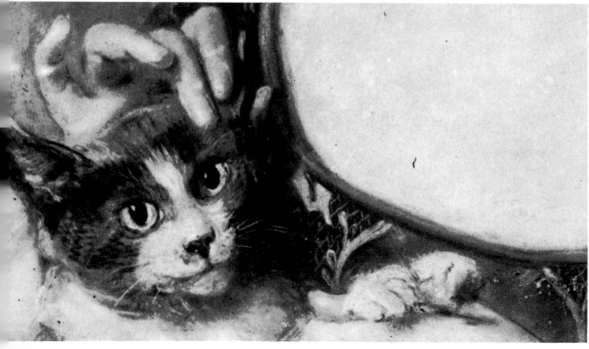

And his *Concert of Cats* remains a stran document.

In Holland Gerard Terborch from 16 painted cats that were neither ruffia thieves nor hypocrites. The pet cat is longer the unluckiest or unhappiest memb of *The Knife-Grinder's Family.* Anoth Dutch artist, Cornelius Wischer, painted cat so marvellously that it has become classic. It is unfortunate that we do n know who designed the medal, very popu in the Low Countries, which pictures a c disdaining bread and overturning wine. T satirical caption reads: '*Pauci cognosce possunt vera bona*' (Few are those who kn the really good things).

THE EIGHTEENTH AND NINETEENTH CENTURIES

In *The Washerwoman* (National Museum Stockholm) Chardin has given us a hap cat. Cochin made an engraving of this su ject in his turn. Chardin's cats are usua wary, circumspect, not as interested in e joying life as they are in looking for som thing to steal. In *The Skate* (the Louv there is a cat with its back arched and paw ready to seize. In *Le friand d'huit* one has saliva on its lips—literally drooli over the oysters. In *Le larron en bon fortune* (The Thief in Luck) the cat is pantry and kitchen glutton rather than boudoir pet.

In the Musée des Beaux-Arts there is painting of 1728 which shows how Chardi following the examples of Desportes a Oudry, always took care to give life a movement to his models. Beside a kitch table covered with a white cloth a c stretches to reach two mackerel hangi from a hook. In *Le lièvre mort* (The De Hare) a famished cat feverishly watches t game that tempts it. The hare and cat we painted with such accuracy that the engrav Lebas, seeing the painting, wanted to buy

Etude de chat *by Jean Baptiste Oudry. Great care has been taken to achieve realism of movement*

at any price. 'It is quite simple,' Chardin said to him. 'I like the jacket you are wearing very much ... let's exchange.' There and then Lebas took off his jacket, and left with the picture.

Watteau did beautiful sketches of cats. At the beginning of the eighteenth century the cat had entered more and more into social life. Fragonard and his master Boucher loved to paint cats, delicately curled up in the lap of a shepherdess, coiled in their mistresses' arms, or idling with her in bed. But, as in Boucher's *La petite fermière* or *La marchande de modes* (1746) these two great masters of drawing too often produced cats that were indecisive balls of fur without volume and above all without expression. Sometimes they were so wretchedly executed that it is hard to tell whether there is a cat or a lap-dog. The only two cats from this period that really look happy are the one in *La Jeune Fille au chat* by J. B. Perronneau (National Gallery, London) and the one by Lépicié in *Le lever de Fanchon* (Louvre).

Apart from occasional exceptions, the cat is treated in a conventional way in European art right up to the nineteenth century. The great majority of artists either ignored it or limited its importance to that of the banality of a decorative accessory. The cat had no more value than a muff or a foot-warmer.

Hogarth, in *The Graham Children* (Tate Gallery, London) painted a cat with a stupid and cruel expression, waiting for the favourable moment to jump on a caged bird. In one of his four paintings, *Scenes of Cruelty*, he singles out for attention a schoolboy whom he calls Thomas Nero who is torturing two cats hung together by their tails from a lampost. Higher up in the picture a cat is being thrown out into space from a third floor window. In the *Child with a Cat* by Martin Drolling (1752–1817), there is a strange pot-bellied cat with big globular

Hireshige's cats. Japanese artists have represented cats in hundreds of ways, always with the greatest fidelity

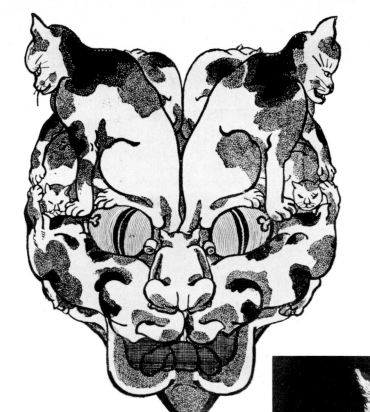

Japanese capri

Detail from The Graham Children *by Hogarth : a cat ready to leap on a caged bird*

eyes and a bulldog's face. The child who strokes it has a bird on his shoulder and is completely its opposite in tenderness, purity and innocence. It is not till the coming of Barlow, the first natural animal painter, then Stubbs and most particularly Morland, that we find in English paintings those placid or happy cats that the English are so fond of.

One of the greatest of all portrayers of the cat was Gottfried Mind, a Swiss artist who left a number of beautiful pen studies and watercolours of cats. He could be called 'the Raphael of cats'. Even so, his carefully observed and skilfully executed studies lack the charming lightness of touch that characterized the work of his equally famous compatriot, Henriette Ronner.

The Swiss can also be proud of two great masters of animal art who came later. Sandoz sculpted and modelled cats with absolute precision in the most preciou materials. Steinlen, Swiss in origin thoug he spent all his life in France, is famous fo his cats.

In nineteenth-century Belgium ther were two good animal painters who love cats. Stobbaert's *Woman with a cat* is ad mirable. And in his *Cuisine d'un zoolâtr* beside an intrigued tortoise and parrot, cat scornfully watches five dogs of differer characters and breeds overwhelm thei master with caresses and squabble amongs each other for his favours. In Van de Bosch cats are superbly depicted but th essential feline qualities are sacrificed to th anecdote. It is not enough for the artist tha the grey of a cat's coat should harmoniz with the white of the candles and books. Th cat must in addition have jumped on to th desk, overturned everything and playe

94

havoc with the scattered manuscripts. Yet another tendentious painting! After the indifferent and disdainful cat comes the cat as devastator and destroyer! The Belgian engraver Félicien Rops seems to have seen in the feline species a symbol of sadism and perversions, often placing cats in some of his equivocal scenes of cruel and morbid eroticism.

Has France done any better? Up to the nineteenth century the cats her artists produced were usually stupid, inexpressive, round blurs of hardly any plastic interest at all. But, at the same time as novelists and poets began to discover the charm of this ideal companion and at last to do justice to the cat, sculptors and painters were also to give evidence of the re-awakening of that first artistic interest, animal art.

For G. P. Saint-Ours, around 1800, the cat was still only a small extra in a group composition. On the night of the fifth of April, 1809, as the artist lay dying, a cat jumping on to his bed and aroused him momentarily from his torpor. In a faint voice he called to the relative watching at his side, 'Cousin, take this cat out of my sight. The colour of its fur clashes with the shades in this bedspread'. And then more softly still, 'Forgive me, Lord, for having wished still to be a painter when I ought only to be a Christian.'

It was with Géricault and his *Le chat blanc* that the scene changed. Without having done anything itself, the cat had arrived at a happy turning point in its history. Painters came to associate it with all the pleasantest colours that they used in their scenes of the new and more romantic life. They tried to capture its characteristics in art and in

doing so contributed more than they knew
to making it loved, even though their own
attitudes were so diverse. Where Géricault
responded to all the melancholy gentleness
of a tender pet, Delacroix saw a tiger.

MILLET, COURBET AND MANET

J. B. Millet, painter of peasants at work, the
serenity of the fields, the poetry of the earth,
placed a cat beside his *La Batteuse* (The
Thresher) and another on a wall in *La
Mort d'un Cochon* (Death of a pig).

Courbet in *The Artist's Studio* attributes
to the cat a last harmful intention. In the
foreground his cat is attempting to catch
hold of a woman's white floating veils. But
it is pleasing all the same because it is a
beautifully executed and very handsome
immaculately pure angora. And we know
how difficult it is to use a white palette and
still show every shadow and every reflection
in a white model.

The comes Manet, whose cat in
Olympia is so very different from Courbet's
angora. This black cat is all silent, secret
sensuality and delight. But do not be mistaken! According to one professor of art
history Olympia is not the woman … it is
the cat! In order to enlarge the black patch
of the cat, the painter placed beside it a
negress, and it was to set off this black that
he added the pinkish white body of the
woman.

The critic had reached this conclusion
after someone pointed out to him that the
cat was not in the centre of the composition,
but was placed near the outside edge. He
recalled that in Titian's *Pala de Ca Pesaro*
the Virgin Mary is also on the extreme right.
It is the same with Christ in one of the
'Feasts' of Veronese in the picture gallery
of Turin. When someone objected that
Manet's model really was called 'Olympia'
the critic answered that this was but another
proof that Olympia was really the cat, because that name was only the nickname
Manet gave the model, because he was as
fond of her as he was of the cat. This theory,
from someone who is both an authority on
art and a cat lover, is perhaps a little partial.
Manet himself was extremely fond of cats,
and many of them appear in his work. But
he did not take a great deal of trouble over
their representation. A few deft brush
strokes were enough to suggest feline movement. One can see why his fellow cat-lover,
Baudelaire, in a delighted but incredulous
aside in a letter to Manet, asked about the
contents of *Olympia*, 'is it really a cat?'

FROM TOULOUSE-LAUTREC
TO PICASSO

Toulouse-Lautrec could not dissociate the
cat from the woman in his poster-portraits
of the disquieting *Miss May-Belfort*. Rodin
also loved cats, and sometimes drew and
sculpted them, but in secret, as if to apolo-
gize. Steinlen (1859–1923) spent his whole
life creating and recreating cats by millions,
mostly in drawings but also occasionally by
modelling them in wax or casting them in
bronze. Between the vigorous Rodin and the

fragile but courageous Steinlen there existed a common bond. Both had always loved
the common people. Both glorified effort,
hardship, courage and sincerity.

Steinlen devoted his talent to the cats of
the humbler people of Paris: the cats of that
secret world of the painters and seam-
stresses, the lovers and concierges of La
Butte de Montmartre. Steinlen's cats were
those of the rooftops, the cemeteries and
the streets. Tabbies, blacks, cats the colour
of smoke or snow, harlequin cats, domino
cats, cats from Spain or from Clichy, toms
with mutilated ears, kittens drowned before
their eyes opened on the light of day, the
walking skeletons of the frightened cats
that haunt the rubbish-bins. Steinlen was
their own artist. In portraying the feline
dynasties of Montmartre, he was, and will
always remain, a priest of that pagan religion
that worshipped Bastet as much as Freyia.

Renoir was also an inspired friend of
women and cats, and towards the end of his
life resembled Steinlen like a brother. He
was a painter of motherhood and love, and
served in his own way the very revealing
world of cats. By placing a patient cat in the
arms of a pretty woman or a child he gives
his model something to react to, and we
come to know her better. We can admire
his method in his *Portrait de Madame
Manet* and in *La petite fille au chat*. Indeed
in so many of his paintings a purring, curled-
up cat emphasizes the softness, the soothing,
almost maternal sensual pleasure of his girls.

Gauguin's brown women of Tahiti are

Long-haired cat with ruffled fur by Francis Picabia

Study of cat's heads by Géricault shows great powers of observation

in complete contrast. And beside them lie languorous felines in whom the storms of nature can loose sudden violence. In the fresco in the Boston Museum which is titled *D'où venons-nous? Que sommes-nous? Où allons-nous?* two cats in the foreground symbolize mystery. In *Fleurs et Chats*, in the Carlsberg Glyptoteck Collection in Copenhagen, two magnificent cats seem to be living orchids. In *Te Rerioa* (Sleep), in the Courtauld Collection in London, there is another still that is all quietness, poetry and euphoric content.

Bonnard's cats whether in *Sieste au Jardin*, *Etudes du chat* or any other of his paintings containing cats, all have the same air of abandon – except when he has actually surprised them in the act of leaping or playing. When an acid critic accused him of painting cats that seemed to be made of india-rubber, he could not have paid a higher compliment. What else are cats made of? Is rubber not at the same time both the toughest of materials and yet the most fluid, the most inert and yet the most responsive, depending on how we choose to use it? For Bonnard a balustrade, a corner of green, some curved feathers and two mischievous cats at play was subject enough for a painting. And for this reason those who love Bonnard are often cat-lovers, as well.

The artists who have painted cats over the last century can be divided into two groups. There have been those who instinctively loved and understood cats and paid hommage to them. And there have been those who felt an antipathy towards them. As if irritated by this lack of sympathy without realizing it, they have interpreted cats in their work in a hostile and sometimes aggressive way.

The most famous of this latter category is undoubtedly Picasso. It is safe to say that in his painting he has never tried to flatter nor hoped to charm. 'Everyone wants to understand painting,' he has said. 'Why do we not try to understand the singing of birds? Why do we love a flower or the night

without trying to understand it? Yet painting, people want to understand.' When he is questioned or criticized, 'I am not looking,' he replies. 'I am not looking; I am finding.'

It is from these quicksands that any attempt to understand the animal art of Picasso must begin. The veterinary surgeon, Dr Guy Cumont, did precisely this in an inaugural thesis which might easily have been written by a professional art critic. Picasso as a painter, sculptor or ceramicist of animals is often thought to be easier to understand than in his portraits and still-lifes, because the deformations to which he submits his subjects are less forced and less divorced from natural representation. But Guy Cumont has shown in an intense study, that Picasso, when depicting animals, purifies and eliminates in the same way in which he modifies realism in his treatment of humans and landscapes. He is not 'looking'; he is 'finding'.

In his illustrations to Buffon's *L'Histoire Naturelle* (1930) or his painting *Minotauromachie* (1935), Picasso's drawing has a classic purity. But looking at the eleven successive states that lead from the photographic bull of 5 December, 1945 to the linear bull of 17 January, 1946, one can only guess at the sincere and tormented research that has contributed to this evolution of style. From then on, his animals are stylized in conformity with an acute sense of their personalities. They become signs, totems, emblems. But even the greatest of the deformations in these abstract images is not the result of eccentricity or caprice. For Picasso, the animal is everything; its shape and movements are one with the idea it symbolizes.

'I want to create a cat like the real cats I see crossing the streets, not like those you see in houses.' he says. 'They have nothing in common. The cat of the streets has bristling hair. It runs like a fiend, and if it looks at you, you think it is going to jump in your face.' This is why, emphasizes Guy

*By Picasso, who makes a
totem of the cat*

Cumont, Picasso has always used for cats a
dark brown colour range broken up by
flashing interruptions of white, whereas his
savage deformations betray his deeply emotional approach to the subject.

Other painters have had more respect for
the morphology of the cat. They have loved
them, and known them well. But they have
always reproduced in their work one particular type of cat. Some have only drawn
short-haired cats, others only long-haired
cats. Some, only cats of one colour, others
cats that are exaggeratedly polychrome.
These occasional painters of animals have
in fact never been interested in the characteristics of cats, but seem bound to some
striking impression that has been made on
them at a very early age, or by some haunt-
ing unconscious memory that has been
forgotten by the rational mind.

Picabia (1879–1953), who so often
roamed the ports and villages of France,
repeatedly painted the same shaggy cat
with green eyes and ruffled hair of a beautiful yellow. This cat is not the pinkish-beige
or *café-au-lait* colour of the Siamese, nor
reddish gold like the Van cat of Turkey.
It is yellow, a canary yellow, violently and
extremely monochrome as if the better to
cry out that this is the only cat, the unique,
the true cat. And after all, who knows? Perhaps the cat of earliest times was yellow,
yellow like the tiger, the panther, the ocelot,
and striped or spotted with black.

For others too, this ideal domestic cat
appears as yellow, or red striped with pink.
Is art here instinctively copying nature? It
is relevant here to note that cats whose coat
colour is in the range from a sulphur or
golden yellow to a sand-colour are those
which adapt most easily to contact and
friendship with man, while the dark cats,
particularly the black ones, have a wild
character. The first are said to be children
of the sun, delight and courage, the others
children of twilight and night, mistrust and
fear.

The appearance of the cat in art is as

interesting to psychology as it is to aesthetics. The cat is often the subject of children's earliest drawings, and it also appears in the work of the mentally ill who have been driven or encouraged to express what disturbs them in graphic or plastic form. Perhaps some instinctive tendency is in evidence here.

The first drawings of children and the work of the mentally disturbed are very different. The child stylizes a cat using a few features and two or three circles. But the vision that a mentally sick person has of the same animal is as much more complicated, overcharged and monstrous as his psychology is more grave. Such a difference in conception throws still more light on the duality present in our attitude to cats. Both the limpidly clear and simple evocation of a cat by a child, and the schizophrenic's nightmarish interpretation are exact and true, because both are sincere.

André Breton makes this point in his *Cahiers de la Pléiade* when he writes of the art of the mentally ill. 'The machinery of artistic creation is here set free from all hindrances. . . . Close confinement and the renunciation of all profit and vanities—despite all that is individually pathetic in these people—become the guarantors of that absolute authenticity that is going by default today everywhere else, and the lack of which corrupts us day by day.'

The mentally ill have a conception of the cat that is outside all we believe we know to be the personality of this animal. The psychological whirlwind into which these pictures drag us is disconcerting. But if we can look impartially and without prejudice at them how illuminating they can be! Art does not consist in a skilful, faithful copy of a model, but in what it discovers and reveals about the mystery in that model. This is why there is sometimes more that is true about the mystery of cats revealed to us in

the works of these disturbed and technically clumsy artists than in the most perfect reproduction of a cat by a master of animal art grown grey in his profession.

The first art of all was animal art. Prehistoric man only began to draw and paint man himself later—after he had given up his cult of animals, after he was freed from his fear and his need of them, after he had triumphed over them. Now animal art is dying out, because man today is interested only in himself. The *Société francaise des Animaliers* was founded in 1921. It counted amongst its famous names those of Jouve, Sandoz, Pompon, Deluermoz, A. Margat, Jacques Nam, Guyot and more. It tried in vain to achieve recognition. But after a few excellent exhibitions which the critics treated to silence, the real animal artists renounced it.

The only ones who can persist today with animal art are those for whom animals are a refuge and escape, leisure, the luxury of the moment, a secret delight.

MARQUET AND COCTEAU

Such a person, apparently, was Albert Marquet. In 1963 his wife, Marcelle Marquet, collected together in Paris canvases and drawings that showed a little known aspect of Albert Marquet—his animal art. Among these is his excellent portrait of Marcelle Marquet herself, bent over some absorbing work of sewing, with her grey cat asleep in her lap, hollowed in the vivid and sumptuous red of her skirt. An equally surprising discovery was that perfect composition in which a white cat is softly buried in the sleep of innocence, but a second black cat, very wide-awake indeed, is turning round, its eyes alight and its paw raised high.

There have been so many others who have painted cats: Suzanne Valadon, Chagall with his tragic phantom-like cats, Grau Sala

Tapestry entitled My Cat *by a young child who used only a few scraps of cloth*

with his Siamese sitting in state on a round table loaded with fruit. There are all the various cats of Jean Cocteau, one of whom is in the church of Saint Blaise-les-Simples near Milly-la-Forêt, the thread-like and famished looking cats of Carzou, Joucin's Parisian cats—each with a famous master, those of the esoteric Monique Watteau, so clearly influenced by Léonor Fini, and the other-worldly and poetic cats of Adrienne Ségur. The latest among symbolic cats are those of Pierre Corsen, who has succeeded in combining in each one the images of desire and sensuality, anguish and courage, suffering and fear.

JAPANESE ART

The Japanese were interested in the cat from the earliest times. They set themselves to interpret its psychology. They observed it, noted each detail of line and colour, literally spied on it to discover each of its expressions and attitudes. They represented it in hundreds of different ways with amazing accuracy: sitting at the edge of a window, fleeing with a fish between its teeth, lying in wait for a bird or leaping after a butterfly. They painted the mother cat feeding her kittens, the fighting tom, the cat overwhelmed with heat or laziness, the cat stretching or yawning. They saw the humourous side, the almost caricature-like appearance, of a cat balancing on top of a roof, or a female cat in heat. They understood the cunning of the cat who turns a deaf ear, and the malice of the cat who lets a mouse escape solely in order to catch it all over again a moment later.

The Japanese have a great deal in common with cats. They project into their creations that capriciousness of behaviour and love of fantasy that, in them as in cats, is so puzzling and disconcerting. They can conceive in graphic terms a cat that is itself made of the heads of cats, whose eyes are bells, and

The cat is always present i[n] drawings of Stei[n]

whose bells are eyes, and many other fantasies of the same order. They patiently carve cats on their netsukes and inros. They engrave imperceptible cats on the buttons of their clothes. They give disguised cats the faces of young girls. In two drawings they turn a wheedling flatterer of a cat into a fiendish dragon.

Not in any period of Japanese art, whether we are dealing with works of the Middle Ages or those of Hokusai or those of the Nishiva Sunsos or the Foujitas of today, do we find that massive incomprehension in relation to cats that in European art separates the greatest masters of the eighteenth century from the painters, sculptors or engravers of the nineteenth and twentieth centuries.

CARICATURE AND ANIMATED CARTOON

Humorists have often been the cat's greatest friends and most sincere defenders, seeing in it only fantasy, gaiety, the pleasure of flouting existence and pride in fending for itself.

Twentieth dynasty Egypt was already producing great frescos, drawn and then heightened with vivid colour, parodying the historic feats of arms sculpted in the temple stone. In Thebes they smiled at battles between cats prudently sheltering behind impenetrable walls, and rats, shooting with bows and brandishing shields, commanded by a Pharoah-Rat who rode in a great chariot drawn by mastiffs. Nothing is new under the sun. Fifteen hundred years later an identical scene reappeared in an engraving in the North of France entitled Fortress of Cats (see page 57). The Russians also had their cat caricaturists in those artists who risked lampooning their sovereign, the harsh Tsar Paul I, in drawings that showed him as a big and fat and terrible cat.

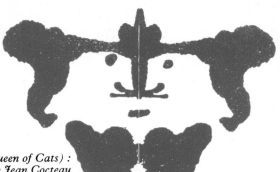

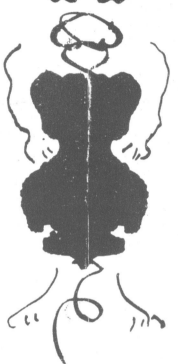

Reine des Chats *(Queen of Cats)*:
a few ink-blots by Jean Cocteau

*A cat is mysteriously framed by
Leonor Fini*

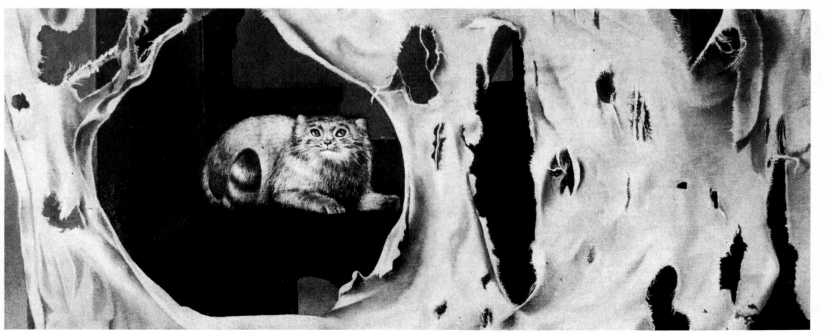

The 'Crazy Cat' as drawn by
Harriman for animated cartoons and
strip cartoons in the United States

'Felix the Cat' by Pat Sullivan was
one of the first great stars of the
animated cartoon

'The yellow kid' by Outcault, one of
the first strip cartoons

The English caricaturist Louis Wain for a long time produced more than a thousand drawings a year. All of these cats wore human expressions and acted in a human fashion until the day that Louis Wain became insane. Then the cats became more and more abstract until finally they were patterns and colours that bore no resemblance to either cat or human. Other cat caricaturists include Siné the visual joker, whom Malcolm Muggeridge has called 'a desentimentalized Thurber', and the talented Dubout, who expresses, through his inexhaustible gentleness and indulgence for every kind of cat, his pitiless, bitter but lucid opinions on the human race (see pages 220 and 224).

Modern times have seen the growth of a new form of graphic expression that evolved from caricature, that of the animated cartoon. Millions of people all over the world are following its development without always realizing to how great an extent artistic skill and the gift for observation are combined in this new art form.

In America there are several masters of the cinematic art who excel in this line, in particular the team led by the late Walt Disney. Today's animated cartoons have come a long way from those of twenty years ago, when the jerky and irregular movement of the animals caricatured was enough in itself to raise a laugh. Nowadays the illusion achieved can, for a few sequences and particularly where animals are concerned, be so complete that the spectator can forget for that moment that these are artificial creatures, entirely the fabrication of man. There lies behind the articulation of their limbs and the play of their muscles, their movement, gait, and mannerisms, a complete understanding of the anatomy and physiology of the animal involved.

The animated cartoon has certainly brought to many people a better knowledge

Tom and Jerry, the cat and mouse whose adventures appear both on the screen and in cartoon strips

'Mandrake the Magician'. Can he bewitch the Queen of the Cats?

of the less obvious aspects of the characters of the cat and many other animals. But it has also awakened in people of our generation a greater interest in lives other than those of human beings. This is in all ways a change for the better.

The animated cartoon is entirely the creation of its film-technicians and draughtsmen. Out of nothing they can create either one cat or hundreds of thousands of cats of all colours and breeds. The artist can give to a fighting or lazing tom any expression or attitude he pleases. It is his decision whether some amorous female cat on the screen twists her backside to an exaggerated degree, gives an exasperated cry or even keeps silent. The animated cartoon is able to emphasize, exaggerate or underplay the feelings of its characters, and impose at will its own symbolism on them.

The father of all the cats of the cinema screen is 'Felix'. This gauche and malicious cat was the great star of the animated cartoon in America during the 1920's, and the first to make use of sound – one year before his then obscure rival, Mickey Mouse. His success was one of the things that influenced cartoons in the direction of the caricatured animal who walks upright on his hind-legs and behaves like a human being.

Marcel Brion, today a member of the Academy Française, wrote in 1928 about

After 1930, the 'crazy cat' disappeared from the screen, but continued his adventures in the strip-cartoon. He had begun his career in the cinema around 1914, and seems to have been created by Pat Sullivan. Later, in the course of his career, he was animated by Harriman, Many Gould, Searle and above all Nolan.

this famous cat: 'Felix is not just a cat, he is the cat. I would like to say that he is a super-cat, because he belongs to no category of the animal kingdom. At times he imitates the gestures of the humans among whom

he finds himself, but he does not stay with them. With a bound, he reaches the realms of fantasy and installs himself there....

'He has escaped the reality of the cat; he is made up of an extraordinary personality. When he is walking like a man preoccupied, with his head buried in his shoulders, his paws behind his back, he becomes the impossible in cats, the unreal in men.

'He is honest, generous, fearless and optimistic. He is ingenious and fertile in resourcefulness. Nothing is more familiar to him than the extraordinary, and when he is not surrounded by the fantastic, he creates it.

'And it is this creative faculty which quite rightly holds us in Felix. It arises from two mental attitudes: astonishment and curiosity. The virtues of poets and scholars. His familiarity with the exceptional has not deprived him of that admirable quality: the capacity to marvel. Felix constructs a universe using only two properties, both originating in him, material signs of the state of his own soul: the exclamation mark and the question mark. Nothing more is needed for building a world!'

THE CINEMA

We cannot expect as much from the cinema of 'flesh and blood'. The camera really does contain a magic eye that lets nothing escape. But animals are not intelligent actors, and not necessarily tractable. To succeed in getting a simple cat to enter, leave, jump, run or stop still sometimes means waiting hours or even days, being endlessly patient and finally achieving what can often be only a disappointing or negligible result.

This is why we have more films about dogs and horses than about gorillas. And it is why this seventh art-form is better suited to showing us the habits of deep-sea fish or the lives of butterflies and bees than the secret ways of the wild cat or the behaviour

'Rhubarb', star of cinema and television films, is at home in swimming pool (above) and decorations (right). Below right, his feline admirers take a closer look

'George' the cat, meets 'Lilly', the cat-girl from the Peep Show

pattern of a Siamese. However, a few directors have successfully taken up the challenge, not by trying to make a cat obey the requirements of any particular script, but by adapting the general possibilities of their theme to the natural tendencies of the cat.

From time to time, however, there does appear a gallant cat, with a face more expressive and more plastic than usual, who really seems to live his role, either out of the spirit of the game or out of love for his master. Such a cat was the incredible Siamese of Walt Disney's 'That Darn Cat'. Such again was 'Rhubarb', the American 'mongrel' cat who at the age of sixteen years (which makes him almost a centenarian in human terms) was one of the most famous of Hollywood's animal film stars. Rhubarb always loved playing the clown. He would leap, swim, chase after a ball like a dog. He could go to sleep, roll on his back, yawn with boredom or adopt an air of fury to order, and like an old and consummate actor could tirelessly begin all over again. He was paid $1,000 a week for each film. And his master has ceased to count the awards of palms and cups and Oscars that film juries, children and Societies for the Protection (and admiration) of Animals have, to this day, heaped on him.

In England a trainer, John Holmes, has made himself an authority on cats for television. He holds that it would be useless to try to teach a cat to do anything other than what it wants to do. Age is certainly not a factor in this matter of training. Kittens who have been taken from birth and looked after with all possible care do not show a great deal of talent. On the contrary, it is the adult cats of unknown origin, rescued from destitution and then lovingly cherished, who have been most adaptable to the profession. The important thing first of all is to discover their natural tastes, and then to encourage these tastes, appearing to 'serve'

the cats all the more; because every cat is susceptible to solicitude. One must not, however, be governed here by appearances. 'Buster', for example, although he looks as if he is furious, is a model of gentleness. 'Stripev', who looks like an angel, is in fact a demon. 'Sam' has made countless films. As for 'Koobie', he is obsessed by the laurels of his American colleague 'Rhubarb'. He will do anything required of him in a film, but only in the role of a clever ruffian.

Several years ago, a very successful and extraordinary long colour film was made in Hungary called 'Kati and the Wild Cat'. It was shot in the heart of the enormous forest of Radvany. And it is hard to know who contributed most to its success: the director Agoston Kollanyi, his camera-man Lajos Vancsa, or the principal protagonist, the wild cat who at the age of two and a half months was faced, for the first time, with the terrifying assembly of equipment used in film-making and with nature on a grand scale.

Czechoslovakia, in turn, made a film called 'One Day a Cat', an astonishing colour fairy-tale in which a cat plays a curious role. When it does not wear the spectacles that its master puts over its eyes it sees people as they really are, and in a different colour depending on their different faults or virtues. When it turns its gaze on them for a moment, thieves turn grey, hypocrites violet and the unfaithful yellow, while lovers take on a pink colour and sincere people turn blue. In this charming idea there reappears the belief that cats have a mysterious power. The eyes of a cat fixed upon us in an implacable, phosphorescent and luminous gaze are always disconcerting. Some find it fascinating, others unbearable. In this film we find ourselves half-way between the fairy tales of our own childhood and those disturbing Black Books of magic spells that wizards used ages ago.

Scene from 'One Day A Cat' by Jasny

Scene from 'That Darn Cat' by Walt Disney, with Hayley Mills

Gigi, played by Leslie Caron, loves cats. From Minelli's film 'Gigi'

THE CAT IN PHOTOGRAPHY

Thanks to the fact that 'snapshots' are becoming more and more rapid, photography today has become the art of capturing the fleeting expression and the revealing movement. Photography is to the cinema what a preliminary sketch is to the final animated cartoon, but with more truth in it and the possibility of greater expressiveness. A good photograph is no longer merely a clear one. There has been such progress achieved in the technical mechanics of photography that perfect exposure can now be guaranteed. The artistic merit of a photograph today lies in the lighting, expression, attitude and characteristic detail that it manages to capture. A good photo will combine in its result a great many different aspects of its subject, yet this must not be immediately obvious in the final picture and should not provoke an immediate analysis. Whether it is a question of a movement, a landscape or a portrait, everything should contribute towards the final synthesis and effect.

The art of photography today has become the art of movement. And during recent years there have been many peace-loving hunters of game who, armed only with a camera, have rightly been prouder of having caught at a distance of 20 yards the flight of an antelope or the charge of a buffalo in their lens than of slaughtering either with a rifle shot.

While painters and sculptors of animals are disappearing or at least becoming rarer

Cats always seem to be particularly interested in photographic equipment. Perhaps they're trying to find that birdie

By placing a sheet of glass over two chairs, a photographer improvises a transparent table on which her subjects can move about: this is how the photograph opposite was taken

every day, the number of animal photographers is on the increase. And many of these specialize or show a clear preference for one or another species.

Ylla gave the lead. This young Hungarian student came to Paris to study archaeology, but she soon discovered her talent for portraying the dogs and cats of Paris. Her photos became famous. Other photographers followed her. They took photographs by the thousand, not only popularizing the breeds that appeared in the various international cat shows, but also revealing to a large public unexpected aspects of the lives of the alley-cats and strays. Cats were now seen as they really are: no more cruel toms, all spreading claws; no more diabolical females. Rather the despairing stare of a cat trying to cross a road, the bewildering equilibrium of another walking with tranquillity on a balcony balustrade at a height of ten stories over empty space, the comedy of a bundle of kittens tangled up in a ball of wool, the euphoria of a mother cat in the hollow of her cushion, the astonished surprise of a small cat nose to nose with a large watchdog, the casual set-backs of a newly-born kitten, full of awkward curiosity, and, from time to time, what every photographer longs for, the 'photo-shock' that needs no caption.

Cat photographers could be listed by their hundreds. Their talent has done more than a century of poems to create a climate sympathetic to the cat.

6 *THE CAT AND MUSIC*

Two great cat-lovers held the same opinion on the mysterious appeal of their favourite animal. For Florent Fels the cat offered the indefinable charm of silence. Gilbert Ganne, author of a penetrating essay on cats called 'Orgueil de la maison' (from Baudelaire's poem, see page 76) goes even further: 'The cat is the only creature which, being loved, can love and keep quiet.' Must love, which is said to be blind, be dumb as well?

THE CAT'S VOCAL POSSIBILITIES

While I am writing, two tom-cats are in the process of fighting at the bottom of the garden for possession of a ball and emitting loud cries. And I am no longer very far from agreeing with Moncrif, Champfleury, the Abbé Galiani and those many others who have attributed to the cat a possible vocal range of between twenty and sixty notes. The range of expression is perhaps even richer still. From the rounded modulation of the low notes of a purr, it changes to the cooing of the turtledove, to become, through growls and spat out cries, that rending howling and desperate clamour that freeze the blood.

Night and day, in gentleness or cruelty, for better or for worse, no other animal is as much of an extremist as the cat.

Sixty notes, was it said? Why not? It must make use of at least that number, particularly during its amorous moments, when it is successively harp then cymbal, giving out sounds so clearly opposite to each other as the tender plaintiveness of the viol and the brassy outbursts of the trumpet. Perhaps this range of vocal expression that both preceeds and accompanies the coupling of cats is composed of just those tones that awaken and continue to provoke desire.

The cat's most distinctive and characteristic music is its purr. Why does no other animal purr? No one knows. Most people think of the cat's purr as a music of contentment, and so it can be. But it can also be purrs of pain. What are the other meanings to be found in this unusual noise? Has anyone been able to analyse them scientifically.

Kittens begin to purr when they are about a week old. From then on, this vocal activity seems to be a matter of choice—a voluntary expression of a state of mind. Some cats even purr when they are in a light sleep. Are they having happy dreams?

The various tones of purrs are fascinating. Kittens purr in a monotone. But after a slight change of voice, they are able to purr on two or three notes. A deep purr can have at least two meanings: if it is a harsh sound, the cat may be in pain; if it is a contented sound, and if the cat drools a bit, it is ecstatically happy.

The volume of the purr also causes wonder. Why does a cat who has been purring inaudibly suddenly fill the room with sound? And how does he do it?

And what of the maiows? The ordinary cat owner will notice a difference between the maiow that greets the master and the miaow that signals hunger. But the miaows exchanged between cats are as many and as various as the relationships that exist between cats.

Animals certainly take no intellectual interest in the art of music, but then music is not essentially intellectual. As Berlioz wrote, music is the art of moving the feelings through sound. It is sadness, joy, euphoria and sensual pleasure. Sensibility to music does not necessarily involve education: it is vibration, it is an individual reaction to each person, involving either harmony and communion or dissonnance and exasperation.

The poet Laprade, who did not like music, said, 'It is the only one of the arts to which animals, madmen and fools seem sensitive.' He pushes the paradox a little far, but the majority of animals are obviously sensitive to sounds. The cat's senses are too easily irritated, from its auditory acuteness to the sensitivity of its whiskers, for it not to react to a marked degree to music. But

Concert Miaulique *(Concert of miaouws), an engraving of the seventeenth century*

to what sort of music? That of imitative harmonies? In that case it should most of all appreciate instruments that sound like its own voice: the Chinese viol, for example, or the Japanese samisen, the modern musical saw or the saron of Java, a percussion instrument that can be used to make strange miaouwing sounds. The saron has the shape of a cat with paws extended and open mouth, and Patricia Dale Green believes this is to give the illusion that the song comes from this mouth. On the back of this so-called cat are small parallel slats that are stroked with a light reed.

The sistrum of ancient Egypt, which was used in the temple of Isis, was likewise used under the sign of the cat. On this oval metal frame were fixed three or four horizontal rods, which were stroked like the cords of a guitar, and which probably gave a particularly disturbing sound. Paintings and sculptures seem to show that these instruments were used in the various rites of the cat-goddess, and also resounded to excite valorous soldiers to greater efforts in battle. Plutarch described this exotic instrument as follows:

'The *sistrum* too shows that the things that *are* must be *shaken*, and never *cease from motion*, but be as it were aroused and stirred up when they slumber and are slothful, for they pretend they drive off and repulse Typhon with the sistra, showing that when Corruption has tied fast and brought it to a standstill, Generation again unlooses and restores Nature by means of Motion. And as the sistrum is circular in the upper part, the arch contains the four things that are shaken, because the part of the universe that is born and perishes, is surrounded by the Lunar sphere, but all things are set in motion and changed within it by means of the four elements, Fire, Earth, Water, Air. And on the arch of the sistrum, at the top, they figure a *cat* having a human face (sphinx), and on the

lower part, below the things that are shaken, sometimes a head of Isis, sometimes of Nepthys, symbolizing by these heads *Generation* and *End* (for these are the Changes and Motions of the elements), and by the Cat, the Moon, on account of the pied colour, nocturnal habits, and fecundity of the animal, for it is said to bring forth one, and then two, then three, then four, up to five at a birth, and always adds by one up to seven (to her litter), so that in all it produces eight-and-twenty young, the which are equal in number to the illuminations of the Moon. This, however, may be somewhat fabulous, but the pupils in its eyes appear to grow full and dilate themselves at the full of the moon, but become thin and dull during the wane of that luminary; and by the human head of the Cat they express the *Intelligence* and *Rationality* of the changes connected with the Moon.'

Cats are sensitive to the sound of different musical instruments, and also to the charm or displeasure of the spoken word and the human voice. In the seventeenth century certain latter-day Orpheuses augmented their natural talents by teaching cats to miaouw in time with them. These people would make their way from town to town, carrying on their shoulders or in their arms five or six purring cats, modulating more or less rhythmically together. The public were greatly entertained by this and used to give these cunning showmen a generous welcome. The posters read:
You who do not realize the value of music,
Come along and hear the magnificent
    concert,
The enchanting tunes I teach my cats.
Since my beautiful voice makes even these
    animals amenable,
I cannot fail to instruct you all.

These performances were much more humane than some which took place in the sixteenth century. Unscrupulous showmen found strange and cruel ways of presenting

Seventeenth-century poster advertising a concert of cats

Engraving from the seventeenth century: concert of cats

The Cat Musicians *attributed to El Greco*

orchestras of cats. Twelve or fifteen unhappy animals were shut up in a box, whose bottom was pierced by as many holes as there were cats. The tail of a cat was passed through each one, and the showman would pull these, more or less strongly and more or less often, to obtain a stupid cacophony of noise. It is hard to explain how in any country any audience could have taken pleasure in such a ridiculous exhibition.

The most indifferent of cats is affected by its master's voice, whether feared or sought after. This is what Marcel Jouhandeau has written in *Minos et moi*. The author's imitation of a blackbird, he says, produces an effect on Minos that borders on the ludicrous. 'Immediately,' writes Jouhandeau, 'as if capsized, he stretches himself out, making strange bobbing movements with his backside and his neck, almost swooning, and, on reaching the pitch of excitement, his claws beat at the sky .... but if my modulations soften, become more languorous, closer to the nocturnes of the nightingale, then I lead him, little by little, at will, to calm himself, and pass from voluptuousness to tenderness.' Further on we read: 'Whenever I sing, he comes and sniffs my song all around my mouth; he tries to find it with his claws, to make off with it.'

Henri Sauguet, a composer who always loved cats, was sixteen and had just discovered Debussy when he became intrigued by the attitude of his much-loved Cody, the black and white cat of his childhood who eventually lived to be twenty years old. When Sauguet played the 'Cortège' of the 'Petite Suite' he saw Cody thrown into complete confusion. He rolled on his back, shivered with pleasure, got up again, jumped on the piano, then on to the knees of his master and licked his fingers on the keyboard. If that hand stopped still? He moved slowly away without haste—and then rushed back again, enraptured, as soon as the enchanting birds began to pour forth again.

Cat musicians in a Russian cartoon

Cody was succeeded by Marie-Adélaïde Pompon, who was very fond of coloratura voices. Just as with Jouhandeau's cat, she tried with quick blows of her paw to seize these things which are intangible to us but which for cats are perhaps material objects – and which we in our ignorance call sounds.

It is possible that, even just for the briefest of moments, the vibration of a sound in the air is accessible to the hypersensitivity of a cat. That, anyway, would be the prosaic explanation of the phenomenon. But how do we explain the instinct for harmony, the taste for what is musically correct, that the composer Reynaldo Hahn assures us he has seen in cats? In the nineteenth century, the famous Mlle Dupuy was completely persuaded of this phenomenon. She noticed that, when she played on the harp a piece that was familiar to the cat, it betrayed its feelings either by giving a purr of sympathy or, on the contrary, by crying out, according to the quality of the playing. When she died, having recognized how much of her success she owed to the independent critique, she bequeathed her cat a house in town and another in the country, and left a substantial income to several personal friends so that they would gladly want to look after the health and comfort of her singular heir.

For several months Casimir Colomb, in an isolated villa, watched the curious behaviour of a wild and unapproachable cat. On evenings when two of his young friends were singing an Italian barcarolle the cat would immediately arrive through the window, jump into the room, rub itself tenderly against the legs of the singers and then, when the last note had emerged, fly off again wildly and even more quickly than it had come, leaving the audience astounded.

This double magic of sounds, the sounds that cats perceive and those they emit them-

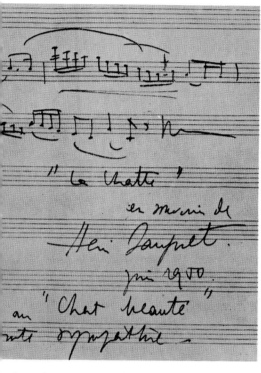

selves, has attracted both modest and celebrated composers, and has given us many
melodies, songs, ballets and other original
works.

THE CAT IN MUSICAL COMPOSITION

One of Scarlatti's compositions, from a collection of Sonatas for harpsichord dedicated
around 1729 to the Princess of Asturias,
is marked only with the indication
'moderato'. Today it is known as the 'Cat's
Fugue' because it is thought to have been
suggested to Scarlatti by the steps of a cat
on the harpsichord keyboard. This anecdote probably arose because of the numerous
passages in double notes, the oddly rising
intervals and the incessant rapidity of the
playing.

Rossini in his later period, wrote many
pieces of 'salon' music. Though slight,
musically speaking, they were gay in theme

and intended for the amusement of the
evening's guests. Such a piece of wit is his
little-known *Duetto Buffo di Due Gatti*
(Comic Duet for Two Cats). Rossini, adapting the miaows of cats to the music of the
human voice, anticipated Ravel by nearly a
century.

Ravel's opera *L'enfant et les sortilèges*
seems to have been the first important lyrical
fantasy on the dancing and singing loves of
the feline race. Although it was based on a
short story by Colette, Ravel would not
allow any commentary whatsoever by the
author. Not once did he invite her to a preliminary hearing. Only one scruple seems
to have struck him. Taking every pain with
the famous love duet between the two cats,
he gravely asked the author whether she
would have any objection if he allowed himself to replace a 'Mauao', which he found
inconvenient, with a 'Mouain' . . . or perhaps
it was the other way around.

*Costume by Paul Colin
for* L'Enfant et les Sortilèges
by Maurice Ravel

7 THE SCIENCE OF THE CAT

If the master asks, 'What is a cat?', the schoolboy may be satisfied with the reply 'A small tamed tiger'. The student, better informed, should say, 'A carnivore of the genus *Felis*'. If the answer is to be complete, he should also add: 'A family clearly distinguished by the specialization of its teeth and claws.' The cat's teeth are totally different from those of omnivores, and indeed are the most specialized teeth among the carnivores.

PHYSIOLOGY

The sometimes frightening mouth of the cat is the same, on a reduced scale, as that of the lion. A fundamental point is that the lips are black in colour. All cats should show this dark colouring of the mucous labials, a colour like gleaming anthracite. Cats without it are degenerate, and will probably die early and without descendants. A cat with pink lips is not worthy to be called a cat.

The cat has only thirty teeth, whereas the dog has at least ten or twelve more. But what teeth they are! And how well adapted! In the upper jaw there are on each side three rather negligible incisors, but a magnificent canine that is wide at the base, tapering to a point at the tip and more or less curved at the back, being slightly less so at the front. The same is true of the lower jaw. But with the molars it is different. There are four on each side above, three on each side below. A person who looks at them closely and touches them with a finger will find that they are sharp and serrated like the teeth of a saw. The inferior maxillary is very slightly thinner than the superior maxillary, so that the molars fit against each other not crown to crown, but with their sides in contact. In this way the teeth cross together and marry up like gear teeth or the blades of shears. This same effect is found in the gentlest of kittens as well as in the lion and the tiger.

With the Siamese, as with the panther, everything contributes to a swift tearing up and cutting effect. Indeed, because of the way the jaws are hinged together, grinding movements are impossible in the cat.

The muscles of the jaws are short, powerful and as hard as iron. They are inserted into widely-spaced zygomatic arches. These muscles give a characteristic shape to the feline skull, which has been said to be as long as it is wide. Nevertheless, in this respect, the head of the Siamese is definitely more 'ophidian' or snake-like when compared with the more 'bull-dog' Persian.

One does not look at a cat's head; one caresses it. 'Short, ovoid and without internal occipital protuberance' say the textbooks. But the most effective way to look at a cat's head is to see it held in the hollow of a large hand, fitting there as exactly as a stone in a peach, and then emerging smoothly through the hole made by the thumb and forefinger with its ears bent flatly back and looking as neat as the head of a snake.

The construction of the cat's body, the way that its bones are assembled together, give it an immense elasticity. In man the vertebrae of the spinal column are held together by ligaments, but in the cat these connections are muscular and therefore elastic. The cat's spine consists of twenty thoracic vertebrae, plus two or three false vertebrae in addition to the normal lumbar ones. This vertebral axis is bound together by small muscular bundles. This is why the cat can elongate its back or contract it, curve it upwards like the arch of a bridge, or even oscillate it along the vertebral line. The structure of the cat's breastbone also contributes to elasticity, the sternebra being elongated by the addition of a small cartilaginous stalk.

Another reason for the cat's marvellous flexibility is the construction of its shoulder joint. This joint permits the cat to turn its

The physiognomy of the cat: in profile and full face

foreleg in almost any direction. The lack of a clavicle also permits freedom of movement. The cat's clavicle is either very small or nonexistent.

The cat's skeleton is remarkably like the skeleton of man. At least, it seems to have all of the most useful elements. The one thing it does not have is a thumb. It does have what might have been a thumb, attached to the inside of the leg at the top of the foot. But the bone never developed, and only a claw remains as a hint of what might have been.

But what they lack in thumbs, cats make up in toes. They usually have four toes, but it is not uncommon to see six toes or even seven. This trait is hereditary.

One of the most interesting things about the cat's structure is the movement it produces. Unlike the dog and horse, the cat walks or runs by moving the front and back legs on one side, and then the front and back legs on the other side. The only other animals that move in this way are the camel and the giraffe. Every other four-legged animal moves its left front leg at the same time as its right hind leg, and the right front leg with the left hind leg.

Approximately 290 bones, 517 muscles and a slight amount of fat make up that agile feline machine which we so admire—and to which we pay tribute when we say that someone 'walks like a cat'. But besides being one of the most agile of creatures, the cat is also one of the most devastating. Its natural weapons are its retractile claws. These sharp claws, connected by exstensible ligaments, can stretch out or disappear back again by the simple contraction of the flexor muscles. So it is not surprising that cats are the most silent of animals. With the claws pulled back like eyelids, they advance, wearing their natural slippers—those thick elastic pads that insulate their feet.

The cat's skin is, like man's skin, made up

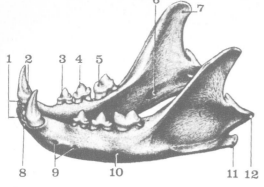

*New-born kittens depend on their
mother. They are born deaf and blind*

of two layers: the dermis and the epidermis.
The function of the cat's skin is the same as
the function of man's skin: to act as a barrier.
Our skin is constantly in a state of regenera-
tion, and the same is true of the cat, with the
difference that the cat's skin is exceptionally
quick to regenerate and to fight off infection
that enters through a wound.

Of course, the main difference between
the skin of man and the skin of the cat is the
hair growth. Man was once covered with
hair, but was it ever as thick as a cat's fur?
Attached to the cat's hair follicles are tiny
erector muscles. Humans have a few of
these muscles on the back of the neck, and
when they go into action, the 'hair stands
on end'. The cat, having these muscles all
over its body, can bristle all over. When
frightened or angry, the erector muscles go
to work–even on the tail–until the cat is
quite terrifying to look at. Is this gift of
nature a psychological weapon? The cat,
although a very small animal, can frighten
off its enemies simply by arching its back,
bristling and hissing.

The cat's tongue is a very useful tool.
Covered with tiny hooks of four different
shapes, the tongue is very useful for picking
up every scrap of food. It is also a remarkably
good cleaning tool.

LONGEVITY

The average lifespan of the cat is increasing
all the time. As in man's case, advances in
medicine are stretching life expectancy
every year. In the past few years, the cat's
life expectancy has increased from twelve
years to about seventeen years. It is not
unusual to find cats much older. Several
astonishing cats have lived to over 30 years
in age, one Los Angeles cat dying in its
34th year.

Although people seem to enjoy comparing the lifespan of animals with the lifespan of man, there is really no way to do so
with any validity. It is simply not true–as

If the eyebrows and whiskers, those indispensable vibrissae, are cut close, the cat is rendered temporarily infirm

When a cat catches a mouse it is not necessarily through smell or sight

Detail from a painting by J. M. Matthias, Méchants Enfants *(Mischievous Children), 1832*

many contend—that one year of a cat's life is equivalent to three of a human life. A year-old cat is an adult animal: it can reproduce and it can take care of itself. A three-year-old child is absolutely helpless.

SENSORY FUNCTIONS

Cats, like many carnivores, are born deaf and blind. The delicate sensory organs are protected in this way until they are ready to be exposed to the air.

But when those first twelve days of natural deafness and blindness are over, how they make up for it! The eyes of a small cat can never be wide open enough, never sufficiently curious, never too impatient in their attempt to see everything. Its little ears, covered with antennae-like tufts, can never be surfeited. Its nervous impulses are constantly being transformed into leaps and bounds and pirouettes. The nostrils of its small nose can never be too vibrant. Its olfactory papillae are always impatiently open for learning everything. In a few days, more quickly than any other domestic animal, a cat begins to accumulate those perceptions, sensations, pleasures and pains that make up experience. It must, in the space of a few months, become sober and wise, discipline its reflexes and gain control of itself.

The physical nature of the cat is contained in the words 'in control'. We have spoken of the structure of its paws, the suppleness of its muscles, its exceptional skeleton, but the cat cannot run particularly fast. In order to escape from danger, or to surprise victims that it could not catch by direct pursuit, it must be able to leap and climb and jump. This is possible because it has a nervous system that is always ready to respond to the orders it receives, and a sensory system that is very efficient. The cat's sense of sight can only be compared with the excellent vision of birds, and its exquisite sense of touch with that of insects.

The cat's sense of touch manifests itself in many different areas. Every hair is sensitive—the eyebrows, the whiskers, the hairs of its cheeks, and the fine tufts of hair on its ears. The function of the indispensable vibrissae (whiskers) are still only partly understood, but we do know that to cut them close is to temporarily incapacitate the cat. Even the tip of a cat's nose is sensitive. It so closely sniffs at the least scrap of food that the phenomenon must be more than olfactory. This prudent and suspicious contact, this need to touch with the nose, so special to cats, has largely contributed to a false belief that the vision of cats is bad and that their olfactory senses are mediocre.

It has been suggested that when a cat catches a mouse that is cowering in the middle of the night in some deep hole, this is not because the cat actually smells the mouse but because the mouse at this moment emits sufficient infra-red rays to alert the thermal sensitivity of the hunter and to guide it—as the warmth of the sun's rays guides a blind man. Whatever the scientific verdict on this theory, a cat can certainly distinguish the smell of nitrogenous products. Its nose catches the slightest suggestion of scent of its master—or the smallest fish closed in a refrigerator. Certain smells to which the finest bloodhounds are indifferent attract or repel the cat. Leeks, asparagus, pinks, eucalyptus, mint, mimosa, lavender, catmint, valerian and tuberoses intoxicate it. It loves the smell of the petrol and oil used in cars, of opium smoke, yeast, the imperceptible odour of freshly slaughtered meat, the musty chlorinated smell of household washing, plaster, fennel, ammonia, the stagnant water from vases. On the other hand, it is indifferent to cold cooked meat. Rum, alcohol, and absinthe are nauseating.

On the subject of the smell of rats and mice, however, it is better to avoid generalizing on what are still doubtful points. It may

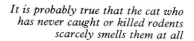
*It is probably true that the cat who
has never caught or killed rodents
scarcely smells them at all*

*The cat can certainly distinguish
the smell of nitrogenous
products, whether dead or alive*

be true that the cat who has never killed rodents scarcely smells them at all. But, whatever the sense that perceives the rodent, it is certainly very strong, for it seems to awaken in the most delicate of Persians the aggressive fervour of the great Oriental ratting cats. This instinct is hereditary in all cats and has merely lain dormant while waiting to be aroused.

A great many other mechanisms seem to be bound up with the complexity of a cat's sense of smell, a sense that does more than determine their hostility to rats or their temporary intoxications. There are cats who will turn suddenly on a hand about to stroke them. Almost always what has happened is that a sudden uncontrolled apprehension, even when concealed, has just modified for a fiftieth of a second the pH (degree of acidity) of the person's skin. Recent works have shown the even more complex role that this olfactory stimulation can play in other physiological functionings, for example, in sexual awakening. It has been demonstrated that the œstral cycle can be disturbed by the chemical stimulation of the mucous membrane with perfume. The French researchers R. David, G. Thiéry and their collaborators have demonstrated the effect produced by the electrical stimulation of the olfactory bulbs of female cats. The conclusions are that the sensibility of these regions is such that it is possible, by means of olfactory stimulation, to waken or profoundly disturb all the delicate mechanisms of the sex hormones.

The ears of the cat are small, short receivers that are pointed at the top, but rounded and open at the base. They turn ten times more quickly in the direction of any sound than the most pointed ears of the best watch-dog. The cat's ear contains almost thirty muscles, whereas the human ear, which hardly moves at all, scarcely has half a dozen. The cat's ear is receptive to frequencies of from 20 to 25,000 vibrations

per second. It is therefore sensitive to ultrasonic noises, whereas most humans are deaf to anything above 20,000 vibrations per second. But it is slightly inferior to that of the dog which is receptive up to 35,000 vibrations per second.

Are white or albino cats, like rattlesnakes, deaf to sound? Many experts think that white cats with blue eyes are, without exception, born deaf. But Alyandro Obolunsky Dadian, the great Chilean breeder and specialist in white Persians writes: 'I have for many years bred white cats with blue eyes.... I have never done away with a single one. All those that I have not kept have gone into the hands of friends, and a great many of the children of my own cats are still living. Not one of them is deaf, not one of them ever has been. In fact, my own cats know the sound of their own names, and each comes only when he hears his own....' So deafness in white cats with blue eyes does not seem to be a rule.

Deaf or not, are white cats as sensitive as others to storms? A normal cat will preen its back or the back of its ear with a wet paw: this sign, harbinger of rain, had already attracted the attention of the Egyptian priests of the temple of Bubastis.

Except in the case of some rare white cats, all cats hear very well indeed. How many contented pets that we have believed to be fast asleep and therefore deaf to all sounds, are, on the contrary, alert to the slightest tremor that they alone can perceive: the familiar car of the master who will be there any minute, the lift which is going to stop at the landing.

I have a story of my own that eloquently demonstrates the powers of the auditory memory of the cat. One of my cats used to come running at meal-times at the sound of an almost inaudible whistle, of the ultrasonic type used in hunting to recall a dog without disturbing the game. For three

months, twice daily, this code was respected by all concerned, and then one day the whistle disappeared, mislaid at the bottom of a drawer. It was only a year later that, completely by chance and in the course of a tidying-up, I found the whistle and casually put it to my lips. It was neither the time nor the place; the door of the room was closed, the window of the room was closed—and yet from the depths of the garden the cat arrived, miaowing his joy at again finding this call that so pleased him. Once again he rushed down to the kitchen, and indeed repeated his behaviour exactly—not out of hunger but out of happiness.

What a fantastic variety of auditory resources must a cat draw on when lost and terrified! Slipping from street to street, it tries to recognize amongst all the unknown things that solicit its attention, the slightest echo that can show it the way. It has been scientifically proved that the cat is capable of distinguishing between two sounds emitted at the same second but separated by fifty centimetres, which represents a chronological difference of ·0000028 seconds.

Tactile sensibility does not seem to vary much between one species and another, whether it is a question of a man's hand or an elephant's trunk. If we touch the wood of a piano or the diaphragm of a loudspeaker, the deep notes give us a vibration which is completely distinct from our auditory perception. Deaf-mutes can easily distinguish, with the tips of their fingers, the deeper tones of the human voice when they touch a singer's throat.

Why is this only the case with the lower notes? It is because they correspond to the lower frequencies, and the tips of our fingers can only register up to a thousand vibrations per second. If we now lift our fingers from the wood of the piano or the diaphragm of the loud-speaker, our ears continue to 'hear', to be receptive to the sound waves, but our

The eye of the cat has very swift accommodation—the power of adjusting the focus to distance

fingers, even when placed the smallest distance away, can distinguish nothing. This is because the mechanism of our ear is much more sensitive than our skin to vibratory stimuli. We hear sounds ranging between twenty vibrations per second and about twenty thousand vibrations per second. We can then, between twenty and a thousand vibrations per second, register the same phenomenon by two different types of sensation: vibratory sensations felt in our fingers and sound in the normal sense heard by means of our ears. But because of its

vibrissae and its sensitive hair, the cat is infinitely more sensitive to vibratory stimulation than we are.

The special visual power of cats is famous. After all, everyone has always known that cats can see in the dark. Or can they? In fact, they cannot see in absolute darkness. But cats can see much better at night than men can. They can see ultraviolet rays and other light invisible to men. This power seems to come from visual purple in the epithelial rods.

The cat's cornea is more developed than

that of the dog. Its anterior chamber is deeper. Its retina is a richer glossy velvet, particularly in the area immediately around the optic nerve. It has a total field of vision of 280° and a binocular field of 130°, so that it has greater visual possibilities than the lion (range of 120°) and greater still than the dog (range of 83°).

The direction of the eye is necessarily determined by the position of the recess or orbit. In man and the monkey, the orbits are in a more or less parallel direction. In carnivores they begin to diverge. In birds it is a more marked divergence still. But a cat has eyes that are almost frontal. A good comparative measure of this direction of the eyes is the angle of the intersection of the tangential planes at the base of each orbit. In man this angle is between 130° and 140°, in the cat it is 105° to 110°, but in the dog it is between 85° and 90°.

The volume of the eye, as well, is remarkable. The eye of the horse and of the ostrich are the biggest that we know, marine animals excepted. But the cat has the biggest eyes in relation to the weight of its body. The volume of the ocular globe is four to five cubic centimetres. Further, it is the relatively small cats who have the biggest eyes.

What can be learned from these details, which are perhaps rather technical for a reader who is not a specialist? The vision of the cat gives it a wide range but little three-dimensional perspective. But this is a more usual type of vision in mammals than is generally believed.

Unlike dogs, cats retain the visual powers of their youth. Cataract, the fate of all dogs after their eighth year, is practically unknown in cats.

Accommodation–the power of adjusting the focus of the eye to distance–is very swift in the cat. Its pupillary reflexes are very lively, and this explains the extraordinary precision with which it is able to gauge the exact distances in jumping.

The cat can distinguish form better than the dog, but less clearly than human beings can. It differentiates quite clearly between squares and circles, whatever their size and in whatever way they are placed. But on a grey fabric in which it can perceive the nuances, it cannot distinguish either stripes or drawings. Its vision in half-light on the other hand, is very sensitive. The extreme development of its cornea and the dilation of its pupil allow it to see where the illumination would be too feeble for our vision.

Can the cat distinguish colours? Professor Bonaventure, of the Faculty of Sciences at Strasbourg, thinks that the cat can only distinguish red, and that all other colours appear to it as a range of greys. It is generally admitted that colour vision does not exist in nocturnal animals. If the cat can perceive colour differences it might be by some other mechanism than that of vision.

It is always difficult to talk of colours and tastes in relation to animals. The cat is not supposed to have much sense of taste, because, as in the case of dogs, food does not stay long in its mouth. It tears, pulverizes, swallows very rapidly indeed, and its digestion is essentially gastric. Also, it has been shown by laboratory experiments that a cat cannot distinguish the taste of sugar. And yet the cat always, in relation to food, gives the impression of wanting to make up its mind.

ELECTRICITY

The cat's electric potential has never been the subject of precise research, and it has never been measured. Therefore, it is with appropriate reservations that I tell the story of the engineer who, after evaluating in terms of 'stroke-units' the electric potential that can accumulate along the length of a cat's back, estimated that two thousand

Not sure whether it is for him!

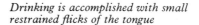

Drinking is accomplished with small
restrained flicks of the tongue

A frightened, or disagreeably surprised cat, rapidly flattens itself, as if it were getting ready to leap

million 'strokes' would be enough to light up a 75-watt lamp for one minute! Its nerve-impulses do not make the cat into a generator, but it is easy to confirm, by stroking a cat's back on a stormy day, that thousands of crackling sparks are produced.

Subject to the same reservations comes the claim of a Derby technician which appeared in the Bulletin of the British Embassy in Paris. While investigating the source of interference that was preventing television stations from correctly transmitting emissions of a certain wavelength, the technician discovered, he said, that the cause of the trouble was a nervous cat whose mistress caressed it in order to calm it. 'These caresses produced enough static electricity to scramble the images of a television station. . . .' The researcher continued to follow the matter up closely, 'because there could exist' he said, 'other cases of scrambling of this kind, it being very possible that the production of static electricity could vary from one cat to another.'

THE INTERNAL MYSTERIES

Keeping to direct observation, we can certainly note the extent to which heat seems indispensable to cats. Everything which gives off heat waves attracts and holds them. When the summer sun has gone it is the stove, the radiator and the fireplace that serve as substitutes. What is the role that heat plays in the physiology of the cat, for whom hunger and thirst seem to be less hard to bear than to be deprived of warmth? We could say that the cat feeds on heat rays. Their effects, which the cat can tolerate to the point of congestion, sometimes succeed in producing nervous disorders which show themselves in a sudden need to leap about, to leave the comfortable room and go out into the cold. For several days after this it is possible to note discreet shivers in the skin, little spasms in the limbs, a partial paralysis of the third eyelid (that is, the eyelid that blinks) and lastly, a clearer symptom: a convergent squint in both eyes. There is no fever, and all the general functions remain normal. The appetite is conserved. An equal number of symptoms show that no infectious agent is involved, and the troubles disappear leaving no sequels.

How is it that the cat is literally able to roast itself beside a hearth under heat conditions that would be intolerable to any other mammal, and yet at the same time it is startled if someone scratches a match beside it? Why, with a hearing so sensitive to the ultrasonic, is it able, when it wants, to be totally impassive to the most deafening din?

Here is one of the most mysterious aspects of the cat. To demonstrate this mechanism, science must study more than the external manifestations that accompany or betray certain emotions in this animal. The phenomenon of fear is one among several such emotions that have been studied in all their aspects.

A frightened cat, or simply a disagreeably surprised cat, begins by rapidly flattening itself as if it were getting ready to leap. Then, almost immediately, it straightens up again. Its hair bristles, its attitude is hostile. If it is incited even further, its pupils dilate to their extreme, its breathing becomes short and rapid, its tail beats the air furiously and in a moment seems to become three times its size. Is it completely terrified? The ears lie back, the whiskers and eyebrows point forward, the menacing teeth are exposed, the back arches, while along the full length of the vertebra there arises a hairy spine which makes the cat look like a dragon. It hisses, spits, howls and pants, as if to intimidate its adversary. And if the menace becomes more specific, it attacks, claws spread, with the swiftness of lightning.

This series of behavioural changes is a matter of everyday observation and familiar to most of us. With closer attention, we will very often note the appearance of interdigital perspiration which goes so far as to mark the pavement or parquet with the

The attitude of a cat can make the boldest watchdog recoil

clear print of paws. This perspiration can be measured to show a scale of the various degrees of fear. All that is needed is a minute crystal of cobalt blue placed in the hollow of a sleeping cat's paw and held in place by a bandage made of a light strip of absorbent gauze. At the slightest unexpected noise, or under the influence of sudden illumination, a perspiration is established. It dampens the crystal and tints the gauze a pale blue. If a dog on a lead should enter the room the crystal immediately turns a lavender or a lilac blue. If the dog suddenly looks like attacking, the gauze becomes pink. Other reactions appear. The heart beats very quickly, the pulse rate rising to 200. Breath-

ing becomes intense and very rapid. The blood sugar count rises by 50 per cent. There is a rise in the number of red blood corpuscles, which can increase by 25 per cent over their normal number. Finally the adrenal glands play their part with a brutal discharge of adrenaline, and we know the effect that adrenaline has on muscular activity.

Experimental operations suggest that the cat owes these very rapid reactions to its two chains of sympathetic ganglia. A dog deprived of its sympathetic nervous system is in no way different from normal dogs, but the cat which has suffered this operation can live an almost normal life only if it is

well nourished, kept warm and surrounded by affection. Reduced to defending itself, looking for its own food and fighting for its own survival, it is scared and helpless, incapable of jumping after a bird or leaping for a mouse. It is an unhappy creature paralysed by the slightest emotion.

Such is the complexity of problems that have occupied the physiologists of the cat for almost a century now. If the mysteries of this animal are one day understood, we will probably owe it to the neuro-endocrinologists. It is they who have thrown light on animal psychophysiology in general, and that of the cat in particular.

SEX

All the superior mammals have a seasonal sexual rhythm. At regular intervals, under the influence of sex hormones that are passed into the blood, the females enter their seasons, or become 'in heat'. Outside these very precise periods, which vary according to the species, the bitch, the mare, the cow and the lioness remain completely indifferent to males. Such an equilibrium seems to be ignored by the female cat. Cats have an anarchic sexuality; and maternity, pregnancy and the feeding of their young provide no necessary checks on their sex life.

In females of other species, whether domestic or wild, sexual activity develops always in the same regular way. With cats, however, the pattern is essentially variable.

One cat at these times will be the essence of gentleness: she is tender and winning and has lost her appetite—as romantic as you could wish. Another will be nothing but scratches, howls, awkwardness and chronic hunger—a complete animal.

A SENSE OF BALANCE

So many other points in the psychophysiology of the cat remain enigmatic.

How is it, for example, that this nervous creature does not experience dizziness under the same conditions as other mammals? Why is the cat so confident on rooftops, skirting fearlessly round the most dangerous gutters, making a tranquil observatory on the most elevated heights, reaching in a few leaps the top of a great tree—yet trembling with terror when it is a matter of coming down again, miaowing its frailty from the roof or ignominiously sliding backwards down the length of the tree trunk? And how does it manage to land squarely on all fours when it falls from the fourth storey?

The French Academy of Sciences during the last century tried to explain why a cat almost always falls on its feet, even if it has been thrown into space with its paws upwards: 'The terror which possesses it makes

bend its spine, while desperately stretching its head and legs towards the point it has just left, as if to find it again; which gives the firm action of a lever!'

A little later the French physiologist Marey, with the help of a film that captured 60 images per second, showed that a cat, thrown headfirst, starts by turning round on itself with the upper half of its body. When this has turned through 180° the back half does the same.

Unfortunately, in spite of this ability, many cats are killed or fractured in falls. It appears that the most important thing to take account of is the height involved. A cat that falls from the sixth storey or higher is pitiably crushed to the earth. It breaks a limb if it falls from the first. But it generally escapes well if it falls from the fourth. From the fourth storey the cat has time to turn itself in space; at the same time this height represents the extreme limit for the elasticity of its muscles and the resistance of its bones.

THE CAT'S PURR

We know very little about the physical mechanism of that muffled rumbling, the purr. It is probably produced by the vibrations of one of the two vocal cords of the cat's throat.

It has been theorized that the superior vocal cords cause the cat's falsetto cry, the plaintive small child's voice of the Siamese, and the purr while the inferior cords produce the growling of angry tom-cats and the cries of the female in an excited state.

Of historic interest only are the rather gratuitous claims of Champfleury, who attributed to the cat the possibility of emitting more than sixty different notes. The number is more probably twenty. Dupont de Nemours went further and claimed to be able to distinguish six consonants (M.N.S. H.V.F.) besides the vowels that are common to the voices of both cat and dog.

But why does the cat purr? What does it signify? It is held to be the expression of contentment, a manifestation of well-being. But the cats with the least tendency to purr sometimes do so on the operating table; and it would be risky to claim that under these circumstances they are purring for pleasure!

Perhaps we should seriously consider the theory put forward by W. R. MacCuiston in a recent issue of *Veterinary Medicine*. According to him, purring is caused by the increase of blood flow in the vena cava, at the point where this large vein narrows to pass through the liver and diaphragm. When, for some reason or another (enjoyment on being stroked, anger, or simply from being already curled up before a fire) the cat arches its back, the blood rushes against the walls of this funnel-shaped vessel and this sets up the vibrations which we can both hear and feel, and which we call purring.

IS THE CAT A SOUTHPAW?

We know today, as a result of the work of American neurosurgeons, that in spite of the great differences between the brains of cats and the brains of men, there is one outstanding similarity. In both, the right cerebral hemisphere governs the left side of the body and the left cerebral hemisphere controls the right side of the body. In man the two hemispheres function to an unequal degree and, according to his skill or manual preferences, one or the other always predominates. In the right-handed person, the left hemisphere is dominant. In the left-handed person, the right hemisphere is dominant. The cat, however, shows a natural adaption to the equal functioning of its two hemispheres, and it would be interesting to know if it is ambidextrous, that is to say as skilful with the paws on its right side as with those on its left. As a result of an experiment in which sixty cats were led to reach for some food morsel of their choice, using either one paw or the other, Professor J. Cole of Oxford University has claimed that the majority of subjects tested used indifferently and with an equal frequency the right or the left paw. The few subjects who seemed to have a slight preference were 'left-pawed'.

PSYCHOLOGY

Here we enter into one of the most delicate of the fields relating to knowledge of the cat.

Modern 'zoopsychology' is well-inspired in its intention to be prudently impartial and objective. It restricts itself to the study of behaviour. It has put a stop to those widespread generalities that attributed to the cat all the virtues or all the vices, depending on the sympathy or antipathy of the observer.

The classic clichés about cats do not date from yesterday. Fables dating from 2000 BC had several familiar ideas about cats. They were said to be malicious, crafty and sly, but respectable. Today's psychologists are not content with assertions such as these. They have studied, amongst other subjects, the language of cats, or more exactly the combination of ways in which cats communicate amongst themselves. And these are sufficiently stereotyped to allow us to think they express definite emotional states.

THE LANGUAGE OF CATS

There are amongst all mammals various signals which provoke appropriate reactions from others of their kind. With cats the most familiar of these signals are of a visual, olfactory and auditory kind.

To the visual group belong attitudes of the head, movements of the ears, body and tail and the various facial mannerisms.

The olfactory type of signals are those smells produced by glandular secretions or excreta. Urine, saliva and faeces, for example, enable cats to differentiate amongst themselves, and are used in defining territories.

The auditory group of signals is made up of various vocalizations, which range from the softest purr to the sharpest cry, through a complete variety of growling, grunting and spitting in between.

From one cat to another these signs hardly vary. They form a kind of code. A systematic study of them has thrown light on certain attitudes whose interpretation has long been left to the imagination of writers. Little by little, in this way, the psychology of the cat is becoming more understandable to us.

SOCIAL BEHAVIOUR

The study of social behaviour is one of the aspects of feline psychology in which most progress has been made, thanks to English and American researchers. Inspired by this work French psychologists have in turn contributed a clear definition of the term 'territory'. Territory, properly defined, is the zone which its occupant defends against all other cats: the red armchair, the oval basket, the right or the left hand foot of the bed, for example – places where the cat considers himself to be really at home. This 'territory' is not, properly speaking, that 'vital domain' (or 'home range'), that zone regularly frequented by an individual or even a group of cats belonging to the same master, or a group of independent cats who come together as a matter of pleasure, interest or curiosity. The 'vital domain' is not considered by each cat as 'his' personal property. It is a terrain certainly frequented by a particular cat, but where others can play, move around and even hunt. These domains can overlap each other without provoking fights. They are a little like a public garden in a village. Finally, the lair, or 'homing', is the precise spot within either 'territory' or 'vital domain' in which a particular cat knows that he can take refuge, to rest or to escape a danger.

It is all the more curious to note this social organization of felines when we re-

member that the cat does not belong to a gregarious species. Unlike the dog or the sheep, the cat specifically does not have a sense of the pack or the herd. Yet twenty or thirty cats, placed under the obligation of living together – as in a public square, behind the palisades of a yard or in a cattery for breeding, adapt ten times better than do dogs. Why? Because there rapidly intervenes among them a respect for the social hierarchy. There exists among cats, more than any other mammal, a natural tendency to accept the existence of superiors and inferiors. It is not heredity that teaches them this law, but experience. The whole structure of the hierarchy can, in fact, be thrown back into the melting pot each time there is a new-arrival, if the newcomer only shows a little courage.

It is not a question here of choosing a leader or a guide. It is a question of accepting a despot, a tyrant. This despot is not necessarily the youngest or the most handsome. Nor is it by preference either male or female. It is the one which dominates all the others.

Order is in general very quickly established. Let us imagine a group of cats living under the domination of one. A stranger arrives. The attitude of the dominator towards the intruder (who may reveal himself to be a challenger) is quite clear: the 'top cat' arches his back and adopts a fixed and flashing gaze. At the next stage of defiance, his tail is raised quite straight, swollen and ruffled; his claws emerge, ready to shoot forward. A further stage brings defiant and menacing spittings. If the two rivals feel themselves to be equally matched at this precise second there is a fight. Otherwise the inferior adopts an attitude of allegiance; its body flattened to the ground it puts on a submissive air.

Immediately afterwards, whether there has been a fight or not, the confirmed or

132

victorious despot marks his superiority in a curious fashion. He seizes the other by the skin of the neck. Whatever the sex of the cat, this hold is made without any particular brutality; it is a matter of principle, as at this stage the result has been tacitly admitted. The accepted despot straddles his inferior for a few seconds and abandons him.

Within this social hierarchy of cats there only exist two degrees. There are no lieutenants or sub-officers; there is no number two or three. There is only the despot. The whole of the rest of the group keep absolutely equal rights and duties. Within this system are the rather distant relationships that exist between cats. The French psychologist Leyhausen has compared them with paranoid humans: 'Friendship between cats can exist,' he wrote, 'but more or less in the same way that it can exist for a not very sociable man who spends his time in provoking others, and who, when asked why he does not have any friends, replies: "I would like to have them ... but they are so ignoble!"' A strange comparison, but one which underlines fairly enough the social behaviour of cats, at least those who have reached an adult age.

Kittens, in their first few days of life, are too feeble to experience this instinctive need to exercise their egoism. It does sometimes happen that, within a litter, a kitten bigger than the others uses his head and shoulders to be the first to reach the best of its mother's teats. But although they already have their little habits and their little preferred territories, kittens retain, up to the second or third month, a kind of friendship, a kind of reciprocal tolerance, which comes to an end the moment they are able to hunt, and therefore to live for themselves.

HUNTING

The behaviour of the hunting cat follows a fixed pattern. First of all it fixes its gaze on

The language of cats among themselves (drawing by Steinlen)

the prey. Next, it approaches, crawling. Flattened to the ground, it stops for a moment, to raise the back of its body. For a few brief seconds, this part of the body oscillates, first horizontally, then vertically, before the cat draws itself up completely for the final jump.

This jump is calculated in such a way that the back paws touch the ground beside the prey, in order to permit the teeth and the claws to attack very exactly and instantly when the cat lands. At the point of descent the four paws are always at the height of the victim's neck.

THE COUPLING OF CATS

We have already touched briefly on the physical side of a cat's love life. But, as with humans, there seems to be more than sex involved in the coupling of cats. However, if it is really true that 'cats live for love' it is probably because their 'affections' are so closely linked with the basic urges. Sexual excitement can lead a tom cat to straddle both male and female animals of completely different species. The female, in heat, goes in search of caresses, and, in the absence of any of the feline kind, will even go so far as to provoke them on the part of her masters. She rubs herself against human legs, purrs noisily and gives little affectionate knocks with her head. Certain breeds, Siamese particularly, give themselves over to complete vocal sessions. As the cat gets more excited, these vocal manifestations increase in intensity. The cat then literally grovels on her stomach, or else rolls on her back to return swiftly on to her paws with a twist of her backside, or again she might lower her head and paw the ground. If one caresses the cat she hollows her back and immediately presents a picture of classic copulation.

Drawn by the cries that accompany this behaviour, and by olfactory stimulation, the tom importunes the female. He sometimes

*Kittens, up to the second or third
month, retain a kind of friendship
with each other*

pursues her for entire days without taking any food, insisting until he is accepted. The act then unfolds very quickly, always accompanied by cries of painful pleasure on the part of the female. Her submission is marked by the male's very precise bite on her neck, which signals victory and possession.

In the days which follow, the mating is repeated until the male, exhausted, and in spite of all advances by the female, finally leaves her for an indefinite length of time.

This, at least, is the way it is with female and male wild cats, or domestic ones that do not live under the same roof. Things are a little different in this interval between bouts of sexual activity when a pair of cats are living together.

It is possible here to draw some kind of parallel with the behaviour of a human couple united in love. This has been perfectly described by Aldous Huxley in *Music at Night* where he emphasizes how much a pair of cats can experience of the things which are so much a part of love – pride, weakness, joy, despair, forbearance and bitterness. Surely this is anthropomorphism. Some felines, however, do behave in this almost human way. It is the 'lion couple' that has indeed become the classic of exemplary marital unity.

But domestic cats, too, exhibit some traits which are comparable to those of human lovers. To doubt similarities, it would be necessary never to have seen a female cat welcome her vagabond male after three days absence, sniff in his fur the smell of other females, and end up by throwing herself, claws foremost, on her guilty mate. It would be necessary never to have seen the intractable male, his eyes half-closed in resignation, submit without flinching to these reprisals, and then, a few hours later, apply himself to washing the face of the female he has been unfaithful to....

MATERNAL BEHAVIOUR

Jamais chatte qui a des petits n'a de bons morceaux (A cat with little ones has never a good mouthful). So goes a French proverb to illustrate the devotion and abnegation of mother cats.

Much has been said on the manifestations of this instinct. We know with what patience, with what deliberate slowness and in what silence also, mothers bring their kittens into the world. Before the delivery, there is the anxious search for a nest, for a discreet corner free from danger. Then there are the loving cares of cleaning and licking, the attention, sustained over every second, with which she assures herself that not one of her little ones is missing. There is the constancy with which she nourishes them, weans them, surrounds them with a profound and faultless affection. All this she exercises with greater tranquillity when the father is beside her to protect and aid her.

In the absence of her mate, it is the family group, the tenderness her master brings her, from which the cat draws this tranquillity, this maternal euphoria of the lioness (who is always assisted by her male). But one never encounters this peacefulness with the tigress, who is immediately abandoned by her mate. The male tiger, in addition, sometimes constitutes a real danger to the cubs.

A cherished and confident cat will often go so far as to solicit assistance, or at least the presence of her master, during the course of her delivery. Nor is it rare for cats to rely on these same humans to watch over their kittens when they are obliged for a few moments to abandon them.

KITTEN PSYCHOLOGY

The notable differences that can be observed in the behaviour of different kittens is, in fact, bound up with the varying conditions of their mother's lives. Wild cats and abandoned cats have kittens that are anxious, fearful and precociously aggressive. Cats accustomed to solicitude and comfort have, on the contrary, kittens of a happy temperament. These kittens interest themselves very soon in playing, either amongst themselves or with the humans who surround them.

The behaviour of the kitten is interesting to compare with that of the puppy or the children of man. The human baby makes contact with the outside world by carrying to its mouth everything that its fingers encounter. The puppy sniffs first; if the smell attracts it, tasting follows. The kitten is far less gustative than the first, and much less olfactory than the second. It wishes first of all to see, before touching. The young cat is visual before everything else. Only later, with prudent paw, but already lively reflexes, does the kitten complete its education.

In general, it is first and foremost from their mother that small cats learn everything, and receive their warnings. The mother cat does not abandon her kittens when they are weaned. From her remonstrances and her encouragements, the kittens receive a very complete education, which in some cases is even abnormally prolonged. Some cats at three to four months old still remain attached to their mother, not out of a true filial instinct, but because of a lack of confidence in themselves or even, more exceptionally, because the mother's milk has not dried up. It has been noted that these late feeders are not particularly shrewd.

LEARNING

Whether domestic or wild, cats are capable of adapting themselves to circumstances. Sometimes their faculty of adaption is better than that of the dog, and sometimes poorer, depending on the circumstances.

Given a problem, like getting in or out of a mechanical box, a cat will examine the

Maternal tenderness and advice

situation in order to arrive at an adequate solution. If it is not frightened, it will be calm, attentive and deliberate in its actions. In the same circumstances the dog hesitates and then panics. Given the problem of obtaining an object by pulling a string, the cat will rapidly discover the movement of pulling the string towards itself if the object is a fair distance away; but if the object falls beside the cat or draws nearer, it will not think of making the association between pulling the string and getting the object. On the other hand, if it is a problem of obtaining an object that has been placed behind a grille or a coarse screen, then dogs and rats see the problem immediately and quickly find a solution. Whereas a cat will only succeed with difficulty.

Yet, if it wants to, the cat sees more than the dog. An Austrian professor named Mendel amused himself in this manner by gathering a varied group of animals in front of a cinema screen and showing them subjects and scenes that were likely to arouse their interest. First, one or two cats appeared in the foreground. The dogs in the audience seemed quite unconcerned. The image that followed was of a big menacing dog—and although the sound was cut off at this point, three out of five of the cats who were watching immediately arched their backs and growled while the fourth, flattened at the back of its armchair, its nose puckered, began to spit out menaces.

CATS WITH HUMANS

Are cats capable, to any extent, of making contact with humans through the inter-mediary of human language?

Who would be rash enough to say? Certainly the cat is easily integrated into human society, but this integration has always affirmed even more strongly the cat's particular nature. It willingly deciphers all those gestures and symbols which allow it to live in our company, but it remains in a cat's society, allied to but distinct from ours. It seems to understand us perfectly, but care not a whit whether we understand it. We may try to decipher its language if we wish, but we may not infringe on those laws which safeguard its dignity as a cat!

P. H. Scott James claims that one of his Persians differentiates quite clearly between three very similar words: 'hungry', 'hurry' and 'Harry'. The insistent miaowing with which it responds every time that it is asked

'Are you hungry?' finds no echo, it appears, when it is asked 'Are you Harry?' or 'Are you in a hurry?'!

Cats, as much as dogs, are subject to 'conditioned reflexes'. The story of the famous cats of Mlle Adélaïde, who lived more than a century ago in Avignon, gives clear evidence of this. Mlle Adélaïde adored cats. She cherished a dozen. to the total despair of her governess, who had a horror of them. While her mistress was away travelling, the governess had the idea of whipping the cats several times a day with her left hand while she crossed herself with her right. Rapidly the cats came to associate this pious gesture with the pain of the whip. When Mlle Adélaïde returned and asked for news of her beloved animals the governess lowered her head.

'What has happened! Are they sick?
'Oh no, Mademoiselle, but they are possessed by the Devil!'
'Possessed . . . you are mad!'
'You will see, Mademoiselle: when I want to say my prayers, they howl and run like mad things.'

Mlle Adélaïde, shrugged her shoulders and turned to her cats, who welcomed her by purring. In order to disprove these mad ideas she decided to say a 'Pater'. Scarcely had she completed the sign of the cross when the twelve cats fled, bristling, miaowing, growling, spitting and trying to escape by all possible exits, as if the devils of hell were in their bodies. Bewildered, Mlle Adélaïde was obliged to agree. The bedevilled cats were drowned in the Rhône.

The governess never knew that she had discovered the principle of the conditioned reflex before Pavlov.

It is certain that cats have memory. Ernest Menault has said: 'The cat has too much spirit to have no heart.' But has it got what we might call 'memory of the heart'? It will be enough to tell this true and recent story of a mongrel cat called 'Fripon', who stayed for nearly a month by the bed in which his mistress died, and who spat and used his claws when finally the laying-out was attempted. Tearing the shroud, furiously scattering all the flowers, the cat seemed suddenly to go mad. Eventually he was successfully chased from the room. For two days he waited in the street, and then followed the funeral cortege as far as the cemetry. Many months passed. For a long

time, every Sunday, the cat accompanied his master to the grave. And then he continued to come alone, every afternoon, to coil himself up, faithful and patient, beside the mistress that he loved.

If encouraged, adult cats of all ages will play with people who love them. After the first playfulness of youth, some cats soon become meditative and grave; they seem to have a horror of useless movement. Yet when solicited by their masters, these same cats can rediscover all the liveliness of their salad days. They run after a ball, leap after a cork, roll about in mock fights, as if they had never outgrown their infancy—as if indeed, in relation to those humans in whom they had confidence, they always remained kittens.

And what is man to make of the intelligence he has noticed in his cats? For a long time people tried to see a proof of intelligence in the weight or volume of the brain. Today we know that the size of the brain means nothing as far as intelligence is concerned. What does however appear to have

some importance is the relation between the weight of the brain and the weight of the body. This proportion averages 1:35 in man, 1:75 in the anthropoid ape, and about 1:110 in the cat. But of how much use are these figures? They cannot explain why a cat is so curious that it must discover the contents of every basket, box or package that it sees, nor why it will attempt the impossible in order to curl up inside the empty basket, or bury itself in the empty box, as if to substitute itself for the original contents.

Our knowledge is equally inadequate as to why a dog is on the watch for the slightest of our gestures, keeps his eye on us all the time and is alert to our behaviour, while the cat remains impassive to all agitation. In spite of all that we have learned about its behaviour as an experienced hunter, we do not yet know what produces in the ratting cat its own peculiar way of killing its victims, a technique that is neither that of the lion, nor the tiger, nor the wolf. And we still have no idea as to why domestic cats have that

curious habit of placing at our feet the animal or bird that they have succeeded in capturing.

There was, on board a ship called the 'Margueritte Molinos', a cat with a strange habit. Every morning he brought before the commandant's cabin the rats he had killed during the night. Then, as soon as the door opened, he picked up each victim again one by one and carried them to the edge of the couch. Was this a sign of gratitude for a previous act of kindness on the part of the commandant? Once, long before, this cat had rather too quickly taken hold of a fish that had just been caught on a line. For two days the cat suffered with a lip that was deeply pierced by the hook, and it was the commandant himself who freed it.

The female cat of a friend behaved in much the same way. One fine morning she brought her mistress a large rat that was still alive. One can easily imagine the revulsion felt by the lady. In order to make the cat let go its victim, she offered it a saucer of milk. And from that day, each morning

Cats love to play—with humans, by themselves or with other cats

he cat appeared holding a rat between its
eeth, which it 'bargained' against a little
milk for its saucer. It was only at the end of
the week that it was noticed that it was always
the same rat!

What specialist would be prepared to say
why it was that the psychology of cats differs so greatly among the different breeds?
The Abyssinian is very sociable. It never
plays at despotism. It is timid, affectionate
and very tender, without being a stay-at-
home. It does not enjoy staying in an apartment. The Persian, on the other hand, is
a 'grand seigneur', delicate, distant, in-
dulging noble attitudes. Maniac in the
extreme, it takes pleasure in this cushion
or that elected place, and if any other cat
is so unwise as to approach, the Persian
lets loose his august rage. The Chartreux
accommodates itself to everything. It is a
simple and good-natured peasant but a sure
friend. Where does its placid equilibrium,
its accommodating nature come from? The
Siamese is suspicious, cunning, observant
in the extreme. It has the voice of a child,

A kitnapping, perhaps?

the lightning-swift reflexes of the tiger. Attractive, demanding, and itself devoted, with the heart of a dog and the mind of a lion, the Siamese is the most jealous of cats.

It would be possible in this way, with a few adjectives, to give a general picture of every breed and sub-breed. Every feline character trait is so precise that it is possible to recognize under the black coat of a lively cross-breed the clandestine contribution of a Siamese or the ancestral blood of an unsuspected angora.

'Gratuitous opinions', might be the comment of those observers who believe only in the results of statistics. But how many of them have really seen cats live: not just one single cat beside their fire but generations of cats with ancestral instincts and habits acquired through both heredity and experience?

Is it not an oversimplification to think of animals as admirable machines; to take them as simple beings who are born, live and die, who merely function and that is all? Cats, like all of us, lead a complicated existence. They have their complexes, their adventures, their sleep and their dreams, in which they live out the secrets which animate their lives.

Who knows what direction progress in our knowledge of animals will take in the future? In the face of the discovery that

some animals are sensitive to ultrasonic sound, it would be rash to make hard and fast claims as to whether particular animals do or do not have access to varieties of sensation which we do not ourselves share or understand.

There are many curious observations to be made about cats. To some extent, they seem to be indifferent to unpleasant surroundings. And yet, instinctively, they are sensitive to luxury, to what is beautiful. It is not a question here of aesthetic preferences, because we cannot think that they appreciate such and such a colour or shape in preference to another, but of a sensitivity to things of beautiful material, valuable because of their richness and warmth. All cats love contact with silk, velvet and wool, and the softness of real fur. All these natural materials are warmer than the cheaper artificial fibres.

Memories? Of what nature are these in the cat? We know the role that is played in sensory selection by that 'law of interest' common to all beings which makes them remember that which they consciously or unconsciously find useful to remember.

This brief chapter cannot be closed without some mention of the cat's taste for independence. It is a certain truth that the cat never gives up its liberty. Whether the cat you adopt is young or old, male or female,

ardent or calm, it makes its own condition in living with you. If your cat should decid[e] that it will go out, you will always have t[o] give in just to put an end to the matter, t[o] stop the endless miaowing, beseeching, demanding in front of the closed door; o[r] even more often simply because, sooner o[r] later (and the cat knows it), there will com[e] that one moment when your watch slips.

Alfonso was just such a cat—a cat of Paris a cat of the Palais-Royal, a cat who please[d] himself. Alfonso, who knew Colette an[d] indeed was at home to all Paris, was a cat o[f] casual parenthood that a lucky destin[y] brought one day to Raymond Oliver'[s] *Olympe* Restaurant. Soon reassured as t[o] the quality of the food and shelter, Alfons[o] after a week of politeness, opted for a night prowler's life. His master had no choice bu[t] to agree. 'Alas, we can do nothing about it! he said. 'When he wants to come in aroun[d] eight in the morning, he comes in. H[e] breakfasts copiously in the kitchens, an[d] then comes up to the first floor. Aroun[d] mid-day he comes down again, and onl[y] goes out at five o'clock. That is his tea-tim[e] (a special reserve of milk and variou[s] pastries). He licks himself and relicks him self, and at last makes for the landing or fo[r] table 12, under which he immediately fall[s] asleep. He tears himself out of it betwee[n] eight and nine o'clock, installs himself com[-]

ortably on the doormat at the entrance, but will not move from it, obliging the client, whoever he may be, to step over him in order to penetrate his domain. Towards midnight, as soon as the lights are put out, he lets the last client leave; then he rapidly decamps, to hide himself under a car and wait for the closing up. It is a question of principle: whether there is rain, wind or snow, he is determined to spend the night outside. Certainly I have more than once tried to force him to come back in; I have closed him into the cloakroom so that he will spend the night in the warmth. Nothing doing. I was obliged to agree. Alfonso is a gourmet, and an affectionate one at that, but first and foremost he is a wanderer in the night.'

There exist for the cat truths which have nothing in common with human truths. The cat does not question us in order to form its own opinion about us. It does not, like the dog, seek to read in our eyes what is good and what is bad. It is not ignorant of the fact that some things are forbidden, but its knowledge is that of someone outside the law, for whom justice is not the judge but the gamekeeper.

PSYCHOLOGICAL DISTURBANCES
What was in the mind of that cat who continued to visit his mistress' grave for years?

To find the answer we would have to be able to draw out of this cat precise details of his memories, to draw together a maximum of information relating to the circumstances which preceeded his strange behaviour. Obviously that would not be easy. We might as well talk about animal psychoanalysis, and this would clearly be to extrapolate and gratuitously to attribute a cognitive consciousness to creatures for whom, until there is proof to the contrary, modern psychologists are agreed in thinking this does not exist.

This is why it is more prudent to speak of 'zoopsychoses' and 'zooneuroses'. Undoubtedly psychoses and neuroses exist in cats. If these have not yet been the subject of well-known researches, it is because feline medicine, along with the medicine of birds, has been one of the most recent subjects for specialization in veterinary science.

In the case of that romantic cat spoken of above, it was, without doubt, a question of confusion. Being incapable of the abstract idea of death, this cat, which in our terms was 'desolate and faithful', went daily to the cemetery, to the exact spot where his mistress had disappeared for the last time, and instinctively he waited there ... for her to come back! It would have behaved quite differently if the disappearance of the loved person had brought about a true neurosis.

Not that the cat is a stranger to psychological disorders. It is naturally neurotic. It even seems, more than any other animal, to be prone to them. To see this it is only necessary to attend a daily veterinary clinic.

The signs are many and various. Nausea, tachycardia, colic, etc., appear after an emotional shock and persist after the cessation of the cause. There may also be a localized falling of hair, cramps, uncontrollable tremblings and urination. Chertok and Fontaine, professors at the *Muséum d'Histoire Naturelle* in Paris, have reported cases in which psychological disturbance brought on asthma, spasmodic coughing, loss of appetite, persistent constipation, sudden and violent itching. Sometimes even the 'third eyelid' slips to cover the iris—a symptom which veterinarians have learned to associate with intestinal disorders. Symptoms such as these often indicate neuroses.

Frequently neuroses are aggravated in very commonplace cases—such as when a cat who has first been attended to at home is later hospitalized. Equally, neuroses can result from the immobilization of a cat who has been castrated, or whose jaw has been held open by an instrument. It is not rare that such simple interventions, as swift as they are painless, result in more or less fleeting paralyses, swooning and sometimes even death.

We find true psychoses as much in the social behaviour of cats as in their sexual behaviour. In their social behaviour, cases of jealousy are often observed. A cat stops eating or even neglects its grooming—although till then its cleanliness has been exemplary—because a dog or a newly-arrived baby now share in an affection that the cat once had all to itself. There are even more inexplicable cases. A castrated cat, who has for six months lived as a sybarite, never leaving its apartment or its old master for a single minute, will one day venture into its own garden and make the acquaintance of a neighbouring female. From that day on he never appears except at meal-times. The winter comes and this same cosseted cat spends hours and nights outside its home in the cold and the rain, for the sole pleasure of finding again the indifferent beauty whose slave he has become—subjugated, emaciated and, for all that, impotent.

It is within the framework of sexual behaviour that we note the greatest number of psycosomatic anomalies and disturbances. And these are more frequent in the case of pure-bred cats than in wild cats or strays.

Homosexuality in small felines of brilliant pedigree is a common observation these days. If one of her fellow pure-breds is 'in heat', it often happens that a female will exhibit the aggressive behaviour of a tom. This, however, does not prevent her a few minutes later, and without the advantage of being in a state of receptivity, of taking up the eloquent posture of an excited female. Similar aberrations, along with the odd heterosexual impulse are widespread among castrated Persians and Siamese. Certain of these cats, indisputably castrated, even retain the possibility of erection for several months after the operation.

To return to females, it has been noted that hypernervous subjects sometimes experience a prolongation, an exaggeration, a disordered expression of the heat cycle. The affectionate interest which the humans may shower on these cats, the soothing attentions, the caresses which paradoxically are intended as substitutes, in fact undoubtedly contribute to fostering this convulsive excitement.

Siamese females are more liable to 'psychoses' than those of any other breed. The frequency of organic lesions in the ovaries in Siamese is possibly not unrelated to these troubles, in which case it would no longer be a question of a purely psychological disturbance. A perfect example is the adult female cat, very gentle, very affectionate, who deliberately urinates in unusual places. In one case this happened whenever she wanted to go out but found the door closed, and certainly when she was left alone in the house. In this type of disturbance, which shows all the determining importance of relations with humans, it is useful to quote the case of a male cat, four years old, which behaved in the following way. During the summer, whenever his master came into the garden, the cat would climb along the trees and jump on to the roof of the house. Once he was there he would miaow gently, complain, seem distracted, and call until someone came to fetch him; although he could perfectly well have extricated himself from that position on his own, and indeed had many times done so. As soon as his master decided to look for him and take him in his arms, the cat would begin to purr, swooning with joy. But if a stranger or a servant came to help him out of his psychosomatic predicament the cat would only increase his complaints.

MATERNAL DISORDERS

The maternal behaviour of cats has attained such heights that humans have conferred a virtuous halo on the cat's maternal instincts. But these maternal instincts are sometimes out of place. False pregnancy is a frequent trouble. Such a 'nervous pregnancy' begins with a cat that is already disturbed and nervous. First she develops an appetite so gross as to approach chronic hunger. She becomes fat. She looks pregnant, and when picked up, she feels pregnant. Towards the end of the fifth week the stomach is clearly distended, while the teats, swollen and painful, are the site of a secretory activity which, though slight, is nearly always present. The false mother then looks about to prepare her bed. Next she gets hold of a soft toy, a slipper or some other object, and she warms it between her paws, licks it and defends it, if required, with spirit. This type of psychoneurosis with 'transference' is the result of an increased amount of progesterone in the blood, a condition about whose origins it is difficult to be precise. Numerous virgin cats, attacked by a psychosomatic disorder of this sort, can successfully give milk to a kitten or any other newly-born carnivore. Some of them even try, for this purpose, to make off with chickens or ducklings—with which they then have no idea what to do.

At the opposite pole to this type of behaviour, we must place the destructive aggressive, indifferent, and sometimes actually murderous behaviour of mother cats with insufficient milk. Cases of cannibalism, so frequent in rabbits and dogs, are rare in cats. In numerous cases a mother cat in the harshest circumstances badly nourished and feeble, will give proof of such obedience to her maternal instincts that we are stupefied. In other cases, however, cannibalism has been observed to be bound up with depression, melancholia or parental psychosis—very frequently, once more, of the jealousy type.

Blin and Faveau, professors at the *École d'Alfort* in Paris, have told the story of a female cat who was the spoilt child of the house and who for a long time was an excellent mother. When she grew old, however she lost her fur and grew so ugly tha

Its taste for independence sometimes leads a cat to the rooftops

Often on the defensive and ready to attack

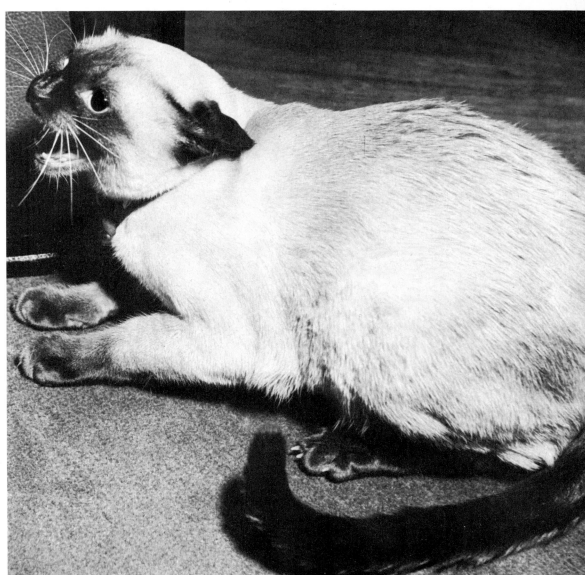

Sometimes, also, simply nervous

gradually she was no longer surrounded by the same tenderness and affection, and the solicitude that had once been given to her was now given to her children. Imperceptibly her character changed. She started by being sulky towards her masters, then she disdained her food, and finally came menacing growls that were frankly aggressive. She could not be prevented from killing three different litters of kittens. At last someone thought of taking pity on her, of starting to take notice of her again, of flattering her. The cat accepted these caresses and within a few days became the excellent mother of earlier times.

These major functional troubles which modify the behaviour and the normal conduct of an animal are certainly related to some extent to what we can observe in the human species. But how far can we stretch the analogy? Some cases have no parallels in human psychology.

Two female cats living under the same roof had a litter on the same day. One had three kittens, the other five. What 'sentiment' or what driving force animated the first when, for weeks on end and several times a day, she took advantage of her neighbour's brief absences to make off with one of her kittens, as if to make an equal redivision of their respective families? Was it jealousy? How do we know? There were so many factors that could have been at work. It would be possible to claim that the cat who had three kittens had far more milk than was needed for feeding her own family and that pure physical necessity set her to looking for numerical reinforcements from among her neighbour's feeding family. Another possible interpretation would be to envisage a sensory attraction of a different kind—an olfactory 'response', or again the effect of a simple auditory reflex when one of her neighbour's kittens began to cry because it was hungry or cold....

But why did she always kidnap only one kitten, and that not always the same one? Did, at some point in time, a physical attraction mix with some psychological activity? The hormonal changes which bring about profound modifications in maternal behaviour do not always constitute an adequate explanation of reactions like these.

Maurice Thomas, a French physiologist, noted the following behaviour of one of his cats. It concerns an excellent mother who during the birth of her first kittens, and during the first five or six days of feeding, behaved like all normal cats. But after this short period, without there being anything in her attitude or condition that could have given warning, she purely and simply got rid of her kittens, which were on average three to four per litter, by a rather extraordinary method that does not appear to have been instinctive. In the course of a series of births, several times dead or dying kittens were discovered lying in the hall, without there being any evident explanation for it. One day, however, Maurice Thomas witnessed the following scene: the mother cat, who lived on the ground floor with her family, seized one of the kittens by the neck and climbed up to the landing on the second floor. Once there she slipped her head through the bannisters, relaxed her jaws, opened her mouth and let the kitten fall, to be crushed against the tiled floor of the hall about ten yards below! In his surprise Maurice Thomas let her do it. She returned downstairs quite calmly, took hold of a second kitten, remounted, and then went for the third kitten. And so all three kittens, at scarcely a week old, were put to death by this astonishing procedure. What comment can we make on such strange behaviour?

THE DREAM

The higher animals dream. Electroencephalography has proved this. But we can only postulate that there exists between the

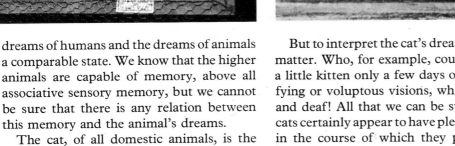

dreams of humans and the dreams of animals a comparable state. We know that the higher animals are capable of memory, above all associative sensory memory, but we cannot be sure that there is any relation between this memory and the animal's dreams.

The cat, of all domestic animals, is the one which most willingly abandons itself to sleep. It is, therefore, the ideal subject for researchers studying the modifications of cardiac rhythm, the respiratory movements, tension, muscular tone, etc., and along with these, the control of the various phases of sleep by means of electroencephalography. Even if we do not yet know what cats dream about, at least we can be certain that they dream. It has even been proved that kittens dream. In fact, from the first hours of their life, neurophysiological activity, with which dreaming is bound up, is already functioning in these little cats, along with the functions of digestion, respiration, circulation, etc. It is always only towards the tenth day of their existence that evidence of dreaming begins to show itself, becoming established after the second week.

But to interpret the cat's dreams is another matter. Who, for example, could claim that a little kitten only a few days old has horrifying or voluptous visions, while it is blind and deaf! All that we can be sure of is that cats certainly appear to have pleasing dreams in the course of which they purr and are completely relaxed, and also more agitated dreams during the course of which they spasmodically flex their claws while the skin is overrun by shivers.

If a cat is brusquely woken from its dreaming sleep, it immediately starts up and remains bewildered and mute, with its eyes wide open and a stunned expression. But spontaneous awakenings, unexpected and unpredictable, also follow a calm sleep. These are awakenings that cannot be explained by the sudden perception of any sound or light or other contact; these are the awakenings in which a cat leaps with a bound from its sleep, the hair bristling, spitting terror and with its tail swollen in the extreme. 'As if it had seen the Devil' it is sometimes said: and so we come to the hallucination.

HALLUCINATIONS

However much one may wish to stick to the scientifically 'known' it is sometimes necessary to have recourse to the embarassment of human analogies in order to explain feline behaviour. How else are we to explain the following sudden attitudes? A cat of a placid and affectionate character suddenly turns into a furious dragon. Another one, quite as trustful, becomes unreasonably terrified. He tries to fly, takes refuge under some piece of furniture and crouches there fearfully, or else throws himself at random on the first leg that passes within his reach, lacerating it as if demented. What name are we to give to the manifestation?

Let us call it a hallucination or delirium of the sensations or even 'sensation without object'.

Personally, I have known a cat that exhibited these bizarre signs of psychological disorder. Completely normal in appearance and of a very gentle character, it seemed to become mad every time a certain young butcher's boy came with deliveries to our

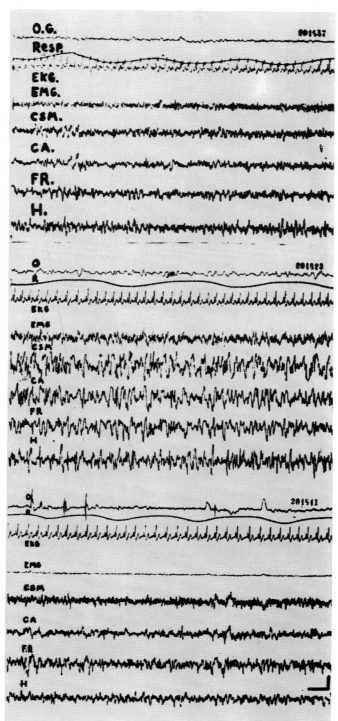

country house. Merely at the sound of his voice or of the doorbell, the cat would leap up and disappear. If he was in the garden he would make off with insane speed, not to be seen again until nightfall. If he was in the house he would fly up the stairs as if catapulted by an irresistible force to take refuge under a bed in the nearest room. Should the door of this room be closed? Then in his blind race he would throw himself against it, or try to cling to it and climb up the wall—all this in a succession of disorganized leaps, which would suddenly give way to an extreme depressive state. The crisis would last for a few minutes only, but while it did, it was spectacular. It was particularly strange, firstly because this inexplicable phenomenon never occurred with other delivery boys, and secondly because the cat, who never left our grounds had no valid reason for associating the sight, voice, smell or presence of this young delivery boy with any horrifying memory.

HYPNOSIS

That the cat is sensible to hypnosis cannot

This encephelogram shows a cat's three stages of brain activity. Note that the waking and dreaming stages are similar, showing rapid cortical and sub-cortical activity

Top: Awake
Middle: Sleep
Bottom: Dreaming

O.G. = oculogram
Resp. = respiration
E.K.G. = electrocardiogram
C.S.M.-C.A. = cortex sensory-motor,
               cortex acoustic
F.R. = reticular formation
H. = hippocampus

Dazzled by the headlamps of a car

As if it had seen the Devil ...

be disputed. In 1914 Professor Mangold of the University of Fribourg hypnotized a great number of intractible tomcats. In 1956 Svorad, studying the question, admitted the fact of animal hypnosis, which was obtained primarily by the classic methods of rocking or rotation.

This method consists of taking hold of the cat with a rapid movement and laying it quickly down on its side or its back. As soon as its first defensive reflexes are calmed, a kind of rocking movement or alternating rotation is imposed on the complete body until, after a shorter or longer time, the subject, far from reacting, abandons itself completely and little by little becomes completely immobile.

To what mechanism can we attribute this paralysis of movements and the will? We do not really know the part played in this cataleptic state by psychological factors on the one hand and physical factors on the other.

We must distinguish between two different kinds of hypnosis. There is that which ends in a kind of inhibition of movements; here the method consists in firmly, but above all without violence, making it impossible for the animal to jump back up on to its paws again and escape away. Then there is the other type of hypnosis, which takes possession of a cat when, for some reason still unknown to us, it quite spontaneously falls into a state of stupour. Both types of hypnosis undoubtedly involve a common, or at least a comparable principle.

There is also a more subtle but very well-known phenomenon which borders on auto-hypnosis. Many are the cats who, after a period of quite normal relationships, after having shown every interest, in so far as they are capable of it, in our daily life, seem suddenly to withdraw from the world. With its paws retracted, its whole body drawn up compactly, its neck almost effaced, and its

eyes either half-closed or wide open and staring straight ahead, the cat does not sleep, it does not doze, it does not even appear to dream. It is deaf to the most unfamiliar noises and to the most caressing appeals. It is transformed into a statue in which there is not even the slightest shiver of a single hair. It appears to be in a trance: it appears to be 'elsewhere'. What astute psychologist will one day decipher the enigma of this natural tendency which domestic cats have of 'cutting themselves off' whenever they please and as they please?

THE SIXTH SENSE

What are we to make of those strange forms of feline behaviour which men of all eras have observed and interpreted, according to the formulae of their time, as diabolical or heavenly signs of second sight?

Scientific documentation has gone as far in hermetically closing its doors to these phenomena as literature, always a little suspect, has seemed to overdo its belief in them.

Claude Farrère, author of 'Bêtes et gens qui s'aimèrent' (Animals and People who have Loved Each Other), has minutely described in his *Journal* the mysterious attitude of 'Kare Kedi'. One night this cat, with startling suddenness, tore himself out of his sleep. He seemed in a moment to become the focus of a thousand confused sensations. He fixed the left-hand wall with a burning eye. Then, with his hair bristling, he leapt to the ground and, as if he followed step by step an invisible presence, he slowly made his way along that particular wall. He did not sniff, he hardly listened, he simply stopped to gaze intently at this wall on which there was nothing at all. Then suddenly Kare Kedi, with a terrifying jerk of all his muscles, leapt backwards and spun round wildly, his tail absolutely stiff. He tried to fly. 'He forgot that I was there,' writes Farrère, 'that I was his refuge. Only after a very long time

Auto-hypnosis? Paws retracted, the whole body drawn up compactly, the eyes half-closed

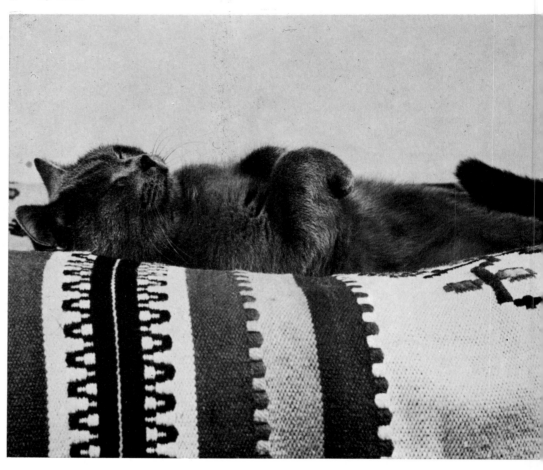

did his wild gaze quite by accident encounter my eyes, and he remembered my presence. Then, with the impetus of a hunted animal, he threw himself on me and huddled against my chest. I myself was afraid! The fear of this terrified cat penetrated my marrow....' The next day Claude Farrère noted in his *Journal*: 'This night the pretty prostitute, my neighbour, has been assassinated.' Several moments later the master and his cat went into the room of the crime. But Kare Kedi had not a single look for the corpse: for him there was nothing interesting in a dead body.

Was this a case of second sight, sixth sense or simply 'supersense'? The sceptical will claim that the cat, with its very fine ears, heard what Mr Farrère did not – whatever it was that was going on in the next room, behind that fascinating, terrifying wall.

'PSI-TRAILING'

The ability that the majority of cats have for finding their way home under the most unlikely conditions remains another mystery. This instinct for returning to the lair, the 'homing' instinct, reaches extraordinary proportions in the cat. Here are some examples that can be verified. 'Pompom', a Siamese belonging first to M. Joseph Villet, was given to M. Villet's brother who lived in Tours. A month later the cat came back to Limoges and took up his place again at the hearth he had known first. 'Moumousse' was accidentally lost in the Maine-et-Loire district while on holiday with his owners. Ten months later he rediscovered his owners, M. et Mme Chirade, in Doubs about 465 miles away. 'Mylord', lost while he was playing around on the Côte d'Azur at Cap-Martin, was too late in making his way back to the villa his owner had rented for the Christmas holiday; so he took up his journey again and arrived back at the home of Mme Voindrot at Saint-Jean-de-Vaux in the Saône-et-Loire during Easter.

Some stupefying cases have been studied by serious American researchers such as Duke University's Professor Rhine and the Doctors Forster and Osis, to cite only the best-known team.

For more than ten years this phenomenon of 'psi-trailing' has been the essential object of their research. Among a hundred and one stories that are difficult to verify, one true story has become famous: that of a New York cat.

This little cat belonged to a New York veterinary surgeon who, being called to take up a post in California, was obliged to abandon it. Time passed, and then one morning

The feline sense of balance is astonishing

five months later the cat appeared at his master's new address. It calmly entered the house, jumped on to the familiar armchair that had for so long been its 'territory', installed itself there and fell asleep.

At first the veterinarian did not wish to believe his eyes. The distance between the State of California and the State of New York is 2,300 miles as the crow flies. But the cat that had walked into his house behaved as if it were completely at home. It had the same fur, the same shape and size and the same look as the one he had been obliged to leave behind him in New York. Then the vet remembered a detail. As a result of a two-year-old wound, his cat had a very clear enlargement of a bone at the level of the fourth caudal vertebra. It was the matter of a moment to place his fingers on the spot where this malformation should be ... it was there!

These astonishing possibilities leave humans in a daze. Is another 'supersense' involved? Neuro-physiologists Presch and Lindenbaum of Germany have investigated the problem experimentally. They had several cats shut up in boxes, transported a long way from their home areas, and then set loose in places where they had never been before. The cats were released in the centre of a labrynth whose twenty-four exits emerged regularly in all directions on to natural surroundings.

In spite of these conditions specially meant to bewilder the cats, eight out of ten of them started by emerging from the labrynth by an exit that already pointed correctly in the direction of their home. This is an experiment that can be repeated. It is found that the cats who hesitate and make the most errors are very young cats, and that the number of errors increases in proportion to their distance away from their homes. The same experiment was once repeated with forty-two cats and gave the

*Cats trained to stay immobile
preparatory to being launched into space*

same results. Another time rats were used. Here again it was found, though without being able to explain why, that the greatest number of errors occurred among those of a young age. But also it was found – and this is a more curious fact – that the number of errors noticeably increased when the test was made in the winter.

Do the vibrissae really play the part of antennae? We know that they have an extraordinary sensitivity. Other animals, whose bodies rarely come into contact with the outside world, can only explore the space around them with the help of these 'feelers'. With little arthropods, for example, who are literally closed into their casing, and with crabs whose carapace is an actual armour, the horny shell is traversed by hairs of which some are olfactory and others tactile.

What a pity that we do not have fuller details about that travelling cat from New York and his bewildering tour across the United States. With such a subject, what experiments would not have been possible?

He could have been habituated to tolerating a small radio transmitter. It would have then been possible to follow his movements without risk of losing him. If it was found that he was directing himself, or trying to direct himself, towards his master, one would have asked the latter to move quickly towards another distant place; and so one could study the techniques employed by the cat in a variety of circumstances.

Then we could perhaps gain access to the real personality of the cat and to one of the biggest secrets of its behaviour. Such a perspective is not, however, entirely within the realm of hypothesis. American neurophysiologists at Yale University are achieving success in a different field. Dr José Delgado installed a complete series of electrodes in the brain of a cat. The operation took place under complete anesthesia, and when the cat woke up, he knew nothing about what had happened. Experiments did not begin until everything had healed perfectly. It is impossible not to feel

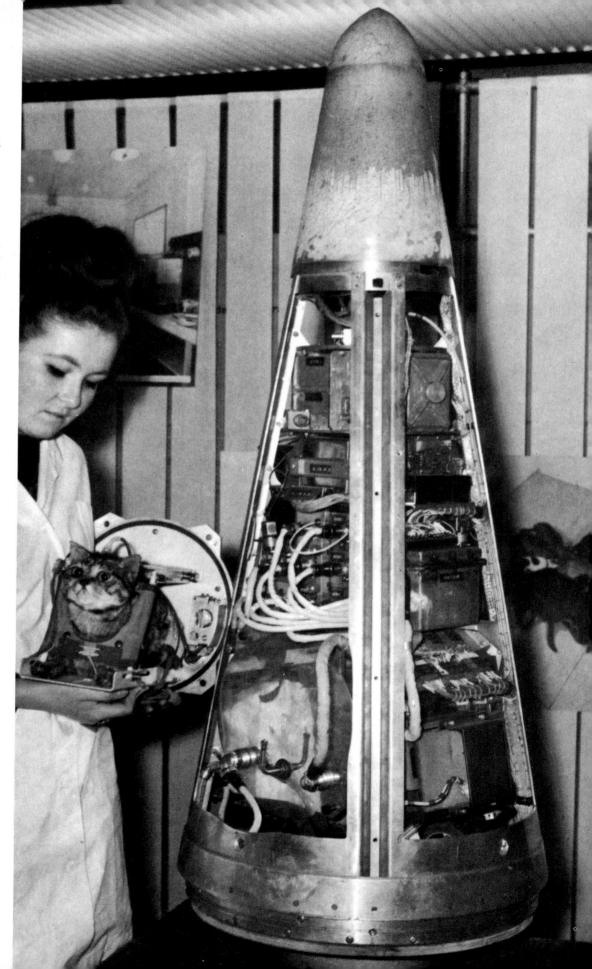

A space-cat in the Palais de la Découverte. This cat was catapulted to a height of 98 miles aboard a rocket Véronique

for this laboratory cat, but those who were present and took part in the experiment confirm that he made no attempt to escape. He even seemed to appreciate the situation, as if appreciating the interest that was being taken in him. Not knowing anything about the surgical operation to which he had been submitted, he behaved as if he were obeying a simple friendly drill: he became a robot.

Around his neck, one might distinguish a small collar on to which is fixed a receiving set with tiny transmittors, to which are attached neat silver wires, each of which corresponds to a cerebral localization and disappears into his fur. By this means, whether in the same room or hundreds of miles away, and by a radio-transmitted command, the cat can experience the need to drink (and he has water and milk placed at his disposal), to eat (he can choose whatever he wants), to itch (and can scratch himself as much as he wants). It is even possible, by stimulating such and such a part of the frontal lobes, to provoke in him an overwhelming affection or an aggressive antipathy and, in the very next moment, to reduce these states.

The importance of this experiment is not that one can oblige the cat to perform such and such a movement, but one can simply, by passing an electric current, waken in him the desire to act in a determined direction.

At present such experiments towards a better knowledge of feline psychology are not being regularly followed up; though they have been renewed with monkeys and, for some time now, with humans. These same minute electrodes are planted in specifically chosen points which relate to the psychic disorders presented by the subjects. In this way it is possible to make tests whose results are extremely illuminating for psychiatrists. These results are at present being published by the New York Academy of Science. It goes without saying that they may provide us with some frightening perspectives on the human mind.

8 THE CAT AND MEDICINE

In the eyes of the early Christians the cat was the son of Satan, the instrument of the Devil. During the Middle Ages the Church began to require that the disciplines of Hippocrates be under the control of theologians. Therefore it is not surprising that the early doctors believed the cat to be a source of many dangers to man's health.

THE HEALTH OF MAN

From the quacks of the fairgrounds and market squares to the greatest of the court physicians, all in the Middle Ages were united against the cat. The sixteenth century surgeon Ambroise Paré wrote 'Cats not only infect by their brains, but also by their hair, their breath and their gaze: as it is, all hair, thoughtlessly swallowed, can suffocate a person, by choking the channels of respiration, but the hair of the cat is dangerous above all others; their breath is infected with a tabific poison.' And Matthiole, a French doctor of our own century, claims to have known women who took such pleasure in cats that they could not sleep without having several sleeping beside them, and who, as a result of the cats' breath mingling with the air, became consumptive and died miserably. Cats also offend with their gaze, to such an extent that some people, seeing or hearing a cat, tremble and have a great fear which arises from an antipathy coming from an influence of heaven.

'The cat also infects those who eat its brain, and these people are tormented with great pains in the head, and sometimes even become mad. To cure them it is necessary to make them vomit; and the true medicament is composed of musk mixed with wine.

'I will say further that the cat is a pernicious beast to children in the cradle because it sleeps on their faces and suffocates them. This is why it is very necessary to be on one's guard.'

Are they really as frequent as is claimed, these deaths in which little children are suffocated in their beds? Above all, are cats as deadly as has been supposed, these animals that are so clean? It used to be said that, because of their contact with rats, they could carry typhus, leprosy and the plague.

Even in modern times all it takes is a slap-dash article or a badly interpreted piece of information for thousands of innocent animals to be menaced with destruction. Before the Second World War Siamese cats once ran this risk because a leper, having come to France from Indochina with one as his companion, had not wanted to be separated from it. That the Siamese cat is bred today is due, happily, to the strong hold they have on our affections and the fact that it was never possible to prove that the cat could be a carrier of leprosy.

Shortly after the Second World War there was a great scare relating to a disease called 'typhus' that occurred in cats. The veterinary surgeons did not take the trouble to explain that this was not the same 'typhus' as the disease humans were subject to. The disease had only been given this name to emphasize the extreme rapidity with which the organism was invaded and the high death rate the disease attained. This name for what was in fact a 'plague' affecting cats was as ill-chosen as it was unjust.

Can tinea (scalp disease) or scabies be caught from the cat? Both these certainly can be caught through contact with cats in a diseased condition, but they can also be caught through contact with other humans: at a hairdressers, in a hotel, or in a badly cleaned taxi. These mild skin diseases can be cured within fifteen days by special treatments.

Infections can be caused by a cat's scratch, but these are certainly not the result of a pathogenic agent particular to the cat or to its claws. Any other animal, or any other object that scratches can produce the same effect. The same type of infection could arise from a scratch from barbed wire, from brushing past a hedge or while picking a rose. But it has doubtless seemed preferable to hold 'the cursed animal' responsible, rather than the poetic rosebush.

An eighteenth-century engraving by J. E. Liottard, The Sick Cat, *after a cartoon by Watteau*

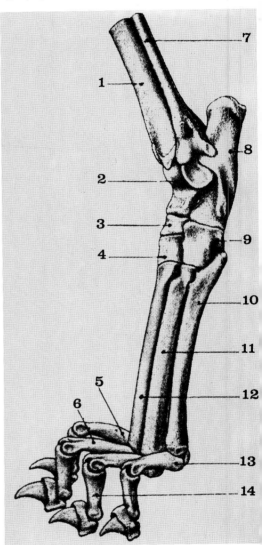

Skeleton of the foot of the cat :
1—tibia ; 2—astragalus ; 3—scaphoid ;
4—cuneiform ; 5, 6—phalanges ;
7—fibula ; 8—calcis ; 9—cuboid ;
10, 11, 12—metatarsals ;
13, 14—phalanges

The movements of its paws are of an extreme delicacy

transparent, resemble the drops of the morning dew; how my nose is like the rose's leaf and my whiskers like the stamens of the flower? These are the distinctive signs of our secret origin, which I would like to reveal to you:

"'One day the Fairy of the Roses was banished from the kingdom of the fairies for a grave offence. Instead of touching with her wand the roses that had gone to sleep for the winter, she had had the notion of sowing the land with weeds! When the queen of the fairies banished her, she warned her that she would never again see the kingdom of the fairies until she had done some great good deed for the human race, in order to atone for the damage she had done. Exiled on the earth, the unhappy fairy led a miserable existence. When she saw, in the countryside, the peasants forced to separate the good grain from the weeds, she was ashamed. One autumn day, caught by bad weather, she knocked at the door of a cottage and was offered the attic. Being a coquette, she then got out of her bag all her finest attire, souvenirs of her past splendour; she clothed herself in her best and fell asleep fully dressed. On waking she found herself in rags. The rats and mice had quite stripped her. She was still lamenting when her hosts appeared. 'We too are victims of the rats.' they said to her. 'There will be scarcely any bread for us this year. They have devoured our harvest.'

"'Then the fairy decided to do something to rid the peasants of this scourge. She took some clay and began to mould and model a little animal, elegant, strong and light, who would drive away the rats by its presence. A hundred times she started her work all over again. Finally, inspired by the tiger, she succeeded in constructing the most graceful and courageous of animals.

"'Then the breeze bent towards her the most beautiful flower. 'I am tired of being

Champfleury (1821–89) was already writing on the subject of the cat's claws: 'But how could we think of reproaching roses with this marvellous system of defence which we so dread in cats!'

Since then Jane d'Hazon, a modern writer, has given us this charming legend. "'Have you never observed", said the cat to his master, "how greatly my claws recall the thorns of the rose bush? Have you never observed how my eyes, which are so

a rose.' said the flower. 'Take my soul and give it to this creature who will move about, and see and hear, so at last, attached as I am to this bush of thorns, I may live the existence I have always dreamed of!'

"'And so it was that the first cat received life, and it was also a great good deed for men. She who had been able to create it was pardoned at last and restored to her kingdom.'"

We must not be astonished if, like the

Claws to the fore

rose whose thorns spoil neither its perfume nor its beauty, the most amiable and the most beautiful of cats sometimes remember that they have claws.

What are, in fact, the diseases that cats can effectively transmit to man?

Rabies? Since the time of Louis Pasteur rabies has almost disappeared, and in those cases where bites are suspect, vaccination against rabies is a sure prevention. It is even possible that in previous times rabies was sometimes confused with epileptic fits, the two diseases having some identical symptoms.

What are the facts relating to tuberculosis? We cannot deny that cats can suffer from tuberculosis and communicate it. Nevertheless in tuberculosis, as it occurs in cats, it is almost always the human bacillus that is the cause. The cat is infected by its surroundings and, except in the case of ocular tuberculosis, the disease takes a rapid and grave course (extreme thinness, coughing, difficulty in breathing, etc.).

Tuberculosis is one disease that cats are more likely to catch from humans than humans from cats. Nevertheless, once a cat has become infected it is very likely to pass the disease on. Therefore, doctors and vets alike will recommend the destruction of an animal with tuberculosis.

Parasites, both internal and external, can constitute a danger to human health. Fleas and lice can be transferred from cat to human, but the problem is not acute and they are easy to get rid of. Nor do mange mites present much of a problem to humans. A very uncommon but irritating insect is the *Cheyletiella parasitovorax*. An affected cat (usually one with a close, fine coat) will suffer from inflammation and flaking of the skin. People who handle these cats may possibly develop irritating blisters and skin eruptions on the arms and neck. However, this affliction is rare and easy to heal.

In Copenhagen a blood transfusion was given to a cat suffering from an inflammation of the liver. The donor was a dog

The birth of monsters among cats is extremely rare. This one has two heads and a normal body

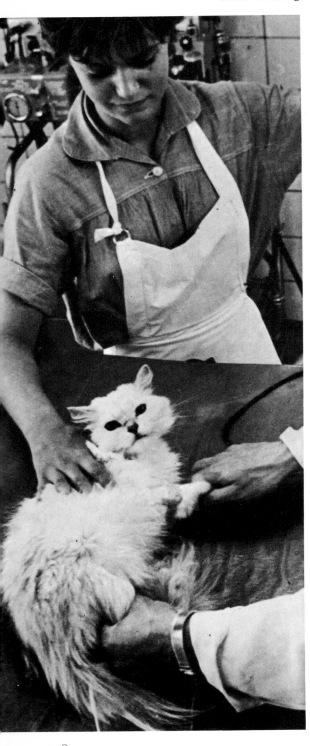

Internal parasites are more dangerous. It is possible for a tapeworm to be transferred from a cat to a human. This condition can be recognized in the cat by the presence of little bundles of eggs which the tapeworm sheds and which appear in the cat's fur. When these are noticed, a vet should be consulted. One way that tapeworm can be controlled is by eliminating fleas and lice which act as an intermediate host between cats and people.

Some people think there is a connection between roundworms and an eye disease that is contracted by children. The larvae of this particular roundworm are thought to migrate through the tissues of the body, and there is some evidence that they may get into the blood-vessels at the back of the eye, causing blindness. The chance of this happening is extremely remote; there are hundreds of dangers to children's eyes that should cause more concern than this one.

It can probably be said that cats of all the domestic animals are perhaps the least dangerous to human health. Their natural suspicion, their instinctive delicacy, make them less likely than the dog to come into contact with sources of contamination. A cat does not sleep just anywhere and on just anything at all. A cat does not drink just any water or any milk that is lying around. A cat never eats dung.

The cat is difficult to feed, difficult to handle, and will not easily tolerate dressing and equipment. It is not therefore as frequently exploited for research purposes as one might expect in view of the low price for which stray cats can be procured. For the purposes of studies in bacteriology, medical research has had recourse to the rabbit, the guinea-pig or the rat rather than the cat, whereas experimental surgery often prefers the cat to the dog or the monkey.

To what medical ends is the cat used? Primarily it is used in research on the nervous system. More often it is used in work on comparative psychophysiology, such as in the famous University of Chicago experiments on alcoholism.

Inspired by the rapidity of the process of association in cats, Professor G. H. Wassermann has several times repeated the alcohol test of Dr Schwartz. The cats, placed in cages, are trained to eat only on the appearance of a luminous signal. The method involved is as follows: by pressing a button with its paw, the cat turns on the light in question and makes its food appear.

Once this first conditioning is obtained, an experimental neurosis is caused. The cats have been habituated to pressing the call button in order to make the food appear, and now another factor is brought into play. Use of the call button still turns on the light and makes the plate of the food appear. But when the cat approaches the food it is im-

mediately hit full in the nose by a jet of water and subjected to a slight electric shock. Astonished and surprised, the cats try, in spite of everything, to feed themselves, but very rapidly give up and, as can easily be imagined, fall into a state of bad temper.

Then comes the third stage. In order to calm the cats and cure them of their anguish, they are provided with solid food or liquids that contain alcohol and others that do not. These foodstuffs are, naturally, freely accessible. At the start the cats choose their food more or less at random. But then, very quickly, they realize that while the alcohol is affecting them they have neither fear nor anxiety. After this, they go by choice to the meals treated with alcohol, even if this means confronting the jet of water or the electric shock.

What is the purpose of experiments like these? To show that a human alcoholic cannot be cured of his disease by means of any medicaments or drugs if he cannot first improve his mental equilibrium. But is it necessary, in order to reach such an obvious conclusion, to upset the nervous equilibrium of so many cats?

Definitely more murderous in effect is the market in cat skins for the treatment of rheumatism: a therapy of doubtful value. The furs of European cats are prepared by the millions and sold throughout the world, often under the pretence that they are the skins of wild cats. It is hard to believe that its wild origin could be claimed to give the skin greater therapeutic powers than if it had come from a domestic cat.

THE HEALTH OF CATS

Until very recently no animal doctor would have dared to ask for fees in return for services rendered a cat. It was not that no one ever thought of alleviating the ills of this proud and discreet animal who knew how to suffer and die in silence. But it was because almost every veterinary surgeon at the beginning of this century thought that this might have meant paying dearly for ignorance.

There have always been people known as animal doctors. In ancient India veterinary science flourished. Treatises on animal diseases were written, and there were hospitals for the various species of animals. In Babylonia, the legal code of King Hammurabi (c 1800 BC) dictated the fees that were to be paid to 'doctors of asses and oxen', and the ancient Greeks had a whole class of people who were horse-doctors. Hippocrates, Xenophon and Aristotle all gave considerable thought in their writings to the subject of animal diseases, and this interest continued to flourish in Rome. The last of the great ancient veterinarians were the Greek vets attached to the Roman armies during the Byzantine period. Among these, whose science was in some ways more advanced than human medicine, was Apsyrtus (AD 330), the 'father' of veterinary medicine.

During the Dark Ages, veterinary science –along with many other sciences–died. It was not until the eighteenth century that interest again revived among the educated classes, and this interest was only inspired by a terrible animal plague that had swept Europe. During the late eighteenth and early nineteenth centuries, veterinary colleges began to be established, but the profession did not regain its lost status until the twentieth century.

Veterinary surgeons have only begun seriously to study the cat very recently. For a long time treatment of cats was simply an extension of the treatment given to dogs; surgery was limited to general intervention for abcesses, sores and wounds, fractures and castrations. The latter were sometimes carried out in conditions even more precarious than those applying to cocks and hogs. It was only with difficulty that practical therapy emerged from the stage of giving calming syrups and purgative pills.

The cat was certainly never, as the dog was, the companion of princes and great people. But in all periods the need to protect, to pamper and to help the cat where needed, has been an instinct in the hearts of girls and women. Already in the seventeenth century the cat, often promoted to the status of a living doll, was the object of care and attentions that were sometimes as clumsy as they were tender. The delicacy of the situation did not entirely escape an element of the grotesque. An engraving by Leblond (1667–1714) ridicules an entire family that are preparing to nourish by force a cat who does not wish to eat. An eighteenth-century drawing by Cochin the younger, called *L'Enfant* (The Baby) shows two little girls busy administering some potion to their pet, and taking the greatest care not to injure it.

In the eighteenth century J. E. Liottard made an engraving (after a cartoon by Watteau) which was called *Le Chat Malade* (The Sick Cat), and which was accompanied by a verse, whose argument is translated as follows:

You watch with joy a dying lover,
Yet for a cat your tears are profuse.
This contrast, Iris, so bizarre, is
    not pleasing.
I am indignant at these stupid alarms.
But when I see this idiot of a doctor
Care for this animal, perfidious and
    evil, I laugh.
If he would stick to cats with his
    dubious science
What good luck for the human race!

Chesteau, too, executed a mocking portrait of a society beauty, more careful to get a doctor for her very uncooperative tomcat than to bring up her unruly children.

In each one of these works, one can notice that the people concerned, to whatever level of society they belong, have prudently bound up the object of their solicitude, for fear of being scratched.

At the end of the nineteenth century almost the only household panacea for feline ailments was catmint or catnip. In the case of digestive troubles the cure was a bath, cooking salt, or bread and butter boiled to a pulp with curdled milk. For the rest, let us pass in silence over a thousand ridiculous prejudices: from the plaster of warm wax on the nape of the neck to combat convulsions and meningitis, to the cutting of the end of the tail to extract a worm (the worm being nothing but the extremity of the spinal marrow, that is in anatomical terms, the 'finum terminale').

Today disorders of the skin, the eyes, the ears, the circulatory, respiratory, urinary and digestive systems, troubles of the nervous system, those of the skeleton or the blood, as well as contagious disease or internal parasites, intoxications and so on, are the subjects of preventive studies and treatments, as well as curative ones which are very close to those in the medicine of man.

Local anaesthesia and general anaesthesia together with antibiotics, have permitted the most daring interventions, from the operation for diaphragmatic hernia to splenectomy, gastrotomy, the pinning of complicated fractures and the replacement of diseased limbs and organs with artificial ones. Oesophagotomies to remove foreign bodies from the thoracic oesophagus, considered for a long time impossible, are today a common practice. Operations such as caesarian section, hysterectomy, ovariotomy, and cystotomy are performed in the clinics every day.

Finally, when there is no hope of cure, when the practitioner thinks that it would be more humane to bring useless suffering to an end, the science of today places at his disposal methods of euthanasia that are as numerous as they are diverse, and all equally painless and effective.

The veterinary colleges of all countries have fixed hours at which they welcome, often without there being any fee required, people of 'small means' whose sick cats are certain of receiving the same care that they

*The care of cats requires the exercise,
under all circumstances, of gentleness,
firmness and patience*

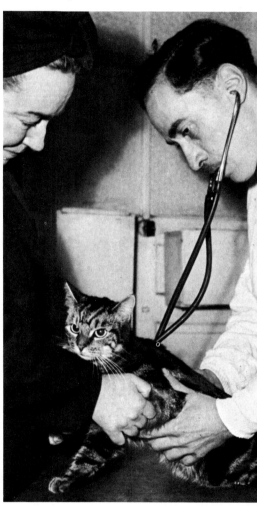

tability, the unpredictable reactions which it has in response to certain medicaments or surgical interventions have nothing in common with animals of the farmyard. The care of cats requires the exercise, under all circumstances, of patience, firmness and gentleness. A cat perceives instantly if the person who approaches it or touches it is experiencing the slightest hesitation, the slightest hostility; and the rapidity of its reflexes then becomes immediate. If the doctor is calm and sure of himself, it closes its eyes, flattens itself, and gives itself up; but if the opposite is true it remains seated on its hind-legs, ready to spring, wrinkles its nose, gives a warning stab with its claws, and draws backwards. At the final stage of fear or anger, it throws itself forward and attacks, lacerating or biting the imprudent person.

A veterinary surgeon for cats must be prepared to deal with the 'zooneuroses' discussed in the previous chapter. Troubles that are the result of a nervous shock might possibly be combatted with calming drugs. Otherwise, the disturbed cat is aided by calm gestures, a gentle voice, caresses if possible and in those cases where the cat has temporarily been removed from his domain, a comfortable habitation where he can, in silence, make himself a refuge and a zone of security. A better knowledge of feline psychology has certainly contributed to the many clinical cures of the past twenty years.

It is not surprising to see that more and more women are becoming veterinary surgeons. Women are also taking the place of the male orderlies and the kennel-men who once constituted the totality of the personnel.

MONSTER CATS

The malformed cat—whether it has rickets, abnormally projected jaws, excessively large head, a hump back or stunted limbs—is the

would get with an independent practitioner. In the big cities such as New York, London, Paris and Berlin, it is possible to make the same appeal to public dispensaries set up by private initiative or to the assistance of the societies for protection of animals which are directed by veterinaries and specialists.

A veterinary surgeon for large animals cannot lightly set himself up as a doctor or surgeon to cats without particular preparation, and above all without a natural disposition towards the animals. The extreme sensibility of the cat to physical pain, its irri-

exception. It is so rare to find real monsters born among cats that any cases of abnormality confirmed in living cats are always made the object of scientific communications or drawings. These are by now almost all in museums or archives.

In 1683, a bizarre litter of kittens was produced in Strasbourg, in which the umbilical cords were inextricably mixed and where the mother was almost entirely deprived of teats. In 1750, a truly monstrous cat, with six limbs—two front legs and four back legs—was the subject of an excellent engraving.

Cats are often brought to veterinary clinics or surgeries in travelling baskets like this

Royal appointment for a seller of cat's meat (1780)

BY
ROYAL APP   OIN
J. W. EVANS
SHORT'S GARDENS—DRURY L
Famleys owning
Cats & Dogs
Freſh
Boiled
Paunſhes
once a
fortnite
Waited on daily and regler.

NO CREDDIT

In 1935, F. Cathelin presented to the French Society for Comparative Pathology a monster, again with six legs, two front ones and four back ones. A few months later Professor Richet presented a case to the Academy of Sciences that was similar. Dr Cathelin, on this subject, has emphasized that such monsters, born viable, are almost impossible to find. He only knew of nine similar cases in the entire world; and of these only two were of the feline species.

COMMON ILLNESSES

Those who keep cats would be well advised to know something themselves of the diseases and ailments to which cats are prone, rather than leaving everything to the vet.

Of course, it would be impossible in a page or two to summarize the technical and scientific knowledge in this field where our knowledge is increasing every day. But it is possible to indicate a few essential facts. And this may help in eradicating some widely spread prejudices and in pin-pointing a few urgent and essential preliminary measures that the owner himself can take – and on which the life of the cat may often depend.

Certain illnesses develop with lightning rapidity. A Siamese that yesterday was playful and enjoyed a good appetite may suddenly appear sad, still, drawn in on itself, its nose dry and its eyes half-closed. It has not eaten today? Never mind. It will eat better tomorrow. And tomorrow, sometimes the cat is dead.

This is the acute form of the famous pseudo-typhus. It is often accompanied by profuse diarrhoea, uncontrollable vomiting, and it sometimes ends with a last loud cry, striking as an ultimate appeal. There are very effective vaccinations against this disease which, in 1935, killed more than a million cats in England and which still rages in France, Germany, Belgium and the United States.

Sometimes, again with a complete loss of appetite that is the first alarming symptom in adult cats, a long filament of saliva taints the lips and the neck. Is it tonsillitis? Or perhaps something stuck in the cat's throat? To determine what it is, the first step is to open the cat's mouth and very rapidly inspect the tongue, the hard palate and the throat. It will not be so easy to do this successfully, however trusting and gentle your cat may be, unless you know the right

method. The left hand literally holds in its palm the nape of the cat's neck and the ears; the right separates the jaws; while the index finger gently presses down on the tongue. Often this is enough to disclose a tongue that is redder at the tip, which is a sign of a virus invasion, or to locate by touch a splinter or fishbone in the throat or tongue. In either case, there should be no attempt to touch anything. The vet should be called, because he is the only one who can save the animal.

Another time it may be a dry, brutal cough that attracts the attention, or perhaps the very classical sneezing with thick mucous discharge that is the symptom of the very frequent catarrh.

The 'common cold' is not an illness to which cats are susceptible, but catarrh is common, usually being a symptom of another disease. In this illness again there should be no delay. Nasal inhalations should be tried. Also, of course, it helps to keep the cat warm and to make sure its diet includes plenty of raw meat and fresh green vegetables. A little daily lemon juice also helps. If the condition worsens, a vet may give the cat a course of powerful antibiotics.

It is equally important not to neglect

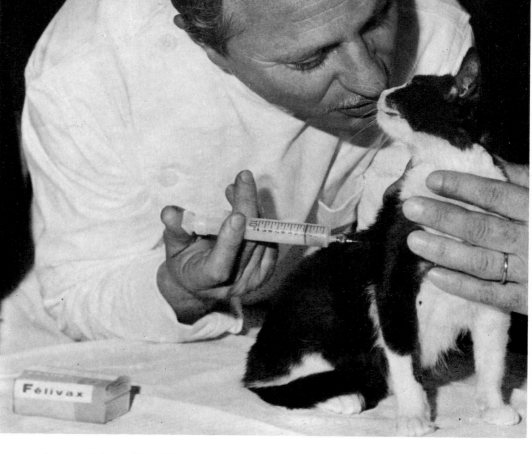

A cat being vaccinated against typhus

A dental examination

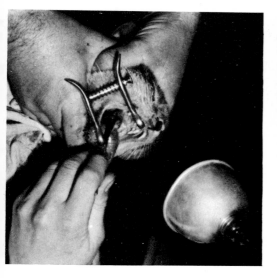

parasitic otitis, which shows in a violent scratching of one or both ears and the presence of a more or less dry secretion, brownish in colour. The parasitic mites that cause this trouble are tiny insects that make their home only in the ears of dogs and cats.

It is also as well to be able to recognize the state of the mucous membranes of the gums and the eyelids. In their normal condition they are pink. An ivory palour is always a sign of a profound anemia, while a yellow colour indicates serious trouble of the bile ducts or the liver.

It should not be forgotten that if the cat licks itself continually, the anatomy of its tongue is such that it cannot fail to swallow a quantity of loose hairs. Vomiting, constipation or enteritis are often of no other origin than this. The best way to get rid of fur balls is with the aid of a very mild laxative. They can be prevented largely through attentive brushing and grooming—so that there is very little if any loose hair for the cat to swallow.

Both for the sake of your own personal hygiene and for your cat's cleanliness, you ought to brush or comb it every day, and this is a good opportunity for keeping an eye on the condition of its skin. The thickness of a cat's fur, even in a short haired animal does not make easy an early diagnosis of a skin disease.

There are two kinds of skin disease—the parasitic and the non-parasitic. Parasitic diseases are contagious—both for cats and for humans—because they are caused by tiny fungi or mites which are easily transferred from one 'host' body to another. The two most common parasitic skin diseases are mange and ringworm. Mange is caused by a burrowing mite that digs out little tunnels in the cat's skin. The irritation causes terrific scratching, which, in turn, can cause a secondary infection. These mites cannot live more than a few days in cold weather, but in warm weather they are very active and difficult to get rid of. Ringworm, caused by a fungus, is just as troublesome as mange, but not as easy to detect. The cat scratches, but not so furiously. The sure way of detecting ringworm is a method that uses ultra-violet light. In a dark room, ultra-violet light makes every affected hair glow fluorescent. Treatment for both ringworm and mange should be prescribed by a vet. Because these diseases are easily spread, it is best to confine the things that the affected cat touches to things that can be sterilized or burned.

The most common non-parasitic skin disease among cats is eczema, a condition which seems to have many different causes. Authorities cannot agree on whether it is caused by diet, biochemical disturbances (which might possibly be inherited), the disturbance of hormone balance (such as may occur in neutering), a malfunctioning of the kidney or adrenal gland in older cats or perhaps even an infestation of blood-sucking parasites such as fleas or lice. Because of the variety of possible causes, there is also a variety of possible cures—none of them guaranteed. Many people give their pets yeast tablets once in a while, but the best advice will again come from a vet.

These few introductory facts about the health of cats are well worth knowing if one wants to take some responsibility for the hygiene, the health, and the happiness of an animal that never implores pity or assistance, but is, none the less, delicate and fragile.

9 *THE BREEDS OF CATS*

In his studies of the cat, Leonardo da Vinci wanted, both as a man of science and as an artist, to explore those laws of 'divine proportion', that 'harmony of parts within the whole' which had been basic aesthetic principles since the time of Plato and Pythagoras. His knowledge of the morphology of the cat, of the articulation of its skeleton and the movement of its tendons and muscles, led him to conclude that 'the smallest of the felines is a masterpiece!'

Colette wrote of the cat that 'it is the animal to whom the Creator gave the biggest eye, the softest fur, the most supremely delicate nostrils, a mobile ear, an unrivalled paw, a curved claw borrowed from the rose-tree....' She also reminded us that 'there are no ordinary cats'.

Ugliness scarcely exists in the cat. Old, wounded or sick, an unaesthetic cat is rare. Scientifically speaking, all domestic cats have an identical morphology; yet no two cats are the same. We have only to look in the streets or our homes to see the kaleidoscopic variety in the coats and colouring of our domestic cats. To the tigers and the lions, to the pumas, jaguars, panthers and cheetahs, nature gave a fairly standard uniform. But for the youngest and the most recent of the species she seemed to borrow from the coats of all.

No one knows what colour domestic cats were originally, but it is likely that the Egyptian cats were a reddish or yellowish colour. Pigmentation has a great deal to do with environment and camouflage; desert cats, such as the Egyptian ones, were probably the colour of the desert. Other colours probably appeared in other areas. But before nature could fix the colour of this tiny species, man intervened, and the results of more or less systematic breeding are seen in the variety of colours, stripes and spots that exist today.

The breeding of cats for show purposes brings an artificial element into our appreciation of the colouring and patterns of their coats. The standards to which the various breeds conform lay down self-colours such as black, white, cream and red and blue. But what a range of colours are covered by these arbitrary names! Grey does not appeal to our taste, so we breed 'blue' cats! Apart from the points of the Siamese and the fantasy of patches on the Tortoiseshells, the Tabby is the pattern our standards usually require. But what have these standards to do with the markings on the coats of most of the free-living, free-mating domestic cats who surround us?

TABBY MARKINGS

The name 'tabby' is said to derive from the name of the Attabiah district of old Baghdad. The Jews in this district made a fine black and white silk with a watered effect. When this appeared in Britain it was called 'tabbi' silk, and the resemblance between the stripes and water marks of the silk and the coat patterns of the cat lead to the use of the name 'Tabby' for the cat.

The pattern that breeders call Tabby markings is to some extent an arbitrarily chosen one, an unachievable design which they attempt to breed their cats to conform with. Yet in the drawings, models and mummies of ancient Egyptian cats, tabby-type markings appear. Some say that the European wild cat markings resemble those of the tabby, except that where lines are continuous in pedigree cats, they tend to be broken up into segments or spots in the wild cat. The breeding of Tabbies must certainly involve a compromise between nature and man: the stripes and spots and bars and rings of the ancestors of our domestic cats have been 'organized' by man in an attempt to achieve the standards of his own aesthetic choice. The almost impossible

Cats of various markings, as drawn by A. Férard. From bottom to top: spotted, oceloid, self-coloured, tiger, tabby

The head of a short-haired tabby

challenge to the breeder is to realize this dream in his pedigree cats.

The classic tabby markings have to show up in dark markings on a paler colour. They consist of specific pencillings on forehead and cheeks. There are two or sometimes three wider but distinct bars across the chest. On the front legs there should be bars of the same width as the alternating stripes of the ground colour. The 'butterfly markings' on the shoulders are oval markings with a spot in the middle that relate to the forehead pencillings to give a butterfly impression if the coat is imagined spread out like a cured skin. A rather similar marking appears on the flanks. The lines of the flanks are rather irregular, and the bars on the back legs tend to be wider than those on the forelegs. Two bands of colour run down the back from the nape of the neck to the root of the tail, and it is difficult to achieve these in distinct and even form. The tail should be ringed with at least four rings and the tail tipped in the colour of the marking, ideally to a depth no greater than that of the rings. Although these markings are only an ideal, progress is being made by breeders in achieving regularity and delicacy of line in individual cats. Nature does better! Whatever the markings actually present in a cat, it is usual to find that the two sides of any tabby cat's coat are remarkably the same in their design.

Other patternings are coming into fashion. Spotted cats are appearing in the 'Any Other Variety' class in shows, as are Mackerel-striped Tabby Cats, which can be very beautiful indeed.

SELF-COLOURS

A study of the possible colours that can appear in a cat's coat brings one up against the questions of genetics. There are thought to be twelve genes for colouration in the hereditary make-up of the cat. White colouring is, to some extent, related to a recessive gene and can only appear when there is at least one such gene in each parent. But generally speaking, the genetic structure of the cat where colour is concerned is not one of clear-cut dominant and recessive genes whose interaction can be easily predicted by breeders knowing the pedigree of the cat. There are many modifying genetic factors which affect the picture. Black, for example, is a sex-linked characteristic, one of the factors contributing to the rarity of fertile males in certain breeds.

Theories as to the non-genetic factors influencing the colouring of cats fluctuate. Jean Rostand has claimed that Siamese kittens, which are born completely white and only develop their adult colouring gradually, will stay white if brought up in a hot-house. Buffon (1707–1788) did not hesitate to state that climate, food and general conditions play an equally important role. 'The Chinese cats of the province of Pe-Chi-Ly owe to the richness of their diet, to the heat and to their idleness, the fact that their ears are hanging and their hair long, while the colours of the cats of Northern Spain, far from having become enfeebled and uniform like the cats of the Orient, have become exalted, more frank and lively, the russet having turned to red, the brown to black, and the grey to white.' This interpretation may not be acceptable today. But factors of environment must have played a part in producing the great variety of colours to be found in the domestic cats distributed over the world today. The hazards of free mating cannot have been the only ones at work.

COAT LENGTH AND TEXTURE

Here we have, to some extent, a simpler genetic picture, as long-hair can be said to be a characteristic recessive to short-hair. If a long-haired cat is mated to a short-haired cat the litter will be predominantly

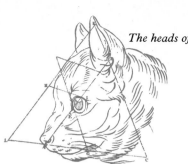

Two Persians: a Smoke and a Black

short-haired. These kittens will, of course, contain, though not display, the concealed recessive long-haired factor, and may be parents of long-haired kittens in their turn. But the picture is not nearly as simple as this. As all breeders know, intermediate hair-lengths always appear, and it is breeding to man-made standards to always attempt to produce only the longest or the shortest coats. Another arbitrary factor is that of silkiness of coat. In no breed, except perhaps the Chartreux, is woolliness of coat accepted by show standards, but in our common household cats how often does it appear!

BODY TYPE

The controlled breeding of cats by man has resulted in the development and fixing of three distinct body shapes. One is close to the 'type', as it is called, of the classic Egyptian cat. To take a breed with 'foreign' type, the shadow of an Abyssinian thrown against a wall irresistably evokes the elegant nervous silhouette of the hieratic cats of Bubastis. The Persian or Long-haired cat has a massive round and thick-set body-type and makes us think of some impassive Buddha, heavy with meditation and wisdom. Dare we say that the type of the British short-haired cat reflects the taste of the country where it was bred? Neat and sturdy and poised, and of independent character?

The factors influencing the body line and structure of the cat are particularly confused. The outline of most cats today is incontestably a long way from the one seen in representations of the cat of ancient Egypt. Yet this is where it is believed the domestic cat originated. These had a long-flowing sinuous body line, deep but narrow chest and triangular head, with narrow skull, long ears and elongated snout. In my opinion the domestic cat cannot successfully interbreed with the European wild cat, yet the shape of the European or British domestic cats of

Three Russian Blues

today, whether pedigree or stray, cannot fail to remind one a little of the wild cat with its heavy-jowled face, large thorax and muscled thighs.

THE SCIENTIFIC BREEDING OF CATS

It was curiosity that first inspired a small number of breeders to try to cross the few natural breeds that were once known across the world. These were principally the Siamese, the Birmans, the Persians or Angoras, the cats of Gambia, the cats of Malta (the blue Chartreux and the red of Tobolsk), the cats of Spain and Portugal, and the cats of the Cape of Good Hope.

Surprisingly quickly, however, these early producers and breeders succeeded in reaching agreement on international standards for the varieties of cats issuing from their mixtures. By now there are very precise standards that impose official canons of beauty on cats of the pedigree or show world. But these inevitably are subject to change. New breeds, the result of crossings, selections, the application of the principles of genetics and other patient researches of breeders, come to be recognized and then developed further. Because of this profusion of new possibilities, the societies and federations that lay down these standards specify that it is not correct to speak of a new 'breed', with its own standard and scale of points, until after the presentation in shows of a series of cats with the characteristics of the breed spaced out over a specific number of generations.

What do we mean by the characteristics that typify a breed? The President of the Cat Club of Paris, Professor Etienne Letard of the École Nationale Vétérinaire d'Alfort has put the answer quite clearly. It is a question, first and foremost, of a hereditary characteristic that can be transmitted uniformly. A new quality which appears to be a possible characteristic of a separate breed

it must be truly new, it must set apart the group of animals which bear it. It is justifiably accepted that when it is only a question of some small detail, of no great importance and which does not catch the attention of the observer, it is inappropriate to create a new breed.

Lastly, to be able to speak of a breed, the group of animals that display the typical characteristic must be reasonably numerous as well as homogeneous. Until this is so, one can only speak of a 'family', of a lineage who display a particular characteristic, but not of a true 'breed'. And not to stick to these rules would result in a disintegration of the species into a multiplicity of breeds which could only be disastrous for the science of breeding.

The science and art of breeding has certainly been founded on a biological and genetic basis. But it contains, nevertheless, an element of the conventional, the artificial: because it is according to his own personal views, his own tendancies, fantasies and tastes, that an individual breeder will attach more or less importance to any new characteristic that appears and decide whether it is or is not worthy to constitute a possible characteristic for a new breed.

THE SIAMESE AND ITS VARIETIES

The origin of the Siamese is not definitely known. The first certain reference to the Siamese in Siam occurs in 1830 in a poem about cats, in which there is distinct reference to the mask and points that are the characteristic features in the colouring of the Siamese.

The type may have been fixed by Pradgadipok, father of a Siamese king, who kept these cats jealously guarded and confined to his palace. Although the penalty for stealing one was death, the boys in charge of them seem to have removed the occasional one from a new litter and sold it in Shanghai to tourists passing through.

does not have to be transmitted so that it shows in the direct descendants. But it is necessary that it should, during a series of organized matings, be displayed again in a later generation for it to be considered 'fixed'. This is the true aim, the really creative role of the breeder. When the characteristic is fixed, when it becomes the common and constant attribute of all the subjects that belong to this lineage, it deserves to be considered a breed characteristic. But if it cannot be transmitted hereditarily, then it is obvious that, whatever its beauty and importance, it cannot be considered a characteristic that constitutes or designates a breed.

It is, of course, obvious that in all species of animals, new and interesting characteristics appear from time to time. If they can be fixed, there is nothing to prevent them being considered as breed characteristics. As a result, the number of breeds in any species can never be finally fixed.

These breed characteristics can be of various kinds. They can relate to the shape of the animal: to its build and style, or to its size. They can relate to the external appearance of the animal: to the skin, individual hairs or fur, feathers, horns, the colour of the mucous membranes and so on. Or they can relate to the aptitudes or habits of the animal: to its physiology or psychology.

Breed characteristics can certainly be of any kind. But for a characteristic to be worthy of being the hallmark of a new breed

In 1884 a pair of cats called Pho and Mia were the first Siamese to reach England. They were brought by Mr Owen Gould, the Consul General in Bangkok, from the Royal Palace there, and were shown at the Crystal Palace in 1885. In the same year, another pair were brought into France for the first time, and presented to the Jardin des Plantes. The fashion for these cats, however, really began in England, where their appearance in public exhibitions aroused great interest. Their popularity so spread that by the end of the 1880s there were quite often nearly a dozen Siamese shown in the two classes for them at the Crystal Palace Show.

The Siamese is alert in character, affectionate and endearingly sociable. Its main draw-back as a pet is its piercing and much-used voice, which seems closer to the cry of a human baby than any animal sound. Walt Disney made use of this human element in their miaowing when he gave speech to the Siamese in the film 'The Lady and the Tramp', and made them whine 'We are Siamese – if you please'.

The Siamese is the prince of cats. Its physical beauty is of a delicate kind that lies in its elegance of line, subtlety of musculature and delicacy of colour. The ideal Siamese, for breeding and show purposes must have a long, lithe, well-proportioned shape that gives a flowing effect. It should always be slender and never fat. The bone structure should be delicate, never heavy. The hind legs should be slightly longer than the front legs, giving the effect of a very slight slope downwards from the tail and haunches to the neck. The feet should be oval. The tail structure is important in Siamese. It should not only be long and tapering with a fine point at the end, but should be a thin tail all the way along. It is a bad fault for the tail to be thick where it joins the body. A slight kink, but only at the very extremity of the tail, is allowed for show purposes. But though the original Siamese cats often had kinked tails, or really short tails (sometimes mere stumps), European breeders have been trying to eliminate this very Oriental characteristic. The head of a Siamese should be literally triangular, and set on a sinuous neck. A bad fault in head shape is for the sides of the face not to be straight enough for the cheeks then curve in towards the nose, giving the face a pinched look, and making the muzzle seem too wide. The ears should be larger than those of any other domestic breed. They should be long, wide at the base and rather pointed at the tip. They should be set well apart, contributing to the wedge or triangular shape of the whole head. The eyes should definitely be almond-shaped as a result of the bone-structure of the sockets; the shape of eye that is commonly thought of as 'Oriental'. They should ideally be a brilliant deep sapphire blue. Eyes that are too pale are a common fault in Siamese, as are eyes that are too round.

Siamese kittens are born almost white, or, more exactly, an extremely pale shade of cream that has a greyish tone. Only gradually do the characteristic colour markings of the adult Siamese, the points, appear in its coat. These consist of a dark mask (that is, facial colouring concentrated over the cheeks and round the features of the eye and muzzle) which should connect up by fine lines to the base of the ears, which again are dark in colour. There is also less dramatic darkening of the feet, legs and tail. The dark-coloured points should stand out in contrast against the paler main colour of the coat, though in most Siamese the main coat colour is lighter on the underside than over the back. It is a fault for there to be a dark spot on the belly, or for there to be any white colouring between the toes.

It is in producing different colours of

At five months, a young Birman is only promise . . .

At three years he has acquired his full majesty

Kittens of any breed are appea.

points that breeders concentrate their efforts when trying to achieve new varieties of Siamese. The classic Siamese is the Seal-Pointed, which should have dark brown points. The main coat colour should be a warm fawn on the back, becoming paler down the sides and a creamy white under the stomach.

The first Blue-Pointed Siamese was bred in England in 1894. The mask and points should be a greyish blue. The main coat colour should be a glacial white shading to a lighter blue than that of the points across the back.

The Chocolate-Pointed Siamese should have points of a milk-chocolate colour and a body-colour of ivory, shading (if at all) to a paler chocolate over the back. The original cat with these characteristics was a male Siamese that was brought into England from Siam in 1897.

The latest variety to receive official recognition are Lilac-Pointed, as they are called in Great Britain, or the Frost-Points, as they are occasionally called in the United States. These should have frosty-grey points with a pinkish cast or tone, and a frosty-white body-colouring, shading (if at all) over the back to a colour matching the points but paler, as in all varieties of Siamese. But in this variety the colouring of the nose and pads should be a faded lilac rather than pink.

THE COLOURPOINT

The establishment of the Colourpoint as a breed was due to the efforts of Mr Stirling-Webb of England. In the United States long-haired Siamese cats, that is long-haired cats with both Siamese colouring and body-type, had been successfully bred, but the breeding abandoned. It was held that the beauty of the Siamese type was lost with the addition of long-hair. Mr Stirling-Webb's intention was to breed cats of long-haired body type as well as coat, but with

the introduction of the Siamese colouring. His attempts were completely successful, and the breed of Colourpoint Long-Hairs was given a breed number by the Governing Council of the Cat Fancy in 1955.

The standard requires the typical body-type of the Persians or 'cobby', as it is called, and emphasizes that any similarity in body-type to Siamese to be considered most undesirable. Also, a kink in the tail is considered a defect. It requires fur that is long, thick and soft in texture and a full neck frill. The possible varieties in colouring are those of the Seal-, Blue- and Chocolate-Pointed Siamese. The main difficulty in breeding Colourpoints at present is to obtain eyes that are not too pale a blue, and that are as large and round as the long-haired type requires. The colour of the eyes should be a clear, bright and definite blue, the deeper the better.

The Colourpoint is remarkably like a breed recognized in France, the Khmer, which has its own standard in that country, though it is not recognized by La Fédération Internationale Féline d'Europe.

THE BIRMAN

The Birman is the Sacred Cat of Burma. There are few of these in either the United States or Britain and they have only just been accepted as a breed. But they have had their standard in France since 1925, and are much shown there.

The Birman is an exotic cat; its origin and the tale of its introduction in Europe are also exotic. Over a hundred of these cats lived in the underground temple of Lao-Tsun in Burma, and the priests believed that the faithful returned to the earth after death in the bodies of these cats. The cats were worshipped by the priests and treated like gods; and indeed the name Lao-Tsun means 'the dwelling place of the gods'. During the rebellion in this area in 1916, a British officer, Major Gordon Russell, helped to quell it, and he made it possible for some of the priests to escape into Tibet, taking their sacred cats with them. In 1919 he went to live in France, and the priests sent him in gratitude two Birman cats.

Much is said on the subject of the relation of the Birman to the Siamese, both in the matter of their origin in the Far East and their breeding history in the West. In the early history of their breeding, crosses with Siamese were undoubtedly used. Whatever

The Khmer, (page 177) is a breed much discussed in France. Is it the happy result of a cross between a White Persian and a Siamese (this page)?

Tree of Coexistence ►
by Eden Box (1962)

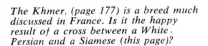

the truth of the matter, in appearance they are long-haired cats with a marking reasonably similar to that of the Siamese. The original Birmans, like the Siamese, were Seal-Pointed, but there is now a Blue-Pointed variety.

The standard requires a long but massive body of medium size. The limbs should be short and powerful. The head should be large and really round, with a curved forehead and short nose. The fawn of the body colour should have a golden tinge to it, which distinguishes it from the Siamese colouring. The mask, points and tail should be seal-coloured as in the Siamese, but the paws should be pure white giving a gloved effect quite unique to this breed. The fur should be long and silky, and is often wavy under the stomach. The frill and brush should be well-developed. The eyes should be of a vivid and deep blue.

THE BURMESE

The breed of cat known as the Burmese is the work of the School of Genetics at Harvard University. The first Burmese, a brown female called 'Wong Mau' with a

body of the slender foreign type, was imported from Burma into the United States in 1930 by Dr G. C. Thompson of San Francisco. As there was no similar male, she was mated with a Siamese. The result was eclectic: as much the one as the other. Then followed the long slow process of selection and remating, accompanied by disappointments and successes but pursued with stubborn persistence until a self-perpetuating breed in the strictest sense of the term was finally created.

The first Burmese were imported into Britain from America in 1947 by Mr and Mrs Sydney France of Derby, and after many difficulties the breed was established. In 1952 it was given a provisional breed number, and in 1954 it was finally recognized by the Governing Council of the Cat Fancy. It is now recognized in France under the name *zibeline*.

The ideal Burmese should have a body line much like that of the Siamese—medium in size, long and slim. The bones should be as fine and the hind legs again slightly longer than the front ones. The tail should be long and thin and pointed at the end, but, for the present, the tails of Burmese are not yet as fine as those of Siamese.

The neck should be long and slender. The head, however, is not quite as long as that of the Siamese. It should definitely be wedge or triangular in shape, much as the head of the Siamese used to be at the beginning of the century. The ears are not quite as large as those of the Siamese, but they, too, should be wide at the base and stand upright from the head. It is important that the eyes should be of the true Oriental almond-shape slanting towards the nose, and they should be yellow in colour. It is a fault for them to be blue or for there to be any squint. Burmese have retained their eye characteristics far better than Siamese throughout the process of breeding.

The coat of the Burmese should be a really

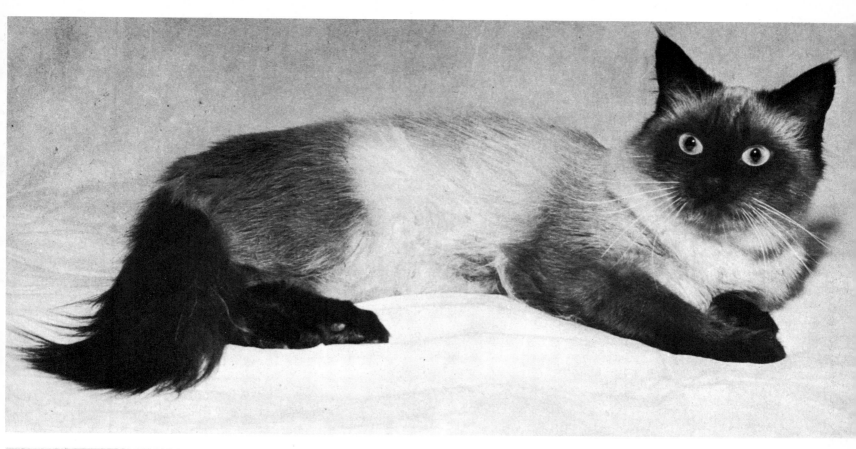

dark seal-brown in colour, though this inevitably shades to a lighter colour on the chest and belly. This colour should be solid over the whole body. In Burmese kittens, who have a paler colour coat, the darker coloured mask and points characteristic of the Siamese can be seen. But as the kitten gets older and the coat darkens they tend to disappear and should not show in the mature cat. Usually,

France's Khmer is remarkably like the Colourpoint

A newcomer : the Burmese or zibeline

A pair of Burmese, in whose artificial creation the Siamese played a part

however, on close inspection they will be found to be still faintly present.

Recently a new breed, the Blue Burmese, has been recognized. It is like the brown in all respects except that its coat should be of a bluish-grey colour, shading to a pale brown or grey on the belly. There should be a silver sheen to the coat. There should be no white or tabby markings, but the mask and points shade to a silver grey.

The Burmese seem to be quite as affectionate as the Siamese, but far more placid in character, which makes them easy cats to show. Their voice is as shrill but they talk distinctly less, which is undoubtedly an attraction to many people thinking of keeping a Burmese as a pet.

LONG-HAIRED CATS

The original long-haired cats in Europe used to be called angoras. Later they came to be known as Persians. Nowadays, for show-purposes, they are referred to as 'long-haired' to distinguish them from the short-haired varieties where necessary. There is some confusion as to where they originally came from. According to Buffon it was Asia Minor. There is good evidence that these cats existed in Persia several centuries ago. It is possible that the name angora is the place-name (corruption of 'Ankara', the Turkish city). But there exist other animals with long silky coats called angoras: angora rabbits, angora guinea-pigs, angora goats.

These long-haired cats were first introduced into Italy towards 1550 by Pietro della Velle. Then they were brought to France at the end of the sixteenth century by Claude Fabri de Peirese, a scientist of many interests at that time. The long-haired cat probably reached England from France.

In 1856, M. Lottin de la Val wrote to the Société Impériale d'Acclimatation saying: 'I have found this beautiful feline species on the great Armenian plateau at Erzerum,

where the climate is conspicuously different from that of Angora.' He noted that the angora was the dominant variety among the cats of Kurdistan. He had seen whites, greys and spotted orange ones. He also saw them in Baghdad though in smaller numbers 'because the inhabitants' he said, 'reproach them above all with being carriers of the plague. . . .'

The angora type of fur was probably the result of a sudden mutation that was fixed by the process of natural selection. An angora is simply a cat with extremely long hair. Sometimes in shows one sees complete monuments of fur, under which it is almost impossible to trace the harmonious anatomy and purity of line that make up the actual body of the cat. But it is in the body of the Persian that the process of artificial breeding by man has had its triumph. The modern long-haired cat is an animal that does not have much in common with the original angora. The latter had a much less round skull and a longer nose. The long-haired cat of today is characterized by its wide spherical skull and almost non-existant nose, as in a Pekinese dog.

The modern long-haired cat is the result of work by English breeders, who produced it within less than half a century. And it is interesting to note that they produced a very similar evolution in the chow-chow, the dog that came originally from Hong-Kong. Like the angora cat, this dog was to start with a loosely-built animal with harsh, half-length hair, a skull narrower than the now massive one, and long, slender limbs. We might possibly say that the parallel change in the two animals reflected English taste in these matters as much as English science. But two factors in the science of breeding probably contributed. The chow-chow, when taken over by breeders, was fed on a meat diet, poor in carbohydrates but rich in fat-soluble vitamins and mineral salts. In addition to this change to a richer diet, it was

A suspicion of a nose in a wide face characterizes the Persian

Sometimes the shape of the Persian is completely lost in the cloud of its fur

subject to the cold, damp climate of Great Britain, so different from the warm dry climate from which it came. Was there at work here, influencing this evolution of both the chow-chow and the Persian, quite independently of diet, some mechanism of natural adaptation in these transplanted animals? We do not yet know the answer. But the same solid, thick-set body, wide skull, short nose, and thick, relatively short limbs were the result in both animals.

The ideal type of body structure of the long-haired cat today is massive and low-set without being coarse. The bones should be solid and strong. The legs should be short and thick in relation to the body-size. The tail should be short, too, and very fully furred – the type of tail that is called a brush. The head should be wide across and round in shape, with a short nose, full cheeks and a broad muzzle. The ears should be small, neat, set wide apart and well-covered with fur. The eyes should be large, round and wide open. It is a distinct fault for them to be small and too deep set. They should be luminous, though the actual colour differs in the different varieties.

The coat is, of course, very important in long-haired cats. The fur must always be long, silky and flowing. The long hair around the head is the frill and should be particularly full. When brushed up it should stand away from the body and neck forming a big full ruff around the head. The tail, too, should be particularly full. Indeed, when brushed out, it should be as wide as the body. The combination of fullness of coat in frill and brush should contribute to the square shape of this short-bodied cat. And,

of course, care and grooming of the long-haired coat is of enormous importance when showing these beautiful cats.

The possible differences in coat colour have led to there being numerous varieties of long-haired cats. And this is the field in which breeders concentrate their attention in trying to establish new breeds. Blue, grey, black, white, cream, red—from London to Chicago, from Tokyo to Paris, the different varieties vie with each other to become the latest fashion.

THE BLUE PERSIAN

The Blue Persian was first shown in England as a breed in its own right in 1889. Before that it had been entered under Blue Tabby or Blue classes that allowed white to appear in the coat. The speed with which the Blue Persian became popular is shown by the fact that by 1899 there were more than a hundred entries in the classes for cats and kittens of this breed. The Blue Persian Cat Society was formed in 1901, largely because of the efforts of Miss Frances Simpson, one of the most dedicated breeders of the Long-haired Blue. The true Blue Persian did not appear in Europe until 1914. But by now it is popular throughout the United States and Europe.

These cats are basically a bluish-grey, but the standard allows for a wide range of colouring from dark to pale coat colour. The coat should be uniform in colour. The ruff should not be paler in colour. The spine and tail should not be darker. When this fault is present the darker hair is usually found to be coarser than the rest of the coat. There should be no white spots on the stomach or throat, as often used to appear when the breed was newly established. And each individual hair should be uniformly coloured. It should be the same shade from the tip right down to the skin. This is particularly difficult to achieve with the paler shades of blue coat. Finally there should be no white hairs

in the coat. These may happen as a cat gets old, or towards the end of the season, when hair is dying and hairs originally blue turn white or nearly white. At one stage in the breeding history of these cats there was, probably because of their success and popularity, over-breeding and too close inter-breeding. The coat began to lose its uniformity and pale grey and yellow patches began to appear.

The eyes of this breed should be a deep orange or even a copper colour. Green or pale yellow eyes are no longer acceptable. And the presence of even a trace of green in a cat's eye should be accepted as meaning that the individual is unsuited for breeding purposes.

In the United States a shortening of the face even more than is normal for the long-haired face, giving a really Pekinese-like look, has resulted in a special group being formed within this breed for show purposes.

Breeders should, as a rule, however, conform strictly to the standards. It is the striving after sensational effects in breeding that produces those Persians that are just flabby balls of fur, with cheeks invading their eyes, colour that is washed out and legs that are bandy or too furry. The production of high quality long-haired cats is a very paying proposition. They are amongst the most popular breeds today because of their aesthetic appearance, their gentleness or character and their resistance to diseases.

THE LONG-HAIRED WHITE

White cats with long hair were probably present in France two hundred years ago at least. And the cats that existed in England in the early nineteenth century were probably first brought from France. Certainly France has always maintained high standards in producing Long-haired Whites.

Two varieties are recognized in Britain, the Long-haired White with blue eyes and the Long-haired White with orange eyes. It

has been claimed, with justification, that the blue-eyed variety is genetically the purer. It is probable that the orange-eyed variety was produced by artificial breeding in an attempt to counteract the deafness that is so characteristic of white cats with blue eyes. There often appear white long-haired cats with odd eyes, one blue and one orange. Opinions vary as to the quality of their hearing but it is certain that it is far better than that of the purely blue-eyed cats. And these odd-eyed white Persians, though useless for show purposes, make good breeders. Not only their hearing, but their type often appears to be better than in the blue-eyed whites. These last are difficult to breed and tend to have small litters. Much work needs to be done on them before they will become popular. But it is not impossible that even their predominant deafness, which seems to be due to some genetic link-up, may eventually be overcome.

The coat colour of both breeds should be pure white, the main fault being the appearance of yellow markings. But the practical difficulty in keeping the coat colour white lies in its tendency to become greasy, and then accumulate dirt in the grease, producing a yellow discolouration, particularly in the tail. To retain show standards the tail may have to be washed and powdered as often as once a week. Although orange-eyed whites tend to have better type than blue-eyed ones, their coats are sometimes a little woolly in texture. The blue-eyed whites often have a truly remarkable silky coat. The orange-eyed Long-haired Whites have one notable advantage over other long-haired cats in that their coat colour is not subject to seasonal modifications. Though kittens may show grey marks at birth, these usually disappear by the time the cat is mature.

The eye colour, which should be deep blue in one variety, and deep orange or copper in the other, is easier to spot for quality in orange-eyed kittens. These achieve

Dody de Padirac, at two months, already has all the characteristics of her breed

With the White Persian, all seems to be calm and voluptuous delight

their adult colouring by the time they are six or seven months old. Whereas the eyes of blue-eyed kittens may continue to deepen in colour until they are over a year old.

THE LONG-HAIRED BLACK

This is one of the oldest breeds of all. In England there were special classes for Long-haired Blacks in the earliest cat shows, and there were many entries. However, many of the breeds that are now popular have only been established within the last seventy years or so.

One reason for the loss in popularity of the Long-haired Black is that they are difficult to breed. True black cats are very rare indeed. The best subjects can become discoloured when very young. The coat starts to show rustiness or brownish patches, the hair becomes dull and dry and very unattractive to the cat-lover. In addition, Long-haired Blacks very easily revert to the older type, with elongated nose and long legs. These facts contribute to making the market for this breed very poor indeed. The standards state that the colour of the coat of a Long-haired Black should be 'lustrous raven black to the roots, and free from rustiness, shadings, white hairs, or markings of any kind'. This is difficult both to attain and to maintain.

One of the first difficulties a breeder encounters is that it is very difficult to judge the future qualities of a kitten before it is six months old at the very earliest. Often it is not possible till later still. Sometimes the adult cat with the most intensely black coats were almost a rusty brown as kittens. Other kittens have a whitish undercoat which they eventually lose. This prejudices the chance of selling kittens, as well as making it difficult to decide which to keep for breeding.

It is often advisable to use, from time to time, a cross between a Black and a Blue when breeding Blacks, in order to strengthen the type of the Black. But this introduces

the risk that the individual hairs will not be pure black but may become paler towards the root.

It is especially hard to achieve black cats without a single white hair in their coats. When these white hairs appear they are often coarser in texture than the fine black hairs, and their presence can be disguised by intensive grooming which tends to remove them.

Strong sunlight undoubtedly has a bleaching effect on a black cat's coat, making it browner. Water also seems to affect the pigmentation, and too much licking or even walking in tall wet grass can lighten the coat, giving the unwanted rusty or brownish effect. Moulting seasons, of course, affect the colour of the coat, too.

The eyes of the Long-haired Black should be a dark orange or copper colour. No other

cat is so esoterically or magically a 'cat' in appearance as this beautiful Persian whose brilliant dark colouring is illuminated by golden eyes. It is resistant to disease. It is among the most courageous, vigorous and ardent of all the breeds, and I personally find it sad that it is not more popular.

However, for those who love this cat, there is one reassuring fact. It is of considerable importance in the breeding of other varieties. Paradoxically, it is to the black cat that recourse is had when whites must be bred even whiter still. It is also used in the breeding of Tortoiseshells. And Always, breeders turn to the Long-haired Black when other unstable varieties begin to show, in coats that should be uniformly coloured, the menacing marks that are atavistic signs of a return to the coats of their ancestors.

THE LONG-HAIRED CREAM

With the Long-haired Cream we are getting close to those breeds that I call 'adapted' Persians; those varieties whose colour does not yet seem to be properly fixed. I find it hard to think of cream as a genuine self-colour. Is the cream not just the more or less temporary result of combining yellow or red with white?

Probably the first Creams appeared in litters produced by crossing Red Tabbies with Tortoiseshells. Cream is one of the colours of the Tortoiseshell coat. A less likely suggestion is that they resulted from a cross between Red Tabbies and White, which certainly could produce fawn and even cream kittens, but the self-colouring would have been rare.

In England this breed's popularity certainly reached its height during the 1920s. The first classes were for Fawns or Creams. Even now the standard does not lay down any exact requirement as to the shade of cream, but only that the colour should be 'pure and sound throughout without shading or markings'.

In practice, breeders prefer the paler shades which are more attractive and brighter to the eye. But it is particularly difficult with the paler coats to retain uniformity of colouring as there is a tendency for lighter undercoats to appear. The use of Red Tabbies in breeding shows in the tendency of Creams to become too 'hot' in colour, that is too red. Also, tabby markings begin to appear. Cross-breeding with the paler Blues is a much-favoured method of preserving or improving type and colour.

My own suggestion to breeders, if I may be permitted to make one, is the introduction of the occasional pure Long-haired Black among the Creams to come. And also I would draw attention to the need to conserve the pigmentation of the mucous membranes, one of the signs of a healthy cat.

The standards allocate 50 points, a full half of the total number, to the colour, coat and condition. This refers not only to the uniformity of colouring, but also to the length, density and silkiness of the coat. Wooliness instead of silkiness of coat is an occasional fault among Creams. In my opinion the pure cream colouring, uniform and without markings, is going to become more and more difficult to fix. But the Long-haired Cream is an extremely beautiful animal, and I wish the breed a long life.

THE LONG-HAIRED RED SELF

The Long-haired Red Self succeeded the Orange, a variety now no longer spoken of. The Red Self is even more difficult to breed than the Cream, to which it is so closely related. Although there are official standards for it in England it may almost be said that no true Red Selfs have been achieved by English breeders. In North America and Scandinavia there has been more success.

ur such as this must have constant care

ese Black Persians with copper-
loured eyes would enrich a legend

A young Cream Persian

The difficulty is in eradicating tabby markings or their remnants from what ought to be a deep, rich red coat without any markings at all. Many are the suggestions that are made for improving the breed, and they include cross-breeding with good quality Long-haired Blacks.

The standards allocate 50 points, half of the total, to the colour and coat alone, which shows the importance quite rightly attached to this prototype, more often dreamed of than actually seen. However, it is certainly possible to hope that by means of rigorous selection and long and patient crossings, there will be success in producing and fixing this pure red breed of cat, whose red colouring must certainly have existed originally as a self-coloured coat (in the same way as whites, blacks, and blues), but has not persisted.

ADAPTED BREEDS

We now come to that group of unstable Long-haired breeds that I call 'adapted' because, in my opinion, they cannot be said to breed true. Cross-breeding with other varieties seems far too necessary in order to maintain the standards, and in some cases is the only method of reproducing the variety at all. This does not seem to me to be in accordance with the classic principles of breeding, which require that a new breed should succeed in reproducing itself over a number of generations before this proposed breed can be claimed as fixed. Are we not threatening the principles on which the science of breeding is based in a desperate search after novelty and sensation? These unstable breeds are certainly beautiful to look at in shows or in the home, but their biological foundation seems quite uncertain.

THE LONG-HAIRED SMOKE
The best period for Smokes in England was during the first twenty years of this century.

But they have lost popularity and are tending to disappear. This is at least partly because they are extremely difficult to breed.

A standard exists both for the usual Smoke, which is the Black Smoke, and for the Blue Smoke. The Black is the more distinctive because of the greater contrast between the black and the silver in its coat. The blue and silver are not so striking a combination. This colour difference is the only difference between the two.

Ideally the body of the Black Smoke should be a deep jet black in colour, shading to silver on the sides and flanks: the mask and feet should be black with no markings, the frill and ear tufts should be silver with the frill being longer than in other breeds, and the cat should have as white an undercoat as possible. The undercoat contributes greatly to the beauty of the cat as it shows through the black of the longer hairs of the back as the animal moves. The silver frill haloes the black face.

One of the main faults in modern Smokes is that the undercoat is a smutty dull grey, rather than a pale silver or pale greyish white. Rustiness of the black is a problem, as with all black coats. But it is a fact that the black of the back is almost never as dark as that of the face and feet, and the individual hairs of the back become paler towards the roots. In kittens the white undercoat does not show. It lightens with age. It is impossible to decide how good a kitten is going to become before it is at least six months old. But it can be said that those kittens whose undercoats begin to pale early on will develop into the best adults.

THE LONG-HAIRED BLUE-CREAM
This variety was recognized by the Governing Council of the Cat Fancy in 1929–1930. The decision still surprises some, including myself.

The British and continental standards for this breed require that the coat consist of

The Tortoiseshell has faithful admirers

The Tortoiseshell-and-White has four colours in its coat

blue and cream hairs evenly intermingled. The effect is rather that of shotsilk. No patches of blue or cream should appear. In the United States, however, the coat is required to be patched with blue and cream, as a Tortoiseshell is patched. The coat of the Blue-cream should always be particularly soft and silky. The eyes should be deep copper or orange.

My own argument against recognition of this breed does not lie only in the fact that its coat is merely a mixture of two colours, rather than showing a genetically pure colouring. It lies also in the fact that there are no Blue-cream males. It is very rare that these should be born at all, and the occasional males that appear die within a few weeks.

THE LONG-HAIRED TORTOISESHELL

The Tortoiseshell is another variety of cat in which next to no males are born. The few that are born are generally sterile, though this is not quite without exception. Here we have another of those breeds in which Nature seems to give up her rights. However, breeders find the production of Tortoiseshells interesting because of the unpredictability in the litters produced. They do not claim that this is scientific breeding.

Good Tortoiseshells are beautiful and rare. Their coat should consist of three colours: black, red and cream, evenly distributed in patches of solid colour over the body, preferably also over the legs, feet, ears and the tail as well. There should be no mingling of hairs of the other colours in the individual patches and no white hairs at all. There should certainly be no markings of the tabby type, or indeed any stripes or rings. A red or green blaze between the eyes is considered very attractive. The hair of the brush and the frill should be extra long. The eyes should be copper or deep orange. To breed these cats it is necessary to mate the Tortoiseshell mother with a

father of one of the relevant self-colours. But there may be no Tortoiseshell from such a litter at all.

The Long-haired Tortoiseshell-and-white variety differs only from the Tortoiseshell in the addition of white patches among the other colours. Not much white is necessary, indeed too much is undesirable. But an even white running from the top of the head to the nose is a great asset.

THE LONG-HAIRED RED TABBY

This is a variety in which English breeders have achieved the best results. Rather surprisingly, it is more popular than the other two Long-haired Tabby breeds. It is the most difficult to breed, because both ground and tabby markings should be a deep rich red, and it is therefore difficult to obtain markings that really stand out. Also, as with the other two breeds, the long coat tends to blur the design. But English breeders have succeeded in fixing a good cat of strong stature. And if the colour tends to become too pale, it is enough to introduce occasionally the blood of a good Long-haired Black for the red markings and ground to be restored to their original brilliance within two or three generations.

The main fault to watch out for is a tendency, common to all the Long-haired Tabbies, for the type to revert: for the re-appearance of a longer head and ears that are too long. The tail is sometimes too long, and the fur of the brush is often inadequately short. This spoils the cobby appearance required in long-haired cats. A white tip often appears in the tail, too, which is difficult to eradicate in succeeding generations and makes the cat dangerous for breeding purposes. White markings on chin, chest or stomach are possible, equally dangerous faults. The main difficulty in producing the correct tabby markings is in obtaining the two clear lines running down the back.

Often this appears as one solid band of colour, not much darker than the ground. The eyes should be of a deep copper colour.

THE LONG-HAIRED BROWN TABBY

The Long-haired Brown Tabby was at its most popular at the beginning of this century. It is no longer so, and considerable work needs to be done by breeders if really excellent specimens are to appear again.

The standard requires a really rich tawny sable in the ground colour, and some think today's colour a little too pale. The delicate dense black markings in this breed seem comparatively easy to obtain. A common fault in Brown Tabbies used to be a white chin, and a paler colour in the chin still often appears. This is the most difficult breed in which to achieve the wide head required by the long-haired type. Green eyes used to be acceptable but now the standards require hazel or copper.

THE LONG-HAIRED SILVER TABBY

Again this breed was more popular at the beginning of the century, but like the other

The Long-haired Brown Tabby should have black markings on a rich, tawny sable ground colour

The Long-haired Silver Tabby should have green or hazel eyes

A Long-haired Silver Tabby masked with black

The Chinchilla, whose coat is so curiously 'ticked' that it appears to be clothed in silver lamé

Long-haired Tabbies, is no longer so. The markings, however, particularly on the body, seem to have been very distinct and of a clear good black.

The standard requires a pure pale silver ground colour on which jet black markings look very beautiful indeed. But breeders find it hard to keep out a yellow or brownish tinge. The requirements for eye colour have changed since these cats were first shown. Originally this was hazel, but then green eyes were introduced and some claim that this was when the breed began to deteriorate. Today's standard allows green or hazel eyes.

CHINCHILLAS

In Britain cats called Chinchillas were known at the end of the last century, but these had markings on the legs and tail and even sometimes on the face. The first Chinchilla that we would recognize as one today was shown in 1902. A Society for silver cats was formed in London in 1919. Chinchillas were at their best in Britain in the 1930s.

The name is a surprising one, and its origin seems to be unknown. This breed's colouring is not dissimilar to that of the chinchilla native to the Andes. But there is certainly no likeness between the Chinchilla cat and the chinchilla rabbit.

The United States and the Commonwealth countries recognize two breeds where Britain recognizes only one. The Shaded Silver has darker ticking and a pale silver undercoat compared with the Chinchilla's white one. This heavy ticking is not acceptable by the British standards.

The standards for the Chinchilla are very precise. 'The undercoat should be pure white, the coat on back, flanks, head, ears and tail being tipped with black, this ticking to be evenly distributed, giving the characteristic sparkling silver appearance; the legs may be very slightly shaded with the tipping, but the chin, ear tufts, stomach and chest must be pure white; any tabby marking or brown or cream tinge is a drawback. The tip of the nose should be brick red, and the visible skin on eyelids and the pads should be black or dark brown.'

Originally the eye colour of the Chinchilla

Drawing by Steinlen: A cat playing
with a ball of wool

Mimile, Pierre Blanchar's tabby,
had her own way of opening doors

was not specified, and the brown eye colours were permissible. But now they must be an emerald or blue-green colour. The bone structure can be finer than in most cobby long-haired cats. Many think this suits the cat's delicate appearance.

Kittens are often born with ringed tails, but this marking usually disappears. More worrying to breeders are kittens with heavily barred legs. If these have not disappeared by the age of ten weeks, they are unlikely ever to disappear completely.

SHORT-HAIRED CATS

It is among the pedigree short-haired cats that the difference between the foreign and the European body types shows up most clearly. The type of the short-haired cat has been much less radically altered by the process of artificial breeding than is the case in long-haired cats. Indeed many people still think of the pedigree British short-haired cat as basically just a common-or-garden sort of cat such as can be found roaming the streets and countryside, or sitting beside their fire.

We do not really know the origin of the domestic cat in Britain, though the most likely theory is that it was brought in by the Romans. There are those who think that because of its scarcity in early times it must have mated with the stocky wild cat then so widespread (though this is not my opinion). What is certain is that by now its body-type is quite different from that of the slim, delicate Siamese, Russian or Abyssinian breeds brought to Europe in comparatively recent times. It does not have their delicacy of structure, long flowing lines, narrow head with large pointed ears or whip-like tail.

The body of the British short-haired cat should be medium in length but strongly constructed and neat in appearance. Essentially it is a sturdy cat, but well-proportioned. The fore and hind legs are of equal length, and the feet are neat and round. The chest is broad and strong. The head is round, the top of the skull being rounded and the ears set wide apart. These latter should be small, even at the base, and definitely rounded at the tip. The eyes are set wide apart, too. The cheeks are wide and well-developed, tapering slightly towards the chin. The nose is short. The tail is medium in length and tapers towards the tip.

The coat should be really short and dense. The fur is often described as 'hard', but what is meant is that it should not be woolly. The hairs should, in fact, be fine.

In the opinion of many people these British short-haired cats are unusually intelligent and responsive in character.

The points system is similar for the various breeds: 50 points are allocated for type, coat and condition; the other 50 relate to the colouring and the eyes.

SELF-COLOURED
SHORT-HAIRED CATS

Four self-coloured short-haired breeds have achieved recognition and a standard from the Governing Council of the Cat Fancy in Britain: black, white, blue and cream. Red is absent. Two breeds of white are recognized: one with blue eyes and one with orange eyes.

To breed an absolutely pure black cat is as difficult for the short-hairs as it is for the long-hairs. It is even more difficult to achieve the standard in that the eyes must be deep copper or orange. Not a trace of green is allowed.

Short-haired blue-eyed Whites are as afflicted by deafness as similar long-haired cats. Though if there should be merely one or two black hairs on the cat's head, deafness is unlikely. The standard requires that the eyes be a 'very deep sapphire blue'. The Short-haired White with orange eyes has only recently been recognized as a breed.

Short-haired Creams are another new breed and still very rare. The main difficulty is to achieve a rich cream that is not too hot in colour. But as the cats are bred like to like, and move further from their Tortoiseshell origin, this fault is likely to disappear. They should have copper or hazel eyes.

SHORT-HAIRED TABBIES

Three of these breeds are recognized in Britain: the Silver, the Red and the Brown. The Short-haired Silver Tabby is the most popular and should have dense black markings on a pure, clear silver ground. The eyes can be green or hazel. The Short-haired Red Tabby is very difficult to breed. The ground colour should be a really rich red, and the markings of an even denser and richer red. This colouring is quite different from that of the common 'ginger' cat which is a much paler orange shade. The most common fault in this breed is the appearance of white on the neck, chest, underside or tip of the tail. The eyes can be hazel or orange. The Short-haired Brown Tabby should be a rich sable or brown in ground colour with very dense black markings. The most prevalent fault is the appearance of odd white hairs in the coat. The eyes can be orange, hazel, deep yellow or green, a fact which probably reflects how few in number are the pedigree cats of this breed. With all these Tabby breeds the clarity of the markings in conformity with the required tabby pattern is of considerable importance when points are allocated in shows.

MULTI-COLOURED
SHORT-HAIRED CATS

There are not as many of these among the short-haired breeds as there are among the long-haired. But the Blue-cream, Tortoiseshell and Tortoiseshell-and-white have achieved recognition. The Short-haired Blue-cream is one of the latest varieties. Its colouring should be produced by a soft,

*Examining the situation in order to
arrive at an adequate solution*

even intermingling of the blue and cream hairs, exactly as in its long-haired counterpart. A wide variety of eye colours are permissible, perhaps because of the newness of the breed. Copper, orange or yellow are acceptable, but not green. The Short-haired Tortoiseshell and Tortoiseshell-and-white again have the same coat colour as the similar long-haired breeds. The eyes may be orange, copper or hazel in colour. There is the same absence of males in these two breeds as in the long-haired ones.

SHORT-HAIRED BLUE CATS

In this category we find a trio of blue cats: the Blue British, the Russian Blue and the Chartreux. Their geographical origins could hardly be more different. The Blue British has been bred from the domestic cats by now native to the island. There is a story that the French breed, the Chartreux, was brought from South Africa to France by the Carthusian monks (whose first monastery was La Grande Chartreuse). In 1756, however, Buffon already indicated it as an ancient breed in his *Histoire Naturelle*. The Russian Blues are said to have been brought to Britain from Russia on cargo boats trading between Archangel and Britain. Indeed they were originally called Archangel cats. The body-types of these three breeds are as different as their origins. Cross-breeding between these different types to improve coat colour is ill-advised as one risks spoiling the type.

THE BLUE BRITISH

This is the most popular of the British short-haired breeds and has the true sturdy neat medium body-build of this type. The standard requires a coat of 'light to medium blue, very level in colour and no tabby markings or shadings or white anywhere.' The eyes should be large and full, copper, orange or yellow.

THE CHARTREUX

The Chartreux is a cat of rural France. I has a stockier body line than the British Blue. It stands solidly on comparatively short, well-muscled legs. Its head is round but set on a thick-set neck and having really full cheeks. It has a very powerful jaw temptingly reminiscent of that of the European wild cat. Its ears are of medium size and set high on the rounded skull. Its fur is woollier than that of any breed described so far. Its colour can be any shade of greyish blue, though the preference is for the pale

*Although a cat of no particular breed,
its line is not without nobility*

*A rare European variety : the Red
with hazel eyes*

*The Chartreux : a French breed, not
to be confused with the Blue British
or the Russian Blue*

colours. The standards are as rigorous as
those for the Blue British in forbidding any
markings or white hairs in the coat. The
eyes must be orange or golden yellow.

THE RUSSIAN BLUE

The body line of the Russian Blue recalls
that of the ancient Egyptian cat. It has the
typical 'foreign' body type, to quote the
standards: 'long, lithe, graceful in outline,
fine in bone and light in build'. The straight,
tapering tail is long in proportion to the body.
The legs should be long and slender, too,
with the hind legs longer than the front ones.
The skull is flat and narrow, the forehead
receding. The face and neck are long, and
the ears should be large and pointed, wide
at the base and set vertically to the head and
should not be thickly furred. The eyes
should be typically oriental or almond-
shaped, and set rather wide apart. They
should be a vivid green in colour. The coat
should be particularly short, and should be
dense and close-lying. The Scandinavian
countries have produced the best 'plush-
like' coats. A medium to dark shade of blue
is required, with the typical clear lustrous
sheen. Bad breeding methods have introduced tabby and other markings, and spoiled
the texture also of the coat of this once pure
breed. This has been caused by the lack in
Britain of Russian Blues for like-to-like
breeding. The Russian Blue is said to be a
strangely silent cat, though perfectly friendly
in character.

MANX CATS

These are the famous tailless cats from the
Isle of Man. The breed is slowly increasing
in popularity throughout the world, and
recently the Isle of Man Cat Association
was formed. There are many legends as to
their origin.

On the Isle of Man itself there are various
traditions as to how these cats reached the
island from shipwrecked boats. According

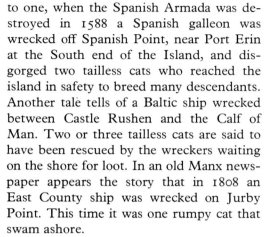

The Chartreux has an almost comic rotundity

The type of the Chartreux has changed since Buffon's time

to one, when the Spanish Armada was destroyed in 1588 a Spanish galleon was wrecked off Spanish Point, near Port Erin at the South end of the Island, and disgorged two tailless cats who reached the island in safety to breed many descendants. Another tale tells of a Baltic ship wrecked between Castle Rushen and the Calf of Man. Two or three tailless cats are said to have been rescued by the wreckers waiting on the shore for loot. In an old Manx newspaper appears the story that in 1808 an East County ship was wrecked on Jurby Point. This time it was one rumpy cat that swam ashore.

Perhaps the least likely tale is the one which credits the Manx cat with being the last of the animals to enter the Ark. Noah, in a hurry because the waters were rising, shut the door on its tail.

What was the origin of this tailless cat? In spite of the theory of the Ark, there is certainly no question here of some mutilation, accidental or surgical, being passed on; rather it is a case of a natural mutation being fixed. And as the attempt to breed Manxes like-to-like over many generations results eventually in litters where many of the kittens die, sometimes even before birth, it is possible that taillessness is genetically allied to some lethal factor in the make-up of the cat.

It is claimed that rumpy cats were once widespread in Cornwall. There have always been Siamese with truncated or atrophied tails. There are numerous varieties of tailless cats in the Malay Archipelago. And a great many cats without tails appear in Japanese paintings.

Auguste Pavie, the explorer, thought that the Manx was related to the Annamite cat; a small, graceful cat with a very small tail. These are believed to have been introduced into the East Indies from Britain by eighteenth-century trading expeditions.

Wherever these cats came from, the question remains: why is there no evidence of their race anywhere else?

Whatever their origin, the Manx is established as a breed. It should be a true tailless cat, having no stump, however vestigial. Instead there should be a distinct hollow at the end of the spine. Ideally, the hindquarters or rump should be 'as round as an orange' the standards state. The back should be short, the flanks deep and, very important, the hind-legs should be much higher than the fore-legs. This gives the Manx its characteristic hopping gait, described as 'rabbitty'. Less important points are that the head should be round and large, but with a longish nose. The cheeks should be very prominent. Snipiness is a bad fault. The ears should be rather wide at the base, tapering slightly off to a point. A very important point is that the coat should be, as the standard states: '"double", soft and open like that of the rabbit, with a soft, thick undercoat'. The prevalence of 'rabbitty' characteristics in the Manx have led to improbable theories as to its origin being the result of a cross between a rabbit and a cat. Any coat or eye colour are allowed in Manxes, and are only taken into consideration by judges when all other points are equal. When this happens the eye colour should relate to the coat colour according to the general rules for British cats.

Breeding Manxes is indeed difficult enough without being complicated by requirements of colour and coat. Cross-breeding being necessary much of the time, the best method is probably to interbreed with a stumpy or imperfect Manx. Even when two perfectly tailless Manxes are mated, the resulting litter may contain a complete mixture of tailless kittens and kittens with any variety of short or stumpy tails. Litters produced by mating these vestigially-tailed stumpy cats with pure Manxes are

*Much has been written about the
origin of the tailless cats of the
Isle of Man*

much healthier than those bred from purely
tailless parents.

BALD CATS

This breed of cats without fur has been
resurrected by Professor Étienne Letard of
the École Nationale Vétérinaire d'Alfort.
There are a few examples in Europe and
America.

These cats are not born completely bald.
The kittens have very light hairs which are
scarcely thickened by the growth of a slight
down during the first two months. After
the kittens are weaned, this inadequate fur
falls away. From then on they are completely
smooth. Sensitive to cold, thin, unaesthetic
and not much admired by cat-lovers, these
bald cats have only a technical interest. They
are a flirtation for the specialist. The mutation has been fixed, but the breeding of bald
cats hardly seems to have a great future.

THE REX

Another novelty breed is that of the curly-
haired cat, or the 'poodle' cat, as it is sometimes commonly called. These have been
artificially bred, and are still rare.

The coat is even shorter than in short-
haired cats. There is no undercoat and the
guard-hairs are shorter than the middle
coat and do not show. The middle coat,
however, is not only wavy but very dense
and particularly fine and silky. There seem
to be two types of coats according to the
body type of the cat. Those with a foreign
type have thinner but more curly coats.
Where the type is like that of the British
short-haired cat the coat is thicker and wavy.
But Rex hair can be introduced into any
breed including Persians. The kittens are
born with curly hair from the start. Even
the whiskers in a Rex are wavy. They are
said to be affectionate, intelligent and not at
all delicate, and unusually easy to train; in
other words, they would make excellent pets.

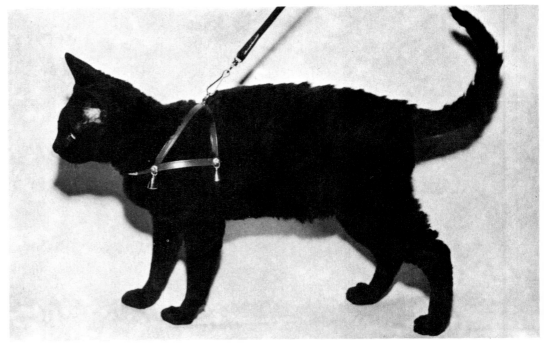

THE ABYSSINIAN

Today the Abyssinian is far more popular in the United States than in Britain, though it only appeared there in the nineteen-thirties. The first Abyssinian on record was brought into England in 1869 by a Mrs Lennard, wife of an officer who served in the Abyssinian war. But it is not a cat native to Abyssinia. It can only be said that it must have originated somewhere in Africa. It was first shown at the Crystal Palace in about 1883, and the Abyssinian Cat Club was founded in England in 1926.

The type in Abyssinian is essentially foreign. Its silhouette is that of the ancient cats of Egypt. It is fine in bone structure and has the long lean flowing body line. The body should never be too large in size or coarse looking. Its head is not quite as long as that of the Siamese, nor are its ears quite as large, though they are equally pointed at the tip. Too large ears would be dispro-

portionate. The tail, compared with the Siamese, is only fairly long, but again it must taper to the tip.

The coat of the Abyssinian is unique. The individual hairs, according to the standard, should be 'Ruddy brown, ticked with black or dark brown, double or treble ticking (i.e. two or three bands of colour on each hair) preferable to single ticking'. This ticked coat is reminiscent of a hare's. The main difficulty for breeders is to eradicate the white chin that often appears. Even in better specimens the chin is sometimes too pale in colour. An even worse fault is the appearance of one or more white bands across the chest, or even white markings on the underside. As always, it is extremely difficult to breed out white markings once they become established. Because of cross-breeding made inevitable by the scarcity of Abyssinians in Britain, tabby markings such as bars on the legs or even ringing of the tail have been introduced into the breed. These

The Abyssinian, with its calm and steady character, is nevertheless audacious, too

are bad faults. The only marking permitted is a dark spine line. The standard requires that 'inside forelegs and belly should be of a tint to harmonize well with the main colour, the preference being given to orange-brown'. The coat should be short, fine and close. The pads in the Abyssinian should be black, and this colour should extend up the back of the hind legs. The eyes should be large, bright and expressive, either green, yellow or hazel.

There also exists a breed of Red Abyssinian whose body colour is the rich copper red correctly called 'rufous'. The ticking should be in darker colours that contrast with the main red colour. The underside and the inside of the legs should be a harmonizing deep apricot colour. The tip of the tail, however, is dark brown, and this colour can continue on up the tail as a line. There should be dark brown colouring round the pads, and this should extend up the back of the hind legs, while the pads

themselves and the nose should be pink.

Abyssinians are unusual cats in character. They demand affection and companionship from humans. They actively seek it out. They continue to play when they are no longer kittens. They make much use of their paws, and often inspect objects with these rather than using, as is normal with cats, their noses. Indeed, they are very active generally and need freedom. They should probably not be kept in restricted quarters. They are unfortunately the most susceptible of all breeds to disease.

SOCIETIES FOR CAT-LOVERS

There exist today throughout the world many societies whose aim is to gather together those who are interested in breeding cats. These societies and federations of societies exist at both the national and the international level and their affiliations

ramify across the globe. Here is a typical statement of the principles: 'To assure the amelioration and the reconstitution of the breeds of cats, to patronize or organize public shows, to establish rules, to nominate specialist judges, to study perfect specimens of the various breeds with a view to elaborating for each breed an official standard, the registration of pedigree cats, etc.' The number of such societies in existence at the moment is enormous, and here are some:

THE UNITED STATES:
The Cat Fanciers Association, The Cat Fanciers Federation, The New York Empire Cat Club, The Lord Islaw Cat Club, The Hudson Valley Cat Club, etc.

ENGLAND:
The Governing Council of the Cat Fancy, The National Cat Club, The Midland Counties Cat Club, The Southern Counties Cat Club, The Croydon Cat Club, etc.

LA FÉDÉRATION INTER-NATIONALE FÉLINE D'EUROPE

A federation to which national societies such as the following belong: Austria: Klub den Katzenfreunde Osterreichs. Belgium: Cat Club de Bruxelles. Denmark: Landsforeningen af Danmarks Racekatterklubbar. Finland: Helsingin Rotukissayhdistys R.Y. France: Fédération Féline Française. Germany: Deutscher Edelkatzenzuchter Verband. Holland: Nederlandse Vereninning von Fokkers. Italy: Società Felina Italiana. Norway: Norsk Rase Katt Klubbar. Sweden: Sverak (Sveriges Rask Kattklubbars Riksforbund). Switzerland: Fédérations Félines Suisse et Helvétique Réunies.

SPECIALIST CAT CLUBS:

There are many societies devoted to special breeds such as the Siamese Cat Club of the U.S.A., The Special Tabbies and Torties Fanciers of Great Britain, and Le Cercle du Chat de Birmanie et Colourpoints of France.

Over the last twenty years it is undoubtedly in the United States that there has been the greatest and most rapid expansion in the breeding of pedigree cats. There is an American monthly illustrated magazine with more than forty pages of text entirely devoted to the subject of breeding cats. Everything that could be of use to catbreeders is there, including of course 'Wanted' and 'For Sale' details, reports on developments in breeding, and reviews of

ssinian kittens are particularly
tionate and remain attached to
mother longer than those of any
breed

books and various publications relating to the cat. Even poems have their place. In the 'Cats Show Calendar' details are given of the dates and places of shows that will take place in the following month; and there are never less than eighteen or twenty of these a month.

The first Cat Show was held in London at the Crystal Palace in 1871. The National Cat Club, Britain's premier cat club, was the first to be founded, in 1887. From this club, in 1910, today's Governing Council of the Cat Fancy was formed. Amongst the clubs affiliated to the 'Fancy' as it is called, the National Cat Club still has special rights. The Fancy organized the first show of its own in 1953 to celebrate the Coronation of Her Majesty Queen Elizabeth II. This Coronation Show was held in the Royal Horticultural Society's New Hall.

To the Governing Council of the Cat Fancy are affiliated many European Societies: The Cat Club of Paris, The Cat Club Vaudois (Switzerland), Felikat (Holland), both the J.Y.R.A.K. and the Racekatten (Denmark), Norsk Racekatten (Norway), La Société Royal Féline de Flanders, Svenska Kartklubben (Sweden). There is an association between the Fancy and La Fédération Internationale Féline d'Europe, or F.I.F.E. for short.

Those who are devoted to the interests of the science and art of breeding pedigree cats can only hope that international liaisons will become closer still. It is in the interests of the cat.

10 THE SIGN OF THE CAT

It is always to ancient Egypt that we must return in order to understand the many ideas that have become attached to the cat. We have already described the cat's remarkable rise from prehistoric obscurity to the status of a worshipped idol, but the question we have not asked is whether there was a difference between the cat and the sign of the cat—did the Egyptians make a distinction between the real animal and the symbolic totem?

To answer such a question we would have to undertake a thorough study of the religion of the ancient Egyptians. And even then we could never be sure about the thought processes of a civilization that was formed 'before philosophy'.

The worship of the cat seems less extraordinary if we remember that the primitive religion of Egypt was primarily an animistic nature worship. The spirits of nature were either life-giving, like the cat and the cow, or dangerous to life, like the crocodile and the cobra. The particular power of each totem was derived from the particular attributes of the animal. Amulets, carved in the shapes of these gods, were designed to give the wearer the attributes of the god. Thus, a woman who wore the cat amulet hoped to become fortunate in love, fashion and all things feminine.

But the cat also served the Egyptians as a symbol of life. In *The Book of the Dead* (written during the period of the New Empire: 1567–1085 BC) there is a drawing in which the cat, symbolizing the sun, is killing the serpent, representing darkness.

THE CAT IN HERALDRY

Perhaps the first cat in heraldry was the red cat that graced the arms of the *Felices seniores*, the most famous of the Roman legions. But, in general, domestic cats have not been as popular in heraldry as have the lions and the leopards. When they do appear, they are usually a play on the name of the family—such as Scotland's clan Chattan.

In the Middle Ages, as can be imagined, there were hardly any armorial bearings proudly displaying their nobility under the sign of the cat, so abhorred by the Church. But time passed and, towards 1530, a German tale, 'The Tower of the Cat' by Bertrand Walkliet, explained the presence of a black cat in a blazon that has today disappeared:

A powerful and important prince one day decided to build the highest tower in the world. He sent out appeals. The reward offered was appropriate; the weight in gold of the first battlement realized. The candidate, however, would pledge his life against the solidity of his work. A mason from the North presented himself to the prince, and said 'My Lord, for the weight of a battlement in gold I will construct you such a tower as no cathedral or royal fief has ever seen the like.'

The tower was soon complete. The top seemed to touch the high clouds, and those returning from the Holy Land compared the pyramids of Egypt to wretched molehills on seeing this proud work which seemed to be too marvellous to be anything but supernatural. Satisfied, the prince said, 'I will defy the thunderbolt, the Emperor and the world from the height of this tower.'

He then proceeded to his finance minister and told him to prepare the gold that had been promised to the mason. However, following some friendly advice, he decided first to consult his astrologer. Was the tower sound? 'It will be seen to fall as soon as the first storm brings the west wind,' claimed the astrologer.

Disturbed by this prediction, the prince decided to see the mason again. He found him rebuking his men for wanting to throw a black cat from the top of the tower. 'It is a wicked and vile action,' he cried at them. He had taken the cat under his arm and was just leaving when the prince, favourably impressed by this kindness, approached. 'Your gold is ready, friend', said the prince.

Sign drawn by A. Willette for the famous Montmartre cabaret Le Chat Noir *(The Black Cat)*

A money-box asking passers-by in London for contributions for the protection of cats

'But before I keep my promise I would like to see how your tower holds up to the first wind.' 'I will vouch for it with my head,' said the mason from the North. 'It is strong and will prove sound.'

In the month of October an appalling storm broke out. The prince, followed by all the court, immediately rushed to see how the structure would hold. They waited in vain through a whole day and part of the night. At dawn the tower still stood, and the courtiers left.

Naturally the most furious of them was the astrologer, who was now more decided than ever to bring about the downfall of the mason. When night came he went to the tower in secret with a keg of powder, lit the fuse and fled. Arriving at the palace, he thought fit to give the alarm to the prince. 'The tower is cracking!' he howled. 'The tower is swaying . . . the tower is going to fall!' Everyone ran to the windows to watch the spectacle, but the tower did not move. The prince was already bitterly reproaching the astrologer for having disturbed him for nothing when the mason appeared, his black cat under his arm and an extinguished fuse in his hand. He demanded justice, and told the following story: As he was sleeping tranquilly in his tower he was woken suddenly by the desperate miaowings of the cat.

Immediately he got up, discovered the incandescent fuse and had only just time to extinguish it and rescue the cat from its pain – for it too began to burn. Then he had discovered the keg of powder. It was a miracle that he had not been blown up with the tower. 'My Lord, give me the money', he said, 'and I will return home.'

The prince gave a cry. Slowly he looked over the witnesses to the scene. His gaze stopped on the astrologer whose palour had already betrayed him, and on the spot the latter confessed. He was hanged. The mason received his gold and, in addition, found himself awarded land and a title with a right to carry arms which displayed a tower and a cat.

The ancient dukes of Bourgogne placed the cat in their blazon, with this device: All by love, nothing by force. In the *Dictionnaire des figures héraldiques* by Th. de Renesse almost all the arms of France, Germany, Holland and Italy in which the cat appears are mentioned. There are not a hundred of them.

These are the arms bearing the heads of cats: the Dekater family have the head of a cat in silver on an azure ground. The Platen have two heads of cats facing each other. The Kater carry three heads.

Other arms carry a complete cat who,

according to its posture is said to be: *rampant* (standing in profile, on the left hind-leg), *effaré* (leaping), *assis* (sitting), *passant* (walking towards the dexter side, with tail and dexter fore-paw raised) or *hérissonné* (bristling, with its back raised higher than its head).

Among the arms which have interesting mottoes are those of Le Chat de Kersaint (a sable cat on silver) whose device is 'Mauvais chat, mauvais rat' (A bad cat, a bad rat) and those of the Catto family of Scotland, whose motto is 'Touche not gloveles'.

' Certain armorial bearings carry a cat holding an object. The Brockmann family have a cat sitting on a mound holding a mouse between its teeth. The Chazot have a cat knawing a bone. The Katte of Vicritz have a cat seated on a cushion stopping a mouse. Others that have this type of blazon are the Katte de Wust, the Katz de Kazenthal and the von der Katze.

Other armorial bearings present an extra-ordinary cat. The Chaffaux have a cat armed with a scythe in front of a house. The Chaurand have always had a silver cat accompanying the golden lion on their blazon.

The Dobekatz have a cat wearing a collar and leaping from the top of a rock. The di Gatti have a cat on a bridge beside a river. The Heigl have a cat with a woman's face wearing a bonnet. The Pachahamer have a cat with a human face wearing a pyramidal hat.

Other arms carry two cats. Those of the de la Chatardie de Paviers d'Angoumois have two silver cats and those of the Katzeler have two cats facing each other.

There are others who have three cats in their arms. The Adams have three cats on a ground of azure laid on ermine.

There are so many other families whose names seem more or less connected with that of the cat: Auchat, Chazot, Matoux, Mieulle, Miaule, Catta, Caton, Gatti, Gattoli, Gatellier, Katz, Katzen, Katlen, etc. If they all had blazons the cat would be as great a heraldic beast as the lion.

A lucky mascot on the bonnet of a car

Sign of the restaurant 'Mediterranée' in Paris

The cat brings a feeling of calm— even to a pin-ball machine

THE PRACTICAL CAT

Some of the old inn signs in France display the cat in a variety of strange roles. There is the sleeping cat, which will surprise no one. But there are also the cat turning the roast on the spit, the cat playing the hurdy-gurdy, or sometimes even the harp, the grinning cat and even a hunchback cat for an inn in Lille.

In England, in the village of Albrighton in Shropshire, an inn-sign claims 'The finest pastime under the sun—Is whipping the cat at Albrighton'. This sign commemorates a strange and very old custom according to which, every Mardi Gras, an unfortunate cat was whipped to death.

In Lyon an inn-sign *La Chatte Blanche* (The white cat) was put up in 1872. But it shows two cats adorned with earrings, in memory of two real cats who at one time paraded in a jewellers window wearing earrings.

One of the most famous Parisian signs is that of the 'Chat noir', the famous cabaret of Montmartre where the satirical spirit of this century first showed itself and Rodolphe Salis received the entire world. The independence of the 'Chat noir' was the cause of its success. Its sign displayed a cat with a goose in its mouth; the goose symbolized the bourgeoisie.

The cat had appeared as symbol of an entirely different order during the French Revolution. In 1793 Fabre d'Eglantine, wanting to commemorate the saints of the Roman calendar when it was to be replaced by the republican calendar, presented his colleagues with an animal calendar. This calendar, though welcomed with enthusiasm, had a short life. In it the pig took the place of Saint Catherine, the goat that of Saint Florent and the cow that of Saint Geneviève—the cat replacing Saint Félix!

In Japan the classic name of 'Neko' (which means both the male and female

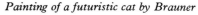

The cat appears on the seal of Sessa, Venetian printers

Painting of a futuristic cat by Brauner

*The cat as symbol of a double
personality by Pierre Corsey*

cat) is given to the geishas because, to charm their guests, these seductive young women play the 'shamisen', from which they extract tender miaowing sounds and which are partly made of real skins of cats.

THE CAT IN PHILATELY

The postage stamps of the different countries are symbolic authorities which carry to the four corners of the earth the portrait of a great man, or a celebrated monument or an image that draws attention to some national product.

The cat did not for long remain excluded from this honour. But it is surprising that the Sudan and Egypt, cradle of the domestic cat, have not thought of adopting it as their emblematic messenger in this field.

The Republic of Liberia presents a stamp showing a gilt cat, the *Felis aurata* or African Golden Cat. It is a small wild cat which is very similar in appearance to Temminck's golden cat, described in chapter one.

The upper parts of the body vary between a grey-brown colour and a chestnut red. Its stomach is flecked with dark spots which are denser towards the flanks. This African forest cat is found in the fringes of forests that extend from Guinea as far as the Congo.

The Republic of Cuba, on the occasion of the fiftieth anniversary of the Jeanette Ryder Foundation (1957), brought out a stamp with a picture of this famous animal protrectress seated with two dogs beside her and carrying a cat under her left arm. It is stamp number 458, 4 centavos.

In 1961 the Grand Duchy of Luxembourg issued a polychrome stamp (number 596, 150 F.) showing a striped cat with a reminder about animal protection.

Poland has, since 1964, been using ten very interesting polychrome stamps. These are admirably engraved and picture the cat at its most attractive. Number 1332 (30 groszy) represents a very beautiful black

cat with yellow eyes. Stamp number 1333 (40 groszy) shows the orangish-red face of a young cat desperately calling – perhaps for its mother. Number 1334 (50 groszy) depicts a classic Siamese with blue eyes. Number 1335 (60 groszy) represents a yellow and white alley cat with orange eyes. Number 1336 (90 groszy) is completely occupied by the head of a White Persian with gold eyes. Number 1337 (1·35 zloty) shows the head of an Orange Persian with gold eyes. Number 1338 (1·55 zloty) bears a picture of a grey striped kitten, scarcely a few weeks old, with a frightened look in its blue eyes. Number 1339 (2·50 zloty) shows a cat of no breed, a small tiger, beige striped with black, who appears to be following his own path and deigns to turn his head to see who has dared to challenge him. Number 1340 (3·40 zloty) is a gold-eyed Blue Persian, who fulfills all the standards for his breed. Number 1341 (6·50 zloty) is a lucky charm of a stamp showing a short-haired cat of the purest black with huge green eyes and a velvet tongue.

The Low Countries, in 1924, issued several stamps dedicated to animals. Number 793 honours the cat.

Spain issued an air-mail stamp (number 80, one peseta) which commemorated the famous flight of Lindberg. In the bottom right hand corner there is the silhouette of a cat.

Yugoslavia issued a very beautiful stamp on which the silhouette of a maroon cat stands out from a yellow ground. This is a stamp of ·30 dinar.

The Yemen, in a very artistic series (1–4B, 1–8B, and 1, 2 and 4B) popularizes the images of the Siamese, the Chartreux and the most representative Persians, such as the White, the Blue and the Orange.

Rumania has combined an exact knowledge of felines with a sense of humour in an attractive series (5, 10, 40, 55, 60, 75

The cat is often used as a philatelic messenger

bani and 1 lei 35, 3 lei 25). They are inspired by the complete range of feline psychology, from that of the royal Persians to the humblest stray cats.

This documentation of postal stamps has kindly and almost entirely been contributed by Dr Houdemer and Professor Bressou, and details completely the postal stamps currently dedicated to the cat. There are, in addition, some private stamps showing cats. For example, there is the famous stamp issued by the Danish Society for the Protection of Animals in which three seated cats and a crescent moon are engraved on a purple ground. This stamp (10 Bre Beskyt Dyrene) was presented in London by Mr Hans Hwass at a recent meeting of the national directors of the powerful and very active I.S.P.A. (International Society for the Protection of Animals). The stamp carries across five continents evidence of the affectionate interest that the various animal-loving groups in Scandinavia have always taken in cats.

MODERN SYMBOLS

In modern times the sign of the cat is everywhere. Where it once was carried in martial colours, it now appears in trademarks and commercial advertisements. Heraldry has given way to the brand label.

The cats on Christmas cards and other greeting cards bearing a message of good will are undoubtedly popular. It would be foolish for us to maintain that millions of cat calendars are sold because the cat is a good-luck symbol. Rather, it is the instant appeal of the cat that has turned it into a commercial success.

How did this remarkable change in taste occur? Why does this ancient god and medieval devil now have 'instant commercial appeal'?

The feline renaissance began in the nineteenth century. It was in the air. It was part of the general sentimentalism that followed in the wake of Romanticism. In England, more specifically, it was Queen Victoria's influence as much as anything else. Everyone knew that she doted on cats. It was during her reign that cats became an emblem of romantic cosiness. And today, if those cats on the calendars and greeting cards stand for anything at all, it is this same romantic cosiness.

But in other fields the sign of the cat has grown up and become more sophisticated. In publicity and advertising the cat is used more than any other animal. What other animal can be associated with so many of the qualities we look for in the products we buy? What other animal has charm, beauty and mystery, as well as cleanliness? More important still, what animal is so photogenic—especially when in motion for the television screen? In fact, no other animal could so successfully sell us beauty products, soap, detergents, cream, carpets, fuel, washing machines, cigarettes and shoe soles.

The cat is beginning to stand for so many things that one could almost say it was a symbol of life itself. So it was for Giacometti. A few days before his death he said on French television: 'If I knew that a cat was closed up behind a painting by Rembrandt and in danger of asphyxiation, I would not hesitate to destroy the canvas immediately to liberate the animal'. He was not indifferent or hostile to Rembrandt, but for him life had more value than art.

If the cat is not yet a symbol for life, it is certainly a symbol for the good, luxurious or plush life. There is no new form of comfort, no progress in the art of living that could not publicize itself to good advantage by drawing on the secret contentment of cats.

FASHION

Today cats are a popular subject for all sorts of ornaments, knicknacks, toys and jewellery. The naïve, big-eyed china cats of the Vic-

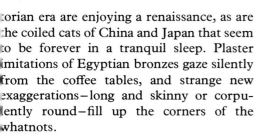

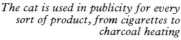
The cat is used in publicity for every sort of product, from cigarettes to charcoal heating

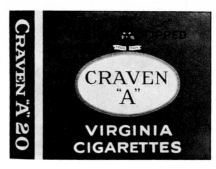
torian era are enjoying a renaissance, as are the coiled cats of China and Japan that seem to be forever in a tranquil sleep. Plaster imitations of Egyptian bronzes gaze silently from the coffee tables, and strange new exaggerations – long and skinny or corpulently round – fill up the corners of the whatnots.

In the sixteenth century Japanese craftsmen were already making hollow porcelain cats with empty eye sockets. When a tiny oil lamp was placed inside one of these figures, the cat took on a delightful transparency. The trembling flame, seen moving in the empty eyes, gave an animation that was more than enough to make the rats flee. Scientific progress has brought only superficial changes in this ingenious design. Today in Japan an electric cat miaows ten times a minute, and its eyes light up with each miaow.

In the bestiary of cuddly toys, it is possible to find a cat that miaows or cries out when its stomach is pressed. There are also cats that purr when lain on their sides. Rubber balls in the shape of cats heads are designed as toys for dogs.

Cats made their entrance into the world of jewellery when they were worn as amulets in ancient Egypt. Golden bracelets or collars were hung with dozens of kittens, symbols of maternity. But the content of the symbol has changed. What was yesterday an emblem of fecundity is today only a pretty bauble, signifying little more than a gentle affection. From the great jewellers of New York, London and Paris to the most popular merchants of costume jewellery, there exists a common tendency in the interpretation of the cat. The whiskers and eyes are emphasized, the body is represented by a single sleek line.

The ideal of feline beauty is not all that fashion has borrowed from the cat. It has not always been enough for women to strive for the slow graceful walk, the supple thighs,

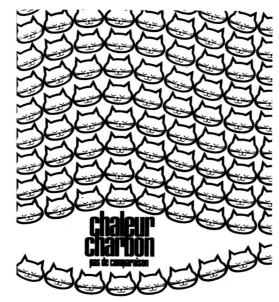

chaleur
charbon
pas de comparaison

UFF. PUBBL. ALBERTI

casa, dolce casa

Col suo aroma inconfondibile
e col suo lieto colore di sole
lo Strega completa
l'ospitalità della vostra casa
e la rende più intima,
più calda, più serena.

LiquoreStrega
delizioso digestivo

The cat can be a symbol of shoe
comfort or simply an emblem of
elegance

Sign of a hatter

the lengthened shape of the eye. They have also wrapped themselves in its skin.

Under Pericles the skins of cats were used for clothing, but, like shepherds' sheepskins, they were only made up into coarse jackets for servants. Later, perhaps from the shoulders of some rather too beautiful slave girls, the furs of cats passed to the shoulders of their mistresses, and a fashion was born.

In the Middle Ages shivering Europe clothed itself in all the skins possible. After ermine and marten, otter and cat brought the highest prices. Even during the strict reign of Charlemagne, women were so taken with the fur of otters and cats and spent such sums on them, that in the year 808 the Emperor decreed: 'It is forbidden, in all seasons and in all places, to sell the finest doublets of otter fur for more than 20 sols, or fur mantles of cat skin for more than 50 sols'.

This decree largely attained its end. From the end of the ninth century, there is no further mention of adornments of this kind.

But this wisdom was ephemeral. In the twelfth century fur made a come-back. The furrier came to be as much in demand as the jeweller. In order to meet the growing requirements, common pelts such as hare, dormouse and squirrel were discovered, and the wild cat was savagely hunted down. The domestic cat, with fur either long and silky or short and close-packed, also paid a heavy price. It took a top place in the fur industry of the world.

Since then, sheared or not, the strong fine skin of the cat, after being properly dyed and treated, is so well worked over for the market that it can be mistaken for ocelot, and even white fox!

In England, where cat-lovers shudder at the thought of wearing their pets' pelts, it has long been the practice to spin and weave the hairs of cat and rabbit in with wool, cotton or silk.

11 FRIENDS AND ENEMIES OF THE CAT

Between the domestication of the dog and the domestication of the cat, the time that passed was a hundred times greater than the time that passed between the invention of the wheel and the invention of the supersonic plane. But the distance which separates the cat from the dog in the heart and mind of man is not solely a matter of chronology.

From the dogs of the caves or the peat-bogs to the warlike watchdogs of the Assyrians and the languid greyhounds of the Orient, the dog has never ceased to advance in human society.

As hunting became organized it grew to be the passion of princes, and dogs became associated with this intoxicating pastime. Men opened to their favourite bloodhounds the doors to both their castles and their hearts. This was the dog's first step from a status of service to the status of friend. Today the dog is completely at home under the roof and as the companion of man.

This book has told the history of the cat, and a very different one it is. Humiliated, misunderstood, for centuries subject to attack in Europe, it has not yet ceased to jump at the sound of our voices and fly in terror before our shadows. How could they have confidence in us, or the reliability of our friendship? Why and how is it that some humans love cats while others detest them?

THE HOSTILE ONES
Happily, the enemies are fewer than the friends. Of the enemies, there have been those who, without much consideration, turned against cats and those who conscientiously tried to understand and define their aversion.

Julius Caesar held them in horror. But then the Romans never understood the cat.

Ambroise Paré, the surgeon who looked after Henri III of France towards the end of the King's life, was notorious for his

antipathy to cats. For him everything about the cat was danger, poison and dirt. Was Henri influenced by him in his attitude towards cats? If not, then why did this gentle king, like his brother Charles IX, completely lose consciousness even at the sight of a cat?

Ronsard, so alive and so gentle, shared this type of physical repulsion: 'I hate their eyes, their forehead and their gaze – Seeing them I fly elsewhere – Trembling in nerve, in vein and limb – Never will cat come into my room.'

Abdülhamid, grand sultan of Turkey at the end of the eighteenth century, felt a real terror of cats. And against this type of inexplicable reaction there is in fact no question of calling up the resources of courage.

Voltaire, who so often set himself up as the apostle of tolerance, had only feeble arguments with which to oppose the grace of the cat. 'How,' he ironically exclaimed, 'can we be interested in an animal who did not know how to achieve a place in the night sky, where all the animals scintillate, from the bears and the dogs to the lion, the bull, the ram and the fish!'

The French zoologist Georges Cuvier (1796–1832) dedicated lengthy pages to cats, but they were characterized more by his mediocrity as a writer than his skill as a scientist. He saw them as 'mistrustful and savage' and ends his very partial description this way: 'Cats among themselves judge each other exactly as we judge them'.

Buffon attacked in turn. 'The cat is a faithless domestic animal that we only keep from necessity in order to use it against another even more inconvenient enemy that we do not wish to keep at all. . . .' Throughout this tirade, we are taught that the cat is a rascal, a thief, a dissimulator, 'who does not look straight and appears to have feelings only for himself, loves only conditionally and only enters into relations (with people) in order to abuse them'.

The portrait of the cat belonging to Mademoiselle Dupuy, who left in her will 15 francs a month for her cat

*An anonymous engraving of 1420 :
a cat seems to be teaching its young
the sport of mice-catching*

*The tomb of the cat belonging to the
Marquise du Deffand. The cat died
in 1707*

*Richard Whittington, Lord Mayor of
London, who owes a great deal of his
popularity to his cat*

ALLERGIES AND PHOBIAS

Two great leaders of men were quite overwhelmed by cats: Napoleon and Lord F. S. Roberts. They made no mystery of the matter. The great English Field-Marshall, who defeated the Boers, couldn't breathe if a cat merely entered a room or was found hidden there. And Napoleon's feelings are well-known. He loved dogs but broke into a cold sweat at even the sight of a kitten.

Are we today any better informed on this strange phenomenon? We have at least given it names. When fear of cats becomes morbid and is accompanied by symptoms of hysteria such as severe emotional disturbance, paleness, profuse sweating, nausea and sometimes even fainting, we call the condition aelurophobia. There are, however, those unfortunate souls who may like cats very much, but are allergic to them. Allergies are not at all well understood, but it is clear that some do relate to psychological factors, and some do not. To give a name to these reactions is not necessarily to understand them.

POPES AND CARDINALS

As well as this negative reaction, there also undoubtedly exists a natural affinity for cats. Is this affinity a purely physico-chemical phenomenon? Is it an emotional or aesthetic response? Is it made up of something of all these? We do not know. But what we are certain of is that it exists. Whoever loves cats loves them neither by reason nor by education nor by choice. Whoever loves them does so from instinct, and never by halves.

The true friends of the cat are legion, to such an extent that it is impossible to know where to start, even when we confine ourselves only to the famous.

First let us do justice to the Church. She has not always systematically dishonoured the cat as a demon. In the Museum of Saint-Germain-en-Laye in northern France there is a stone altar sculptured with cats at which baptisms were celebrated between the end of the eleventh century and the beginning of the twelfth.

A great many of the princes of the Church have loved cats. Was the first among these Gregory the Great (Pope from 590 to 604) or Gregory III (Pope from 731 to 741)? Tradition has it that each of these, renouncing all his worldly possessions, kept as his only friend and sole wealth one small cat.

Another pope who was fond of cats was Leo XIII, whose favourite companion was his tabby 'Micetto'. This obscure kitten, born in the Vatican, was tenderly brought up by His Holiness and lived in a fold of his robes. Chateaubriand, who adopted this cat, told his history. It is believed that his stuffed skin is preserved in the chateau of Combourg, where Chateaubriand lived during part of his youth. Finally, the Abbé Gautier recalls that Saint Philip Neri loved his female cat very dearly; and it is said to be due to the tomcat of the worthy Pope Pius VII, brought from Rome to Paris after the conclave of 1800, that the sixth arrondissement of Paris is so heavily populated with cats.

The gentle affection of Thomas Wolsey (1471–1530) for his cat was famous throughout England. She was present in his arms throughout the most important audiences, reigned on high in his cathedral, and was present at all his meals. This illustrious cat enjoyed such prerogatives that the Envoy Extraordinary of Venice noted in his memoirs: 'Certainly nothing like it has been seen since Caligula. . . .'

In France it was Richelieu, another great cardinal and minister, who imposed cats on the public. He installed dozens of cats at the court, first to the horror of the courtiers, but then to the great joy of the ladies. There

Sir Walter Scott loved to have the company of his cat while working

Richelieu installed his cats at the Court of France

was 'Lucifer', a beautiful jet black Angora, the very discreet 'Gazette'; 'Soumise', who shared his master's couch, 'Pyrame' and 'Thisbe'; 'Rubis' who purred like a pot of boiling water, 'Rita', who curled herself up on all the edicts and decrees and many others, including 'Perruque' and 'Racan', so named because their mother had given birth to them in the wig of the Marquis de Racan, a poet of doubtful merit.

We know more about Richelieu and his celebrated cats than we do about any other part of his sentimental life. Each morning, almost as soon as the Cardinal opened his eyes, and particularly when he was unwell, a handful of kittens was brought to play on his bed. His other cats, male and female, gambolled about together in a neighbouring room, under the charge of two gentlemen selected for the purpose, Abel and Teyssadier. Between 1624 and 1642 the door to advancement was open to whoever offered the minister the most playful kittens or the most caressable cats.

Sometimes this indulgence was mildly abused. Old Mlle de Gournay applied for a pension and the cardinal granted her two hundred crowns. The Abbé de Boisrobert pointed out that this was rather puny, and

so Richelieu added on another fifty *livres*. The abbé was then constrained to remark that something would also have to be done for Mamie Paillon. 'Mamie Paillon?' 'Yes, my lord. She's a cat, and a rather delicate animal.' 'Then let's add another twenty *livres*,' laughed the cardinal. Boisrobert still hesitated. 'The thing is ... Mamie Paillon has some kittens.' 'Kittens? All right. You shall have another *pistole* for each of them.'

Before dying, Richelieu made generous provisions in favour of his protégés. His cattery at that time still contained fourteen animals. A privileged few were to enjoy throughout their lives an income of twenty *livres*; the others were to have a right to ten, and two guardians were to be paid to provide them with care and comfort until such time as they rendered up their souls. Alas for the cats of the terrible Cardinal, they did not live to enjoy his bequests. Marguerite Yerta-Mellera has told how one evening the doors of the cattery yielded to the pressure of the drums of the Swiss regiments, and a massacre took place to the echoes of the screeching of cats and the laughter of men. The affair drew to a close with a monstrous stew at the inn of the 'Boudin généreux' in the Rue des Poulies.

HEADS OF STATE AND MINISTERS

From Richelieu another French minister took up the cause. Louis XIV's finance minister, Colbert, was, for utilitarian reasons at least, a friend of cats, too: he ordered that three or four efficient toms must be kept on every ship.

Under Louis XV cats had the freedom of the city because the Queen, Marie Leczinska, loved them. At first indifferent, Louis XV probably became interested in cats to please the Queen. Each morning he would welcome a big white cat into his bedroom.

One day while the Duc de Noailles, with his forehead pressed to the window pane, was watching the rain pour down on Versailles, the king slipped up noiselessly behind him, grabbed him by the neck with his hand and, at the same time, quite as violently gave a resounding furious miaow of rage. The unhappy Duc de Noialles was so completely terrified, thinking himself attacked by one of those toms that frightened him more than anything else, that he fell rigid to the ground. Was it a heart attack? It proved so difficult to rouse him from his faint that Her Majesty, stricken, believed it was the end.

Detail from a painting of Marie-Josephe de Saxe, the Duke of Bourgogne and their cat. During the eighteenth century cats had an honourable place at the French Court (painting by La Tour)

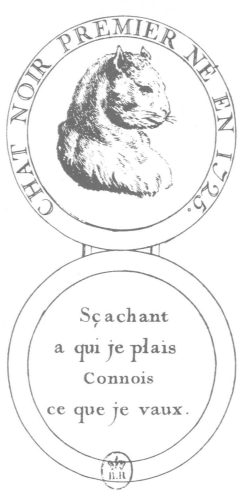

CHAT NOIR PREMIER NÉ EN 1725.

Sçachant
a qui je plais
Connois
ce que je vaux.

Medal with the inscription: 'Black Cat I, born in 1725'. This medal dates from the reign of Louis XV

However much of a mocker he may have been, would Louis have amused himself with this practical joke if the interest which the queen had for her pet cats had not aroused a passing sympathy in her husband?

Indulgent and good as she was, the gentle Marie Leczinska did not allow the slightest infringement of etiquette. Now this etiquette forbade leaving the slightest object on any of the seats in the Queen's bedroom. One day a haughty and irritable duchess placed her pelisse on one of the stools which were lined up beside the bed. A servant came in, saw the cloak – which was lined with white satin and trimmed with fur – and immediately took it into the antechamber.

One of the Queen's cats passed by. Cats, as we know, love satin and warm fur. He found the material to his liking, voluptuously rolled on it, tore it, and finally forgot himself to such a degree that the satin was irrevocably spoilt. The duchess returned, discovered the damage, tore the cloak from the hands of the valet who offered it to her

and, red with anger, went to find the queen.

'Look, Madame, at the impertinence of your 'people'! They have thrown my cloak on to a bench in the antechamber where your Majesty's cat has made this of it!'

Marie Leczinska did not flinch. She replied in a calm tone: 'You must know, madame, that you have "people", but I do not. I have "officers" of my bedchamber who have bought with their charge the great honour of serving me. They are men who have been well brought up, and they are not ignorant of the fact that, chosen from among the greatest ladies of the realm, you should have been accompanied by an equerry, or at least by a *valet de chambre* who would receive your cloak from you; and that in observing the forms proper to one of your rank you would not have been exposed to seeing your possession thrown on to antechamber benches. *A vous revoir!*'

Of the cat there had been no mention, but for the duchess this was disgrace. One could not with impunity accuse the favourites of Marie Leczinska.

A century later, Queen Victoria was to become the protectress of the cat as pet. After her death 'White Heather', the white cat who had been first in the Queen's favours, was piously taken in by all the royal family. Surrounded by English solicitude, White Heather lived to a ripe old age in Buckingham Palace and died sincerely regretted by Edward VII.

There will be fewer kings in the future. But the leaders of democracy, too, have found in the cat that silence which can be a refuge and that discreet unwearying presence that is true friendship.

One winter's evening during the American Civil War, Abraham Lincoln discovered in General Grant's camp three small cats paralysed with cold, and he adopted them.

In France, Georges Clémenceau, known himself as the 'Tiger', shared the passion for feline friendship. A year after the First World War he fell for the charms of a beautiful Blue Persian. She was brought from London in great secrecy; and 'Prudence' (by 'Nicholas Nickelby' and out of 'Sally Brass', as they say of horses) was, with his ginger-coloured Skye Terrier, among the most beloved and familiar friends of the President.

It was with 'Gri-Gri', the Siamese of the French statesman Raymond Poincaré (whom he spoke of as 'intelligent as any man') that these *café-au-lait* cats from the Far East conquered the French Republic and those who served her. Leon Blum, France's first socialist premier, would have no other breed. And on the morning when his wife entered a Paris clinic for an urgent operation, he suffered a double anxiety because his Siamese cat slipped from a piece of furniture and fractured a femur.

Lord Chesterfield left a pension to his cat. Winston Churchill was so attached to his ginger tom that through the worst of the London blitz he insisted on personally taking him to a safe place. This cat also sat

'Nemo' is a member of the Harold Wilson family

The official burial of a Whitehall cat in the cemetery for cats in London

Cemetery for cats and dogs in Paris

NANOU

in on many wartime cabinet meetings.

Theodore Roosevelt loved at least two cats–Tom Quartz and Slippers. 'Slippers' was a grey cat with six toes who roamed about a great deal, but always knew when it was time to put in an appearance at a big diplomatic dinner. On one historic occasion the entire impressive procession of ambassadors, plenipotentiaries and ministers had to be rerouted around the centre of the carpet– where Slippers was rolling luxuriously.

Harold Wilson is attached to his Siamese 'Nemo', and several members of his cabinet (including Douglas Jay and Anthony Greenwood) are also dedicated to their cats. These are privileged cats. These are the lucky cats who roused the envy of that Italian Ambassador who, when asked, 'What would you like to be later, if you were allowed to live your life over again?' replied: 'I would like to be a cat in London ... or a cardinal in my country!' But this diplomat seems to have forgotten that Mussolini loved cats like an Englishman. And that Lenin (for cats have no political leanings) never felt so inclined

to meditate on the happiness of men as when he had a cat on his knees.

INTELLECTUALS, WRITERS AND ARTISTS

Cats are the natural companions of intellectuals. They are the silent watchers of dreams, inspiration and patient research.

Louis Pasteur had only indulgence for his favourite cat. Einstein appreciated the worth of this companion of his most exultant moments, when the turmoil of his ideas swept him out of daily life to lead him to the edges of the Infinite. Doctor Schweitzer knew only two precious ways in which to take refuge momentarily from human misery: his piano and the childish playing of his cats.

Ingres was always a lover of cats. One New Year's Day, when he was a director of the Ecole de France in Rome, he was preparing to present himself to the Prince Borghese when a distracted servant came to tell him that 'Patrocle', his favourite cat, had suddenly died. Ingres was so over-

chat mean

whelmed by the news that, tearing off his cravat and coats, he ran and shut himself into his bedroom. Throughout the whole of that first day of the year he cancelled all calls and receptions in order to weep his fill for the loss of his dear friend.

However, it is in the world of letters that the cat seems to have found the greatest number of defenders. After the death of Laura – the lady who dominated his poetry – Petrarch surrounded with concern and solicitude that poor cat of no breed that his friend had confided to him. Its skeleton is still preserved in the town of Padua.

It was only with the beginning of the sixteenth century that writers began to welcome as friends, openly and without embarrassment, the first few representatives of the abhorred race of cats. Joachim du Bellay (1522–1560) was the first to write in their praise. His attitude to his own '*Gris argentin petit Belaud*' (Silver grey little Belaud) was all tenderness and indulgence. Belaud slept in his master's bed and ate at his master's table. When he died, du Bellay did not hide his grief. The poem he wrote as a testament to his cat is two hundred verses long, and in it he says:

For three days now I have lost
my well-being, my pleasure, all my love,
My heart is almost breaking in me
When I speak or when I write
For Belaud my small grey cat
Belaud who was, by chance,
Nature's most beautiful work
Thus made, as cats are made,
Belaud whose beauty was such
That she is worthy to be immortal.

Montaigne was not content merely to admire the grace of his cat, 'Madame Vanité'. Once he had gained her friendship, he wanted to know her soul. It is possible to claim that the author of the *Essais* was the first, and perhaps the only man of his

period, to advance into feline psychology, persuaded as he was that 'cats communicate amongst themselves, and quite certainly reason. . . .'

The eighteenth century saw the triumph of philosophy. Did it contribute to the reinstatement of that cat that the seventeenth century seems to have disdained? The cat was certainly not chased out of the house, indeed it made its way from the cellars to the kitchens, and from the kitchens to the salon.

One of the eighteenth century's greatest figures, Samuel Johnson, loved cats to the point of madness. When his cat 'Hodge' began to show signs of growing old, Dr Johnson decreed that his only food from then on was to be oysters! And from that day, in order not to inconvenience his servants, Johnson (who had heartily mocked Horace Walpole because the latter had said of his cat 'Selima' that she was a nymph) went himself each morning during the winter to buy fresh oysters, opened them personally and offered them one by one to his cat.

Besides La Rochefoucauld, Crébillon, Jean-Jacques Rousseau and Montesquieu, there was the hypersensitive Abbé Galliani, who said: 'It's a good thing my cat was found this morning. Otherwise I would have hanged myself .

Another good friend, to whom cats of many generations owe a great deal, was Auguste Paradis de Moncrif. In 1727 this hitherto somewhat obscure author wrote a book entitled 'Les Chats', which swept him immediately to the fore. From that day he was known as '*l'historiogriffe*', or 'chronicler of the claw', and became a stock character for popular ridicule. Wherever he went people miaowed or purred, or even spat at him in simulated fury. If he became visibly annoyed they pretended to placate him with soothing words, 'Puss, puss . . . calm down

then, calm down . . .' and gently stroked their fists as if they were paws. With some courage Moncrif kept his head and, being a good man, he sometimes offered to correct his foolish deriders. Gradually, he grew reconciled to the irritations of fame, especially when the Académie Française opened its doors to him. His literary elevation did not, however, prevent a final band of jokers from interrupting his inaugural speech by loosing half-a-dozen terrified cats across the floor.

Such an episode is frequently all that is needed to launch a fashion. People came more and more in their salons to discuss the mysterious attractions of the cat, and its strange taste at one and the same time for independence and comfort. As the years went by, people affected to care deeply about respecting the personality of their pet, and took great pride in being the protector and friend of an animal whose status they vowed never to diminish.

Mme Deshoulières, who composed a tragedy in which all the characters were cats, did not hesitate to tell her husband in her letters to him, that the greatest concern of her life was the happiness of her 'Grisette'.

The wife of the Field-Marshall of Luxemburg swathed her 'Brillante' with such tender regard that an admirer, in a moment of jealousy after he had seen the cat walking with her in the garden, wrote to the animal: 'Luxemburg is your mistress . . . How I wish she were mine'.

Ladies of quality, and also of the bourgeoisie, could no longer ignore the heartfelt passions of their friends. The Princess Palatine had started the fashion by announcing that 'cats are the most entrancing animals in the world'. The Marquise du Deffand gave her beribboned and perfumed cats complete freedom to do as they pleased on the satin sofas of her boudoir. The Duchess de Bouillon took great pleasure

in watching her tomcats do battle for the favours of her prettiest female. Mme Helvétius decked out her cats like fine ladies, and visitors to her salon, in search of an easy-chair or couch, had first to remove (with suitable apologies) dozens of great fat cats. In summer these were got up in absurd silk costumes, and in winter they wore thick fur robes, each adorned with a flowing train.

Mme de Staël, who had boasted of never having caressed an animal, complained when imprisoned in the Bastille of an invasion of rats. A cat was placed at her disposal, and from then on she sang the merits and the hidden charms of cats.

Mme Récamier, that languorous cat of French literary and political circles in the early nineteenth century, kept a place on her famous couch for 'Dorothée'. Chateaubriand sounded the call to arms in favour of his cat 'Childebrand'. 'Buffon mistreated the cat,' writes Chateaubriand to the Comte de Marcellus. 'I work for its rehabilitation. I hope to make it into an acceptable and honest animal, and quite the fashion of the time.'

From then on there rose a great chorus from writers in praise of all cats. Hoffmann wept for 'Murr' as one weeps for a child, and did not survive him by more than a few months.

Victor Hugo cherished several. After 'Chanoine', who sat enthroned on a dais of crimson satin, there came 'Gavroche'. On one of the birthdays of his granddaughter, he brought Gavroche to her, holding between his paws a huge bouquet of flowers, to which was pinned this card: 'From Gavroche, boulevard de la Mère-Michel'.

Mérimée praised the qualities of his cat, though regretting that he was really too sensitive. Saint-Beuve had them by the dozen. His favourite was 'Palemon' and an affectionate tabby about whom he wrote in

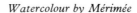
Watercolour by Mérimée

Victor Hugo's cat

his *Chroniques*. One evening Palemon brought home with him a female cat who, two months later, presented him with six kittens. Incapable of destroying them, Saint-Beuve placed an advertisement on his front door in the Rue du Montparnasse which read: 'Small cats here to be given to people who really love them'.

Théodore de Banville, the French poet who linked Romanticism and symbolism, always had some kitten or other lying on his papers. But the three champions who all their lives defended the cat were Barbey d'Aurevilly, Théophile Gautier and Charles Baudelaire. Barbey d'Aurevilly had a great love for 'Demonette' who lies at Asnières in the cemetery for dogs. Théophile Gautier saw in the cat 'a philosophical animal who does not distribute his affections lightly'. He cajoled 'Seraphita' for a long time, but it was 'Eponine' whom he preferred. She received his visitors in his antechamber and led them politely into the salon where she made them patiently wait. Having begged Théophile Gautier several times without success for a libretto for an opera, Massenet came one day to visit him. When the author opened the door of the salon, he found Eponine and Massenet having a long and friendly conversation. The gentle Massenet had won the day! Gautier began work at once. The work was swiftly finished under the title *Le Preneur de Rats* (The Rat-Catcher) but the opera was never performed.

Charles Baudelaire was not only the greatest poet of the beauties of the cat. He also loved them in practice. A mysterious and rapid understanding always established itself between him and them. Champfleury has given us this detail: 'Suppose a cat appeared at the entrance of a corridor or crossing the road? Baudelaire would go towards it, talk to it, draw it to him by caresses, and soon would take it in his arms where he could fondle it ... even against the

lie of the fur!' Decidedly, Baudelaire was attuned to cats!

Edmond de Goncourt had never had any animal as a pet before his cat 'Mie'. Yet it seems that 'Mie' was the only being that this famous naturalist writer embraced at the moment of his death.

Hippolyte Taine said in memory of 'Puss', 'Ébène', 'Mittone' and so many others that he had loved and looked after: 'I have studied many philosophers and many cats. The wisdom of cats is infinitely superior!'

The historian Michelet, and Mme Michelet in particular, provided a happy home for nearly a hundred and thirty cats; but they had no more after the brutal death of 'Pluton', killed during their absence from Paris by an irascible gardener.

Alexandre Dumas the younger, allowed his cat the freedom of roaming the streets. Every evening 'Mysouff' left their home in the Rue de L'Ouest, and came to meet him in the Rue de Vaugirard, miaowing with joy as soon as he saw him appear at the top of the Rue d'Assas. But Mysouff seemed to have a sixth sense which told him when Dumas was not coming home for dinner. At these times he did not bother to go out, but would curl up on a cushion and wait anxiously, 'like a serpent biting his own tail'.

Ernest Renan, the nineteenth-century philosopher who wrote the *Life of Jesus*, had 'Corah' for a companion. This firm rationalist did not hesitate to affirm that his cat had a better sense of time, that she followed the rhythm of the hours and days and weeks better than he did.

François Coppée, who usually sheltered half-a-dozen cats, wrote under the luminous eye of 'Blanchat' and 'Isabelle'. 'Lilith' watched over Mallarmé. Maurice Rollinat, Guy de Maupassant, J. K. Huysmans and Anatole France needed the presence of a cat in order to work.

In his numerous voyages over the world,

Pierre Loti, the novelist, brought back, from 'Balkis' to 'Mahmoud', cats of all possible coats and colours. He admitted in confidence however, that he trembled before 'Pamouk', his impressive Black Persian. 'Rosette', on the other hand, had the gift of soothing him. This little female cat was so gentle that Loti had the idea of improving several passages of 'Ramuntcho' (adapted from one of his novels) at the Odéon by having her on the stage. Unfortunately, Rosette, who had behaved perfectly during rehearsals, had uncontrollable stage-fright on the evening of the dress-rehearsal and had to be withdrawn from her role.

Like Colette, Pierre Loti was one of the few authors of the century really to appreciate, as connoisseur and friend, the secret companionship of cats. After his long cruises, it was always with joy that he returned to them in his small house at Rochefort. Here would be a variety of cats of various origins that, sheltered and nourished by his Aunt Claire, lived together with those lean and frightened cats, brought back from the Far East, that only he was allowed to caress. One of the latter group was that 'Moumoutte chinoise' whose story he tells in *Le livre de la pitié et de la mort* (The book of pity and of death).

Paul Léutaud, who lived so literally among his cats that he came to resemble them in many ways, delighted in the apparent calm, the scrutinizing gaze and the ready claws of the hundreds of down-and-out cats that lived with him.

André Billy has said of Léautaud: 'The intellectual anarchist that he had been since he was young turned into the *petit bourgeois*. ... Old age aggravated his prejudices and eccentricities.' It also seems that old age aggravated his sensibility to the point of sentimentality. Like Joachim du Bellay and like Hoffmann, Paul Léautaud wept for the death of his favourite cats with a desolation

Jacques Prévert loved to hold dialogues with the cats he met in chance encounters

that was absolutely sincere. Five months after one of them disappeared, he was still able to say 'When the idea returned this morning as I came back from buying the newspaper ... disappeared since the 10th of June! What grief! No, no, I have not forgotten him, I am not consoled!'

Battered and soured, a misanthrope, un-reflecting and impulsive, Léautaud at the end of his life had really become one of this community of cats amongst whom he was both the happy victim and the acknowledged despot. Of this solidarity with his cats, this shared way of behaving in the face of the uncertainty of the hour and the menace of tomorrow, Paul Léautaud made a personal confession: 'When I leave them, they will have need of nothing and nobody. I have made provision for them in my will: each one of them will eat, sleep, live and die in peace....'

How many cats must Colette have cherished: from 'Fanchette' and the country cats of Sido, to the final Chartreux who had the honour of being the last to purr on those famous blue sheets of writing paper on the desk. Colette had known, fed and caressed the majority of the cats who appear in her works: the cats of Claudine, 'Kiki-la-doucette' – the Persian, the 'Pegots' cats of the Monts-Boucons, the female cat of the Rue de Courcelles, for whom she once fought like a lioness and who followed her down the Rue de Villejust, those who travelled in a basket and accompanied her to Belle-Ille-en-Mer, those whom she found again at Saint-Tropez, and even the alley cats. Even the cats who never lived are now more alive than the living and will never die because they are immortalized forever in the stories of Colette.

The death of a cat touched Colette more deeply than the surliness of her welcome might lead one to think possible. In 1939 she wrote to Leopold Marchand and alluded

Drawing by Dubout, who studied cats in every one of their attitudes

Leonor Fini was always surrounded by cats

Detail from a painting by Bonnard

to the death of 'Zwerg': 'Everything which has happened with "Zwerg" will happen eventually with "La Chatte", who is not nearly as healthy as Zwerg was. We ought only to allow ourselves to become attached to parrots and tortoises. It is true that we could not bear to leave them living on after us in unhappiness. Nothing in love can be arranged. Let us therefore be unhappy with grace, etc.'

Jean Cocteau, who perhaps like Maurice Goudeket learned to love cats through his contact with the luminous world of Colette, was not, in his own opinion, 'one of their maniacs'. But, as he said, he had 'one by chance, then two, four, five. . . .' From the Siamese to the Blue Persian, and passing by the children of these two, he eventually ended up one fine day with that royal cross-breed, a 'kind of black semicolon, who would only eat if one placed the meat in front of his mouth'. For someone who merely found cats amusing, it would seem difficult to have been more greatly their slave.

Paul Morand willingly admitted his weakness. It was very rare to spend a day at a cat show without seeing, across the decorated cages where the greatest champions sat in dignified boredom, bending over some White Angora with orange eyes, the fine intelligent face of this writer who seemed to know all the secrets of men . . . and of animals. He raised more than a hundred cats and wrote of those who can to some extent be called his brothers: 'I love cats because they are silent, and because of this, misunderstood—misunderstood because they disdain to explain themselves.'

Marcel Pagnol, the dramatist who wrote *Fanny* and other comedies, lives in the Midi, where men are too happy among themselves to be interested in any other animals. He has never passed for a passionate animal lover. And yet, on his sunny property, there

lives a typical country cat, who feeds off lizards, voles and sparrows, respects the work of his master, follows in his tracks and seems to search his friendship out.

Here we have a curious aspect of feline psychology. Setting apart actual permanent hostility and menaces meant to drive them away, certain cats seem to take a wicked pleasure in troubling those who are indifferent to them, or even actual enemies. Is this an attempt to seduce them? Is it just a matter of chance? I think not. Francis de Miomandre, contemporary French novelist, was frightened of them, and cats quite maliciously followed him with their assiduous attentions. The poet Maeterlinck could scarcely be said to have liked them, yet the cats of the surrounding gardens came unceasingly to pester him.

In general, however, French writers (especially those of the nineteenth century) have adored the cat. English and American writers have been rather more non-committal in print, but just as fond in practise.

All three of the Brontë sisters loved cats, although Emily was less demonstrative than Charlotte and Anne; references to favourite cats often appear in the diaries of the latter two. Mrs Gaskell, in comparing Charlotte with the more mysterious Emily, wrote of their love of animals: 'The feeling, which in Charlotte partook of something of the nature of an affection, was, with Emily more of a passion. . . . The helplessness of an animal was its passport to Charlotte's heart; the fierce, wild, intractability of its nature was what often recommended it to Emily.' This comment makes sense to anyone who has ever pondered on the differences between the author of *Jane Eyre* and the author of *Wuthering Heights*.

Samuel Butler, whom Bernard Shaw described as 'the greatest English writer of the latter half of the nineteenth century', kept and loved several cats. His long cor-

The art dealer Ambroise Vollard loved to caress his cat

Colette never ceased to love and write about her pets, from her first country cats to her final Chartreux

respondence with his friend Miss Savage (whom he was notorious for *not* loving) contains many references to cats. In 1885 he wrote to her: 'No, I will not have any Persian cat; it is undertaking too much responsibility. I must have a cat whom I find homeless, wandering about the court, and to whom, therefore, I am under no obligation. . . . I have already selected a dirty little drunken wretch of a kitten to be successor to my poor old cat. I don't suppose it drinks anything stronger than milk and water, but then, you know, so much milk and water must be bad for a kitten that age—at any rate it looks as if it drank: but it gives me the impression of being affectionate, intelligent and fond of mice, and I believe, if it had a home, it would become more respectable. . . .'

Charles Dickens had no aversion to cats, and there was one kitten, in particular, that adopted him. It followed him around like a dog and sat in his lap when he was working or reading. Dickens told the story that one night when he was working in this way, the candle suddenly went out. He relit the candle, stroked the cat—who was looking at him pathetically—and went back to his book. A few minutes later, as the light became dim again, he looked up just in time to see the cat deliberately put out the candle with its paw and then look up at him appealingly. On this second hint, Dickens broke down and gave the cat the attention he so obviously desired.

In *Puddn'head Wilson* Mark Twain claimed that 'A house without a cat, and a well-fed, well-petted, and properly revered cat, may be a perfect house, perhaps, but how can it prove its title.' This great American writer had a love for cats which was real, though understated. Of his own cats he wrote: 'They had no history. They did not distinguish themselves in any way. They died early—on account of being so overweighted with their names, it was

thought–"Sour Mash", "Apollinaris", "Zoroaster", "Blatherskite", . . . names given them, not in an unfriendly spirit, but merely to practise the children in large and difficult styles of pronunciation. It was a very happy idea–I mean, for the children.'

H. G. Wells had a marvellous cat that was a great asset in social situations. Whenever one of Wells' guests talked too loudly or too long, this cat would make a great show of jumping down from his chair–with as much noise as possible–and walking to the door. Wells named his last cat 'Mr Peter Wells', and on one occasion he swiftly corrected a visitor who addressed the distinguished animal as 'Master' Peter Wells.

Edgar Allan Poe's love of cats was less mysterious than his use of them in his writing. His favourite was a large tortoise-shell named Catarina, who shared his home and his poverty. It was said that, when Mrs Poe lay dying, her only source of warmth were her husband's coat and Catarina.

Thomas Hardy's love for his cat was expressed in 'Last Words to a Dumb Friend', quoted in chapter four. When he grew very old, this great novelist and poet was given another cat–a grey Persian with orange eyes, who was absolutely devoted to him when he was dying, and who disappeared soon after his death.

TODAY'S PERSONALITIES

Today the cat lovers are legion; a roll-call of the well-known people who like cats would fill another book this size. Let us be content to note that actors and actresses have always had a special relationship with cats–from Ellen Terry and Sarah Bernhardt to the glamorous personalities of today: Sophia Loren, Peter O'Toole, Anna Magnani, Jean-Louis Barrault, Claudia Cardinale and Dirk Bogarde, to name only a few.

12 TOWN CATS AND COUNTRY CATS

How many domestic cats are there in the world? What is their fate today?

In the U.S.A. recent statistics give their number as over 30,000,000, to only 17,000,000 dogs. In Great Britain, 4,250,000 cats share with 4,000,000 dogs in the affection of a people famous as animal lovers. In France the cats outnumber the dogs by 7,500,000 to 6,000,000.

Some of these are very well cared for, as we know. People keep cats for all sorts of reasons, but basically because people need cats. A recent study of the psychology of pet ownership was made by a pet food manufacturer in Britain and concluded that domestic animals are 'an outlet for feelings not acceptable in human society ... nothing we can do will embarrass them ... therefore we need not feel embarrassed ourselves ... pretence and our pretensions are dropped.' Another manufacturer, in the course of market research, asked cat owners 'Why do people keep a cat, do you think?' Giving more than one answer sometimes, people reacted as follows:

43% because of loneliness
26% to keep away mice and rats
21% because of a general fondness for
     animals
19% as company for children
5% to make the place look home like.

In yet another study, by yet another pet food manufacturer, the subjects were asked to agree or disagree with a set of statements designed to sound out cat-owner psychology. Twenty per cent of the people questioned strongly agreed with the statement 'My cat needs me', while only two per cent strongly disagreed. Twenty-three per cent agreed that 'cats are sensitive to human emotion', thirteen per cent agreed that 'cats are easier to get on with than people', and nearly fifty per cent strongly agreed that 'cats are very good company'. Fifty-seven per cent agreed with the strange statement that 'by looking at a cat you can tell about its owner', and forty-one per cent agreed that 'cats understand what you say to them' (though they presumably take no notice).

So much for the people who make homes for cats. But what of the cats that have no homes?

In Dallas, Texas, alone, 175,000 cats without masters were counted in 1965. Has this state, in which cattle and horses reign supreme, a particular hostility towards cats? Not at all. The explanation lies in the fact that, in 1964, a municipal law limited to four the number of cats one was allowed to possess per home.

It is possible to reduce the birth-rate of cats by, for example, refraining from keeping a pair living together in one home, or, if one possesses both males and females, by entrusting to a veterinary surgeon the task of ensuring celibacy. But there still remain the stray cats, the free cats.

The more the inhabitants of a town love them or put up with them, paradoxically preferring to turn them over to the hazards of luck rather than to destroy them, the more of these cats there are. And this produces that plethora of unhappy beasts, free to reproduce themselves and increase their numbers in those places where they are most loved, but not necessarily best cared for.

THE CITY LIFE

Paris is a startling example. Paris, where there are districts that still keep the character of rather swollen villages (Montmartre, Ménilmontant, Montrouge, Montparnasse), can compete with Dallas in its concentration of cats per square mile.

Cats do not pay taxes, and so we cannot know precisely what number of them there are. But the figure of a half million is probably an accurate enough estimate for the feline livestock of Paris.

There are over 30,000,000 cats in the
United States and 4,250,000 in
Great Britain

In Belgian towns there is often a
street specially dedicated to cats

Amongst the number of the more-or-less ownerless cats of Paris we must count the sixty odd, who, due to their ability to inspire terror in rats and to the zoophilia of the Assemblée Nationale, have been called 'the feline dynasty of the Palais Bourbon'. The majority of them are black, a fact noticed by M. Neuwirth, one of those who brought the law for the protection of animals before the Assembly. Their best friend is the Assembly barber. No official budget provides for their upkeep, but scraps from the parliamentary restaurant have proved enough to keep them reasonably fed.

What of those cats who are warm in winter, and whose masters in summer worry whether 'this fish is still fresh enough', or who say, 'perhaps we should give Puss some chicken liver, just for a treat and a change'? Happy cats, like happy people, have no history.

But there are the others, the hundreds of thousands of others: cats of the gardens and public squares, cats of the alleys and the dock-side, the street-arabs and the down-·and-outs or, as they are known in Paris, the 'gavroches' and the 'clochards'. Their hunger, misery and cold never quite lead them back into a wild state. They continue to be born, to live, to love and to die surrounded by the total indifference of the humans who have deceived them. And this is the real drama, this is where the responsibility lies. Generations of civilized people, people with hearts as well as minds, are guilty of an unthinking crime. This animal that they knew how to turn to their own account, that they welcomed beside their fire and that over the centuries they have turned into a domestic animal, lives today disarmed and disabled in our towns and cities and without appeal against its sufferings.

This is the drama of all homeless cats adrift in our huge modern cities. It is the drama of the cats of Paris: 'that Buchenwald of cats' as Colette called it. It is the drama of those cats, young and old, who are disposed of in the small hours of the morning by being thrown into the depths of the ditches of Vincennes, from which they have no hope of climbing out. It is the drama of those cats of the desolate stretches of the Buttes-Chaumont, and even more, sad irony, of the Rue des Alouettes, the street of the larks. It is the drama of the cats of the metro station of la Chappell. These cats have been to such an extent ignored and yet omni-present, that after the First World War Joseph Delteil was able to write: 'There are evenings when Paris smells of cats.'

But there are other cats whose life on the streets is not one absolute misery. Beside the trembling, emaciated wrecks of the utterly homeless cats, there are others who take to the streets to some extent by choice. These are not cats that have been abandoned They have an address, a roof over their heads, some sort of title of residence. They can give their references: 'I am the cat from the docks of Rue des Jeûners ...' or 'I am the cat from pavillion 56 in the central allé If Les Halles . . . .'

At least one of Paris's street cats knew how to take care of itself. The famous legend of this cat is evoked in the name of the 'Rue du Chat-qui-peche' (The Street of the Fishing Cat). Have there been others who have been driven to this unlikely art? Fishing i certainly not unknown among felines. The fishing cats of Asia spring to mind immediately. And reports are often heard o the fishing habits of jaguars in the Amazon area of South America. Both Feliz de Azara a Spanish naturalist who lived in Paragua from 1781 to 1801, and later a French

Roofs are everywhere a favourite meeting place

In Istanbul the cat is king

engineer, F. de Lincourt, claimed to have surprised jaguars behaving in the following way: Lying down on the bank of the river, the hungry jaguar beats the water with a nervous and impatient tail. The fish, thinking it is fruit falling, dart for it. The jaguar, with a swift movement of its back and paws, makes the most of their imprudence. Perhaps the Paris 'Fishing Cat' behaved in the same way. In some times and in some parts of the city he would not even have had to go to the river. For it has happened that cellars and underground store-rooms have been turned into ponds stocked with fish when the Seine was in flood.

These cats who live off the streets are not cats without civil rights; they are simply independent. Certainly they eat here, there and everywhere, but they return at the trot when they hear a familiar sound or a voice calling them. They know how to escape, with a light wriggling movement, the odd impulse to caress them; they know how to evade delicately unwanted attentions, to keep their distance without giving the appearance of fear or repulsion ... one must not cause offence! These are the cats of the markets of the high villages of Provence, the little ports, the very rare public gardens where they are tolerated by the keepers.

CATS OF THE MEDITERRANEAN

It is the cats of the Mediterranean coastline who have the least to complain of. Those of Egypt, of Alexandria, Cairo, Port Said, those more or less direct descendants of the sacred cats, live on little under a sky eternally blue.

The cats of Turkey suffer perhaps from the cold of Ankara, but the fisherman are their friends. In Istanbul the cat is king. There are hundreds of them, on the quays, round the factories, in the residential areas. The inhabitants feed them. The cats arrive for dessert when the white cheese appears on the tables. They return, drawn by the smell of cooking meat. All around the stalls and shops they wait for the scraps of those fish for which Istanbul is famous. Milk, unhappily, is fairly rare, but the yoghourt is as creamy as could be wished; which is why one so often sees a seller of curdled milk escorted by dozens of cats, their noses in the air, their tails as straight as tapers. Cats are numerous in the cemeteries, which are sometimes found in the middle of the towns.

I myself have quite often seen a curious habit in Turkish towns. From an open window on the second or third floor a basket is let down on the end of a cord. A cat is being let down, in his own private lift, to take a stroll in the district and amuse himself while his indolent mistress avoids the drudgery of making the descent herself.

Istanbul is the paradise of cats. Here every sailor, every shoemaker, every baker, every fruit-seller loves to keep a cat on his shoulder, or to feel it purring between his feet, a big fat cat swollen with subdued affection. Here the taxi-drivers would smash themselves into a wall in the narrow streets rather than injure a little kitten sleeping in their path.

Some Turkish cats, like some of the bigger cats, such as tigers, have the ability to swim. Before the Second World War, Miss Laura Lushington of Weston Turville in Buckinghamshire brought back with her a dozen Turkish cats to England. Today their descendants swim in her swimming pool by her side. She has found these cats to be strictly fish-eaters: rats and mice can sleep peacefully in their presence.

There are countless cats in Greece. From the Piraeus to the Acropolis where they

*In Italy cats are multiplying,
surrounded by indulgent indifference.
Venice, in particular, is their paradise*

sleep in the sun they descend at night to prowl round the little restaurants. There are not many to be found in the principal streets. But when, in 1959, an underground station was installed in the Omoura square in the centre of Athens, a disused tunnel had to be permanently blocked up, and it was found that nearly a thousand cats had made it their clandestine home. Public opinion was aroused and a wave of affection for animals made itself felt. Squads of volunteers mobilized themselves, and within two or three days, without the slightest violence, they succeeded in getting control of almost all the cats and finding a master for each one.

In Italy cats have always been able, without too much difficulty and thanks to the indulgent indifference of a people disarming in their charm, to live and multiply. Are the emancipated cats of Florence or those of the Forum of Rome unhappy? It is improbable. It seems that there are a million and a half of them, and that their number continues to increase. Once some of their enemies decided to do away with the sun-saturated cats of the Coliseum but the affair, in 1960, was brought before the Council of Ministers. The Government of Italy wisely decided to keep its cats. They were part of the landscape.

Since then an association for feline defence, the 'Ida Carboni League', has been founded. Before the Olympic Games were held in Rome some members of this league kidnapped the bulk of those cats threatened by the building operations that were about to start, and took them to the 'City of Cats'.

About twelve miles from the capital, at Ostia, Umberto Reck and his wife have given shelter to an impressive number of cats that would otherwise have been homeless. There are at least 500 there. And yet it is not rivalry and squabbling but joi-de-vivre and peace that are in evidence in this collective life. R. P. Audras, who is familiar with this paradise for abandoned cats, confirms that their

simple presence in this area has completely cleared the surrounding six miles of the thousands of rats and mice that used to infest it. Every other day a veterinarian passes to check on the health of the residents. He examines the bronchial tubes, tends minor injuries, cossets appetites. He is greeted by a chorus of gentle miaowings and little cries of impatience, as if to welcome and thank him for his gentleness and friendliness.

For a long time, the cloister of San Lorenzo in Florence was the traditional asylum for abandoned cats, and nothing was more curious than to see them arrive at mealtimes when the clock struck the first strokes of midday. In 1958 a priest did not hesitate to have himself tied round the middle by a strong rope and lowered a full 35 yards down the side of a town clock in order to go to the rescue of an unhappy white cat who, by accident or folly, had for 24 hours been miraculously balancing on an overhang.

In Venice, cats are as greatly loved as little children. The health authorities have made several attempts to organize the capture or the killing of cats in order to clear the town of these pests. But the Venetians are so firmly attached to their vagabonds, even the scabbiest and mangiest, that these campaigns always meet with complete failure. The animals, spitting and scratching, are hidden in dark courtyards or in chests, ahead of the arrival of the commandos of the city health department. And so the Venetian cats increase in number every year.

Some of them live a strangely isolated and ghostly existence, rarely putting their noses out of doors and then only on narrow inaccessible balconies. The greatest number are half wild and live off charity in the old sewer pipes, from which sympathetic people have removed the grills, or in the inextricable recesses of gardens gone wild. Every morning one can see them throw themselves like wolves on the most indigestible food – offal,

fish tails, noodles wrapped up in old newspapers—that housewives have put out for them. On a winter's afternoon near Saint Mark's an old woman will come to feed cats in gardens that are beginning to turn green; and a man in a beige overcoat will divert the flow of a nearby fountain so that the water, running into a dip in the paving stones, forms a drinking-basin for the cats. The cats of Venice are not cold. Nor are they hungry. Yet, although they seem to be satisfied to the point of turning up their whiskered noses in disdain at a plateful of spaghetti placed at their door, the cats of Venice are

rarely fat. Apparently it is only at Christmas and on festival days that they grow a little plumper. The only ones who become even slightly stout are the ones who take to the churches and become hunters of rats.

The cats of Israel are perhaps the strangest of all. In Tel-Aviv and in Jaffa the stray cats are neither timid nor suspicious. You can caress them in passing and even take them in your arms. Multicoloured and optimistic, they seem to take equal pleasure in the taste of a tomato, a fish or even an ornage! Extremely precocious, they can reproduce from the age of five or six months, and rarely deny

themselves this privilege. They never come into the houses. They live outside, circulating from garden to garden and terrace to terrace.

They have peculiar habits. They never scratch. If they want to free themselves from some importunate embrace, they bite. They rarely fight with each other, and then they make it up very quickly. They are at the opposite pole from the cats of Europe who sniff, hesitate and seem to regret having to take the food you offer them. The Israeli cats come like dogs when called and enjoy eating from a human hand.

231

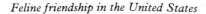

Special attentions for the cherished pets : the publicity for cat products is continually expanding and changing

ZOOPHILIA

What are we to say of the cats of Northern Europe? These countries are famous for their love of cats.

The cats of Belgium are big and fat. Their fur shines. They are epicureans who purr and love to be caressed. The cats of England and Germany are as home-loving as their owners. The cats of Sweden are the happiest cats in Europe. Stockholm is its capital of cats. If, by chance, a cat should be lost in this city where cats reign supreme, twenty people immediately appear to set off in search for it. The police launch an appeal, the press an investigation. Should the cat really be lost, really abandoned, someone will be there to offer it shelter, comfort it and reassure it. By the next day it will have been placed. This is a love of animals that is intelligently organized. It could fruitfully be a source of inspiration to so many of the other great cities of Europe.

In France, the animal protection organizations have made a great effort in this field. In 1960 the 'Association des Amis des Bêtes', 34 Rue de Grenelle, Paris, for the first time and with the support of the store, Magasins de Printemps, instituted a service for the free placing of abandoned cats. Every single day the various societies receive dozens of kittens and adult cats, particularly females, whom they are obliged to put to death swiftly and painlessly. The police regulations and those of the health authorities restrict to seventy-five the number of cats that can be given refuge in each of the various registered shelters.

This example has been rapidly followed. A similar organization, the Société Protectrice des Animaux, 39 Boulevard Berthier, Paris, was set up with the co-operation of another store, Magasins de la Samaritaine. This initiative has made possible the rescue of about 10,000 cats each year, because they have been found homes. Every year during the summer holidays, when more cats than

ever are abandoned, and whenever there are cat shows in Paris, these same groups carry out a particular campaign. With the help of newspapers and television, they launch a 'three days of adoption' in which they save numerous animals.

In England, there is the Royal Society for the Prevention of Cruelty to Animals, the oldest Society of its kind in the world. The scope of its work is enormous and extends as far as India, where travelling veterinary clinics bring help to animals in the most remote areas.

The Blue Cross Animal Welfare Society and the P.D.S.A. (Peoples' Dispensary for Sick-Animals) have a similar field of activity. Founded in 1917, the P.D.S.A. runs more than 80 permanent dispensaries, 28 travelling dispensaries and five modern hospitals. Each year it brings help to 200,000 cats and finds homes for between 75,000 and 80,000. Finally, in 1927, there was founded a specialist organization, 'The Cats' Protection League' which has numerous affiliated bodies in England and Ireland. It is dedicated exclusively to providing medico-surgical help to cats.

In the field of animal protection England has done more still. In 1959, on the initiative of some of the directors of the R.S.P.C.A., the I.S.P.A. (International Society for the Protection of Animals, 106 Jermyn Street, London) was formed simultaneously in London and Boston. This brings together representatives of the principal societies for animal protection in all countries. Each nation has its elected director who is responsible for the liaison of his country's organizations with the centralized services of one of the hemispheres. The London centre is concerned with work in the United Kingdom, Europe and the Afro-Asian countries. The Boston centre is responsible for the U.S.A., Canada, South America and the Far East.

The action undertaken at world level by

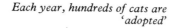

*Each year, hundreds of cats are
'adopted'*

*Others find temporary refuges, and set
up residence there*

the I.S.P.A. is enormous. It concerns itself with the fate of cats in North Africa, the exportation of sheep in Tunisia, the winter famines that hit the reindeer of Norway, the laws and decrees of France relating to the slaughtering of animals, the plight of the last gorillas in the Congo, the world massacre of seals and whales, the clandestine traffic in cats for experiment in Germany, and so on. In particular it is to the I.S.P.A. that we owe the organization and the financing of what was called 'Operation Gwamba', which saved thousands of wild animals in Africa from death by drowning. They were threatened by the flooding induced by the great constructional works that were re-shaping the topography of the land.

In many countries efforts are being made to prevent all kinds of acts of cruelty to animals. Sanctions, more or less severe, exist for the punishing of violence and brutality. But certain acts, which bring about suffering, still completely escape jurisdiction. The most common of these is the abandonment of cats. In the eyes of many people this small act of cowardice seems innocent and excusable. But in terms of the law it should none the less constitute an offence. This has been the case for a long time in English law, and in that of certain states of America.

In Britain, where cats are more pampered than in any other country, the astonishing and shameful fact is that a significant number of owners either abandon or destroy their cats before going off on summer holiday. The reasoning, if such a word can be applied, seems to be that many people feel the cost of kennelling to be too high, especially when they probably paid nothing for the cat in the first place. (The situation is different for dogs, simply because they are more often purchased.) The R.S.P.C.A. has has noted that at holiday periods there is an increase both in abandonments and in the number of requests to the society's clinics to have pets destroyed.

One unfortunate factor is that the cat population does not enjoy the special status extended to dogs, although its claim, in terms of numbers, would seem to be as great. Stray dogs are a police responsibility and must, under law, be kept alive for seven days. This is chiefly to give owners an opportunity to claim them back, although in effect a dog may be kept alive for a considerably longer period if the R.S.P.C.A. takes it into care.

Cats, on the other hand, are more difficult to rehabilitate. They breed more freely and present a greater demand for new homes, especially from owners who find themselves overrun by all-too-frequent issues of kittens, and have to apply for help. And in view of the tremendous availability of cats and kittens, the animal societies achieve a fairly high success rate, notably the R.S.P.C.A. who in 1966 found new homes for 20,409 unwanted cats.

Legally, the position has improved since 1960 when it became an offence not only to maltreat a cat, but also to abandon one in a way likely to cause suffering. In 1966 the R.S.P.C.A. secured 904 convictions under the Protection of Animals Act, of which 124, or roughly one in seven, were brought for cruelty to cats. Offenders now face a maximum penalty of a £50 fine and three months' imprisonment. And if, on a second or subsequent offence, the culprit is found unfit to own a cat he will be deprived of the right of ownership.

A similar judgement was made in France for the first time by the tribunal of Aix-en-Provence when, on the 6th July, 1962, it condemned to a 60F. fine and 100F. damages, someone who tried to lose his cat a long way from home in order to be able to leave on a voyage without any worries. Unfortunately such sentences do not only depend on the law of a country, but also, and above all, on the temperament of the judge and on his personal feelings towards animals.

It is precisely from this moment of aban-

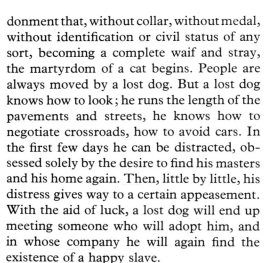

The stray cat is sometimes treated as an enemy

But often it arouses sympathy

UM SPENDEN
WIRD GEBETEN!

elft uns
...rlassenen
Katzen

donment that, without collar, without medal, without identification or civil status of any sort, becoming a complete waif and stray, the martyrdom of a cat begins. People are always moved by a lost dog. But a lost dog knows how to look; he runs the length of the pavements and streets, he knows how to negotiate crossroads, how to avoid cars. In the first few days he can be distracted, obsessed solely by the desire to find his masters and his home again. Then, little by little, his distress gives way to a certain appeasement. With the aid of luck, a lost dog will end up meeting someone who will adopt him, and in whose company he will again find the existence of a happy slave.

But the cat! With its absolute inability to cope with the dangers of a street, the coming and going of vehicles and passers-by, the abandoned cat goes to ground. He waits. Everything around him is isolation, danger, menace. Where will he find aid – from some charitable souls, perhaps themselves hunted by the police, who may bring him something while hiding themselves? The cat, who does not have the instinct of the pack, will nevertheless come sooner or later to join up with other brothers in misery. The instinct for the preservation of the species will eventually come into play. Other cats will be born of these embraces, other cats who will in their turn know this same fate and become battling toms or wild females, condemned to live exactly like rats!

A cat who belongs to no one belongs to the whole world. The result of this paradox is tragedy. These cats, until yesterday domestic, become the victims of poison, traps, the murdering spade-blows of angered gardeners. But the charitable soul, surprised in the act of feeding them, simply because she has taken pity on them, becomes the object of remonstrances, vexation, pursuit.

Are these cats domestic animals? Certainly not! They have no further connection with domestic property, and the civil and penal codes ignore them. Recent French legislation may bring benefits. One generous attempt punishes 'all acts of cruelty towards a domestic animal or towards any other animal which is dependant on man'. But it rests incomplete and silent on the subject of those cats with no home, those cats that are joined together as 'feral cats'.

Another unhappy situation is the blind distribution of poisoned food, meant for foxes and other wild flesh-eating animals but which, every year, kills an even greater number of cats and dogs.

Quite as repellent is the fact that the few misdeeds with which cats can be charged should weigh so heavily in the balance against them, when one thinks of the services they have rendered ... and which we have forgotten. Logic flounders.

It is true that when man intervenes in the natural order of things, a fiasco often results. In Africa, where the lions and the zebras lived together in freedom, there were always lions and zebras. Where man has passed there are neither lions nor zebras. In the forests, the woods and the fields, where insecticides are spread in profusion, too many birds and bees are killed without the suppression of the insect that it was our intention to kill.

It would, by thinking along these lines, be easy to find fair reasons why cats should, once and for all, be protected. It is sufficient for there to be a cat in the garden for the moles and the voles to disappear. It is enough for there to be a cat in the house and, from the cellar to the attic, rats and mice are soon gone.

LONG LIVE THE CAT

While I write these concluding lines there are seven cats playing around me who are at home, even though chance brought all seven of them to me. Lying half under my arm, 'Grizon', the despot over us all, warns me that the time has come to finish this

234

Even in distress, the cat retains its enviable equilibrium

book. A code exists between us: in silence she has half raised and lowered her eyelids three times. Against my leg, a hard contact and the slight shiver of a tail raised in impatience: this is 'Philibert the Younger' whom no one has had the courage to condemn to celibacy. A heavy, muffled 'plouf' and then an echo, the dry 'toc' of a rickety chair being abandoned: this is 'Gros Richard', the obese Tortoiseshell that some imperious need, or some sensory hallucination, has just torn from his eunuch's dreams and propelled towards the kitchen. In an hour there will be the hypocritical little miaowing, first timid and then imperative, of 'N'a qu'un oeil' (Only one eye) the independent one. She is one-eyed as a result of a contretemps with a blackbird when she was very young, but it has not diminished her fire in any way. Of the remaining three, each with his own history, two are still waiting in the garden under the moon. The third has already gone to sleep ... on our bed! These are seven happy cats who live in an age that is basically sympathetic to their race.

If periods of history had totems appropriate to their tendencies, then we would live in the era of the cat. It is the era of plaintive songs and cries, of animal movement and suggestive purrs, the era of independence and pride, of violence and beauty; above all, it is an age with an inextinguishable thirst for living.

Will the man of the future be wise enough to adopt the gentleness, serenity and calm which are the secrets of the cats' equilibrium?

ACKNOWLEDGEMENTS

39a: Alfort Veterinary College

141, 234c: Agence Ali

106a, 144a: Agence France Presse

21a, 46a, 88, 91a, b, c, 93b, 95c, 112, 218a, 223a, 225a: Archives Photographiques

23a, 32a, 84b, 90a, 94a, b, 113a, 118a, b, 121a, 128, 129, 154, 166, 168a: Arts Decoratifs

61b, 106a, c, 108b, 109b, 110, 124a, 143b, 156a, 183b, 195b, c, 230a, 231a, 232b, 233b: Atlantic Press

21b: Athens Archaeological Museum

144b, 177a, 201a: Atlas Photo

16c: Baufle

10, 127, 143a, 167a, 188, 191, 193a: Bavaria Verlag

79a: Nicholas Bentley/Faber and Faber Ltd.

125, 135, 208b: Bern

14, 17b, 34b, 36c, 38a, 40b, 41a, b, c, 48b, 49a, 56, 57, 61c, 64a, b, c, 65a, b, 66, 67b, 80a, b, 81a, 82a, b, 84b, 85a, b, 95b, 112a, 114c, 126a, 133b, 152a, 159, 160, 161a, 198a, 206a, b, 208c, 212a, 214, 216a, 217a, 218b, 222a: Bibliothèque Nationale, Paris

24: Biltgen

62: Bips

118c, 119a, 156c: Prof. Bressou, 'Anatomie descriptive du chat'

147b: A. Briou and H. Ey, 'Psychiatrie Animale'

19b, 28a, 30a, 30c, 31a, 68a, b, 69: British Museum

122a, 228a: Cecchetti

166b: R. Chaynes

162a, 176b, 177c, 180b, 185a, 190a: Colyann

50, 61a, 75, 119b, 133, 136a, b, 137, 138b, 139a, b, 157, 167b: Gunnar Cornelius

209b: P. Corsey

96a: Courtauld Institute

105a: Dell Publishing

15, 16a, 17a: Des Bartlett/Armand Denis

107d: Disney Productions

55: Documents Geigy

104: Doubleday, New York

233c: Europress

27b: G. Freund

32b, 53a, 92a, b, c, 93a, 96b, 98b, 99a, 113b, 207b: Giraudon

44: Grosvenor Gallery

102: Guggenheim Museum, New York

79b: Kathleen Hale/Country Life

18, 19a, 52: Hassia

78, 120b: Hollinger

23b, c, 31, 46b, 47, 74a, 79a, 84a, 115b, 124b, 140a, 147a, 149, 164, 200d, 226, 232a: Holmes Lebel

42a, 60b, 108a, 121a, 152b, 153, 158a, b, 163b, 219b, c, 230b, 231a, 234b, 235a: Keystone

213: W. Klein

25a, 26a, b: P. Koch

98a, 109a, 174a, 180a, 186a, 188, 221b, c, 222b, 256: La Vie des Bêtes (coll.)

33, 148b: E. Landau

209a: Maeght (coll.)

221a: Magnum

156b: Marquet (coll.)

26a: Mason, 'The Ancient Civilization of Peru'

39b: R. Mayne

37a, 37d, 48a, 49d, 106b, 107a, b, 114a, b, 220b, 224a: Dr Fernand Méry

80: Munich Museum

28b, 30b: Musée du Louvre

5, 103a: 'New Yorker'

104a, b, c: Opera Mundi, King Features Syndicate

65, 76a, b, 77a, b, 81b, 97a, 103b, c, 115a, 190b, 203, 208d: A. Peyraud

60a, 150b: M. Pons

97b: Pougnet

53b: Prado Museum

42b, 45a, 131: Presshusset/Bo Jarner

35a, 43, 56b, 71b, 216c, 217b: Radio Times Hulton

39b, 58, 59, 73b, 79, 116, 121b, 123a, 138a, 182, 146a, b, 168b, 172, 175, 181, 182a, 201b, 223b, 224b, 229b, 234a: Rapho

86a, 87a, 105b, 206c: Resnais

12, 67a, 87b, 101, 219a: Ribière

207a, 208a: Ricci

100a, b, c: Dr Roumeguer

27a: Rouvière

90b: Royal Library of Windsor

67c: A. Segur

36b, 38b, 123b, 126b, 147c, 169a, 170, 171, 173b, 174b, 176a, 177a, b, 178a, b, 179, 182b, 185b, 186b, 189a, b, 192a, b, 193a, b, 194a, b, c, d, 197a, b, c, 198a, b, 199a, b, 200a, b, c, 202: Serafino

114d, 115c: Seuil

16b: Si Merrill

20: E. Smith

34a, 35b, 36a, 40a, 45b, 69a, 70a, b, 71a, b, 72a, b, 84c, 86b, 90d, 95a, 97b, 100d, 107c, 112b, 150a, 162b, 194a, 195a, 204, 210a, 211a, b, c, d, 212a, b, 216b, 220, 232 c, d, 233a: Snark International

90c: Stockholm Museum

132, 145, 148a: J. Suquet

94c: Tate Gallery

120a, 143c: Tierbilder Okapia

144b: United Press

22: Vatican Museum

75a: Verroust

11, 73a, 225b: R. Viollet

15: Van Vormer

122b, 227a: Von Hagen, 'The Incas'

74a, b, c, 83: Frederick Warne & Co. Ltd

147c, 161b, 163a: D. York

151, 235b: Zalewski

In colour:
Si Merrill (p.16–17); Hassia (p.48–49); Suquet (p.144–145); Snark International (p.80–81, 176–177); Giraudon (p.96–97); Photothèque R. Laffont (p.56–57; 120–121; 208–209; 224–225)

Jacket and cover illustration by Doumic/Atlas Photo

Paul Hamlyn wish to thank the following people for permission to reprint in the English edition:

Selection from Saki's *The Square Egg* reprinted by permission of The Bodley Head

Selection from 'Last Words to a Dumb Friend' from *The Collected Poems of Thomas Hardy* reprinted by permission of the Trustees of the Hardy Estate, The Macmillan Company of Canada Ltd and Macmillan & Co. Ltd

'The Cat and the Moon' from *Collected Poems of W. B. Yeats* reprinted by permission of Mr M. B. Yeats and Macmillan & Co. Ltd

Selection from 'The Malediction', originally published by Martin Secker & Warburg Ltd in *Three Players of a Summer Game*.© 1945, 1948, 1954 by Tennessee Williams

'The Naming of Cats' and other extracts from *Old Possum's Book of Practical Cats* by T. S. Eliot reprinted by permission of Faber and Faber Ltd